SHAKEN
& STIRRED

Colette
CADDLE

POOLBEG

First published 2000
by Poolbeg Press Ltd.
123 Grange Hill, Baldoyle,
Dublin 13, Ireland
Email: poolbeg@poolbeg.com

This edition published 2002

3 5 7 9 10 8 6 4 2

A catalogue record for this book is available from the British Library.

ISBN 1-85371-958-7

Set by Pat Hope
Printed by Cox & Wyman Ltd, Reading, Berkshire

www.poolbeg.com

SHAKEN
& STIRRED

About the author

Colette Caddle lives with her husband and sons in Co. Dublin.

For Elizabeth Lynott
The best Mother in the world

Chapter One

Pamela Lloyd-Hamilton blotted her lips with a tissue and then leaned forward to inspect her make-up in the mirror. She frowned at the faint crow's feet at the side of her eyes. Laugh lines, her father called them. Well, she didn't find them very funny! She put on the heavy gold earrings that Douglas had brought from New York. She quite liked them though she'd have liked them more if they'd come in a Tiffany's box. She put on her engagement ring and a ruby-studded eternity ring, sprayed Opium behind her ears and down her cleavage and then slipped into the jacket of her grey Donna Karan suit. She checked her appearance once more: dark hair pulled back in a perfect chignon with small tendrils hanging loosely around her thin face, pale blue eyes emphasised with grey eye-shadow and black mascara, and large mouth painted in Chanel's latest plum shade. She nodded, satisfied with her appearance. She looked elegant and feminine but professional. Perfect.

Douglas shifted in the bed and she took a step

towards him but he rolled over and started to snore. She shrugged, picked up her bag and suitcase and let herself out of the room quietly. It was seven-fifteen and the taxi was due at half-past. She went quietly down the impressive, mahogany staircase, took her laptop off the hall table and slid it down on to the top of her trolley-case. She checked her mobile phone was charged and put it into her handbag. The charger she slipped into the side pocket of the case. Happy that she was organised, Pamela went into the kitchen, her high heels tapping loudly on the tiled floor. Her breakfast consisted of four vitamin capsules washed down with a glass of fresh orange juice. She'd have coffee on the plane. She moved across to the dresser and picked up the pad and pen. The top page was covered with Irene's untidy scrawl. Cooking instructions for last night's dinner. Pamela tore off the page and tossed it in the bin. Then in a neat, precise hand she wrote:

Irene,

Dinner party on Saturday at eight. Liz Connolly is taking care of the catering.

Please:

— polish the silver — including the napkin rings

— iron the white linen cloth and napkins

— wash the glasses — the John Rocha Waterford crystal set

Many thanks, P. L-H.

Pamela felt like underlining the *L*. Irene Rooney was unimpressed by double-barrel names and always called her Mrs Hamilton. Pamela had told her on several occasions that her name was *Lloyd*-Hamilton, but it fell on deaf ears. It irritated Pamela but it was a small price to pay. Irene was a hard worker and a good, if plain, cook. So when she called out 'Mrs Hamilton' in her whiny voice, Pamela bit her tongue, smiled tightly and thanked God for a reliable daily.

She tore off the page and tacked it to the notice-board. Then she wrote a separate note to her husband.

Douglas,
Staying at the Caledonian in Edinburgh. Back Friday.
Don't forget to organise the wine for Saturday.
Love P.

Pamela walked back into the hall just as the doorbell rang.

The taxi driver eyed her up and down appraisingly when she opened the door.

"Mornin', love."

Pamela barely glanced at him. "Could you take my case out, please?"

"No problem," he said cheerfully, hoisting it up in his arms.

"Be careful, for God's sake! Can't you see it's on wheels? There's no *need* to lift it. That laptop is worth thousands!"

The man glared at her, put the case down and dragged it out to the car. "Toffee-nosed bitch," he muttered to himself.

Pamela brushed past him and slipped into the back seat. He slammed the boot closed and got into the driver's seat. "Where to?"

"The airport." Pamela took out her mobile and dialled the office. Gina should be in by now. She'd better be. The Marketing Moves seminars were starting in the O'Reilly Hall in UCD on Monday, and Pamela hadn't seen any proofs yet. Gina rarely let her down, but Pamela hated cutting things fine. She was a stickler for detail and she liked to check everything. Jim Reynolds was expecting to see the screen layouts this afternoon and she wasn't comfortable that he'd be seeing them before she did. Well, it was too late now. She'd have to get Douglas to check them. She tapped her fingers impatiently as she waited for Gina to pick up.

"Conference Management Limited, hello?"

"Jack? It's Pamela. Can I speak to Gina?"

"She's not in yet, Pamela."

Pamela tut-tutted. "Get her to phone me on the mobile as soon as she gets in."

"Will do. Bye, Pam . . ." Jack looked at the phone in his hand. Pamela had already hung up. He shrugged, lit a cigarette and went back to playing Lemmings on his PC.

Pamela fumed silently as the taxi made its way down East Wall Road. Where the hell was Gina? How could she be late, today of all days? She'd have to talk to Douglas about this. It was time they reviewed Ms Barrett's future in CML. Pamela had always had her doubts about the girl. She'd been hired by Douglas, probably more because of her pretty face than her talent. But Douglas wouldn't save her if she screwed this job up. Marketing Moves was one of their biggest customers and

Pamela would be furious if Gina let them down. She toyed with the idea of calling Jim Reynolds and fobbing him off for a couple of days, but he was a temperamental old bugger, who'd probably blow a fuse.

Pamela's thoughts were interrupted by the shrill of her mobile. "Yes?"

"Pamela? It's Gina."

"Oh? And where have you been?"

And a very good morning to you too, Gina thought to herself. "I was at the airport," she said aloud.

"What? Why?"

"I left a disk for you at the information desk. It's got the Marketing Moves screens on it and a Word document with the handouts."

"Oh," Pamela said taken aback at her employee's enterprise. "That's great. I'll call you as soon as I check them. Bye."

"Don't mention it," Gina said to the dial tone.

Pamela stepped out of the taxi, paid the driver and walked briskly into Departures, pulling her case along behind her. She picked up the disk at the information desk and went over to the Aer Lingus Business Class check-in.

"Good morning, Mrs Lloyd-Hamilton. Seat 1C as usual?"

Pamela rewarded the girl with a small smile. "Yes, please. Is the flight on time?"

"Yes, it is. You can go straight through. They'll start boarding in about twenty minutes."

Pamela made her way quickly to the gate. She should

have time to look at the presentation and call Gina before they boarded. Choosing a seat in a quiet corner, she took out the laptop, started it up and slipped the disk into the portable drive. Her machine was set to automatically open the Word and PowerPoint packages so all she had to do was open the relevant files.

She checked the slides first, and her face relaxed into a smile as she looked through the presentation. There was no doubt about it, Gina had surpassed herself this time. Pamela made a mental note to talk to Douglas about giving her a pay rise. She closed down the show and went in to have a quick look at the notes that would be bound and given to each delegate. After a few moments she closed down the machine and called the office.

"Gina? That's fine. Why don't you sit in on the meeting this afternoon? Douglas will do all the talking but you could answer any of Jim's technical questions."

"Well . . . eh, I suppose . . ."

"Good, that's settled then. Tell Noreen to call me at ten. I'll talk to you later. Bye."

Pamela hung up, and slipped the laptop back into its case just as the flight was called. She boarded the plane and bestowed a brilliant and rare smile on the bewildered flight attendant. It was going to be a good day, as long as Douglas handled Jim Reynolds properly. But there was no worry there. Handling people was Douglas Hamilton's speciality. He had a way of taking the heat out of any situation and charming even the most difficult of clients.

It was in such a situation that Pamela had first met him. She'd been personal assistant to the MD of a small accountancy firm when Douglas Hamilton had been contracted to computerise their payroll system. David Hanlon knew nothing about computers and disguised his ignorance by complaining loudly and treating all IT people as if they were trying to con him. Douglas had been the poor unfortunate who was in charge of the project and Pamela had cringed as she heard her boss belittle and bully him. Douglas had seemed impervious to the insults and carried out his job efficiently and well within the time-frame specified, earning a grudging respect from Hanlon and admiration and interest from Pamela.

The more time Douglas spent in the office, the more Pamela noticed his brilliant blue eyes, his tanned, athletic body and the easy smile that usually played around his lips. He also seemed to have a bottomless pocket, a fact that Pamela had spotted immediately. Douglas drove a large car, had an incredibly flamboyant lifestyle and wore the most beautiful clothes. He looked every inch the successful businessman. When he'd suggested casually to Pamela after a particularly tough day that they go for a bite to eat and a drink, she was amazed when they'd ended up in the Shelbourne Hotel drinking *real* champagne. As Pamela had sipped the sparkling liquid and enjoyed the attentions of this good-looking and wealthy man, she decided that this was one fish that she wasn't going to let slip away.

From that night on, Pamela and Douglas went out at

least once a week. When he drove her home, Pamela never invited him in and only let him have a quick cuddle before she sent him home frustrated. It left her more than a little frustrated herself. Because for the first time in her life, Pamela was falling in love. But she knew she was doing the right thing. Pamela Lloyd was on a campaign. This was the man she was going to marry. And if he wanted her, he was going to have to make a firm commitment. No ring, no sex, it was as simple as that. Pamela wasn't some prim little virgin, but she'd had only three lovers and she'd protected her reputation carefully. It was all very well saying that this was the age of equality, but no man wanted to marry a woman who'd been around the block a few times.

When Douglas offered Pamela a job in the company he was setting up, she was totally devastated and wondered how she'd misread the situation so badly. She wanted a husband and all Douglas wanted was a PA!

But she was worrying unnecessarily. Douglas had recognised in Pamela a kindred spirit – ambitious and single-minded. It was time he settled down and Pamela would be a valuable asset to his company and a very suitable and beautiful wife. She wasn't the kind of woman he usually went for – much too thin. His tastes were for more curvaceous and hot-blooded women. But then, there was the kind of woman you slept with and the kind of woman you married. One had little to do with the other.

So six months after they'd met, Pamela went to work for CML as General Manager and, six months after that, she'd married Douglas in an elaborate and expensive ceremony.

Pauline and Gerald Lloyd had been delighted with the match. Douglas was exactly the kind of man they wanted for their daughter. Well educated, successful and personable. And Pauline was delighted that Pamela had decided to use the double-barrel surname. It was very classy.

Initially, Douglas and Pamela moved into an apartment in Rathgar and put all their money back into the business. Within two years, CML was in profit and they were able to search for a house. Pamela knew the moment she set eyes on the six-bedroom detached residence in Ballsbridge that she'd found just what she'd been looking for. The Sycamores was an old red-brick lodge in its own grounds, a high wall protecting it from the busy world outside. The trees that had given it its name lined the bottom of the garden and behind them ran a small stream.

"It's wonderful," Doug had said delightedly. He was very much a city person, but it was nice to be surrounded by so much greenery and yet be in the very heart of the capital.

Much to Pamela's horror, the previous owner had modernised the house beyond recognition and she lost no time in calling in a building contractor. Her first instructions to them were to strip out the false ceilings and gas fires and reveal the wonderful old beams and magnificent fireplaces. The kitchen, however, she fitted out with the latest equipment. Stainless steel pots swung over the workstation in the centre of the room and heavy black and white tiles covered the walls and floor. She also installed a large white range, much to Irene's annoyance. Pamela didn't have to cook on the damn thing. She'd only bought it because ranges were all the rage that year. The bathrooms – there were two and an en-suite – were decked out in the best of tiles. Pamela spent hours in Brown Thomas, Laura Ashley and the auction rooms selecting the curtains, wallpapers and furniture. A landscaper was brought in to overhaul the large gardens, install an ornamental pond complete with fountain – ageing it in accordance with Pamela's precise instructions – and trim the hedges that bordered the impressive driveway.

Word soon spread about Pamela's sumptuous home. The Sycamores featured regularly in all the best magazines, the articles punctuated by numerous photographs. Pamela was pleased though not surprised. She'd known exactly what she'd wanted for some time, and she'd researched the task with the same determination that had made her a successful businesswoman. She was satisfied with the results, but had not rested on her laurels. Her home was redecorated every eighteen months, and she added to her collection of antiques at every opportunity.

Douglas listened to her plans and wrote a lot of cheques. But in the end, he had to admit it was worth every penny. The restoration work transformed the place and Pamela's talent for interior design had created an old-world charm. The overall effect was a home that was both stylish and comfortable with success written all over it. The only aspects Doug involved himself in were the layout of his study and the wine-cellar – a small room off the kitchen. He also chose their cars. A grey Jaguar XJS for him and a sporty, red, soft-topped BMW for Pamela.

Their names appeared regularly in the gossip columns, for they were invited to all the best parties, openings and premieres. Pamela couldn't believe her luck: she was a partner in a successful company; a leading light in society; and her husband was not only rich, he was handsome too. They were the golden couple of Dublin 4 society and they were envied, admired and ridiculed in almost equal measures.

Pamela roused herself as the plane began its descent into Edinburgh. She clicked open her compact and touched up her already perfect make-up. The flight was ten minutes early which meant she'd be at the hotel in plenty of time to check everything out before her client arrived. She nodded her thanks as the attendant retrieved her case and, as always, was the first passenger off the flight. Within minutes, she was through customs and greeting the driver that Noreen had booked. It was nearly ten o'clock and it would take about thirty minutes to get to the hotel. That should be ample time to talk to her secretary and deal with her post and any other issues that couldn't wait until Monday. As she got into the car, her mobile rang, exactly on schedule. As was everything in the well-ordered life of Pamela Lloyd-Hamilton.

Chapter Two

Gina pulled on her jacket and went down the hall to bang on her brother's door. "Tim? Get up. You're going to be late. Again."

Her brother groaned. "What time is it?" he muttered from under the duvet.

"Seven," she lied glibly. "Gotta go. See you later." She let herself out the front door and made her way down the short flight of stairs.

Mrs Morris was just coming in with her dog. "Damn lift's out again."

"Mornin', Mrs Morris. Ah well, the exercise is good for us." She smiled at the old woman and kept moving. If she hesitated, Moany Morris would keep her talking for ages and she really couldn't spare the time this morning. She had a lot to do. She giggled as she struggled with the steering lock on her Volkswagen Polo. Tim would kill her when he realised it was only half six. She pulled out of her parking spot and headed for the airport. Pamela would be delighted to get this disk. It would definitely earn her a few brownie points. Pamela could be a right pain in the ass, but Gina understood her obsession with deadlines because she felt exactly the same way.

It was probably the only thing the two women had in common. Though Gina took pride in her work, she wasn't driven the way Pamela was. She worked hard but she also enjoyed having a laugh, going out to lunch with the lads and having a drink after work on a Friday evening. Life was too short to be chained to a desk.

But Pamela didn't want anything to do with her employees. She didn't know about their personal lives and she didn't want to. and she couldn't understand why Douglas bothered to socialise with them.

And though Malcolm and Jack both agreed – after several rounds – that Pamela was a good-looking woman, they thought she was a bit of a cold fish and very stand-offish.

Gina, on the other hand, was attractive, bubbly and passionate. Not a bit like her boss. Her brown eyes sparkled with lively intelligence and good-humour and the deep huskiness of her voice was always a surprise to those hearing it for the first time.

She was quite short and curvy – a fact that depressed her – but it seemed to bring out the protective instincts in men. And the fact that she was completely unaware of the effect she had on the opposite sex added to her attraction and made her just as popular with women. But though she had no problems in attracting men, she still couldn't manage to keep a relationship going for more than a few months.

"I think I get too serious too soon," she told her friend Hannah. "I scare them off."

And while she sat at her desk dreaming of the latest love in her life, Jack Byrne, CML's technical guru, gazed longingly at her over his coffee mug.

Gina thought very highly of Jack. He was a great mate, a computer genius and he'd taught her a lot. Even Pamela thought he was talented. Gina sighed as she overtook a van. It was a pity Pamela didn't appreciate her like that. It was really beginning to get to Gina the way Pamela constantly checked up on her. Gina felt she'd proved herself over and over again. It was about time that Pamela stepped back and let her get on with the job. Gina indicated and turned into the airport. She checked the clock on the dashboard and was pleased to see that she was making good time. With a bit of luck she'd be in work by eight. She might even get a parking space. Gina always started work early. She said it was to avoid the heavy traffic and to get a parking spot near the office, but it was really because she belonged to the minority group of people who actually loved their job.

Gina manoeuvred her car into a tight spot, delivered her package to the information desk and was heading back towards the city-centre ten minutes later. She thought, with a mixture of excitement and anxiety, of the day ahead. Now that she'd finished the presentation for Marketing Moves – she didn't expect Pamela to have any changes – she could concentrate on the sales promo for the interior design company. She was really looking forward to that. It would allow for a lot more creativity than the usual boring financial stuff that was CML's bread and butter. Gina grinned as she realised that it would probably mean Jack wouldn't get any of his own work done. He loved getting involved in this type of thing. He'd quiz Gina about what styles she was going to use, get completely engrossed in discussing the overall theme and then he'd hang over her shoulder while she worked. It was just as well Pamela was out of the office or she'd go mad. Doug was much more relaxed and actively encouraged brainstorming sessions. Sometimes he even joined in and then Gina would get a glimpse of the creative man he used to be. But these days Doug spent all his time going after new business, wining and dining clients and meeting with his investment analyst. He rarely went near a computer now unless it was to check his e-mail, study the financial spread sheets or cruise the Net.

Doug and Jack got on really well but Gina wasn't quite as comfortable with her boss. He had a habit of making personal remarks about her appearance and teasing her about boyfriends and he flirted outrageously.

When Gina complained to Jack, he told her she was overreacting.

"It's just the way he's made. He doesn't mean any harm. He'd never actually try it on."

Gina had looked at him, amazed at his naiveté. She'd seen Doug in operation with girls who weren't put off by a wedding ring and it was pretty obvious that he didn't take his marriage vows too seriously. Jack would tag along to night-clubs with Doug and fall asleep in a corner while Doug checked out the talent. Pamela didn't seem to mind these outings. Gina often wondered if she knew Doug played around. If she did, it didn't seem to bother her.

Gina pulled her mind back to the present as she turned off St Mary's Road into the small cul-de-sac. She slipped her car into a spot just vacated by a Merc, and ran up the steps to CML.

"Mornin'!"

Jack looked up from his game. "Hi, Gina. Call Pammy baby on her mobile."

"Jeez, already?"

"She called a while ago and was very unimpressed that you weren't in yet."

Gina rolled her eyes. "God, maybe I should just move my bed in and have done with it!" She picked up the receiver and dialled Pamela's number and explained where she'd been and why. Moments later she hung up and went over to the coffee pot. "I don't know. That woman's getting worse."

"She's getting to that funny age," Jack said knowingly.

Gina laughed. "For God's sake, Jack. She's only thirty-eight."

"Yeah, well. There must be some reason why she's such a difficult oul' bitch."

"That's so sexist. The same treatment from a man and you'd just say that he was a demanding boss."

"I'm not sexist! Ah, come on, Gina. You can't seriously be defending the woman."

"No, I suppose not. She *is* an awful cow. But then, she's got Doug to put up with."

"Doug-las," Jack corrected in his best Dublin 4 accent. "I don't know. I think he got the short straw."

"You would." Gina poured a cup of coffee and carried it over to her desk. She cleared a spot in the chaos and set it down carefully, before switching on the PC.

"So what have you got on today?" Jack wheeled round to face her.

"The promo for Simone Wallis Interiors."

Jack whistled. "We *are* going up in the world. And do we have a free hand?"

"We?" Gina arched an eyebrow.

"We," Jack said firmly. "You know I give you all your best ideas."

"Really? Maybe you should do the whole thing, so."

Jack leaned back and stretched his arms back behind his head. "Ah, no. I'm more of an ideas man. Wasted on the humdrum of detail."

"Well OK, ideas man. Get thinking. Simone seems happy to let us loose on this."

"Pity we don't have a few more customers like her. Let's have a look at the content then."

Gina and Jack were engrossed when Noreen Dunne arrived at precisely eight forty-five.

"Good morning, Regina, Jack," she said brightly and received grunts in reply. She shook her head and went back out to her desk in reception. She'd never understand those two. She didn't even know what they did half the time. Still, Mr Hamilton seemed happy with them, and that was good enough for her. She hung up her raincoat carefully and patted her hair as she sat down at her desk. She looked suspiciously at the PC in front of her and switched it on with a hesitant finger. It had taken Mr Hamilton a long time to persuade her to part with her word processor – she'd only just got used to that – and take on this beast of a machine. After a lot of patient tuition from Jack, she could now master the rudiments of diary management and the word-processing package but she still didn't trust it.

"Noreen, you have to call Pamela on the mobile at ten."

Noreen frowned at Gina's familiarity. She never addressed Mrs Lloyd-Hamilton by her first name. Well, there had to be some standards, didn't there? "Thank you, Regina," she said primly.

Gina grimaced at the name only Sister Martha in primary school had used. But there was no use correcting Noreen. She would always call Gina, Regina; Doug, Mr Hamilton; and Pamela, Mrs Lloyd-Hamilton. It was her way. She was one of the old school.

At nine-thirty a breathless Malcolm Patterson hurried into the office. "Is Doug in?"

Jack glanced up. "Mornin', Mal. No, not yet."

Mal breathed a sigh of relief and made for the coffee pot.

Gina smiled. The company accountant spent most of his life worrying about the figures, about Doug and usually both! "Relax, Mal. What's the problem?"

"Oh nothing." Malcolm put down his mug and

shuffled out of his anorak. "Just Doug wanted to see next month's budget first thing."

"And it's not ready," Jack said.

Mal sighed as he straightened his tie and tucked his shirt in. No matter what size he bought, it always seemed to work free of his trousers. "No, it's not. I meant to stay late last night and do them but Caroline wanted to go out."

Gina and Jack exchanged looks. Caroline was Malcolm's domineering wife who seemed to keep poor Malcolm on a very tight rein.

Gina smiled sympathetically. "Never mind, Malcolm. I'll distract him for you. I've got a presentation to show him and then we're meeting with a client this afternoon."

Relief spread all over Mal's face. "Cheers, Gina. I owe you one. Now I'd better get down to it." He cleaned his glasses carefully and switched on his PC.

Gina turned back to Jack who was tapping his pen against the screen.

"I really think we should use some animation."

She shook her head. "Too expensive, Jack."

"Have they given you a budget?"

"Not yet."

"Well, then. Oh come on, Gina. It's not often we get the chance to show what we can do."

"Yeah, but maybe subtlety is the better way to go," she argued. "We should get hold of some of their work and see what *their* style's like."

"Exactly right, Gina."

Gina whirled around to see Doug standing in the doorway. She reddened. "Oh, hi, Doug."

"Good morning, Gina. Morning, troops. How are we all this fine morning?"

"Yo, Doug," Jack replied with a grin.

"Morning," Malcolm murmured, trying to blend into the background.

Doug smiled broadly as his secretary appeared at his side. "Morning, Noreen."

"Good morning, Mr Hamilton," Noreen simpered before going to pour him a coffee.

Doug went into his office, threw his jacket carelessly on the back of his chair and came back out, rolling up his sleeves. "Have you seen any of Simone's work, Gina?"

"Only in magazines," Gina admitted. Simone Wallis Interiors was way out of her league.

"So let's get hold of every magazine spread done in the last six months," Doug said sitting down beside her. "We could go to Simone and ask her, but I'd like her to see that we're on top of things."

"I'll get on to the news monitoring service. They should be able to chase up what we need."

"No, no, Gina. You concentrate on the presentation. Noreen can chase up the articles."

Gina smiled apologetically at Noreen as she put the coffee down at Doug's elbow. "If it's no trouble . . ."

"I'll take care of it, Mr Hamilton," Noreen said quietly and went back out to her desk.

Doug winked at Gina and she blushed. When he looked at her she felt like she was the only woman in the world. She knew he had the same effect on all the women in his life, no matter what age. Well, except maybe Pamela. It was a weird marriage for sure. Gina would be jealous as hell if her husband behaved like that. Greg wouldn't, she was sure of that. Now why, when she thought of marriage, did Greg Hamilton come to mind?

Doug's younger brother had worked in CML last summer and Gina had really fancied him. He was different to his brother. The same yellow-blond hair and cornflower-blue eyes but that's where the similarities ended. Greg was taller – easily over six foot – and his hair was long. A bit like Michael Bolton before he got it all chopped off, Gina thought dreamily. Greg was a romantic. A free spirit. Every summer once he was free of the monotony of school life, he travelled. Gina thought he was the most sophisticated and mysterious man she had ever met. It was a pity they hadn't had a chance to take their relationship further.

"Don't you agree, Gina?"

Gina jumped. "Oh, eh, yes. Sure." She nodded furiously and wondered what she was agreeing to.

Doug jumped to his feet and flashed her another smile. "Good. Then that's settled." He whirled around to face Mal. "Right, Mr Patterson. I'm all yours."

"Oh, Doug. Sorry," Gina interrupted with an apologetic smile. "Could we just go through the Marketing Moves presentation? Pamela wants me to sit in on your meeting with Jim this afternoon and I'd like to make sure that you're happy with everything first."

Doug looked at Mal. "Is that OK with you, Mal?"

Mal smiled. "No problem, Doug. Take your time."

Doug sat back down beside Gina and moved his chair closer so that their knees almost touched. "I'm sure everything's fine, Gina, but let's have a look."

Gina shifted uncomfortably. Why had she chosen to wear a short, tight skirt today rather than her usual jeans? She moved closer to the screen so that her legs were tucked well under the desk.

Doug moved closer still. "OK, Gina. Show me what you've got."

Gina smiled weakly and opened the Marketing Moves file.

Chapter Three

"Drink up, Gina. It's your round." Jack drained his glass and put it down on the table.

"You have hollow legs." She looked at his thin frame.

"It's good metabolism. I'm like a fine-tuned machine and I need fuel."

Malcolm stood up. "I'll get these. I've got to head off soon. Caroline wants to go shopping."

Jack looked at him, horrified. "On a Friday night? Are you mad, man?"

"She's had a tough week, Jack. Rachel's had chicken-pox and Caroline hasn't been able to get out at all."

"Well, tell her to get a baby-sitter and come and meet us. We'll go for a Chinese."

"Ah, no. I'd better not." Malcolm hurried off to get the drinks, knowing full well what Caroline would say if he suggested she join them.

"I hope I've got better things to do than to go out with that pair. I don't think I've ever seen Jack in anything other than torn jeans. And as for Gina Barrett! The girl is full of herself."

Mal thought Gina was lovely but he didn't dare say so to Caroline. She'd get into one of her moods and not let him near her for days. And God knows, they didn't have sex that often as it was. He paid the barman and carried the drinks back to the corner table. "So what are you two going to do tonight?" he asked, wishing he could tag along.

"Well, I might go and meet Tom and the gang. They'll be down in O'Dwyer's. What about it, Gina? Want to come along?"

"Dunno. My class are meeting for a few drinks in The Hairy Lemon."

Jack took a long gulp from his pint. "Then let's go to both. A pub crawl."

"How are the classes going, Gina?" Malcolm took a sip from his pint and checked his watch. He could afford another ten minutes.

"Not bad."

Jack snorted. "I think you're wasting your time. You're not cut out to be a programmer. You're too normal. And you're bloody good with graphics."

"But I'm not getting very far in CML and there don't seem to be many openings for graphic artists. Programming is the way to go. That's where the money is."

"Money isn't everything," Jack said sagely. "It's a lot more important to be in a job you enjoy."

"Amen to that," Mal said glumly. He wasn't sure he'd

ever actually enjoyed his job. An 'A' student at school, excelling in maths, it had seemed inevitable that he would go on to study accountancy. At least his teachers and parents all thought so. And he couldn't think of anything else to do. But it was so boring and he did envy the way Jack and Gina got completely lost in their work. But it was too late for him to change course now. He was nearly forty with a wife and child to support.

"I do prefer graphics," Gina was saying, "but I'm just fed up with CML. Well, with Pamela anyway. And it's about time I got a raise."

"Me too," Jack agreed cheerfully.

"So why don't *you* leave? You'd walk into another job with all your qualifications." Gina couldn't understand why Jack stayed. Some of the guys he'd been at college with were earning almost twice as much as he was and they didn't have half his brains. He'd easily get another job. Unlike Gina. She'd started work straight after she left school and the only training she'd ever got was on the job. And so in a moment of desperation and depression, she'd signed up for the programming course. But she didn't really like it. Not that she'd admit that to anyone.

"It suits me," Jack was saying. "I only live down the road, I work the hours I want – what more could I want?"

"Money," Gina and Mal said in unison and laughed.

Mal pushed his glasses up on his nose. "Seriously though. CML are doing very well at the moment. Doug could easily afford to give us all a raise."

"But Pammy baby won't let him."

"That's about the size of it," Mal agreed. Doug was a tough business man but he was fair-minded and he knew the value of good staff. Pamela, however, wasn't too interested in the employees apart from what she could get out of them. If Doug talked about salary increases, Pamela usually managed to talk him out of it.

"Bitch," Gina said glumly. "And that's why I'm studying programming and keeping an eye on the recruitment pages."

"Seriously?" Jack frowned. CML was a nice place to work but he wasn't so sure he'd want to stay if Gina left.

"Damn right. I've told you, Jack. I've had enough. What about the other morning when Pamela rang in and was annoyed that I wasn't there? It was seven-thirty, for Christ's sake."

"She just doesn't think." Jack didn't particularly like the woman but he didn't take her abruptness too seriously.

"I've been looking around myself," Mal admitted.

"What? Jeez, you're all deserting me. Why, Mal?"

"Caroline wants to move house and I can't really afford a bigger mortgage on my current salary."

"But your house is gorgeous. Why does she want to move?" Gina had dropped Mal home once and loved the little semi-detached house that overlooked a large green.

"We could do with more space," Mal explained though actually Caroline just wanted to move to a more exclusive address.

"Something you want to tell us, Mal?" Gina nudged

26

him. "Is there the patter of tiny feet on the way again?"

"Oh, no." *More's the pity*, he added privately to himself. Rachel was three years old and Mal thought it was high time they gave her a brother or sister. It might calm her down to have a bit of competition. But Caroline kept putting him off. There was always a reason to wait a bit longer. "Caroline says it's best to get a bigger house before we plan any more children."

"She would," Gina said under her breath. Poor Mal. He was always working overtime to pay for his wife's 'necessities'. Why was it that the nice guys always ended up with the selfish cows?

"Well, good luck, Mal, but I'd hate to see you leave." Jack patted his back awkwardly.

"I'm not leaving CML just yet, but if I don't get out of here now, Caroline will kill me!"

Gina laughed. "Seeya, Mal."

"Bye, Mal." Jack watched him push his way towards the door. "Poor man. That one's an awful old nag."

"Yeah. Now, are we having another pint here or heading down to Dwyer's?"

"Ah, sure we'll have one more before we go."

"Right, I'll get them."

Jack watched as she pushed her way to the bar. He couldn't imagine CML without her. He realised that they'd probably never be more than friends but the thought of not seeing her every day . . . that was different. He'd just have to make sure she didn't leave. Maybe he could drop a word in Doug's ear. Whatever Mal said about Pamela's influence, Doug wouldn't want to lose

Gina. Yes, that was it. He'd mention casually to Doug that Gina was getting itchy feet. That should do it.

* * *

"The smell is great, Liz." Douglas lounged against the kitchen table and watched Liz Connolly's every move.

"Thanks," Liz mumbled and bent down to get the roast out of the oven, conscious of his eyes on her rear.

Doug watched her appreciatively. She was a good-looking woman, with curves in all the right places and now that husband of hers was out of the picture . . .

"Douglas, stop bothering Liz. Hello, Liz. Everything all right?" Pamela stood in the doorway, watching them with shrewd eyes.

Liz smiled warily. "Everything's fine, Mrs Lloyd-Hamilton."

Doug smiled at his wife. "My, but you look good enough to eat, darling. Is that a Chanel?"

Pamela nodded, pleased. Douglas had such a good eye. She didn't know any other man who would be able to recognise a couture item, never mind name the designer. "Yes. Do you like it?"

"Absolutely. You look gorgeous." Douglas looked at his wife with the same proprietorial admiration with which he looked at his Jag. Pamela was sleek, beautiful and sophisticated. "Can I get you a drink?"

"Mmnn, yes. Just a small G and T." Pamela followed him into the dining-room, Liz already forgotten, and examined her reflection in the antique mirror over the fireplace. She raised an eyebrow when she saw Douglas refilling his own glass. "You're knocking them back a bit, aren't you?"

"I'll need it if you've put me next to Marjorie."

"Oh, she's not that bad. Besides, it's worth it if Jim puts some business our way."

"True. I hope you're going to pay him 'special' attention tonight."

"But of course. It will be easier than playing referee with Jeff and Anna."

Doug groaned. "Oh, lord. Did you have to invite them? I can't understand why they don't just split up and be done with it."

"Jeff would never walk away from the business. He's made a great success of it and it can't be long before Anna's father retires and leaves him to run the whole show."

Doug laughed. "And *that's* why they're invited. Prospective clients."

"Exactly."

"Goodness, Pamela! You're never off duty, are you?"

"Would you want me to be?" she countered.

"Certainly not." He dropped a light kiss on her brow and moved around the table to look at the other name places. "Tony and Michelle and John and Sophie."

"Sophie and Anna are good friends," Pamela explained. "I thought it might defuse things."

"And Tony and John are both die-hard golfers."

"Yes, they can bore each other to death and leave the rest of us in peace." She shook her head as Douglas held up the gin bottle and frowned slightly as he poured himself yet another measure. God, she hoped he wasn't turning into a lush. Douglas was an excellent host, but he could get a little bit silly when he had a few drinks on him. And it was important that he remained in a reasonable condition if they were to woo Jeff and Jim. Still, he looked well tonight. The navy blazer and mint-coloured Ralph Lauren shirt emphasised his tan, and the white-blond hair – still curling at the bottom from his shower – gleamed in the candlelight.

"The presentation for Jim Reynolds went well," he was saying. "He was very impressed with Gina."

Pamela arched an eyebrow "Oh, yes? Was it her work or her boobs that impressed him?"

Doug laughed. "Probably both. She's come a long way though. I wonder if we should involve her more with the customers. She has a great personality."

"Yes, and she looks good too."

"Pamela." Doug gave her a reproving look.

"Well, it doesn't hurt, Douglas," she said matter-of-factly. "It might be an idea to get her more involved with our male clients. But I'll have to talk to her about those dreadful clothes." She shuddered slightly.

Doug didn't see much wrong with the way Gina dressed. Still, a couple of business suits with short skirts might look quite sexy. "You can easily take care of that, darling. Your taste is impeccable."

"Maybe you should do the same for Jack," she said dryly.

Doug grinned. Jack did look a bit rough and ready.

His tightly cropped hair – he looked almost bald – made him look like a punk. And his clothes looked as if they'd never seen an iron. If it wasn't for his wide smile and twinkling eyes, you'd cross the street to get away from him! "Nobody *expects* him to look well. He's the original, stereotypical programmer and I don't care what he looks like as long as he does the job."

They were interrupted by the doorbell. "That'll be John and Sophie. They're always early. You get the door, Douglas. I'll just check on Liz."

Doug grinned as he made his way out to the front door. Check on Liz. Rubbish. Pamela just hated her guests to think that she was standing around waiting for them to arrive. No, she would enter the room about five minutes after he'd poured the drinks, fiddling with an earring and looking mildly surprised that her guests had arrived. He knew all her little tricks. He'd look on amused as the other women eyed her designer dress jealously and the men looked her up and down appreciatively. She was wearing a lot better than any of the other women in their circle. Several had let themselves go when they'd had kids and some of them looked positively middle-aged. But not Pamela. She'd hardly changed in the fourteen years he'd known her. It gave him a great deal of satisfaction.

Pamela was complimenting Sophie on her dress when the other guests arrived. Doug ushered them in and served drinks while Liz passed around the appetisers.

"Pamela, you look ravishing as always. I swear you

get younger-looking every time I see you," Anna gushed.

Pamela smiled sweetly. "Thank you, darling. You should wear red more often. It suits you." She looked with distaste at the broken veins on the other woman's face. "And how are you, Sophie? I haven't seen you since the christening. How is the little angel?" Pamela couldn't remember if it was a boy or a girl, never mind the little brat's name.

"Oh, he's wonderful," Sophie replied, her eyes sparkling and went on to give minute details of the child's feeding and toilet habits. Pamela stuck it for another five minutes before excusing herself. She signalled Douglas and he joined her in the doorway.

"Jesus, the knives are really out with Jeff and Anna tonight!" he murmured.

Pamela pasted a smile on her face. "Well, I prefer their bickering to Sophie's monologue about her baby's diarrhoea!" she said through gritted teeth. "Get everyone to sit down. I'll tell Liz we're ready to start."

Doug nodded and moved towards Sophie with a wide smile. "Come on, folks, time to sit down. Sophie! You look marvellous. How's that beautiful little baby of yours?"

Doug topped up Jeff's glass of port and poured Jim a hefty measure of brandy before topping up his own glass. It hadn't been a bad evening. As usual, Pamela had mixed people well and the conversation was quite relaxed. Well, except for the occasional barbs that Anna threw at her husband. Jeff ignored her and proceeded to get drunk.

Doug wasn't far behind him. He was hoping the brandies would numb the pain. Bloody indigestion. It must have been Liz's fresh bread. He'd wolfed down several chunks of it in the kitchen when he'd got in from his tennis match. He took another mouthful of brandy and mopped his forehead with a napkin. It was bloody hot in here. He excused himself and went to open another window.

"Don't, darling," Pamela called. "The heating is gone off and it's getting quite cool in here." She shivered delicately and he closed the window again. He went out to the kitchen and poured himself a glass of water.

"Are you OK?" Liz stopped packing away her equipment when she saw the colour of Doug's face.

"Yeah, just a bit of indi . . ." He paused, embarrassed. "Just ate too much of your lovely food, Liz," he amended.

Liz frowned. "There's some Alka-Seltzer in the press. The food was OK, wasn't it, Mr Hamilton?"

"Yes, of course. And please stop calling me Mr Hamilton. It's Doug." He sank into a chair and caught his breath as the pain gripped him like a vice. "Nothing to worry about, Liz. You go on home. I left the cheque on the board for you."

"You're sure?" Liz wondered if she should call Pamela.

"I'm sure. Goodnight, Liz. And thanks for everything."

"Good night, Mr . . . er . . . Doug."

Doug took another mouthful of water and went back to join his guests. He'd go for a brisk walk when they were all gone. That would sort him out.

Pamela watched him closely. He looked terrible and he was throwing back the brandy at an alarming rate.

Better get rid of the guests before he fell asleep, or worse, started telling his dirty jokes. She yawned delicately and looked at the slim Rolex on her wrist.

Marjorie took the hint immediately. "Come along, Jim. It's time we were going." She went over to Doug and gave him a hug. "Thank you for a lovely evening, darling."

"Anytime, Marjorie," he answered and kissed her soundly on the lips.

Marjorie blushed like a schoolgirl and turned to give Pamela a peck on the cheek. "Night, night, pet. Such a lovely dinner. Liz *is* wonderful, isn't she? I'd use her myself but Jim insists my cooking is better."

Only because fish and chips is his idea of a good meal, Pamela thought bitchily. She smiled sweetly at Marjorie. It was worth putting up with her nasty little digs if they got some business out of Jim.

The others started to move and within an hour, Pamela and Doug were alone.

"Another success, darling," Doug said putting his arm around her.

Pamela smiled wryly. "Well, at least Jeff and Anna didn't resort to a food fight. Let's go to bed. We can clean up in the morning." Pamela slipped off her shoes and carried them towards the mahogany staircase.

"I think I'll get some air. Clear my head."

Pamela tut-tutted. "You shouldn't drink so much. Don't stay out too long. And don't forget to put on the alarm when you come in."

"I won't." Doug put on his jacket and let himself out

into the cool night air. He walked at a brisk pace towards the river. The pain in his chest had subsided to be replaced by a dull ache, his stomach was sick and his head hurt like hell. He must be coming down with something. Maybe he should go and see Joe.

Joe McCarthy was an old friend and as soon as he'd set up his practice in Ballsbridge, Doug signed himself and Pamela onto his list. Not that either of them really needed a GP. They were as healthy as horses. He stopped and leaned heavily against a wall, suddenly breathless. Yes, he'd definitely drop into the surgery tomorrow. Joe should be there between ten and eleven. Some antibiotics would do the trick. He turned and started back towards the house.

Chapter Four

Joe McCarthy threw the stethoscope on the desk and sat down. "I want you to go in for some tests, Doug."

"Oh, do I have to, Joe? I've a busy few weeks coming up and I'm going to Marrakech next month."

"I'm not talking about the next few weeks, Doug." Joe's serious brown eyes looked steadily into his. "I want you to go in today."

Doug stared at him. "It's Sunday, Joe. Why would I go in today? Aren't you overreacting?"

"I don't believe so. I'll give the cardiologist a call. He owes me one. We'll get you into the Blackrock Clinic this afternoon and start monitoring you immediately."

Doug's eyes widened. "Cardiologist?"

"Yes. Look, Doug. I think you may have had a heart attack."

"What? That's absurd! I think I'd have noticed!"

"Not necessarily. Not everyone falls to the floor clutching their chest. Anyway, humour me. If you're right, you'll be out in a couple of days and no harm done."

"I'm sure you've got it wrong," Doug said faintly. "I feel fine now."

"Well, I hope I *am* wrong. Tell me, is there any history of heart disease in your family?"

"Well, yes. Dad and his brother both died of heart attacks and my mother is taking tablets for angina." Doug looked anxious as Joe made careful notes.

"What about your brother and sister? Any problems there?"

"I don't think so. Greg's only thirty-five and as fit as a fiddle. I don't know about Janet. I haven't talked to her in a while. She lives in Montreal, you see. Anyway, she's only thirty-eight and quite healthy as far as I know."

Joe nodded and continued to make notes.

"So what now?" Doug asked nervously.

"I'll call the Clinic and Alfred Grimes. You go home and put some things in a bag and I'll call you in an hour."

"This is serious, isn't it, Joe?"

"I'm not happy with your ECG," Joe admitted. "The sooner we get you checked out, the better. Don't worry. We'll sort you out. Are you driving?"

"No, I walked."

"Well, just let me lock up here and I'll drop you home. Is Pamela there?"

Doug was even more alarmed now. He only lived ten minutes up the road. Christ, what was Pamela going to say? She hated sickness. Kept well clear of hospitals. If friends or family were sick, she sent a card or a huge bouquet of flowers, but she never visited.

"Doug?"

"Oh, yes. Yes she's in. But she's going out later."

"I'm sure she'll be able to make other arrangements."

Doug doubted it. Pamela wasn't the kind of wife who'd drop everything to run to her ailing husband's bedside. He said nothing.

"OK. Doug. Let's go. Are you all right?"

Doug forced a smile. "Sure. Fine."

Pamela looked up from the newspaper when she heard the front door. Unusual. Douglas usually went to his club for Sunday lunch. She rarely saw him before seven in the evening.

"Douglas? Is that you?"

"Yeah."

"I wasn't expecting you. There's some salad in the fridge if you want it. You'll have to help yourself, I'm going out."

"I'm not staying myself," Doug said grimly from the doorway. "I have to go into hospital."

Pamela sighed. "What have you done to yourself this time?"

Doug had put his shoulder out only last month playing tennis.

"It seems I may have had a heart attack," he said with a nervous laugh.

Pamela put down the paper. "What do you mean?"

Doug sat down on the arm of a chair. "I wasn't feeling too good last night. I thought it was indigestion. Anyway, I still wasn't great this morning so I went up to see Joe. He did an ECG. He thinks I may have had a mild attack."

Pamela swallowed hard as she tried to digest this piece of information. It was obviously a mistake. She'd never had the blind faith in McCarthy that Douglas had. The man was overreacting. That was it. Douglas was in the best of health. "So what happens now?" she asked quietly.

I have to pack a bag and go into the Blackrock Clinic." Doug was a bit put out at how well Pamela was taking the news. It was true she was a cool customer but he'd just told her he'd had a heart attack, for God's sake!

"When, now?" Pamela looked at her watch. She was meeting Jean Fisher for lunch in Rolys in an hour.

Douglas smiled frostily. "It's OK, Pamela. I'll take a taxi. I wouldn't want to upset your plans."

She looked up sharply. "Don't be silly. Of course I'll take you. I can easily put Jean back half an hour. And you can call me on the mobile when you're ready to leave."

"I won't be out today. They have to do some tests. Even if it's a false alarm it will be Tuesday before I get out."

"Oh." Pamela began to feel sick. It hadn't occurred to her that he'd be in more than a few hours. Douglas was fine. There was no need for all this.

Doug softened when he saw her worried expression and took her hands in his. "I'm sure I'm fine, Pam. I've probably just been drinking too much. I should have listened to your wise words." He looked at his watch. "I'd better throw a few things in a bag."

Pamela jumped up. "No, I'll do it." She ran upstairs, took three pairs of neatly folded pyjamas from the hotpress and put them in a small overnight bag. Then she went into their bathroom. They both travelled so much, there were always supplies of small soaps and miniature toothpaste tubes in the house. Pamela checked Doug's toilet bag, discarded some items and added new ones. When she went back into the bedroom, Doug was changing into beige chinos.

"Will I pack the charger for your mobile phone?" she asked brightly. Lord, you'd think he was going on a business trip. Instead of into hospital. In for tests. In for tests on his heart. She took a deep breath. It was important that she stayed calm.

"May as well," Doug said with a laugh. "I'm sure phone calls in the clinic are about as expensive as a five star hotel." The phone rang. "That'll be Joe. I'll get it."

Within thirty minutes, they were on their way and an hour later, Doug stood on the steps of the clinic and watched his wife drive away. He'd told her not to wait though it would have been nice if she'd insisted. But a look of pure relief had crossed her face.

She kissed his cheek and held his hand tightly for a moment. "I'm sure everything will be fine. I'll call you later."

He'd returned her reassuring smile and got out of the car. Now he felt a bit lonely as he checked in and followed the administrator up to his room. He sat on the edge of the bed and grabbed the remote control. There was no point in getting undressed yet. He might as well watch the football.

"Mr Hamilton?" A young pretty nurse breezed into the room.

Doug flashed her a smile. "That's me. But you can call me Doug."

"Hi, Doug, I'm Karen. Please get undressed and get into bed. I need to attach you to a monitor and Mr Grimes will be in soon to examine you."

Doug looked at her with raised eyebrows. The great Alfred Grimes was coming in to see him on a Sunday. God, he *must* be dying! "Any chance of a coffee, Karen?" He asked with his most winning smile.

The nurse smiled back. "I'm afraid not. You need to fast until we know what tests Mr Grimes wants to run. Just water for you for the moment."

"Great."

Doug was taken aback with the speed of things after that. Blood was taken – lots of it, he was given another ECG and now he was attached to a monitor that made some disconcerting noises from time to time. Then Alfred Grimes arrived and read his chart, nodding and muttering to himself. Finally he looked at Doug over his spectacles. "Well, Mr Hamilton. It seems you've had a little belt."

"Oh?"

"Yes. I'd like to do an angiogram. See exactly what's going on in there."

Doug wondered idly why these medical geniuses always spoke in such clipped sentences. It was as if their time was too precious to waste on real conversation. Doug made himself concentrate. An angiogram. A bloke he played squash with had had one of them. "That's where you put a tube in the leg?"

"The groin area actually. Simple enough procedure. We inject a dye and then we can see if there are any blockages."

"And if there are? What then?"

"Let's not jump the gun, Mr Hamilton. Let's just wait and see."

"I'd prefer to know what the possibilities are," Doug insisted.

Grimes sighed and perched on the side of the bed. "Well, it could be congestion of one or more arteries and a change in exercise and diet may do the trick. On the other hand, we may need to carry out angioplasty, or possibly a bypass. We won't know until we get in there and take a look."

"I see."

"Nothing to worry about. You get some rest and I'll see you in the morning."

Doug waited until the door had closed after him before he picked up the phone. "Joe? It's Doug Hamilton. They're going to do an angiogram. Tell me about it."

Half an hour later, Doug hung up the phone. Joe hadn't been able to tell him much more than Grimes. He'd said all the reassuring things about heart surgery. It wasn't a big deal any more. Straightforward procedure. Very successful. But Doug didn't feel very reassured. He didn't believe it would be just a matter of changing his lifestyle. OK, so he probably drank a lot and ate too much junk food, but he took plenty of exercise and was as fit as a fiddle. He hadn't smoked in years. No, this was definitely going to mean surgery. He just knew it. He picked up the phone to call Pamela.

"I'm sure it will be fine, Douglas," she said unconvincingly when he'd filled her in. "You're as strong as a horse. Maybe you just need a holiday. You've been working long hours lately."

"Yes, maybe," Doug replied, knowing that's what she wanted to hear. "I'll call you tomorrow after the procedure. Grimes said he'd do it first thing."

"That's good. Well, sleep well. I'll talk to you tomorrow."

"OK, darling. Don't forget to lock up. Goodnight."

Pamela put down the phone, poured herself another drink and sank back into the armchair that she'd been sitting in since she'd left Doug at the clinic. She'd cancelled her lunch with Jean – there was no way she could carry on a normal conversation today. Her mind went over and over what Douglas had told her. A heart attack. Tears welled up in her eyes and she started to pray for the first time in years.

Doug looked at the clock on the wall. It was only nine o'clock and the night stretched out uninvitingly in front of him. He switched on Sky News as he knew there was no way he was going to sleep. He needed some distraction. Something to stop him thinking about tomorrow.

The night nurse checked on him a number of times, but it was after one before she was able to turn off the TV and slip quietly out of the room.

* * *

"Douglas is in hospital," Pamela blurted out as soon as she walked in the door. She'd considered not telling them about Douglas, but the words had just come out as if she had no control over them.

"What?" Gina stared at Pamela. "What happened?"

Pamela gave a small nervous laugh. "They think he may have had a heart attack. They're going to do an angiogram.

"Oh, Pamela! I'm so sorry."

"Oh, Gina." For one short moment Pamela felt herself weaken, but this wasn't the place and Gina certainly wasn't the person to confide in. She bent her head and busied herself with her Filofax. It would have been better if she hadn't said anything to them but they'd have found out soon enough. Douglas would be on to the office from his hospital bed as soon as he could. Lying around doing nothing was not her husband's style. She took a deep breath and forced her professional smile back on her face. "Well, he's in the best place. It's probably just a false alarm."

"He's as strong as an ox," Jack assured her.

"Yes. Yes, he is. I better re-schedule some of his meetings. Excuse me." She hurried into his office, leaving Jack and Gina looking at each other.

"What do you make of that?" Gina whispered, as the door closed after her.

Jack pulled his chair closer to Gina's. "I don't think she realises how serious this might be. An angiogram is a very invasive procedure. They don't do it unless they have to. My uncle had one last year."

"And what did they find?"

"Two blocked arteries. They ended up doing a bypass."

"Crikey. Do you think that's what they're going to do to Doug?"

Jack shrugged. "Hard to know. He's very young."

"Forty-two," Gina pointed out. That was pretty old to her. "Still, he doesn't look it. No, I'm sure there must be a mistake. Doug's the picture of health. And he always seems to be playing squash or tennis or something. People like that don't get heart attacks."

"Don't you believe it," Jack said sagely. "What about that marathon runner who just dropped dead in the street. If it could happen to him . . ."

"I suppose."

"What's up?" Malcolm came through the door and stopped short when he saw their grave expressions.

"Doug's in hospital. Suspected heart attack."

"Jesus! Is he OK?" He pulled up a chair and sat down beside them.

Gina got him a mug of coffee. "Don't know yet. They're doing tests."

Malcolm cleaned his glasses distractedly and squinted at her. "But he's so young."

"Exactly what I said." Jack sighed. "Kind of makes you think, doesn't it?"

It certainly made Malcolm think. Doug was only three years older than him, and he was a real health freak. Malcolm didn't do any exercise at all and Caroline was always nagging him to lose a bit of weight. Maybe he should join the local gym.

"What do you think, Malcolm?"

"Sorry, what was that?"

"I was saying, I'll pick up a card at lunch-time. We could all sign it."

Malcolm smiled at Gina. "Good idea. Does Noreen know?"

"No, it's her day off. God, she'll be destroyed. Should I ring her?"

Jack shook his head. "Don't be silly. It's just tests. He's not on his deathbed! Don't blow it out of proportion, Gina."

Gina looked affronted. "I'm not. It's just that Noreen's absolutely nuts about Doug. She'll be devastated."

"Well, maybe she won't have to be," Malcolm pointed out. "He might be in the clear by the time she comes in tomorrow."

"Do you really think so, Mal?" Gina had lots of reservations about her boss but she still felt sorry for him. She wondered if anyone had told Greg.

Pamela came into the room and looked at her employees sitting around chatting.

"We were just telling Malcolm about . . ." Gina broke off at the stern look on Pamela's face.

"Yes, well now you've told him, let's get back to work. And Jack? I've told you before. I don't want you smoking in the office." She turned on her heel and went into Doug's office, closing the door firmly behind her.

"Bitch," Jack muttered. "I've only had one this morning. She couldn't have smelled it."

"No, but she might have noticed that." Gina pointed

at the butt he'd left sitting on the side of the desk.

"Shit! Why didn't you tell me it was there?" Jack threw it in the bin.

Gina grinned, switched on her machine and watched Pamela chatting away on the phone. She looked the same as she did every other day. Not in the least flustered or worried. Gina smiled wryly. No, Pamela could never be accused of being an emotional female. But she must be worried about her husband. She had to be. She was obviously just one of these people who didn't like to show their feelings. That was fair enough in Gina's book. It would be a very boring world if everyone was the same. No, Pamela must have hidden depths. She had to have. After all, she'd managed to hold on to Doug this long. And he seemed happy. Despite his roving eye, he never seemed to get seriously involved with anyone.

At lunch-time, Gina went out and got a card. She picked a funny one. Doug wouldn't be into anything soppy. When she came back she got the lads to sign it, added her own name and presented it to Pamela.

"Just to wish Doug well."

Pamela looked slightly bewildered. "Oh, right, thanks. I'll give it to him this evening."

"Have you heard anything?"

Pamela shook her head. "I tried his mobile, but it's switched off."

"Ring the hospital. They'll tell you what's happening."

"There's no rush. He'll call me when he's free. Thanks for this, Gina." She tucked the card into her handbag. "Now if you'll excuse me . . . "

"Sure, right." Gina backed out of the room and shut the door. The woman was definitely an odd fish. Gina would have been up at the clinic all morning waiting for news. How on earth could she concentrate on work at a time like this?

"How is he?" Malcolm asked through a mouthful of tuna salad roll. He'd decided to give meat a miss today.

"Dunno." Gina flopped down in her seat and pulled the foil off a bar of chocolate. "She hasn't heard anything."

"I wonder is that good or bad?"

"Who knows? Where's Jack gone?"

"Out for a walk."

"Crikey! That's almost exercise! What's got into him?"

Mal looked at the roll in his hand. "I think we're all feeling a bit vulnerable."

Gina popped a piece of chocolate into her mouth. "Ah, rubbish. Life is for living. There's no point in worrying."

"That's easy for you to say. You're only a youngster. Your time will come, though. You'll start to worry about these things. Start to check for wrinkles and grey hairs."

Gina laughed. "Me? Never! I'll grow old gracefully. You just have to learn to accept your lot, Mal. Take what life throws at you. It's the only way."

Malcolm smiled and thought he'd probably been just as blasé when he was her age. Mind you, there was some truth in what she said. He was a terrible worrier. Especially now Caroline wanted to move house. It scared the hell out of him when she started talking about fitted kitchens and conservatories. He didn't know where the money was going to come from. And if they took out a bigger mortgage he couldn't see how they'd be able to afford another child for at least two years.

"I'm telling you. Worry and stress are the real killers," Gina continued.

"But you couldn't call Doug a worrier. He doesn't get stressed, he's in good shape, he exercises."

"Mmnn. True. Which goes to prove I'm right. You just never know what's around the corner so there's no point in worrying about it."

Chapter Five

"A bypass?" Doug looked at the consultant and tried to take in the significance of his words.

"Yes. It's the best course of action. Nothing to worry about. I'll get the nurse to bring you in some literature. It will tell you all you need to know."

"When?"

"Not for a few weeks. You need time to recover from this little episode and then I'm away for a while. I'll get my secretary to call you in a couple of days with a date."

"So can I go home now?"

"Well, yes, I suppose you can. Don't go back to work, though. Plenty of rest, good food and some long walks. That's what you need."

"But I have to go in to work. I have to make arrangements."

"You wouldn't have been able to make any arrangements if the attack had been a serious one," the consultant pointed out blithely. "Now be a good fellow and leave the work and worry to someone else. Use this period to build up your strength. The better you are going into this operation, the better you'll get through it."

"So do I have to take anything?"

"Sorry?"

"Tablets?"

"Oh no. You can take an aspirin each day if you like."

"What about, eh, drink?"

"A glass of wine with your dinner. Keep it to one, mind."

Doug looked at him glumly.

The consultant smiled broadly. "Don't worry, old chap. You'll be as right as rain in no time. I'll fix you up, good as new and then you can go and undo all my good work. See you in a few weeks."

Doug sank back on the pillows, feeling suddenly weak. He touched his chest, tentatively. It was hard to believe there was so much damage inside. He felt fine now. This wasn't supposed to happen to him. OK, so his dad had died of a heart attack. But he'd eaten mountains of fried food and never exercised. He'd also been overweight for most of his adult life. But Doug had taken care of himself. He'd always been reasonably careful what he ate and, OK, he liked a full breakfast occasionally and drank too much, but didn't everybody? He went on the dry every so often and exercised constantly, so why him?

His thoughts turned to the business. How was Pamela going to manage? Grimes had said he wouldn't be able to return to work until a couple of months after surgery. And now he was saying that he shouldn't work before the surgery either. That meant Marrakech was definitely out. Dammit! He'd have to talk to Pamela. She'd have to get in extra help. Maybe Greg was available. He was only subbing at the moment. Taking another one of his 'breaks'. He hadn't stayed in the same school for longer than a year. Still, his relaxed attitude towards his career meant he might be able to help out in CML. And he'd probably be glad of the extra cash. But while Greg could help out in the office, he couldn't be trusted to go on any of the trips. Maybe they could get Gina more involved. She'd impressed him with the way she'd handled Jim Reynolds. That would leave Pamela free to take over some of his workload. Yes, that was a definite possibility. They could always hire someone at a lower level to help out with the design work. It would work out a lot cheaper. He shifted the pillows around to make himself more comfortable. Yes, they'd manage fine without him. Pamela was well capable of looking after things. She was an excellent organiser. It was just the hands-on design work she didn't know much about. That was his forte and that's why they'd always made such a great team. He picked up his mobile to call her and discuss it and then put it down again when he remembered the reason for the staff changes. His bypass. He found it hard to believe. He felt bloody marvellous. But in a matter of weeks, Grimes was going to rip open his chest, stop his heart and perform major surgery. For the first time, Doug felt small fingers of fear tighten around his chest. What if he didn't make it through the operation? What if some bloody trainee left a scalpel inside him? What if he had a bad reaction to the anaesthetic? Some people did. He'd never really been sick before. You couldn't count sports injuries.

The nurse came in carrying some pamphlets on heart surgery. She sat down on the edge of the bed. "How are you doing?" she asked gently.

"Oh, fine. Probably still in shock. You never think it's going to happen to you."

"It's quite a straightforward operation. You just need to go in with the right frame of mind. Think of it as a second chance. It's like getting the slate wiped clean."

"So I can get stuck in and start mucking it up again," Doug said with a wry grin.

Karen smiled. "Well, that's up to you. You don't have to turn into a paragon, just be a little more careful. Take some exercise."

"But that's just it, Karen. I'm always bloody exercising. Tennis, squash, the odd bit of golf. And so, at the risk of sounding like I'm feeling sorry for myself, why me? OK, I don't always eat the right foods and I do like a drink, but Christ, I know lots of guys who are much more likely candidates than me."

The nurse frowned. "Do you have a family history?"

"Yes. Bloody genes."

Karen patted his hand and stood up. "No point in dwelling on it. It's happened. What you have to do now is turn it into something positive."

Doug looked at her with raised eyebrows. "You'll be telling me to get in touch with my inner self next!"

She laughed. "See you later."

Doug's smile faded when she left. He picked up the phone once more. No point in putting it off any longer. Pamela had to be told.

Pamela walked back into her office and sat down. She didn't know why she'd gone straight out to tell everyone. It wasn't like her. Maybe it was the shock. It was so hard to think of Douglas being anything other than fighting fit. She couldn't remember the last time he'd taken a day off work. She glanced up to see Gina's concerned face staring in at her. God, why had she insisted that the office walls were glass? The idea had been to cut down on dawdling and increase production but now she felt as if she were in a goldfish bowl. She doodled on the pad in front of her and went over in her mind what Douglas had said. It wasn't very much. Just that they wouldn't do the operation for a few weeks and there would be several weeks of convalescence afterwards. No, he'd told her very little. He was more concerned with the business and how she'd manage without him. His idea was a good one. Greg knew the set-up and would be a great help, and Gina, with a little grooming, should be able to handle some frontline work. She'd have to get on to the agencies about hiring a junior. Someone bright, who could work well with little supervision. There was no reason why everything shouldn't run smoothly in Douglas's absence. Everything would be fine. Pamela looked down at the pad, destroyed with her scribbles. She tore off the page, tossed it in the bin and went back to work.

"Do you think she's OK?" Gina asked no one in particular.

"She's probably checking out the life insurance policies as we speak."

Gina scowled at him. "Jack! That's an awful thing to say! I'm sure she's worried sick."

"She hides it well," Mal said dryly.

"Oh, you two! You're so judgmental! Poor Doug. I wonder how he's taking this. It must be so frightening for him."

Jack drained his coffee mug. "It would scare the shit out of me."

Malcolm promised himself he'd call that health club and join up. "He's going to be laid up for months," he said morosely.

"You think? I thought it was only weeks these days." Gina vaguely remembered a neighbour back home having the operation.

"It is," Jack confirmed. "My uncle was back at work ten weeks after the operation."

"That's over two months," Mal pointed out.

Jack rolled his eyes. "Don't split hairs, Mal. It's no time at all for such a serious operation."

"It means he's going to be missing for the Lifesavers conference in Marrakech," Gina mused.

"And probably the advertising convention in Vegas too," Jack added. "Who's going to handle that?"

"You?" Gina suggested.

Jack snorted. "I can sort out the technical problems but that's about it. Anyway, Pammy baby wouldn't let me anywhere near a customer!"

Mal laughed. "That's true. Mind you, if you got yourself some designer jeans she might."

Jack looked down at his torn Wranglers and faded jumper. "What's wrong with me?"

Gina tousled his hair. "Nothing, pet. We love you just the way you are."

Jack looked longingly into her face. "Honest?"

"Honest." She blew him a kiss and went over to the printer.

Jack sighed and Mal gave him a pitying look. Poor bugger was nuts about the girl and she didn't even realise it. Sad really. They suited each other. Jack needed someone to take him in hand and Gina was the girl to do it. She seemed to go for smoothies though, if the guys she'd brought along to the pub were anything to go by. And she'd been totally smitten with Doug's brother. Funny that. Doug and Greg were very alike, both mad for the women. Gina hated this in Doug but she seemed oblivious to it in Greg. Mal polished his glasses. Women! He'd never understand them.

Gina wondered if she should go in and see if Pamela was OK. She'd nearly bitten her head off before. Still, she could bring her in a cup of tea and then if she wanted to talk . . . Gina saved the file she was working on and went out to put on the kettle. She rooted around in the press for the Earl Grey tea bags and then went in search of one of the dainty china mugs that Pamela favoured.

"You shouldn't have," Jack said as she carried the tea across the office.

"I didn't." She smiled sweetly and walked past him.

"Licking up to the boss, eh? God, you really *do* want a raise."

Gina made a face at him, knocked gently on Pamela's door and went in.

"Yes?" Pamela said without looking up.

"I just thought you might like some tea."

Pamela looked at her vaguely. "Thanks, Gina. Put it over there." Pamela went back to work.

"Any more news?" Gina asked tentatively.

"No."

Gina sat down.

Pamela looked at her. "Was there something else?"

"Oh, no, sorry. Just, well, I wanted you to know, Pamela, that we're all behind you. You don't have to worry about work."

Pamela suppressed a smile. "Well, thank you, Gina. That's nice to know. I think if we all just carry on as normal . . ."

"Yes." Gina smiled at her.

"Get on with the job," Pamela said pointedly.

Gina nodded enthusiastically.

"Like *now*, Gina," Pamela said, giving up on subtlety.

Gina flushed and stood up. "Right. Sorry." She walked out of the office and just resisted the temptation to slam the door after her.

Pamela sighed. God, was it going to be like this until Douglas got back? She'd go nuts if everyone kept asking her if she was OK. Why shouldn't she be OK? She was well used to running things.

Jack grinned as Gina slammed things around her desk She'd never learn. Pamela was never going to become her bosom pal, not if her life depended on it! Gina was beating her head against a brick wall. Jack looked at her sympathetically. She was a real softie at heart. She always saw the best in people. Jack didn't really think that Pamela was all that bad but even he was surprised at how coolly she was taking Doug's illness. It was as if she didn't care at all. Poor old Doug.

Gina tapped furiously at her keyboard and fumed inwardly. That was definitely the last time she'd hold out the hand of friendship to that woman! What was her problem? They'd worked together for four years now and Pamela still kept her at arm's length. Well, she kept everyone at arm's length but you'd imagine she'd be happy to have a girlfriend at work. It definitely wouldn't be Noreen – she'd be horrified if Pamela even tried to get friendly – so that just left Gina. Although Pamela didn't seem to have *any* girlfriends, Gina mused as she chewed on her pencil. Just 'contacts' or other women who moved in the right circles and shopped in the right boutiques. You couldn't call *them* friends. Sad really. Gina threw down the pencil in disgust. Lord, she was doing it again. Feeling sorry for Pamela and the bitch couldn't give a damn about her! That was it! From now on she was going to look after Number One and her first priority was to negotiate a promotion. If she didn't get it, she'd leave. She saved the file she was working on, stood up and grabbed her coat and bag. "I'm off. See you tomorrow."

Jack looked up in surprise. It was only five o'clock and Gina rarely left the office before six. "Everything OK?" he called as she walked out the door.

"Everything's just peachy!" she retorted without looking back.

Chapter Six

Susie Clarke turned up the volume on her Walkman in an effort to drown out the sound of the fight going on downstairs. What in God's name was wrong with him now? She continued to paint her nails a vivid lime green and tried not to listen to her mother's plaintive tones. How many more years was she going to put up with this carry-on? Susie couldn't understand it. She'd have walked out on him years ago. He was a miserable, crabby little man, who thought the world owed him something. Why, only God knew. He was a lousy husband and he'd never been much of a father. He'd just managed to get his wife pregnant five times, and then complain that she couldn't keep the kids in order. His job – he was a plumber when he could get the work – wasn't enough to keep them, so Susie's mother did a bit of cleaning in Cadbury's to bring in a bit more money. Of course, Christy Clarke wasn't at all happy about this. People would think he couldn't look after his own family. Well, he could, and if the bloody woman didn't waste money on herself they'd be able to manage just fine.

Susie had heard it all before. Her earliest memories were of her da coming into the house shouting and her mother telling them all to get up to bed. Susie and Marie, her older sister, would hurry the smaller children up the stairs and then creep back on to the landing to listen to her da roaring and shouting. Susie often thought he was going to hit her mother, but as far as she knew, he never had. But then, he didn't have to. Florrie Clarke was terrified of him and would have done anything to keep him happy.

It made Susie sick. She loved her ma, but was disappointed that she was such a doormat. Why in God's name did she stay with the oul bastard? Susie wouldn't take that crap from him or any other fella. Only one boyfriend had ever got rough with her and a swift knee in the balls had shown him that he'd tried it on with the wrong girl.

Susie blew on her nails and then swung around to the mirror to apply her make-up. She plastered on foundation and then applied a vivid green eye-shadow that did nothing to liven up her blue-green eyes. The dark, almost purple lipstick was a startling slash against her sallow complexion and the heavy black mascara gave her an almost punk appearance. She pulled her stringy blonde hair back into a high ponytail and then dressed quickly in a shiny tracksuit that did nothing to hide her bulging hips and full stomach.

With only a cursory look at her reflection, she picked up a heavy backpack and ran swiftly down the stairs. "See ya later," she called.

"Susie? Susie, wait."

She sighed and turned back to her mother who was closing the kitchen door gently behind her.

"What is it, Ma?"

"Will ye pick up some fish and chips for the tea on your way home? Get some fresh cod. Yer da likes that."

Susie looked at her mother irritably. "Who cares what *he* likes? It would be better for all of us if he choked on the bloody bones!"

Florrie Clarke crossed herself and looked anxiously at the kitchen door. "Don't talk about yer father like that, Susie," she hissed. "Show a bit of respect."

Susie rolled her eyes. "I'll pick up the fish and chips. I should be back around six."

Her mother pressed ten pounds into her hand and smiled apologetically. "Good girl."

Susie let herself out and started running as the bus appeared around the corner. The sooner she could afford to leave home the better. But she'd have to get a job first. A good job. She wasn't going to end up serving in McDonald's or Bewley's. No bloody way. She was going to be very successful. She pushed her way on to the crowded bus and squeezed into a seat beside a large, scowling woman. She gazed out of the window but she didn't see the traffic or the trees. She saw herself in a smart office wearing a smart suit. It would be a large, sunny office in the centre of town. Not the north-side of town, oh no, the south-side. Somewhere off Fitzwilliam Square or Baggot Street. The office would be modern, full of the latest computers and the staff would all carry briefcases and mobile phones and drink in places like the Horseshoe Bar or the Bailey. She would drive a nice little car and live in a small but pretty flat in one of the trendier parts of Dublin. She pushed to the back of her mind the main reason why her dream might not come true. *Don't think about it, Susie.* The bus jolted and she realised that her stop was next. She hurried down the bus, jumped off and started the ten-minute walk to the college, brightening at the thought of the day ahead. She knew she was probably the only one in the class who felt this way. They all looked at her as if she was nuts when she asked questions or stayed back after class, but she didn't care. She was fascinated by computers. She'd taken to working with spreadsheets like she'd been doing it all her life and she was very creative when it came to desktop publishing. But it was the presentation packages that she liked best. Corel Draw, PowerPoint, Adobe PhotoShop and Illustrator. These were the packages that really fired her imagination.

She would always be grateful to the career guidance teacher who'd convinced her that she should go on and study computers.

"It's the way of the future, Susie. You'll need to feel comfortable with computers no matter what job you end up in. A course like this under your belt will open a lot of doors for you."

At the time, Susie had no intention of taking her advice. Go back into the classroom out of choice? No bloody way! But after trawling through the job columns for several months she'd decided to give it a go. It was at a time when there was a lot of help from the authorities to get you off the dole and into full-time work and she was lucky that there were still a couple of places available on the Fás Information Technology course.

She was also lucky that her teacher, Chrissie O'Malley, loved what she did and knew what she was talking about. Susie was immediately drawn to the gutsy, friendly woman.

For her part, Chrissie was delighted with her new student. Susie absorbed information at an incredible rate and was way ahead of everyone else on the course. She also stayed back after class, plaguing Chrissie with questions.

Chrissie was only too happy to answer. It was refreshing to have a student show some interest and there was no doubt that when it came to computers, Susie was a natural, though Chrissie could understand why she hadn't done well in school. She was easily bored and it was the mind-blowing scope of computers that held her attention. And despite Susie's alarming appearance, she was a nice kid with a good sense of humour. At least she was once you got past the massive chip on her shoulder.

Susie's course finished next week and she looked forward to the future with a mixture of excitement and fear. Chrissie had helped her apply for a few jobs, though Susie had turned her nose up at some of her teacher's suggestions. They were at a very low level and the work would be boring. But Chrissie pointed out that it would be a foot in the door, and once they saw her talent she would progress quickly enough. Susie knew she was right and grudgingly agreed to apply for anything and everything.

So things were going according to plan. No, that was a load of rubbish. Susie sighed in frustration as she pushed open the door of the classroom. She'd screwed up. Literally. Because her period was late. Three weeks late to be precise. She was furious with herself. She'd sneered at Mary McNally up the road when she'd got caught out and now here she was in the same boat. She didn't even know who the bloody father was! Well, she did. He'd had glorious blue eyes – she was a sucker for blue eyes – curly black hair, and a cheeky smile. His name was Derek – or was it Declan? – and he'd bought her several Bacardi and Cokes. She'd been delighted when he'd detoured to Dollymount on the way home. He'd parked on the deserted beach and they'd kissed passionately. He was a great kisser. Susie clambered happily into the back seat with him. Shivered deliciously when he pushed up her skirt. And giggled uncontrollably when the condom had split.

Well, the last laugh was definitely on her. She'd never seen the guy again – didn't particularly want to either – but it still meant she was left to face a sticky situation alone. So much for all her big dreams of a great job and a fancy flat.

The obvious move would be to get rid of it, but Susie couldn't do it. She wasn't the greatest Catholic in the world, but her mother and the nuns *had* managed to instil some sense of religion in her. Abortion was a definite no-no. Even her da, who never went to Mass, would be disgusted with her. Mind you, he was going to kill her one way or the other.

Her best bet would be to go away somewhere, maybe London, and have the baby without anyone knowing. But how would she manage on her own? She'd no money and she'd never get a decent job now. She was going to have to tell Chrissie. God, she'd be disgusted with her.

Chrissie looked at her, her eyes full of dismay. "Oh, Susie. Are you sure?"

Susie nodded mutely, embarrassed and ashamed.

"How long?"

"Dunno. Only a few weeks, I think."

"Well, the first thing you have to do is go and have a check-up." Chrissie looked at the young girl in front of her with a mixture of pity and annoyance. She'd had such high hopes for Susie and now this. What a mess. "What do you want to do?" she asked quietly.

Susie gave a small laugh. "What *can* I do? I'm a good holy Catholic girl."

"I see. OK. And will you keep the baby?"

"No. I dunno. Oh, bloody hell, Chrissie. All I wanted was a good job and a better life."

"You can still have that. It may take a little longer . . ."

"I don't want to wait any longer! If I don't get out of that house soon I'll go mad."

Chrissie looked slightly alarmed at Susie's vehemence and was surprised to see tears in her eyes. Susie normally presented such a tough front. "Let's take this one step at a time," she said soothingly. "Make an appointment to see a doctor and we'll take it from there."

"But what about the job applications?"

"We'll go ahead with them. You wouldn't have to give up work until a couple of weeks before the baby is due. And you'll be entitled to maternity leave. It isn't the Dark Ages, love. This kind of thing happens all the time."

Susie looked at her doubtfully. "But who'll want to take on a pregnant girl?"

"You'd be surprised. Anyway, let's worry about that when the time comes."

"I suppose I don't have to tell them immediately."

"No, love. It's best to be honest. No one likes having the wool pulled over their eyes."

Susie looked at her, dejected.

"You should tell your parents too."

"Oh, no! Not yet, anyway. Me oul fella will go mad."

"What about your mother?"

Susie shrugged. "She'd probably be OK about it, but she'd never stand up to me da."

"OK. Well, let's leave that for the moment. You organise an appointment with the doctor and we'll talk again when you know for sure."

"Right." Susie stood to leave and then turned back. "Thanks, Chrissie. I didn't know who else to talk to."

"No problem, love. Take care of yourself." Chrissie watched sadly as Susie dragged herself down the corridor. It was such a shame. Chrissie hoped that there was a broad-minded employer out there who would look at Susie's talent and skill and not her stomach. And what was going on in the poor girl's family? The father sounded like a right tyrant, though Susie didn't seem afraid of him. It would make things a lot more difficult if he threw her out. Chrissie passed a weary hand across her eyes. Tony would kill her. He was always saying she got too close to her students, taking their problems on her own shoulders.

"But," she'd said to her husband on many an occasion, "someone's got to look out for them. They've been let down by the education system already and it's a bloody miracle that they've made it as far as my course. I can't let them down too."

And Tony would smile tenderly and tell her she was an old softie, and she'd hug him and say that's why he'd married her.

Chrissie packed her notes into her battered briefcase, turned off the lights and locked the classroom. She walked slowly down the corridor wondering if Susie would ever realise her dream, or whether she would end up like her mother, with a useless husband and a gang of noisy, snotty-nosed kids.

Chapter Seven

"Tim, where the hell are you? You know I wanted to leave early." Gina strained to hear her brother's reply. The noise on the phone was terrible. He sounded like he was at the bottom of a pit. Bloody mobiles!

"I'm not coming, Gina."

"But it's Easter, Tim! Mum's expecting you. You know how she likes the family to be together at Christmas and Easter."

"Just tell her something's come up. I'll be down next weekend."

Someone, more like, Gina thought grimly. "You can tell her yourself, Tim. I'm not doing your dirty work for you. Tim? Tim?"

Gina banged down the phone, put on her coat and jammed her hat down over her unruly curls. It was still only four o'clock. With a bit of luck she'd get out of Dublin before the worst of the weekend traffic.

"Fancy a quick drink before you go?" Jack suggested hopefully.

"Not today. I'm heading home. Have a nice weekend, guys."

"Bye, Gina," Malcolm smiled.

"Goodbye, Regina. Happy Easter." Noreen managed a small smile. Probably the first since she'd heard the news about her beloved boss.

Gina was going to pop her head around Pamela's door but changed her mind. Pamela would probably only look pointedly at her watch. Nope. Gina had had quite enough of Mrs Lloyd-Hamilton.

She frowned crossly as she made her way out to the car. Damn Tim. This was really going to put a damper on the whole weekend. Peggy Barrett loved to see all her children but there was no doubt that she had a soft spot for her only son. Gina had been questioned at length last weekend about where he was and who he was with. Peggy wanted to know all about the girl he was seeing. Gina secretly pitied the woman Tim eventually married. She'd never be good enough for her mother. She climbed into her Polo, put on the heating full blast and waited for the window to clear. It was obviously Tim's new girlfriend that was keeping him in Dublin. It was over a month since he'd been home. It definitely must be serious. Oh, well, to hell with him. She wouldn't let it spoil her weekend. She needed to recharge her batteries if she was to face Pamela on Tuesday morning. She wondered – for the umpteenth time – what the meeting was about. Pamela rarely called formal meetings and it was even more unusual for her to ask to see Gina alone. "I wonder what I've done now," Gina muttered as she put the car into gear and pulled out without indicating.

Even though it was still early, it took an hour to get out of the city and the traffic on the N7 was heavy. Gina slipped a Robbie Williams cassette into the stereo and let her mind wander. She was looking forward to the weekend. Hannah would be home too and they'd be able to catch up on all the news.

Hannah Kennedy had been Gina's best friend since their first day of school. She worked in London now as an investment analyst and didn't get home too often. It always amused Gina to think of Hannah in such a responsible job. She'd been totally wild in school and given her parents a lot of sleepless nights. Gina would never forget Mrs O'Connor's face when Hannah came home at sixteen with a tiger tattooed on her shoulder. Gina was full of admiration. She'd never have had the nerve to do such a thing.

Now Hannah was a well-groomed businesswoman and wore her thick, auburn mane trained back into a plait or a chignon. Gina often looked at her willowy friend enviously. It would be so nice to be tall. Tall women always looked more poised and sophisticated. Even when Gina wore her highest heels, she was barely five foot five and she still had to look up at Hannah.

"The best goods come in small parcels," her mother told her cheerfully.

"It's better to be petite," Hannah said. "It brings out the protective instincts in men. My height frightens a lot of guys off."

Gina grinned. "It doesn't seem to frighten Fergal Macken off." Hannah's latest boyfriend was completely besotted.

"Yeah, but he's taller than me which proves my point."

Gina supposed she was right. She'd never really had any problems getting a man. But keeping him, now that was a different story. Her relationships never seemed to go the distance. She'd thought Mark was the one, but he got much too possessive for her liking. And David was the opposite. His idea of commitment was holding her hand! Gina overtook a truck and thought of Greg Hamilton. If only they'd had the opportunity to get to know each other better. She'd felt a spark the moment she'd met him and she was sure he'd felt it too. But there hadn't been much opportunity to do anything about it. Gina had booked three weeks' holidays and had been back-packing in Greece the week after Greg started work in CML. And then Pamela had sent her on a course the week after she got back. Apart from a few pub lunches with Mal and Jack in tow, she'd hardly seen him outside of work. It was typical. The most eligible man she'd met in years and she hadn't been able to get him on his own for more than five minutes. Mind you, if she had, she probably wouldn't have done anything anyway. She always got very tongue-tied when Greg Hamilton was around. He was so gorgeous. So worldly. So intelligent.

Gina moved down a gear as the traffic slowed on the approach into Kilkenny. What on earth was she doing day-dreaming about Greg? He was history. God knows when she'd see him again. No, it was time to forget the past and look to the future. Maybe the man of her dreams would be in Horan's Hotel tonight. She grinned as she thought of the men that usually frequented the place. Teenagers with acne or crusty old bachelors on the look-out for a good cook, preferably with a bit of land! No, all she had to look forward to this weekend was a good chinwag with Hannah. Thankfully she was leaving Fabulous Fergal in London, so it would be a real girl's weekend.

Gina drove slowly through the city and out onto the road to Callon. After a couple of miles, she turned into a narrow lane, followed it for another mile and then swung the car into the yard at the side of her home. Sparky, her ancient labrador, ambled over to greet her.

She patted him fondly as she climbed out of the car. "Hiya, mutt. Caught any mice lately?" She dragged her bag from the back seat and walked around to the kitchen door. The smell of apple crumble hit her nostrils as soon as she walked into the kitchen. That was Tim's favourite. Oh dear.

"Hello, love. You look well. Where's Tim? Putting the car away? Or has he gone to the pub already. Honestly, that boy! He could at least have said hello."

Gina returned her mother's hug. "He couldn't make it, Mum. He sends his love."

Peggy Barrett stared at her. "But it's Easter! How could he? I suppose it's that new girl of his. *She* didn't want him to come home. What's wrong with her? Doesn't she want to meet us? Are we not good enough for her?" .

Gina sighed. "I don't know, Mum. But he says he'll be down next weekend." *And he will. If I have to drag him down by the hair.*

"That's not the same at all."

"When's Mary coming?" Gina decided it was best to change the subject.

"She isn't," Peggy Barrett said shortly. "Jamie's got chicken-pox."

"Oh poor little Jamie! And where's Dad?"

"He's giving extra tuition to a couple of Leaving Cert students."

Gina smiled. Typical of her dad. If his students didn't pass their maths and science exams it wouldn't be his fault. He took great pride in his work and if the students showed any interest at all, he'd work with them round the clock to help them succeed. Greg was probably the same. Gina was sure he must be a great teacher. Mind you, if she'd been in his class she'd have done nothing but gaze into those gorgeous eyes all day. Her dad would like Greg. They'd have so much in common.

Peggy tucked a strand of strawberry-blonde hair back into her bun. "I suppose it's just the three of us, so," she said dejectedly.

Gina hugged her. "And we'll have a grand time."

Peggy smiled at her daughter. "Let's have a cup of tea while we're waiting for your father."

Gina rummaged in her bag and produced a botttle of wine. "How about something a little stronger?"

"Why not?" Peggy fetched two glasses while Gina struggled with the cork.

"Will Dad be long? I'm meeting Hannah at ten."

"Oh, Gina! Surely you're not going out at that hour? And on Holy Thursday night. It's the church you should be going to."

"I'm just going over to Horan's for a little while," Gina said defensively. "I haven't seen Hannah in ages, Mum. We've a lot to catch up on." Gina sighed as her mother continued to shake her head. If Tim were here her mother wouldn't have objected to *him* going out. And she'd probably have waited up for him and made him some tea when he got home.

"Well, I hope you'll be coming to the services with me tomorrow."

"Of course," Gina said, eager to pacify her.

Her mother nodded and took a sip of her wine. "So am I right? Is Tim still seeing this girl? Is that why he stayed in Dublin?"

"I think so. I've talked to her on the phone a couple of times. She seems very nice."

Peggy snorted as if that was highly unlikely. "And what about you? How's work? How's your boss?"

"He has to have a triple bypass."

"Oh, God love him!"

"Yeah. He's going to be out of work for a good while. I'm not sure how we'll manage without him."

"As long as they don't expect you to put in longer hours." Gina worked too hard already, as far as Peggy was concerned. She was always in that office. It's no wonder she was still single. "Michael Ford's home from America. For good," she added.

"What?" Gina was confused by the sudden switch in conversation. "What's that got to do with CML?"

"Nothing, silly. I was just saying . . . You and Michael used to be great friends."

"That was when we were kids, Mum."

"So? He's a fine-looking man and apparently he's very successful. He had his own business in Boston."

"If he was so successful, why did he come home?" Gina said dryly. She wasn't in the mood for her mother's matchmaking.

"Apparently he wants to settle down here. He's homesick."

He's not the only one, Gina thought. She was only in Dublin – just a couple of hours' drive away – but she often missed home. Dublin was great but sometimes it was just too big. Whereas in Kilkenny it was hard to walk twenty yards without meeting someone you knew. Mind you, that had its disadvantages on occasion.

"And he's setting up a business in the town. I'm sure he'll need experienced staff," her mother was saying.

"We're hardly in the same line of work. Anyway, I have a job."

"A job you're always giving out about," her mother retorted.

"I just said I'm overdue a promotion, but even so . . ."

"And your father would be thrilled to have you home."

Yes, he would. Tim might be his mother's favourite but Gina was the apple of Ron Barrett's eye. Maybe she *should* think about coming home. There'd be no worries about traffic jams or getting parking. It was always busy in Kilkenny, but nothing in comparison to Dublin these days. And with no rent to pay she'd be able to give her mother more money. But it would mean losing her independence. She'd have to move back into the family home. There was no good reason not to.

After Mary had got married and Gina had moved to Dublin, Peggy had got the builders in. They made Gina's tiny room into a bathroom and put a connecting door through into Mary's old room. Now it was like a self-contained little apartment. Gina's favourite part was being able to soak in the bath for as long as she wanted. There was only a shower in her little flat, and a pretty pathetic one, at that.

So there was plenty of space and the added attraction of home cooking. Gina tried her hand at cooking occasionally, but for the most part she and Tim lived on TV dinners, pizzas and curries. Coming home to *real* food was always a treat.

Gina was topping up their glasses when her father came in.

"I hope you've kept some for me," he joked. "I could do with it. Hello, gorgeous." He hugged his daughter affectionately. "How are you?"

"Great, Dad. Working hard?"

Ron Barrett took off his overcoat and hung it on the peg by the kitchen door. "Wasting my time, more like. Paddy Mooney and Jimmy Riley need a bit of help with their maths. I set them some questions from past papers to help them get used to working within the time limit, but they were more interested in getting out on time to make the disco."

Gina smiled at her father's worried expression. "I'm sure they'll do fine."

"We'll see. Where's Tim?"

"He couldn't come."

"Ah. Would it because of this new girlfriend? It must be love. Don't you think, Peggy?" He winked at Gina.

Peggy banged the pots around. "Love! Don't be silly. He's too young to think of settling down with one girl."

"For God's sake, Mum, he's thirty!"

"Yes, well, there's still plenty of time," Peggy said defensively.

Ron took a sip of the wine Gina had poured him. "Speaking of settling down, young Michael Ford is home."

"So Mum was saying. Is he really back for good?"

"Well, he's bought Foley's old shop."

Peggy put a platter of tender roast beef on the table. "That dump! It's falling down. Get the vegetables, would you, Gina?"

"There's a fair amount of work needed all right," Ron agreed, piling beef on to his plate.

Gina ladled out the peas and carrots. "He must be loaded if he can afford to renovate that place."

"Aye, he's a good catch," her father said, his eyes twinkling.

"Don't you start," his daughter warned.

"I was saying to Gina that he might be looking for staff," Peggy said, joining them at the table.

"Not for a while. It's going to be months before that place is habitable. Lovely bit of beef, Peggy."

"Well, eat up. There's enough of it," his wife said mournfully.

Ron took another drink. "That's a nice wine, love. I

saw Hannah getting off the bus as I was coming in, Gina. Are you two going out tonight?"

"Just down to Horan's."

"That girl's done very well for herself." he added.

Peggy sniffed. She didn't see why Hannah had to go all the way to London for a job. Weren't there plenty of good jobs in Ireland? "Is she still going out with that English fella?"

"Fergal is Irish, Mum. Yeah, they're still together."

"It won't be long before she's going up the aisle."

Gina sighed. Her mother wouldn't be happy until she was married off. Mary had married when she was just twenty-two and Peggy thought it was very odd that Gina was still single at twenty-eight. But she was probably right about Hannah. Gina had never seen her friend so smitten. It definitely seemed as if Fergal was the one.

"He *is* wonderful," Hannah said when they were sitting at the bar in Horan's later that evening and Gina was filling her in on the conversation. "But I have to say your mother has a point. Mike Ford was always a looker. Have you seen him lately?"

Gina shook her head. "Not for a few years."

"He always fancied you. Remember the way he used to hang around after drama class to talk to you. "

Gina laughed. "We were fifteen, for God's sake! What is this? A conspiracy to get Gina Barrett married? All enquiries welcome from single males between sixteen and sixty." But she was smiling. Mike was a fine thing. Well, he had been the last time she'd seen him.

Hannah laughed and pushed a stray auburn curl out of her eye. Dressed in jeans and a plain white T-shirt, with her hair loose around her shoulders, she looked about eighteen.

Every head in the place had turned when the two women entered the bar. So very different, but both attractive in their own way.

"Is there anyone on the scene at the moment?" Hannah asked.

Gina made a face. "Not a man in sight," she complained. "I can't remember the last time I went to the cinema and didn't see the film."

Hannah hugged her. "Oh, poor Gina!"

"It's OK for you, you've got fabulous Fergal," Gina admonished.

"That's true – oh my God."

"What," Gina watched as Hannah's green eyes turned to saucers.

"You'll never believe this," her friend hissed.

Gina laughed. "Oh, please, Hannah. Give me a break. I suppose Mike Ford just walked in."

"Did I hear my name mentioned?"

Gina whirled round to see the man himself towering over her. "Mike! How are you?" Well, that answered that question. He was even better-looking now! Some men were like that. Improved with the years. Mike had filled out – he'd been fairly gangly as a lad – but now he was quite athletic-looking. He was tanned from his years in the States and there were golden streaks through his thick, brown hair. Gina figured he was about twenty-nine. He'd been in the year ahead of her in school. She was glad now that she'd changed into tight black jeans and her new red top.

"Grand, Gina. Yourself? You're looking well." His brown eyes were warm. "How's it going, Hannah?"

"Not bad at all. We were just gossiping about you. I believe you've bought the old shop on Patrick Street."

"Jeez, word travels fast in this place! Yeah, I'm setting up a small design studio. Can I get you ladies a drink?"

"We just got one, thanks." Hannah moved a stool in between herself and Gina. "Why don't you join us?"

"Cheers." Mike ordered a pint of stout.

Gina smiled at him, shyly. He was much taller than she remembered. "So do you think there'll be enough business to keep you going?"

Mike sat down between them. "I should think so. There are a lot of businesses in the area that are fed up with having to deal with Dublin every time they need new stationery or an advertisement designed."

"That's true." Hannah watched him shrewdly. She was used to getting a lot of attention from men, but there was no doubt who Mike Ford was interested in. He'd hardly taken his eyes off Gina since he'd walked in. Hannah clapped her hands against her head dramatically. "Lord, I completely forgot! I promised Fergal I'd call him. Excuse me a moment, would you?"

Gina stared after her. She knew for a fact that Hannah had called him just before she'd left the house. "You're home for good, then?" she asked, taking a sip of her drink.

"Yes and no. I have a partner who's setting up in Dublin. I'll probably be commuting quite a bit."

Gina grinned broadly. Now that *was* good news. "Really? Whereabouts in Dublin?"

"Just off Baggot Street. Near Searson's."

"That's a coincidence. I work near there!"

"Really? What do you do?"

"I work for a conference management company."

"Who?"

"CML."

"Doug Hamilton's outfit."

Gina looked surprised. "You know Doug?"

"Yeah. Nice guy. I did some work for him a few years ago. He's doing well for himself. So what do you do?"

"I'm on the design side."

"That's interesting." He looked at her speculatively. "And do you like it?"

"I'd like it more if the pay was better."

Mike laughed, his dark eyes dancing. "I'll have a word with him, if you like."

"Don't you dare. Anyway, he has enough on his plate at the moment. He had a heart attack."

"Good God! Is he OK?"

"Yes, but he has to have a bypass."

"The poor guy. So who's running the show while he's out?"

"His wife, Pamela."

"Oh, yes. The lovely Pamela. I remember her. Old Doug did quite well for himself there."

"You think so?"

82

Mike grinned. "Not your favourite person, eh?"

"Not at the moment."

"Who are we talking about? The wicked witch of CML?" Hannah slid back on to her stool.

"You got it in one," Mike confirmed. He'd actually liked Pamela Hamilton a lot. She was a conservative woman but very intelligent with a subtle sense of humour. And there was something vulnerable about her too. But it didn't surprise him that she was a tough boss.

"I keep telling Gina that she should leave if they don't promote her. What do you think, Mike?"

Gina kicked her. "Oops, sorry Hannah."

"Well, I'd certainly keep my eyes open and my ear to the ground."

"That's exactly what I *am* doing. I've no intention of moving for the sake of it. I'll leave when I find the right position."

"Do you want to stay in Dublin?" Mike watched her intently.

"Oh, she doesn't mind, do you Gina? In fact she was just saying she quite fancied coming home."

"Really?"

Gina glared at her interfering friend. "Well, maybe. But there isn't anything for me here."

"Don't be so sure," he said cryptically.

Hannah smiled broadly at her friend. "Isn't it great to see Mike again, Gina?"

"Yeah, great." Gina blushed.

"Well, I'm very glad I ran into you." Mike smiled straight into Gina's eyes.

"Me too." Gina nodded.

Hannah looked from one to the other and stood up, putting a hand to her head. "If you don't mind, guys, I'm going to leave you to it."

Gina's mouth fell open. "What?"

"Yeah, I've a bit of a headache. I think it's probably all the smoke in here. You don't mind, do you, Gina?"

Gina looked at her friend's innocent face. Headache! What a load of baloney! She smiled sweetly. "No, of course not, Hannah. If you're not well you must go home. You do look a bit rough," she added bitchily.

Mike stood up. "Would you like me to walk you home?"

Hannah looked alarmed. "Oh, no! Sure it's only down the road. I'll be fine. You two stay here and enjoy yourselves. Gina was so looking forward to a night out. If you could walk Gina home later, though, it would put my mind at rest."

Gina glared at her and Mike grinned broadly. "Well, you can rest easy, Hannah. Of course I'll walk Gina home."

"Oh, good." Hannah winked at Gina. "I'll phone you tomorrow," she said and hurried out of the pub.

"Have we just been set up?" Mike asked, settling himself back down on the stool.

"Yes, and none too subtly either. Sorry, Mike. Don't feel you have to stay with me. I'll just finish my drink and be off."

"You will not. I made Hannah a solemn promise. I can't possibly go back on that."

"Are you sure you don't mind?"

"I'm sure. I just came in for a quick pint and instead I end up spending the evening with the best-looking woman in Kilkenny."

She looked at him suspiciously. "I think *I'm* being set up now. Are you sure my mum didn't pay you to bump into me tonight?"

Mike threw back his head and laughed. "No. Why? Is she afraid you're going to be left on the shelf?"

"Something like that. Well, I am ancient. Twenty-eight. There's really no hope for me now."

"That's true," he said and she belted him playfully.

"Watch it!"

They stayed in the pub until closing time, talking about old times, people they'd known and then Mike told her about the business he was setting up. "I'll be in Dublin quite a bit," he said with a searching look. "Maybe we could get together . . ."

"I'd like that." Gina smiled.

They walked home in a companionable silence, Mike occasionally breaking it to point out a star. Gina was disappointed when they finally reached her gate. "Thanks, Mike. Would you like to come in?"

"No, I'd better get back. I have to head up to Dublin in the morning."

"That's a pity," Gina looked up at him.

"It certainly is," he murmured, pulling her closer. "But I would like to see you again. I'll be back in Dublin in a couple of weeks. Can I call you?"

"I'd like that," Gina said, conscious of his breath on her cheek and the smell of his aftershave.

"Great." He bent his head and kissed her, a soft, gentle kiss.

Gina's eyes were still closed when he released her.

"Goodnight, Gina Barrett," he said softly.

"Goodnight," she whispered and watched him stride back up the lane. She waited until he was out of sight before going into the house, her fingers touching her lips. What a lovely kiss. What a nice guy. And how exciting that he wanted to see her again. She had to agree with Hannah. He was very good-looking. Not in an obvious sort of way. Not like Doug Hamilton. No, Mike's features were subtler. His hair was curly, his eyes a warm brown that twinkled as if he was always enjoying a private joke. His nose was quite large, his chin strong and he looked like a man who spent a lot of time outdoors. Which was funny considering he was really an artist. But then he had an artist's hands with long, sensitive fingers. Gina hummed happily as she spooned coffee into a mug. She was wrong after all. Love stories really could begin in Horan's bar!

Chapter Eight

Pamela looked at the pile of CVs on her desk. The agency had sent over fifteen, but whether any of them were suitable she really didn't know. Douglas had always looked after that end of the business. She'd get Gina to have a look at them and if she found anyone worth seeing they could set up the interviews for later in the week. At exactly ten o'clock, Gina knocked on the door and came in.

"Good morning, Gina. Sit down."

Gina pulled up a chair and set her pad down on the desk.

Pamela tucked a tendril of hair behind her ear with a perfectly manicured hand. "In order to keep things running smoothly while Douglas is out, we need to make a few changes around here. I'd like to get you more involved in organisation."

"But I'm snowed under as it is!" Gina protested.

Pamela gave her a cool look. "Please let me finish,

Gina. Obviously we don't expect you to do this on top of your existing workload. We are going to take someone on to work under your supervision."

"Oh."

"This obviously means a lot more responsibility for you and you will have to do some travelling and probably put in longer hours. I've discussed this with Douglas and we've come up with a package that we think is fair." She handed Gina an A4 typewritten sheet.

Gina's eyes widened as she scanned the page. "Operations Manager?"

"Yes."

Gina looked at the salary increase. Five thousand pounds! That was an extra four hundred quid a month – just over two after tax.

"Is there a problem?"

Gina stared at Pamela. "No. No, it's great. Thank you."

Pamela gave a thin smile. "Don't thank me, Gina. Believe me, you're going to earn it."

"Yes, of course. I'll do my best."

"Now I need you to go through these CV's. See what you think. Get Noreen to set up interviews for later this week. Anyone you think is suitable can be called back next week and I'll see them then."

"OK." Gina didn't seem capable of anything more than monosyllables.

"You'll need to, eh, change your image, Gina." Pamela's eyes scanned Gina's tight jeans and flimsy top. "You're going to be dealing with clients, so a couple of business suits would be more professional."

"Oh. OK."

"And you'll need a lightweight suit for Marrakech."

Gina gasped. "Marrakech?"

"Well, of course. You can hardly organise it from here," Pamela said impatiently. She looked at Gina's stunned expression and hoped that she was doing the right thing. "Any questions?"

"Eh, no. I don't think so. Oh, how's Doug?"

"Douglas is fine. He may be dropping in later."

"That's great."

"OK, Gina. Why don't you have a look at those CVs and we'll talk later?"

"Right." Gina got up and went to the door, clutching the precious piece of paper and the bundle of CVs.

"And Gina?"

Gina paused in the doorway.

"Congratulations," Pamela said, her smile genuine.

Gina smiled broadly. "Thanks, Pamela. I won't let you down."

Jack looked up as Gina flopped back down at her desk, flushed and eyes sparkling. "What's up? You look like the cat that got the cream."

"You are looking at the new Operations Manager of CML."

"No kidding? Congratulations!"

"Thanks," she said shyly.

"Well done, Gina. The drinks are on you this evening." Malcolm grinned at her. As he was the one who looked after the payroll, he'd known about her promotion for a few days now. He figured it would probably be best if she didn't know that Doug had wanted to give her eight thousand rather than the five that Pamela had persuaded him was sufficient .

She beamed at him "No problem. And guess what, Jack. I'm coming to Marrakech."

"Thank God for that. I wasn't looking forward to three days alone with Pammy baby." Jack beamed at her. A few days alone with Gina. There *was* a God!

"It's going to be brilliant! I've always wanted to visit North Africa and Marrakech is supposed to be an amazing city."

"You probably won't see much of it," Malcolm warned her.

"Well, we're arranging a tour for the delegates and as I'm organising it I'll have to go too, won't I?"

Mal nodded soberly. "It's your duty."

"It's going to be awfully hot." Jack hated the sun. With his fair colouring he always burned.

"Lovely," Gina said, hoping she'd have time to use the hotel pool.

"So who's going to do your work while you're away?"

Gina held up the sheaf of CVs. "We're hiring a new recruit. I have to see if any of these are suitable and arrange interviews."

Jack picked up a CV and scanned it. "I wouldn't bother with this one."

Gina took it off him. "I said, *I* have to check them out. You'd better get back to work. Pamela will go nuts if that projector isn't fixed by lunch-time."

"Oh, would you listen to her, Mal. A bit of

promotion and she's throwing her weight around already!"

During her lunch-break, Gina walked up to Grafton Street and wandered into a few boutiques. She hadn't a clue what to buy. It was all very well Pamela saying a couple of business suits, but Gina didn't know where to get something fashionable *and* affordable. She wished that Hannah was here. She'd know where to go. Hannah had a great sense of style and was never intimidated by shop assistants. There were suits of every colour in Marks & Spencer but Gina thought the styles were a bit old-fashioned and the skirts were definitely too long. Pia Bang she avoided. Pamela shopped there and it was way out of Gina's price bracket. She went into Principles and was immediately drawn to a pale mauve trouser suit. This was more like it! She looked at the price tag and cringed. Still. It was an investment. She picked a sleeveless white top to go under it and made her way to the dressing rooms.

An hour later she marched back into CML, her new purchases stowed safely in the boot of her old Polo. As she'd closed the boot with difficulty – the lock was almost falling out with rust – she wondered if she could afford to buy a new car. After all, she was management now. She had to look the part!

"Another lager, Gina?" Jack stood up and pulled a tenner from the pocket of his jeans.

"Yes, please."

"I'll get those."

"Doug! Good to see you. How are you?" Jack pumped his boss's hand.

"Pretty good, thanks, Jack. Congratulations, Gina."

"Thanks, Doug," she said shyly.

"Another pint, Malcolm?"

Mal checked his watch. "No, thanks, Doug. I've got to get home. Good to see you though."

"Thanks, Mal." Doug went up to the bar and ordered the drinks.

"He looks well." Jack sat back down beside Gina.

Gina helped herself to more peanuts. "He's a bit pale. I wonder if Pamela knows he's here."

"She'd go nuts if she saw him drinking," Malcolm said putting on his jacket.

"I doubt that she cares."

"That's not fair, Jack," Gina protested.

"Ah, now that she's promoted you she's a great woman, is she?"

"Oh, shut up."

Jack did as he saw Doug approach with the drinks.

"So, Gina. Are you looking forward to Marrakech?" Doug asked as he settled himself next to her.

"Oh, yes."

"You'll love La Mamounia. It's like a palace. Apparently Winston Churchill stayed there."

"Really?"

"I'm looking forward to visiting the *souks*," Jack said enthusiastically. Once the conference was over, he wouldn't be needed and he'd no intention of hanging around to make small talk over the canapés. He was going exploring.

"They *are* an experience," Doug agreed. "But for God's sake don't eat any food off the stalls in the market square. I did that the last time and I spent the remainder of the trip in the loo!"

Gina looked horrified. "How awful!"

"And remember to drink plenty of water. It's easy to get dehydrated. So, Gina. Have you found any likely candidates in those CVs?"

"Well, I think there are four worth interviewing."

"Yes. I had a quick look at them. I hope you don't mind me rummaging through your desk." Doug gave her his most charming smile.

"Of course not."

"And there was one in particular that looked very promising."

"Gary Williams?"

"That's the one."

"Yes, he has a lot of experience." *Maybe a little too much,* Gina thought privately. The last thing she needed was a junior that second-guessed her. She didn't need the competition. She had never had anyone work for her before and she was a bit nervous about being a boss.

"Well, experience is important, but make sure you find someone that you can work with," Doug advised.

"And someone with a bit of imagination," Jack added.

"True," Doug conceded. "Knowing the packages inside out is not enough. They need to be able to get the most out of them."

"But how do I find *that* out at an interview?" Gina

wasn't at all sure how she was going to recognise the right candidate.

"Give them something to do," Jack suggested. "Why don't you get them to re-design the Lifesavers' logo. The one they have sucks."

Doug nodded thoughtfully. "You might have something there, Jack. Why not get them to do a couple of slides for the Marrakech conference, Gina? That will show if they've got any flair and also if they understand what the conference is about."

Gina grinned. "I'm not sure *I* know that. Insurance presentations have always confused me."

"They bore the hell out of me," Jack muttered. "Nothing but bloody figures. So unimaginative."

Doug laughed. "Don't knock it. We make a lot of money out of these insurance junkets. So what do you think, Gina?"

"I think it's a great idea. If they can come up with something lively and imaginative for insurance, they should be able to turn their hands to anything."

"Great. Just don't give them any real figures."

"Of course not." Gina looked affronted. As if she'd hand out confidential information!

"Sorry." Doug took her hand and kissed it. "I'm sure you'd never do anything so silly."

Gina almost snatched her hand back. "That's OK. Excuse me. I must go to the little girls' room."

She looked at her flushed face in the mirror over the hand-basin and wished Doug wouldn't do things like that. It made her feel so uncomfortable. But he did it so casually that it almost seemed churlish to make a big deal of it. Especially when Jack told her that it meant nothing. She must be the oddball. Hannah would probably take that kind of behaviour with a grain of salt. Laugh it off. She applied some foundation in an effort to tone down her flushed cheeks and refreshed her lipstick before returning to the table.

"I'll probably be going in for the operation the week after you get back from Marrakech," Doug was saying.

"How long will they keep you in?" Gina sat back down beside them.

"Roughly ten days."

"You must be nervous," she said.

"Not at all. It's not such a big deal. Half the chaps in the golf club have had it done. The worst part is not being able to have sex for six weeks!"

"Well, I'd be terrified," Jack said, none too tactfully.

Gina shot him a look. "I'm sure you'll be fine. Back in work before you know it."

"I hope I'm back before that brother of mine puts me out of business!"

Gina's heart skipped a beat. "Is Greg going to help out, then?" she asked casually, Mike Ford fading into the back of her mind.

"That's the idea. It will make life easier for Pamela while you guys are on the road."

Jack grunted into his pint. That's all he needed. That sleaze-bag would be throwing his weight around and coming on to Gina all the time. The really sick part was she'd probably encourage him. He looked at her eyes sparkle as she drank in all Doug's information about his brother. It was disgusting! "I've got to go."

"So soon, Jack? What about you, Gina? Let me get you another drink."

"No . . . I . . ." Gina looked pleadingly at Jack.

"Oh, come on. It's a celebration. Oh, sorry . . ." Doug excused himself as his mobile rang. "Yes? Well, I'm not ready to go yet . . . What? . . . When? . . . OK, then . . . I'll go straight there. Bye." He hung up and shrugged his shoulders. "Sorry, Gina. Duty calls. My mother's not too well."

"Oh, I'm sorry. I hope it's nothing serious," Gina said, thanking God and Mrs Hamilton for her escape.

"No, but I'd like to check up on her. See if there's anything she needs."

Gina nodded sympathetically. He couldn't be too much of a scoundrel if he was so good to his mother, she supposed.

"I'm afraid further celebrations will have to wait," he was saying. "I'll take you to lunch some day. We can discuss the interviewees."

"Eh . . . if you like . . . "

"That's settled then. I'll call you. Congratulations again." He kissed her cheek. "Bye, Jack."

"See you, Doug."

Gina picked up her jacket. "Do you want a lift, Jack?"

"No, it's OK," he said moodily.

They walked out of the pub and stopped beside her car. "Oh, God. How am I going to get out of it?" Gina moaned.

"Out of what?"

"Lunch with Doug, of course."

"For God's sake, Gina. It's only lunch! Get Pammy baby to go too if it bothers you so much."

"Jack, you're a genius. That's it. That's exactly what I'll do. Brilliant. Thanks. See you tomorrow."

Jack watched her as she started the car, waved and pulled into traffic. He waved and wandered off in the opposite direction, shaking his head.

* * *

Doug pulled up outside the impressive three-storey, red-brick house in the quiet square in Ranelagh. His mother was only seventy-five, but whenever she had one of her attacks it always seemed to leave her a little frailer. He wished Greg would move in with her. He'd be a lot happier if there was someone there at night. Mind you, with Greg's social life, it probably wouldn't make much difference. Greg, while fond of his mother, didn't concern himself greatly with her welfare. And with Janet – their only sister – in Montreal, it was left to Doug to keep an eye on Sheila Hamilton. Not that it was a hardship. He'd always been closer to his mother than the other two. Maybe it was because he was the only one who really remembered his father. Janet had only dim memories of her father, and Greg none at all.

Doug was ten when Charles Hamilton died and it had shaken him to the core. How could someone as big and strong as his father die? He'd become very protective of his mother after that and shadowed her everywhere. Sheila had lovingly called him the little man of the house and talked to him often about his father.

"Mother? It's me." Doug went upstairs and opened the bedroom door gently.

Sheila opened her eyes and smiled when she saw her eldest son. "Douglas! What are you doing here? Don't tell me that silly man called you."

Doctor Bradley was under firm instructions to call Doug if ever his mother was unwell.

"He's only following instructions – leave him alone." He dropped a kiss on her forehead and sat down on the side of the bed. "How are you?" He searched her face for signs of pain.

"I'm fine, Douglas. I just got a little short of breath and that silly woman phoned him. There was really no need. She's such a fuss-pot."

Since Sheila's first serious angina attack three years ago, Betty Murray came in every day to cook and clean and, though neither woman would ever admit it, they were great friends.

"Betty did the right thing. Did Bradley give you anything?"

"Oh, some more damn pills. They're over there." She gestured weakly towards the bottle on the dressing-table.

Doug frowned. She was very pale and her lips had an ominous blue tinge. He examined the label on the bottle of pills but the name meant nothing to him. He'd ring the doctor from the car. "Can I get you anything? Some tea?"

"I'd prefer something stronger."

"Mother! Oh well, I suppose a glass of port wouldn't hurt."

"And it helps me sleep," she assured him with a twinkle in her eye.

"OK. One very small port coming up."

An hour later when she was sleeping peacefully, Doug took his hand carefully out of hers, tucked the covers up around her and slipped out of the room. On the way out to the car, he phoned the doctor.

"Mr Hamilton, hello."

"How is my mother, doctor?"

"She's fine. Quite amazing really considering the number of attacks she's had. But I suspect she's not taking it as easy as she should."

Doug sighed. He'd have to have another talk with her. Only the other day he'd caught her weeding the garden. Betty tried to keep an eye on her but his mother was a very strong-willed woman. "What tablets did you give her?"

"Just something to help with the breathlessness. She should be feeling better in a couple of days. I'll call Betty tomorrow and I'll drop in again on Wednesday."

"Thank you, doctor. I appreciate it." Relieved, Doug started the car and headed home. He was feeling quite tired himself now and he hoped Pamela hadn't made any plans for later.

* * *

"It's just a couple of drinks, Douglas. We don't have to stay long." Pamela blew on her wet nails and picked up her magazine gingerly.

"Couldn't you go on your own?" he said wearily.

"Oh, for God's sake! If I hadn't called you about your mother you'd probably still be in the pub!"

Doug knew she was right and normally he'd enjoy going to the club, but tonight he just wasn't in the mood. Still, it was easier to go than put up with one of Pamela's moods. "OK. Just let me grab a shower."

"There's plenty of time. Jim and Marjorie won't be there until nine."

Doug loosened his tie and climbed the stairs slowly. If they weren't meeting until nine he'd be lucky to be in bed by midnight. He chuckled as he thought of the number of times he'd only be getting started at midnight! But somehow clubbing had lost its attraction. If he was honest it wasn't so much the tiredness. It was the fear. Every pain, every twinge sent him into a cold sweat. But while he was afraid of getting another attack, he was even more terrified of the operation. But he couldn't tell Pamela this. She'd just look at him, a vacant look in those pale, blue eyes. She didn't seem to have taken on board the seriousness of his condition at all. To her, it was an inconvenience. A glitch in her schedule. Her energies were devoted to minimising the disruption to CML and their social life. Doug felt more than a little sorry for himself. The only one who really cared about him was his mother and he'd warned both Greg and Pamela not to tell her anything. There was no point in worrying her. He got into the shower and turned the cold tap on full. He needed something to energise him if he was to get through another evening of platitudes and trivia.

Pamela put down her magazine and stared miserably into space. Douglas seemed a lot better – he certainly looked it – but he'd changed. Normally he was out every night of the week – often without her – but now he just wanted to hang around the house listening to his damn CDs. Pamela just couldn't understand it. She'd created a wonderful life for them, just the way he wanted it. Why wasn't that enough any more?

Chapter Nine

Susie twisted and turned in the small cubicle trying to see herself in the mirror. The red jacket was probably a mistake. As always, attracted to bright colours, she'd bought it on impulse, but it stretched tightly across her hips and after the bus ride it was very creased. The long black skirt – the only thing vaguely formal in her wardrobe – was more grey than black from too much washing. She sighed. She certainly didn't look like executive material. She checked her watch again. She'd walked past CML three times already – it was much too early to go in – craning her neck to look through the windows. Finally she'd walked away and wandered into a little Italian café for a cup of coffee. Now she stood in the ladies' trying to tidy herself up and dabbing unsuccessfully at the cappuccino stain on her blouse. She was tempted to get on the bus and go straight home, but she'd never be able to face Chrissie if she did. She took a deep breath, closed her jacket with difficulty – why hadn't she bought a larger size? – and marched back into the café. She'd come this far, she might as well go through with it.

Gina looked curiously at the young girl in reception. She seemed plain on first inspection until you saw her eyes. They were the most amazing blue-green, like a stormy sea. And when she'd smiled nervously at Noreen, she looked quite pretty. Gina watched her surreptitiously, taking in the garish nail varnish, the cheap jacket and unfashionable skirt. She certainly didn't frequent the same shops as Pamela, Gina thought with a giggle. She picked up the girl's file. Her CV was basic and the only reason Gina had decided to interview her was because of the course she'd attended. It was highly thought of and Gina knew a couple of people who'd been through it and they'd turned out well. It would be great if Susan Clarke was as good, but Gina didn't hold out much hope. She was quite depressed with the candidates so far. Still, there was a glowing reference from Susan's teacher. That had to be a good sign. But she was saving the best for last. Gary Williams – the candidate Doug had commented on – was due in at twelve. And hopefully he would live up to his CV.

Gina opened the door and smiled at the girl. "Would you like to come in now, Susan?"

Gina asked the same questions that she'd asked the other candidates. She had them written down in front of her, terrified that she'd forget something. This was the first time she had ever interviewed and she found the whole thing a bit daunting. The only small comfort was that the candidates were probably more nervous than she was.

"Do you know anything about CML?" she asked for the third time that morning.

Chrissie had prepared Susie for this one. "A little. You've been in business thirteen years and your main customers are financial institutions."

Gina's eyebrows arched as Susie named CML's five biggest accounts.

"You're the largest conference management company in the country and you also have a couple of accounts in the UK."

"That's right. We've had a number of conferences in London and Edinburgh and as a result we attracted some new accounts who were impressed with CML's efficiency and the standard of our presentations. Which brings me to the slides I asked you to design."

Susie pulled a disk out of her bag. "I have them right here."

"Excellent. What package did you use?"

"PowerPoint."

"OK. Let's have a look." Gina took the disk, slipped it into the drive and opened the file.

"This is very good," she said, trying not to betray her excitement. Susan's slides were streets ahead of the other candidates'. She had used only three colours and her special effects were tasteful and effective. The other candidates' had fallen into the trap of using every colour available. They didn't understand that less was often more. Gina was surprised, given Susan's dress sense, how muted and classy the screens were. That's what comes of judging a book by its cover, she admonished herself. "I like your use of colour." She smiled at the other girl. "What did you think of the logo?"

"Not a lot," Susie retorted before she could stop herself.

Gina laughed. "It's unanimous, so."

Susie smiled nervously, relieved that she hadn't put her foot in it.

"OK, well I think that's everything, Susan. We might need you to come back next week. Would that be OK?"

"Sure."

"Now, is there anything you wanted to ask me?"

Again Susie was ready. Chrissie said it was important to ask questions and they'd rehearsed a couple.

She asked if CML had any plans for expansion and what steps had been taken to deal with the problems the introduction of the *euro* was likely to cause.

Gina stared at the young girl, gobsmacked. No one else had asked anything that intelligent. She answered as best she could and then stood up. "Well, Susan. Thanks for coming in. We'll be in touch."

"There was just one other thing," Susie mumbled.

Gina sat down again. "Yes?"

"I'm pregnant."

"Oh," Gina said, at a loss. "Congratulations," she added quickly.

"It was a mistake," Susie said bluntly. "I'll be giving it up for adoption. It won't get in the way of me doing a good job. All I'll need is the minimum amount of maternity leave."

This all came out in a rush and Gina's heart went out to the girl who was looking at her hands, her face scarlet. She didn't know quite what to say. "When are you due?"

"October."

"Right. Well, thanks for telling me. We'll be in touch."

Susie's heart sank as Gina shook her hand. That was that. She'd never hear from her again. She walked back out on to the street, tears filling her eyes. CML was just the kind of place she'd always wanted to work in. The pale-blue walls and the darker blue plush carpeting, the black ash desks and the soft leather chairs in reception, the secretary who looked like Miss Moneypenny and the beautiful girl in the gorgeous lilac trouser-suit who had interviewed her. Add to that the wonderful aroma of freshly-brewed coffee and it was like her dream come true. But she'd seen the shocked look on Gina Barrett's face when she'd told her about the pregnancy. The tears spilled out and she wiped them away angrily. It was her own bloody fault. She'd blown any chance of getting a decent job the night she'd climbed into the back seat of that Brava. She'd no one to blame but herself.

Gina sat for a long time looking at the slides that Susie had prepared. They were really brilliant. So far, she was the ideal candidate. Well, she was until she'd dropped her bombshell. There was no way Pamela would agree to hire her now. It would have been difficult enough to persuade her, given Susan's appearance and her accent. Pamela was very snobbish about such things. But Gina felt sure she would have been able to talk her round. But not now. She closed the file with a sigh and hoped fervently that Gary Williams turned out to be as good as he appeared on paper.

Gary Williams was everything his CV said he was and more. The slides he'd prepared were excellent, if a little dull. He was immaculately dressed in a grey suit, blue shirt and matching blue tie. He was handsome and articulate, oozed confidence and Gina took an immediate dislike to him. She said as much to Jack and Mal over lunch in the pub.

"Well, if you don't think you'll be able to work with him, you shouldn't hire him," Mal said through a mouthful of chips. His plan to adopt a healthier lifestyle had fallen by the wayside.

"But if he's the best candidate," Jack interjected, "you can't discriminate against him because he's confident."

"I'm not," she protested. "Oh, I don't know. And he's *not* the best candidate, not really. There was a girl that came up with the most amazing presentation."

"So hire her." Jack couldn't see what the problem was.

"There's no way Pamela will let me. Her qualifications are pretty basic and she's nineteen, single and pregnant."

"That's discrimination too," Jack said.

"You tell Pamela that," Gina said caustically. "I'm sure she'll see your point of view and hire her immediately."

Mal laughed. "And she's really talented?"

Gina nodded. "Honestly, Mal. It was the best stuff I've seen in ages. Understated but so effective."

Mal nodded thoughtfully. "Why not talk to Doug? He'd be more broadminded."

Gina looked doubtful. "Maybe. If she looked like Claudia Schiffer."

Jack looked disappointed. "She doesn't?"

"Let's say she's different. She's about my height, a bit on the heavy side and has a rather . . . individual style."

"But she's good?"

"She's very good, Jack."

"Then get her back for another interview and ask Doug to sit in on it. When's he taking you to lunch?"

Gina grimaced. "Monday." She'd tried to get out of it, but Doug was insistent. Pamela wouldn't even be there – she was away until Wednesday. "But Pamela said *she* wanted to sit in on the second interviews. She'll go nuts if I go behind her back."

"So what? It's better to put up with her temper for a couple of days than to end up working with someone you hate."

Mal stood up. "Anyone for coffee?"

"No, I need to go to the shops before we go back. Anyone want anything?"

"Chocolate, please." Gina handed Jack a pound.

Mal groaned. "How can you eat so much chocolate and stay so skinny?"

"Dunno," she said cheerfully. "Get me a coffee with cream, will you, Mal?"

"It'll catch up on you when you hit forty," he warned.

"That's years away. I'll worry about it then." When she was alone, Gina thought about what Jack had said. He was right. She was the one who was going to have to work with the new employee, not Pamela. Maybe Doug *would* be more receptive. If she showed him the slides first, he'd realise how talented Susan Clarke was. Then he could meet her.

"These are great, Gina. Much better than any of the others. Though Gary's have a certain style."

"Yes," she agreed reluctantly. She'd thought it only fair to show Doug both presentations.

"But there's no doubt that this girl has a gift."

"Exactly," Gina agreed excitedly.

Doug looked at his watch. "Come on. I've booked a table at Chez Nous."

Gina's eyes widened. That was one of the most exclusive restaurants in the city. "I've set up the first interview for two-thirty," she reminded him.

"No problem. If we're late back Noreen can make him coffee."

Gina followed him out to the gleaming Jaguar and resigned herself to a cosy lunch for two. Well, at least they wouldn't be able to drink.

"Just a glass of Chablis, Gina. It will go beautifully with the turbot, don't you think, Stephanie?" He smiled broadly at the beautiful owner.

"Indeed it will," she agreed, smiling sympathetically at Gina. "Maybe some mineral water as well?"

Gina nodded gratefully.

"That's a beautiful suit." Doug said when they were alone. "The colour looks great on you."

Gina was wearing the latest addition to her wardrobe, a lemon trouser suit with a thin aquamarine pinstripe. "Thank you."

"It's quite warm in here. Will I take your jacket?"

"No, I'm fine," she said hurriedly, thinking of the skimpy top she was wearing underneath. The last thing she needed was Doug ogling her boobs all through lunch. She wondered if she ought to tell him about Susan's predicament now or wait until after he'd met her. She watched him taste the wine and nod his approval. Surely he shouldn't be drinking in the run-up to such a major operation? Still, maybe he'd feel more benevolent towards a young girl in trouble after a few drinks.

"A penny for them?" His eyes twinkled at her over his glass.

He really was a very good-looking man. Gina had noticed him get several appraising glances from the other women in the restaurant. "I was just thinking about the candidates."

"You're leaning towards the girl, aren't you?"

She nodded.

"I hope it's for the right reasons, Gina. Don't be intimidated by the thought of a man reporting to you."

Gina was surprised at his perceptiveness. She *had* wondered if she would be able to handle someone as strong-willed as Gary working for her. "I've never been a boss before. It's a little hard to get used to the idea."

He laughed. "After a few weeks you'll be wondering how you ever managed without help. Your biggest problem will be leaving them alone to get on with it."

"Did you find it hard to delegate?" she asked curiously.

He laughed. "Never. I was always too busy thinking about the next deal. The next job. I was usually relieved to off-load some of the work. Still, I do miss the hands-on stuff. Working at a PC all day is a lot more straightforward than dealing with people."

Gina frowned. If someone as smooth and successful as Doug found it difficult, how was *she* going to cope?

Doug smiled at the look of panic on her face. "You'll do fine, Gina. I have just one piece of advice for you. When you're organising an event, always bear in mind that the delegates should enjoy themselves. They may have been sent along against their will and it's our job to make sure that they go home happy."

"I'm sure it's no hardship for anyone to be sent to Marrakech, stay in the best hotel and eat and drink as much as they want free gratis!"

He laughed. "No, but not all conferences are like that. When a delegate has to travel from Cork to Dublin for a seminar on EU funding and it's snowing and the traffic is lousy, they're not so happy."

"I suppose not."

"That's the real challenge. If you manage to hold people's attention – even though the content is boring. If you look after them well and treat them with respect, then you've succeeded in your job. CML can't be held responsible for boring material but we can be blamed for unimaginative presentation, poor service or bad food."

Gina nodded. "I'm really looking forward to the challenge, Doug. Thanks for giving me the opportunity."

"You've earned it, Gina. Pamela thinks so too."

Gina sincerely doubted it. She was quite sure that there would have been no mention of promotion were it not for Doug's impending operation. She nodded and smiled anyway.

"But you and Jack better behave yourselves in Marrakech. I don't want you coming home in the family way!"

Gina laughed nervously. "Speaking of being in the family way . . ."

Doug waited until the door closed on Gary Williams. "He's very good, Gina. I don't know why we're bothering to see this girl."

"Oh, please, Doug. I asked her to come in. It would be cruel to send her away without even seeing her!"

Doug looked at his watch impatiently. It was bad enough that they'd had to rush an excellent lunch, he wasn't in the mood to waste time on Gina's lame dog. Still, these were her first interviews. He shouldn't be too hard on her. She was allowed one mistake. "OK, OK, but I can only give her ten minutes."

"Thanks, Doug." Gina smiled gratefully and went out to collect Susan.

Doug stood up and shook hands with the girl.

"Susan, this is Douglas Hamilton, our Managing Director."

Susan smiled nervously. The MD! Bloody hell!

"Nice to meet you, Susan. Thanks for coming in. I've seen your presentation and Gina has filled me in on your, eh, background. Maybe you'd like to tell us what appeals to you about working for CML."

Susan took a deep breath and started to talk. Chrissie had said that she must make an impression. She was going to do that if it killed her.

Doug looked her up and down as she talked, taking in the garish makeup and crumpled jacket. She wasn't a bad-looking kid. If she was taken in hand and lost a bit of weight she might look presentable. But he thought of her waddling around the office heavily pregnant and shuddered.

"Don't ye think so?" Susan was looking at him, her eyes angry. She knew damn well he hadn't heard a word she'd said.

"Yes, yes indeed," he replied smoothly. "And why do you think we should give you the job, Susan?"

Susan studied her vivid blue nails for a minute before answering. Then she lifted her head defiantly and looked him straight in the eye. "Because I'm a good designer, a hard worker and if ye can get past the fact that I'm pregnant ye'll realise I'm the best person for the job." She leaned forward and looked at him beseechingly, her large eyes filled with desperation. "Look, Mr Hamilton. I need this job. I'm desperate and I need the money. So I'll work twice as hard as anyone else. I'll even clean the bloody floors if you want! Just give me a chance. Please."

Doug smiled slowly. The girl had guts. And she

didn't seem quite so plain when she was angry. Her cheeks were red and her eyes sparkled with temper. What a strange colour they were. "Right. Could you wait outside for a moment please?"

She nodded dumbly and left the room, closing the door with difficulty because her hands were shaking so much.

"Maybe we *should* give her a chance," Doug said thoughtfully.

Gina looked stunned. After Susan lashing out like that, Gina was sure Doug would dismiss her out of hand. "Really?"

"Yeah, why not? Poor kid seems to be having a rough time. But she has a temper, Gina. You may regret your choice. Let's start with a six-month probation and see how she gets on."

Doug smiled indulgently. This was the perfect solution. The probationary period would probably take them up to her maternity leave and then they could let her go. And Gina would be delighted that he'd accepted her recommendation. Perfect.

"Shouldn't we arrange for her to meet Pamela first?" Gina said nervously. Pamela was going to kill her for doing this behind her back.

"Don't worry about Pamela. I'll fill her in. Now, why don't you call the girl in and we'll give her the good news?"

Susie almost skipped down the steps of CML. "Yes! Yes! Yes!" she said, clapping her hands and ignoring the curious looks from passers-by. A wonderful job and a great salary. £15,200 a year! Amazing!

Pamela clenched her fists and forced herself to remain calm. "Let me get this straight. You came into the office when you were supposed to be out on official sick-leave. Carried out interviews that I'd expressly told Gina I wished to attend. And hired a pregnant girl with no experience."

"That about sums it up," Doug said cheerfully. "Oh, don't make a song and dance about it, Pam. She's on six months' probation. If she doesn't work out, we'll get rid of her."

"You undermined my authority, Douglas," Pamela said coldly. "And Gina had no right to involve you in the first place."

"I didn't give her much choice. Don't take it out on her." He slid his arms around her and kissed her. "Don't fight with me, Pam. I didn't mean to undermine you. Sorry."

She smiled grimly. "Stop meddling, Douglas, and go home."

He sighed. "OK. But promise you won't have a go at Gina."

"I promise. Now get out."

"That's a charming way to talk to your husband." He kissed her again and sauntered out of the office, whistling.

Pamela's smile disappeared. Her husband was going soft in the head. What in God's name had he been thinking of? Hiring someone who was pregnant! And at a time like this when they were going to be short-staffed.

She'd probably be out of work more often than she was in! Morning sickness, doctor's appointments, blood pressure. And when she *was* in she'd probably be throwing up in the toilet or complaining about the effects the VDU would have on her baby! Christ, they could be leaving themselves wide open to all sorts of claims. She'd better get Noreen to check into the Health and Safety Regulations. And then there was the maternity leave. No, this wasn't on at all. At least Douglas had hired her on a probationary basis. Pamela would see to it that she didn't survive six months. The last thing she needed or wanted was a pregnant woman on the premises.

"Gina, I appreciate you're trying to dress more in keeping with your new role, but maybe something a little more . . . conservative. Like grey or navy." Pamela eyed the lemon suit critically. The girl looked as if she were going to a wedding or a garden party! "And you'll need long-sleeved tops for Marrakech. Bare arms don't go down very well in Muslim countries."

Gina bit back an angry retort and turned to leave.

"One more thing, Gina. I don't appreciate the way you went behind my back with the interviews."

"I didn't mean . . ."

"I don't want to discuss it. But if the girl doesn't work out I will have to review your position."

Gina stared at her.

"That's all," Pamela said coolly. "Close the door after you."

Chapter Ten

Greg Hamilton parked his Honda Goldwing outside CML and took off his helmet. He'd been nuts to buy the bike – it was way out of his price bracket – but he just couldn't resist it. Doug had pointed out that he could have got a mortgage on a house instead, but what did he need a house for? His little flat was quite adequate with its giant TV, leather sofa and huge bed. He thought of the beautiful redhead he'd just left lying on it. She'd said a sleepy goodbye and he'd smiled down at the long white limbs tangled up in the duvet.

He ran up the steps and strode confidently into reception. "Hello, Noreen darling. You're looking as beautiful as ever."

Noreen frowned at her boss's younger brother.

"Good morning, Mr Hamilton." She ignored the compliment and looked him up and down disapprovingly. Jeans in the office – how ridiculous! And that hair – it was much too long. So girlish. So untidy.

Greg perched on the edge of her desk smiling as she

hurriedly moved all her papers out of harm's way. "So did you miss me, Noreen?"

"Of course, we all have, Mr Hamilton," she said primly. "How long will you be with us this time?"

"As long as I'm needed. You know me. Always ready to lend a hand."

Always ready to get some easy money, more like, Noreen thought grimly. Greg Hamilton was nothing like his brother. Not in the least dependable and impossibly immature. He must be in his late thirties at this stage and he still lived the life of a teenager. And he was a hopeless womaniser. Noreen hoped Regina wasn't going to fall for him all over again. She was a nice girl and much too good for the likes of Greg Hamilton. Anyway, Noreen didn't approve of office romances. The work always suffered.

"Is Pamela in?"

"Mrs Lloyd-Hamilton is at a meeting in town."

"OK. Well, I'll just go and say hello to the gang. A mug of coffee would be nice."

Noreen turned back to her typing. "I've just made a fresh pot. I'm sure you know where the mugs are."

He grinned at her bent head and sauntered into the main office. "Hi, folks!"

Jack grunted, barely glancing up from the cable he was fixing.

"Hello, Greg." Malcolm shook his hand politely.

Gina smiled brightly at him. "Greg! How are you?"

He kissed her cheek and then dropped into the chair beside her. "I've a terrible hangover. I could murder a cup of coffee. Old dragon-face out there won't get me one."

"I'll get you one." Gina hopped up and went in search of the nicest mug.

Greg smiled at Jack's disgusted expression. "So, Jack. What's new?"

"Nothing."

"Still doing the same old job? You should get out and see a bit of the world, mate. You're too young to be stuck in a nine-to-five."

"I'm quite happy," Jack said defensively.

"Really?" Greg looked at him astonished, before swinging around to face Malcolm. "What about you, Mal? Any news?"

"Nothing much. Business is good. The figures for the first quarter were better than expected." Mal watched the glazed look of boredom on Greg's face. "How are things in the academic world?"

Greg yawned. "Oh, the same old routine."

Gina came back carrying the coffee. "Here you go, Greg."

He smiled warmly at her. "Thanks, honey. You're very kind. And even more beautiful than I remember. So tell me all the news. How are you?"

Gina flushed. "I'm fine. And I just got promoted."

"Really? That's great news."

"Yes, I'm the Operations Manager now."

"Well, congratulations. We'll have to celebrate. How about lunch? Just you and me."

Gina nearly fell off the chair. "That would be nice," she said, trying to sound cool.

"Great! I'll get acquainted with the sales figures and I'll come back to get you at twelve-thirty." He stood up and headed for Doug's office with Noreen hot on his heels.

"I'm not sure you should be in here . . . "

Greg smiled coolly. "Where did you spring from, Noreen?"

Noreen flushed. She had deliberately hung around the kitchen so that she'd be able to see exactly what young Mr Hamilton was up to.

"Oh, relax, Noreen. He's my brother. He asked me to check things out."

"Well, maybe I can show you . . ."

"I'll manage on my own, thanks," he said closing the door firmly in her face.

When Pamela arrived, her mouth settled into a grim line when Noreen told her where Greg was.

She walked briskly into Doug's office. "Good morning, Greg." She leaned over his shoulder and snapped the folder shut on the CML financial statements.

Greg smiled easily. "Hiya, Pammy. Just familiarising myself with things. You look as gorgeous as ever."

"Thanks." Pamela made a mental note to keep the offices locked and she'd get Jack to change the security passwords on the system too. "Douglas has prepared a detailed report for you on what he wants you to work on."

"Right."

"It's on your desk. Outside."

"I'd be much more comfortable in here." He lounged back in Doug's leather chair.

Pamela wondered how large their phone bill would be if she left Greg Hamilton unsupervised all day. "That's not possible," she said firmly. "Douglas doesn't like *anyone* using his office. About your salary . . ."

He grinned. "Don't worry your pretty little head about that, Pammy. Doug and I have an arrangement."

Pamela sighed. That meant Douglas had promised him a lot more than was necessary. It probably would have been cheaper to hire an outsider. She looked with some distaste at Greg's clothes and bit her lip hard as she watched him kick the edge of the black-ash desk with a heavy boot.

"Can I presume that you'll dress a little more formally when you're meeting clients? You do *own* a suit, don't you?"

"I have two. And one of them is only five years old."

She smiled grimly. He loved winding her up. Always had. "Great. Well, don't let me keep you." She opened the door.

Greg stood up lazily and ambled out into the main office. Pamela followed, pausing to lock the door after her. Greg was much too inquisitive. She didn't like being called Pammy either but she knew if she said anything that Greg would use it more than ever. She had very little time for the youngest member of the Hamilton family – he was a wastrel. There was something odd about a man of his age living such a Bohemian life. He seemed to have no real ambition. No goals in life. He was nothing like his brother. But he was a charmer and very good with clients and unfortunately they needed him. But hopefully not for too long.

"I'll leave you to it, Greg. Tell Gina if you need anything."

Greg eyed Gina's breasts appreciatively. "I will."

Gina blushed like a schoolgirl and Pamela went into her office shaking her head in despair.

"Let's go to lunch now, Gina."

"I can't go yet, Greg! It's only twelve."

"So?" he said petulantly. "I bet you've been here since the crack of dawn. You can't let them walk all over you, you know. You're entitled to a decent lunch-break. And anyway, sitting in front of a VDU for too long is unhealthy."

Gina didn't think Pamela would be too impressed, but hell, he was right. She did work hard. She was entitled to a break. "OK. Give me a minute." She grabbed her bag and went into the toilets.

Greg grinned at the sour expression on Jack's face.

Gina brushed her teeth furiously with her finger, one eye on her watch, and felt a momentary pang of guilt. Being so excited about going out to lunch with Greg seemed a bit unfair to Mike. Especially the way she'd been dreaming of him for the last few weeks. But then, Mike hadn't called as he'd said he would, so why should she feel bad? She didn't owe him anything. He'd probably forgotten all about her, so to hell with him! She brushed her hair – for once her unruly curls were behaving themselves – hurriedly applied lip-gloss and sprayed herself with *CK One*. She took one last look in the mirror and thanked God she'd worn the lilac suit again. She'd done it to annoy Pamela – not suitable indeed! – but the warm look in Greg's eye was a bonus. She took a deep breath, opened the door and strolled casually back into the office. "Ready?"

Greg opened the door for her with a flourish and Gina left the office completely unaware of Jack's misery. They headed down towards Baggot Street, Gina chatting nervously as they walked. She wondered where he was bringing her. The new Chinese perhaps or maybe that gorgous little wine bar. She was acutely disappointed when Greg stopped outside the first pub they came to.

"Is this OK?" He smiled that wonderful smile that turned her legs to jelly.

"It's fine." She smiled back and followed him through the smoky room to two grubby stools at the end of the bar. She climbed on to the stool, hoping fervently that it was cleaner than it looked. Lilac didn't hide the dirt very well. She studied the blackboard menu above the bar. Whatever else about the pub, its food was usually good. The shepherd's pie was home-made and the lasagne always mouth-watering.

"I think I'll just have a sandwich. I don't like eating stodgy food at lunch-time. How about you?"

"A sandwich is fine with me," she assured him, watching hungrily as the guy beside her tucked into a juicy burger and a large plate of chips.

Greg smiled approvingly. "And what would you like to drink?"

"A bottle of lager, please." If she was going to starve she was at least going to have a drink!

When they got their drinks, Greg lifted his pint of stout. "To you, Gina. Congratulations on the promotion. It's about time. Doug and Pammy don't realise how lucky they are to have you."

"Thanks." She smiled at him over the rim of her glass. She preferred drinking out of the bottle but was afraid he mightn't approve.

"And off to Marrakech, eh? Pity I'm not going. There are so many places I'd like to show you."

Gina sighed. She wished he was going too. It would be so romantic. "But I *am* going to work," she reminded him.

"You know what they say. All work and no play . . ."

She grinned. "I'm not sure Pamela would agree with that."

"Ah, Pamela. A formidable woman. She scares the hell out of me."

"I doubt that very much. I don't think anyone or anything scares Greg Hamilton."

He smiled lazily. "You're wrong, you know. I'm terrified of snakes."

"Me too. The two-legged variety," she said dryly.

He laughed heartily. "You're so funny, Gina."

"I am?"

"You are. Funny, beautiful and clever," he murmured, moving closer.

"What are you after?" She tried to laugh off his compliments.

"You," he said before biting into his sandwich with perfect white teeth.

Gina smiled distractedly and turned her attention to the lifeless salad sandwich in front of her. Was he actually chatting her up? He'd never come on this strong before. She nibbled her sandwich, throwing him what she hoped was a coolly amused look. "You mean there's no woman in your life at the moment? I find that hard to believe."

Greg thought of the gorgeous Annabel, her luxuriant red hair, long limbs and wonderful tits. "No one," he said sadly. "It's hard to find a partner these days, Gina. I mean where do you go to meet people? A club? Most women are very careful who they go home with these days and rightly so. The only way to meet someone is through friends or family or . . . work." He smiled at her. "So what about you?"

"Sorry?"

"Are you involved with anyone?"

"Not seriously." *Not at all.* She thought glumly of how she'd sat looking at the phone for the last two weeks, willing Mike Ford to ring.

"Two lonely souls."

"I'm not lonely," she protested.

"Oh." He looked crestfallen. "And I thought we might be lonely together."

"Oh." Gina almost choked on her food.

Greg laughed. "Don't look so worried, Gina. I'm not

going to eat you! I wouldn't mind taking you out sometime, though."

"That would be nice." She wondered if he could hear her heart pounding.

"Great. That's settled then."

They strolled back to the office in the sunshine and Gina wondered if he was going to make a definite arrangement before they got there. She didn't want him to say anything in front of the others. "Have you seen the latest Bond movie yet?" she asked, panicking as they got nearer to CML. Surely he was going to say something!

"No. I can't stand that commercial crap," he said dismissively.

"Me neither," Gina said meekly. Dammit, why hadn't she mentioned the latest arty-farty movie? Something black and white with subtitles was probably more Greg's kind of thing. He was so sophisticated.

They walked up the steps of the building and Greg paused on the top step and bent to kiss her lightly on the lips. "Congratulations again, Gina. I'll call you."

"OK," she stammered. Call her? They were going to be working side by side for the next few months! Why did he have to call her? They went inside and she watched him disappear into the gents' loo. *Damn, damn, damn.* She slammed her bag down on the desk.

"Nice lunch?" Malcolm asked with a lewd wink.

"Lovely, thanks," Gina answered, with a bright smile.

"So where did he take you?"

"Oh, we just went to the pub."

"Miserable so-and-so," Jack muttered.

"No, he's not," she hissed. "I just wasn't very hungry."

"You weren't hungry! Did you just see a pig fly past, Mal?"

Malcolm ducked obligingly.

Gina glowered at them and went back to work.

Pamela watched them return and was tempted to call Gina in. They'd been out for nearly two hours! Damn Greg Hamilton. He'd only just arrived and he was causing trouble already. She'd have to get Douglas to have a word with him. He might have more luck. Greg would just laugh if she tried to reprimand him. But Gina was a different matter. Pamela expected her to behave like a manager, not a silly, lovesick schoolgirl. But she would have to wait until tomorrow. Pamela had a hair appointment at three and was meeting a client for drinks in The Morrison at five. Then there was dinner with George and Daphne later. Hopefully Douglas wouldn't back out of this one. It seemed unlikely though, because he was very fond of George, and Daphne was a very beautiful woman. And Douglas, Pamela thought grimly, couldn't resist beautiful women. She sighed. It was just as well Douglas was going into hospital soon. Pamela didn't think she could take much more. His behaviour was becoming stranger every day. Well, it would all be over in a few weeks and then things could get back to normal. Well, as normal as they'd ever been. She should arrange a holiday for the two of them when he was better. Somewhere hot and exotic. It would do him good and, God knows, she'd need the break after holding the fort for so long. Between Greg's antics, Gina's love life and, to top it all, a pregnant teenager starting on Monday, Pamela was sure she'd be grey by the time Douglas returned to work.

Chapter Eleven

Susie had been sitting in reception for fifteen minutes before Gina finally came to collect her. Gina stopped dead in her tracks when she saw her. Gone were the shabby but conservative clothes, to be replaced by a lime-green top and blue, flared jeans. Gina realised she was staring and quickly pulled herself together. "Sorry, Susan. Things are a bit hectic at the moment. Come on in. Welcome to CML."

Susie muttered a reply and followed her into a large office. Three men looked up as they came in and she was immediately conscious of how dowdy and fat she probably looked next to the beautiful brunette in the pale grey suit. Gina was so small it made Susie feel enormous beside her.

"You'll be sitting here next to me," Gina was saying. "We'll be sharing a PC for the moment, but I've ordered one for you."

Susie's eyes widened. She'd have her own machine!

"I'll bring you up to speed on what we're working on at the moment and then I'll get you to type up some notes."

Susie was disappointed but Chrissie had warned her that she'd be expected to turn her hand to anything.

Gina saw the look on her face. "Don't worry. You'll be doing some design work tomorrow."

Susie nodded mutely.

"So how are you feeling? Any sickness?"

Susie's expression was guarded. "I'm OK. I won't be looking for any time off, if that's what yer askin'."

"I didn't mean that!" Gina looked startled. God, she was touchy.

"Whatever," Susie mumbled. "And ye can call me Susie."

"Susie. I like that." Gina smiled but Susie just looked at her suspiciously.

"Oh, Jack, I think I've made a huge mistake. She's terrible!" Gina chewed miserably on a chocolate biscuit as she told Jack about Susie's first day.

"It's probably just nerves. She'll settle down."

"I'm not so sure," Gina replied with a sigh. Susie had been positively hostile yesterday. God only knew why because Gina didn't. She'd been really nice to her. But any attempt at friendship had been thrown back in her face. Maybe she and Pamela had something in common after all.

"My very first decision as Operations Manager, Jack. It would be terrible if I'd got it wrong. Pamela would just love that, wouldn't she?" Gina pulled distractedly at her hair. "What if Susie doesn't make it to the end of her probation? Doug would be disgusted with me. I practically begged him to interview the girl!"

"Don't you think you're overreacting a little?" Jack said kindly. "It was only her first day. And this is her first job. Give her a chance."

Gina tapped her boot nervously and looked at the large clock on the wall. It was only eight o'clock. Susie wasn't due in until nine. "I suppose. But she'd better be in on time. I'm going to make sure she doesn't put a foot wrong. In fact I'm going to get her through this bloody probation if it kills me!" She knew if she didn't she could probably kiss the manager's position goodbye. Her thoughts were interrupted by the intercom buzzer.

"That'll be the post. I'll go." She went out and swung open the front door.

"Morning." Susie pushed past her and went straight into the office.

Gina stared after her. "Morning," she replied, finally finding her voice.

Jack winked at Gina. "Morning, Susie. You're starting early."

Susie flashed him a shy smile. "The buses aren't as packed if ye get up early. I even got a seat this morning."

Gina gawped at her. That was the most she'd heard the girl say since she'd arrived yesterday morning! What did Jack have that she didn't?

"Would you not take the train?" Jack was saying. "The station's quite near here."

"The nearest station to my house is two miles away."

"You could cycle to the station," he said helpfully.

Susie grinned at him. "You couldn't leave a bike at the station, not in our neighbourhood. If it was still there when ye got back the wheels would be gone! Anyway, I can't see me being able to cycle anywhere soon, can you?" She looked down at her stomach.

Jack went red. "Oh, yeah. Sorry."

"That's OK." She gave him a friendly smile.

Gina looked on in amazement. "Eh, right, Susie. Do you want to get yourself a cuppa and I'll show you what I want you to do?"

"I'm ready to start now." Susie informed her stiffly and settled herself in front of the PC.

"OK, then." Gina pulled her chair over beside Susie's and opened the Lifesavers file. "This is the presentation that we'll be giving in Marrakech next month. Remember, you already did a couple of slides for us."

"I remember, but this isn't my work."

"No, this is mine."

Susie flicked through the screens, clearly unimpressed.

Gina ignored the implied insult and carried on. "Pamela has some corrections. She's marked them on this hard copy."

"So do ye just want me to key in the changes?"

"That's right," Gina said through gritted teeth. What the hell did the little bitch expect? To run the bloody place on her second day?!

"And she's happy with the colours, is she?" Susie's voice was incredulous.

"Yes. She is." *Don't lose your temper, Gina. You're management now.*

"Really?"

"Really. When you've finished making the changes,

print out two hard copies. One for me and one for Pamela. She sits in that office over there."

Susie nodded and Gina turned back to her own desk, wondering what had possessed her to take on such an cheeky little cow. If her attitude didn't improve pretty quick she was going to have to say something to the girl. Gina dreaded the thought. She'd never had to tell anyone off before. She sneaked another glance at Susie. Pamela would be meeting her for the first time this morning. What on earth was she going to say? If she didn't like the way Gina dressed, she was going to just love Susie's wardrobe!

This morning the girl was wearing fluorescent pink jeans, platform boots – were you supposed to wear high heels when you were pregnant? – and a threadbare, white jumper, that clung to every bulge. Large silver moons hung from her ears and three multicoloured bracelets jangled as she typed. Her make-up today was even more garish: dark kohl outlined her eyes and luminous green eye-shadow was slashed across the lids. The nails on her surprisingly pretty hands were painted black. Oh, yes. Pamela would be really impressed!

Susie keyed in the changes and tried not to feel too let down. Gina had promised she'd been doing presentation work today. And this definitely wasn't presentation work! A kid could do this. If only she'd let her change the design. Her work had been much better than this. She sneaked a look at the older girl and allowed herself a small smirk. Gina might be better-looking but she wasn't as talented. But that was small comfort when Susie wasn't allowed actually to *do* anything. She finished the changes, printed off a hard copy and checked it thoroughly before leaving it on Gina's desk. She printed off a second and was delivering it to Pamela's office when Malcolm came rushing through the door and almost knocked her over.

He put out a hand to steady her. "Oh! I'm so sorry. I didn't hurt you, did I?" His eyes flickered to her stomach.

She chuckled. "No, of course not. I'm grand."

"Good. Good. That's good." He stood grinning at her like an idiot. "Well. I'd better get on. I'm always late, I'm afraid. No matter how early I set the alarm."

Susie smiled.

"Right. So, I'll see you later." He hurried over to his desk.

Nice guy, Susie thought, as she set the pages down on the large desk in Pamela's office. Nothing to look at. Not like his boss. Now Doug Hamilton was a real looker – for an old guy. Malcolm was old too, overweight – but then she couldn't talk – and his brown hair was thinning. Yes, he was a bit of a dork, but nice with it.

"Susan?"

She swung around to see a beautiful, elegant woman standing in the doorway.

"It's Susie. Howaya."

Pamela looked her up and down, taking in the yellow-blonde hair, the garish make-up and the cheap, gaudy clothes. Good God, she even made Jack look respectable! "How did you get in here?" she asked coolly.

Susie reddened. "The door was open. Gina told me to leave this on yer desk." She held up the print-out.

"Very well." Pamela brushed past her and took off her jacket. "Welcome to CML," she said, not sounding at all welcoming. "We expect hard work here. We're a small team and it only works if everyone gives two hundred percent."

Susie nodded. "Yes, Mrs Hamilton."

Pamela sighed. "It's *Lloyd*-Hamilton, actually, but you may call me Pamela. Well, go on then. I'm sure you've got plenty to do."

Susie left, closing the door behind her. Pamela stared out the window at their new employee. What had Douglas been thinking of? The girl had better be a good designer because she didn't have much else going for her. Douglas had said her use of colour was amazing but Pamela found that hard to believe if her make-up and clothes were anything to go by.

Susie sat back down at her desk and buried her head in a file. My God, she'd thought Gina was pretty but Pamela Hamilton looked like she'd just stepped off the cover of a magazine. A bit like Joanna Lumley, only her hair was darker. But she had that same classy air. And she spoke as if there were marbles in her mouth! But what a bitch! Her and Doug made the perfect couple. Both gorgeous and both prize snobs.

"Susie? Could you file these, please?" Gina plonked a pile of mail on her desk.

Susie looked longingly at the PC in front of her. "Sure."

"You met Pamela, then?" Gina had seen Pamela's shocked expression as Susie left her office. Still, no surprise there. She'd known Susie wouldn't be Pamela's idea of an ideal candidate. Far from it. But as long as Susie proved herself to be talented and hard-working, there shouldn't be a problem.

"Yeah." Susie started to go through the pile.

"Her bark's worse than her bite," Gina said kindly.

"Right."

Gina sighed in frustration. "I'll leave you to it."

Susie didn't look up.

Gina swung the PC around to face her and started work, unaware of the resentful look that Susie shot at her.

At lunch-time, Susie walked down to the shops, promising herself a large cream-cake to cheer herself up. *Stop being so bloody difficult,* she told herself. *It's only your second day.*

"Hello, again."

She looked up and smiled as she saw Malcolm coming towards her. "Howaya."

"So how's it going? Are you getting on OK?"

"Yeah, I suppose. I'm not doing much, really. Just filing and stuff."

"It'll settle down in a few days. Everyone's running around like headless chickens at the moment because of this Lifesavers gig in Morocco."

"Oh."

"In a couple of weeks it'll feel like you've always worked in CML. You must come down for a drink on Friday – get to know everyone."

"Maybe."

136

"Well, you're welcome. Seeya later." Mal smiled again and strode off towards the office.

At least he seemed normal, Susie thought, as she ambled on towards the cake shop. Not like those two fashion plates. And Jack was OK too. She walked into the shop but when she got the smell of baking, she felt her stomach turn. She hurriedly pushed her way back outside and stood against the shop window taking a few deep breaths. Maybe she'd just have an apple instead.

"She seems really nice."

Gina looked at Mal with raised eyebrows. "Susie?"

"Yeah. Nice kid. Very shy."

"Are we talking about the same girl?"

Jack grinned at her miserable expression. "Oh, come on, Gina. Give her a chance. Remember, you were the one who hired her."

"Don't remind me."

"What did Pamela say?"

Gina sighed. "She wanted to know why I'd hired a punk rocker. I think it was the make-up that did it."

Mal laughed. "She's colourful all right."

"Wait till Pamela sees the tattoo."

Gina stared at Jack. "What tattoo?"

"Left-hand side of her neck – just under her ear. I think it's a snake."

"Oh, hell, I never noticed that!"

"It's quite nice, actually." Jack added. "Noreen'll just love it."

Gina groaned. "Noreen's already quite shocked by her as

it is. She keeps locking her bag in her desk and counting the pens in reception."

"Why on earth does she do that?" Mal said, disgusted.

Gina shrugged. "Her accent, her clothes, her address . . . take your pick. Susie is not exactly Noreen's or Pamela's idea of the perfect employee."

"But Doug agreed to hire her, didn't he? She must have something," Jack said matter-of-factly. Doug Hamilton wasn't stupid. If he'd hired her she must be good. And despite her unusual clothes and weird make-up, Jack quite liked her.

"She's got a temper. No, honestly," she said when she saw Mal's disbelieving look. "She had a go at Doug in the interview. Told him that if he could forget for a minute that she was pregnant, he'd realise she was perfect for the job."

"She didn't!" Jack laughed delightedly.

"She did." Gina grinned too. It had been quite funny. She'd never heard anyone put Doug in his place before.

"Well, I liked the girl before," Mal said, "but she's gone even further up in my estimation now."

"Ssh," Gina warned as she saw Susie coming back.

Susie sat down at her desk and buried her head in her work again. The silence said it all. They'd been talking about her. It was obvious.

"Fancy a coffee, Susie?" Jack asked kindly as he went off to get a refill.

"No, ta," she muttered.

"Quite right too, Susie. Caffeine's bad for the baby."

"Is it?" She looked at Mal, her face full of concern.

She knew that she wasn't supposed to drink or smoke, but coffee as well?

"So Caroline says."

"Oh." Susie drank a lot of coffee. God, what was she doing to this poor child? It was just as well she was giving it away. She'd make a terrible mother.

"A little wouldn't do any harm, surely?" Gina glared at him.

Mal reddened. "Oh, no. Of course not. My wife's a bit of a health freak. Won't even let Rachel have Coke. Crazy, really. It never did us any harm."

Susie giggled. "My little sister lives on Coke and chips. Mind you, she's an awful terror. She's always either whinging or shouting."

Gina smiled. Two whole sentences. Wow! "My mother says I was an awful child. Always crying."

"Some things never change." Jack ducked as she threw her pen at him.

"So when are you due?" Mal asked, now the ice was broken.

"October."

"That'll be nice. A baby for Christmas." Jack didn't see Gina's warning look.

"I'm not keeping it," Susie said belligerently. "I don't have the money to look after meself, never mind a baby. Anyway, I'm too young to be saddled with a kid."

Should have thought about that before you got yourself knocked up, Gina couldn't help thinking.

Jack fiddled with his lighter and Mal polished his glasses furiously. The silence was deafening.

Susie felt the atmosphere change around her. To hell with them! It was easy for them to judge her. They didn't know anything about her. They didn't have Christy Clarke for a da. They didn't have to give up most of their wages to put food in the mouths and shoes on the feet of little brothers and sisters. Florrie Clarke's eyes had filled with tears when Susie told her how much they were going to pay her. Susie had realised then that putting money away for a flat wasn't on. Her ma had a tough enough life. Now Susie could make it a bit easier for her. She glanced at the three of them and knew that they didn't know what it was like to be poor. They lived in a different world. A world that she wanted to live in too. But she was kidding herself. She didn't talk right. She hadn't gone to the right school. She didn't wear fancy clothes – she'd seen Gina's suit in Principles. It cost a bomb. There was no way she'd ever be let into their world. They wouldn't want her as a friend. She bent her head over the filing so no one would see her tears. Bloody pregnancy – she was always crying these days. And the last thing she needed was their pity.

Mal stirred his coffee and watched the girl speculatively. She wasn't as tough as she pretended. She'd been terrified when he'd told her about the coffee. She obviously worried about harming the baby. Poor thing. She was only a kid herself.

Chapter Twelve

"Gina? It's Mike Ford here."

"Mike! How are you?" She tried to sound cool when what she really wanted to do was scream, *why did it take you so long to call me?!*

"Fine. I'm fine. Listen, I'm in Dublin next week, I was wondering if you fancied going out."

She sighed in frustration. "Oh, Mike, I'm sorry, I can't. I'm going to Marrakech on Saturday."

"Well, as an excuse it beats 'I'm washing my hair'."

Gina laughed. "I'm really sorry," she said and meant it. Though it was probably for the best. If she hadn't been going away she would have said yes straight away. Playing hard to get had never been Gina's forte. And Mike deserved to be kept dangling for a while. He hadn't even apologised for not calling sooner.

"That's OK," Mike was saying.

He didn't sound very upset, Gina thought.

"Some other time maybe. So is this trip business or pleasure?"

"Business," she told him. "But I'm hoping I get a chance to do some sightseeing."

"It would be a shame not to. It's quite an amazing place."

"You've been there?" Somehow it didn't surprise Gina. Mike seemed like the kind of guy who'd done it all. He had that in common with Greg. She seemed to gravitate towards these worldly types.

"Yeah. A few years ago. I'll be interested to hear what you think of it. It's not everyone's cup of tea."

"I don't know why not. It's exotic *and* hot. An irresistible combination as far as I'm concerned."

"We'll see what you have to say on your return. I have to go now, Gina. Enjoy yourself. I'll give you a call next time I'm in town."

"Or I'll see you in Horan's," she said hopefully. Why was it that the men in her life never made firm arrangements?

"Yeah. Maybe. Bye, then."

"Bye, Mike." Gina hung up, disappointed. It seemed to be happening a lot lately. Greg hadn't mentioned going out since their lunch date. And she'd given him enough opportunities. Trailing him out to the kitchen or over to the photocopier. But though he'd always been chatty he hadn't mentioned anything about them going out together. Gina went back to work at her keyboard with slightly more force than was necessary. Twenty-eight and no love life to speak of. It just wasn't fair.

The object of her thoughts sat in Pamela's office looking out at her speculatively.

"Are you listening to me, Greg?" Pamela said irritably.

"Yes, ma'am." He gave her a lazy smile and his gaze went back to Gina.

Pamela frowned. Doug had said he'd warned Greg to stay away from Gina but she wasn't convinced he would listen. She'd just have to make sure they didn't work together. The more distance between them the better and, thankfully, Gina would be in North Africa in a few days.

"Susie will be preparing the slides for your presentation to Quikshop. Doug put together the format. If you've any changes talk to Susie, but I want to see the final presentation."

"I'd prefer to work with Gina. What the hell does that kid know?"

"She's only typing in a few screens, Greg. It's hardly brain surgery. Anyway, Gina's too busy with the Lifesavers project."

She hid a smile as she saw the look of distaste on his face. She certainly didn't have to worry about him chasing Susie! Maybe it wouldn't be a bad idea to keep the girl on after all. She closed her Filofax with a snap. "OK, Greg. That should keep you busy for the rest of the week. Any questions?"

"Eh, yeah. Any chance of a sub? I'm a bit strapped for cash and my rent's due . . ."

Pamela sighed heavily. "I'll talk to Malcolm."

He beamed at her. "Thanks, Pammy."

As he went back to his desk he bent down to whisper in Gina's ear. "How about dinner tonight?" Annabel was away for a few days and he was feeling bored and randy.

Gina shivered as she felt his warm breath on her neck. She should say no. It was ridiculously short notice. "That would be nice."

"Great. Well, why don't we go to the pub after work and then we can decide where to go?"

"OK."

He winked at her and went over to his desk. "A coffee would be nice, Suze."

Susie didn't even turn around. "It would, wouldn't it? Make me one while you're at it. And the name is Susie."

"Susie's a great kid, isn't she?" Mal said to Jack later when they had the office to themselves. "And she's funny too. She really put Hamilton in his place today."

Jack laughed. "Yeah. Great, wasn't it? The asshole deserves it. He treats her like shit."

"He should be married to Pamela, you know, not Doug. They'd really suit each other."

Jack shook his head. "No, I don't think even Pammy baby deserves him."

"Gina seems to think the sun shines out of his butt."

Jack scowled. "Do you think so?"

Mal looked at him sympathetically. "'Fraid so. He's taking her out tonight."

"Bastard."

"Well, it's your own fault, Jack. You've had plenty of opportunity to ask the girl out. Why don't you give it a shot when you're in Morocco?"

"You think?"

"What have you got to lose? Just the two of you in one of the most romantic cities in the world."

"I suppose."

"Go for it. What harm can it do?"

"But what if she's not interested? It would make working together very awkward."

Mal polished his glasses thoughtfully. "That depends on how you handle it. Say you chat her up after a few drinks and she gives you the brush off. You can laugh it off the next morning and tell her you'd had too much to drink. You apologise," Mal shrugged. "And there's no harm done."

Jack looked at him in admiration. "You should be an agony aunt, Mal. Or uncle."

"It's always easy to sort out someone else's problems," Mal said with a sigh. "Now why don't we go to the pub and cramp gorgeous Greg's style?"

"Oh, no. I'd crack up. He'd be all over Gina like a rash."

"Yeah, you're probably right. And she wouldn't be too impressed with us either."

"I wonder where he's taking her?" Jack tortured himself with images of them tucked up closely in a romantic little restaurant.

* * *

"So what do you fancy, Gina? How about a kebab?"

Gina stared at him. This was getting a bit much. They'd been in the pub two hours, they'd had three rounds – she'd bought two of them – and now he wanted to pawn her off with a kebab. Miserable sod! He might be gorgeous and sexy but Gina couldn't stand meanness.

"I'm in the mood for a nice juicy steak actually." She looked him straight in the eye.

He didn't blink. "Really? Well, how about Captain America's?"

A burger joint, Gina thought dismissively. Time to have some fun. "It's a bit far, Greg, and I'm really very hungry. How about The Berkeley Court?"

Gina saw a flicker of panic in the blue eyes.

"Oh, no. I couldn't go there. I'm sure I got food poisoning the last time."

Gina stared at him. Food poisoning in one of Dublin's best hotels? Now she knew he was bull-shitting. She smiled back. "OK, then. What about Latchford's?"

"Where's that?"

"On Baggot Street. It's really nice. Quite reasonable," she added casually.

He relaxed a little. "Oh well, if you say it's nice, I'm sure I'll like it."

"Let's go, then."

"I better ring ahead. Make sure they have a table."

Gina watched him get a telephone directory off the barman and head out to the public phone. *If he says they're full at seven-thirty on a Wednesday, then I'll know he's a miserable bastard.*

He walked back into the room smiling. "Good news and bad news. Latchford's is full but I managed to book a table in Captain America's. We can go down on my bike. It will only take five minutes."

Gina looked down at her short, tight skirt. "I'm not really dressed for going on a bike, Greg."

"Nonsense, you'll be fine. You might cause a few accidents though, with those gorgeous legs."

Gina blushed. Maybe she was being a bit hard on him. After all, he was only a schoolteacher, and Gina knew only too well how badly teachers were paid. He couldn't afford the likes of The Berkeley Court. No, she was being very unreasonable. She followed him out to the bike and climbed on slowly, making sure he got a good view of her legs. "Let's go then."

Gina watched Greg tucking into his ice cream like a little boy. She'd been completely wrong about him. He'd insisted that she have a starter *and* he'd offered to buy wine, but she'd been happy to stick with beer. And after her burger and fries – she'd decided against ordering steak – she'd eaten a marvellously luscious chocolate gateau. Throughout the meal she'd listened to Greg wax lyrical about his travels, tell her funny stories about the kids in his class, and talk wistfully about the book he'd like to write if he ever got the time.

She sighed.

"What?"

"Oh, you've done so much, Greg. My life seems terribly boring by comparison."

"I'm sure it's not. You've done a bit of travelling, haven't you?"

"Greece last year and Ibiza for the two years before that. Not exactly exotic."

"It doesn't have to be. It just has to be an experience. Seeing different places, experiencing different cultures, different cuisine."

Gina smiled as she thought of the lager louts in San Antonio, the burgers and chips that she and Hannah had practically lived on and the fact that their whole holiday had been divided between the pool and the pubs! The only Spanish words she'd learnt were *hola, nada* and *gracias!*

"You have a lovely smile." He stroked her hand and looked into her eyes.

"My teeth are crooked," she said embarrassed.

"They're perfect. You're perfect."

"Don't be silly," she said, hoping he'd go on.

"You're special. I knew the moment I saw you. I was going to ask you out then but I thought you were too good for me."

Gina stared at him. "Me?"

"Yes. You were so pretty and you always seemed to work so hard. I was a little bit in awe of you."

"So what changed?" Gina wanted to believe him but this all sounded just a little corny. She couldn't imagine Greg being intimidated by anyone, least of all her.

"Well, when Doug asked me to come and help out, it was like I'd been given a second chance. It was fate. So I decided to take the bull by the horns and ask you out. And here we are! Poor old Doug. I wish he didn't have to go in for this operation but, like my mother always says, every cloud has a silver lining."

Gina was feeling a little light-headed. Whether it was the conversation or the beer she wasn't sure. She grasped at the opportunity to get the conversation back on a more normal footing. "Is your mother very worried about Doug?"

"She doesn't know." Greg scraped the sides of the bowl with his spoon and licked it with relish. "Doug didn't want to worry her. And my God would she worry! Her darling little boy sick. She'd be devastated."

Gina looked at him curiously. He sounded almost jealous. "He's the favourite, eh? My brother's the same. He's the only boy and my mother thinks the sun shines out of his ass."

"And poor little Gina doesn't get a look in."

"Oh, I do. I'm Dad's favourite. I suppose it's Mary who got the raw deal. She had to grow up pretty fast once Tim and I came along."

"Were you the youngest?"

"Yeah."

"Me too. I thought it was the youngest that mothers were supposed to spoil."

"I think a lot has to do with the birth," Gina said knowledgeably, smiling at the waitress who'd brought more drinks. "If the mother has a rough time she takes it out on the kid."

Greg laughed. "I must ask my mother how it was for her. See if I can prove your theory."

"So if Doug's not going to tell her, how's he going to explain his absence for a few weeks?" Gina knew that Doug saw his mother at least once a week.

"He has it all planned. The story is he's going to the States on business and then he and Pamela are going on to Martha's Vineyard for a holiday. Very cunning, my brother."

"But won't she expect a card?"

"He's thought of that as well. He's installed a PC in her house and set her up with an e-mail address. He can call her anytime he likes and she won't know where he is. *And* she can write back."

"And there's no handwriting to worry about so Pamela can send a message if he isn't up to it. Wow, he *is* clever."

Greg frowned at the admiration in her voice. "A lot of fuss about nothing, if you ask me. I disappear off for weeks at a time and the old lady doesn't know where I am. Doug coddles her too much."

"I don't think there's anything wrong with looking out for your mother," Gina retorted coolly.

He smiled quickly and took her hand. "Oh, I agree, don't get me wrong. I just think that ignorance can be bliss."

"And isn't that what Doug's doing? Hiding the truth from her?"

"Yes, yes he is. You're quite right. It's good of him to be so thoughtful at a time like this. I'm sure he must be worried sick."

Gina relaxed again. "If he is, he's hiding it well. So is Pamela."

"Oh, it would take a lot to worry Pammy. Now if he were going to be in hospital for Royal Ascot week, that would be a *real* problem!"

Gina laughed. "You're terrible."

"You know you have the sexiest laugh?" Greg stroked the inside of her arm with long, tanned fingers.

"Do I?"

"You do. Have you finished? Let's get out of here."

"Where will we go?" Gina finished her glass of beer and focussed, with some difficulty, on his face.

"What about back to your place?" he said huskily, his eyes moving from her lips down to her cleavage.

Gina sobered up immediately as she thought of the pile of dirty dishes in the kitchen; the panties and stockings hanging from the rail in the bathroom and the half-eaten pizza that Tim would inevitably have left on the coffee table.

"'Fraid not. My brother will be there." It wasn't really a lie. There was a very good chance that Tim and Grainne would be in.

"Well then, how about my place?" Greg was pretty sure that Annabel had taken all of her belongings with her and she always changed the sheets before she left. What a woman!

Gina felt a wave of doubt through her inebriated state. This was moving a little too fast. She didn't want Greg to think that she was easy. "Maybe we should leave it. I've an early start tomorrow."

"Are you sure?" He leaned across and kissed the side of her neck, and then moved up to nibble her ear.

Gina sighed. God, it was tempting! He was gorgeous. She pulled back reluctantly. "Yeah. Some other time. It's been a lovely evening, Greg. I've really enjoyed myself."

"I'm glad. Come on. I'll leave you home."

"But my car . . ."

"I don't think you should be driving, do you?"

Gina shook her head and stopped herself from pointing out that he'd had just as much to drink. "Maybe not. But I'll get a taxi."

"Are you sure?" Greg asked.

Gina nodded and allowed him to help her into her jacket.

"Then at least let me walk you to the rank."

As they walked down Grafton Street, Greg slipped his arm around her waist and fondled her breast. Gina felt a tingle run through her and wished she'd agreed to go home with him. But she'd so much to do tomorrow and she'd have to go home, at some stage, for a change of clothes. It just wasn't on. She grimaced as she saw the line of taxis. Typical. She'd been looking forward to a long cuddle while they waited.

"See you tomorrow, Gee." Greg bent his head and kissed her on the lips. Gently at first and then more insistently, his tongue darting into her mouth, exploring. He pulled away abruptly and grinned at the beatific expression on her face.

She opened her eyes slowly. "Bye."

He held the door and stood waving as the car moved away. When it was out of sight he turned on his heel and walked briskly in the direction of McDaids. There was still time for another pint. He wondered if Maeve was working tonight. Now she was *really* hot!

Gina sank back into the seat and listened with half an ear to the taxi-driver prattle on about the traffic. Her head was full of Greg. His eyes, his lips – hers were still tingling – and the raw need she hadn't felt in a long time. But what about Mike? Wasn't it him she *really* fancied? She shook her head as Mike's broad frame and warm brown eyes swam before her, pushing the blond, blue-eyed image into the background. Dammit. Why was she feeling guilty? It wasn't as if she was actually going out with *either* of them. She should be so lucky. "Just take each day as it comes, Gina." She nodded sagely to herself, oblivious of the strange looks the taxi-driver was giving her in the mirror.

Chapter Thirteen

A dry heat rose up to meet them as they got off the plane in Agadir.

"My God, if it's this hot at night, what's it going to be like in the daytime?" Jack pulled off his sweatshirt.

"Isn't it wonderful? Now I wonder where our courier is?"

"Mademoiselle Barrett?"

"Oui?"

"Bienvenue. I am your courier. Michel LeMan."

Gina looked into the dark eyes of an extremely handsome man. "I was expecting a girl . . ."

He shrugged and smiled. "Michel – it is a common mistake. I have arranged refreshments in a private room for your party. Then we will take the coach to Marrakech."

"That sounds fine. I'll get them together. They're all wearing badges."

He nodded approvingly. "That will make things a lot

easier. If you like, I will wait here and you can send them down to me."

Gina nodded and hurried back up the steps of the plane. With the exception of one case of travel sickness and one delegate who, after a few whiskies, got over-amorous with a stewardess, everything had gone smoothly so far. And it seemed as if the very capable Michel had things under control here.

The Marketing Manager of Lifesavers was waiting for her. "Are we ready to go?"

"Yes, Bob." Gina smiled at the stocky young man. They'd had a chance to chat on the flight and got on very well.

His boss was a different story. David Hargreaves was an overbearing, self-important man with a quick temper.

"We'll just have tó keep him happy, so," Gina had said nervously when Bob filled her in on his cantankerous boss.

She smiled now as the stewardess handed her the intercom.

"If I could have the attention of the delegates of the Lifesavers conference? Please disembark now. Our courier, Michel LeMan, is waiting to escort you to a room where we will be served refreshments. We will leave for Marrakech within the hour and be in the beautiful Mamounia Hotel for breakfast."

There was a murmur of approval and the delegates made their way down the aisle and out to the charming Michel.

David Hargreaves paused beside her. "I hope there's

going to be no more alcohol," he grumbled. "Some of this lot are pissed as coots. And this bloody junket is costing me enough as it is."

"He's a real charmer," Jack muttered as the MD disembarked.

Refreshments, to Gina's relief and Jack's disgust, turned out to be mint tea.

Jack winced as he tasted it. "I'd prefer a pint."

"Shut up, Jack!" Gina forced some of the liquid down her throat. "It's their traditional drink."

"What is this stuff?" the whiskey-drinker said loudly. "Doesn't taste anything like tea."

Gina blushed. "I . . . eh . . ."

"This is our favourite drink in Morocco," Michel said smoothly. "It is popular in most North African countries. You will find it very refreshing in our climate. And as most Moroccans don't drink alcohol, I suppose you could say it is our Guinness!"

Everyone laughed and Gina breathed a sigh of relief. "I'm sorry about that," she said when Michel came over later. "He's had one too many on the flight."

"*Pas de problème, mademoiselle.* I'm used to it. Anyway, mint tea is a bit of an acquired taste."

Gina set her barely touched glass down on a table. "Yes."

"I will go and see if the coach has arrived."

"Isn't he nice?" Gina watched him go, admiring his slim build in the white trousers, shirt and black jacket.

"Lovely," Jack mumbled, scowling. He thought he'd left the competition behind.

Michel came back and announced that the coach had arrived. Gina shepherded everyone out and suppressed a yawn as she followed them. She'd hardly slept at all the night before, excited at the thought of her first real assignment. She hadn't slept on the flight either. Maybe now in the dark shadows of the bus she could drift off. It was more than a three-hour journey. That should be long enough to recharge her batteries. She stopped dead in her tracks as she rounded the corner and saw the banger her delegates were climbing into. She got on and took in at a glance the shabby seats and the drab blinds on the windows. The air-conditioning was noisy – or maybe it was the engine making that terrible racket as the air-conditioning seemed to be non-existent. The heat on the bus was stifling.

"Michel . . ."

"Ah, *mademoiselle*. Why don't you sit here?"

"Michel, this is disgraceful."

He frowned. "There is a problem?"

"Well yes, I'd say there's a problem! This bus is ancient!"

He smiled. "But very reliable. And thankfully the air-conditioning is of the old kind." He shivered. "Moroccan nights can be so cold."

Gina looked from him to the perspiration standing out on Jack's forehead. "Cold?"

"Oh, leave it, Gina," Jack muttered. "It's not a long journey and at least the sun isn't up yet. Everyone's tired. It's too much hassle to organise another bus at this stage."

Gina looked over at where the MD was almost

asleep. Thank God for that anyway. "OK, but I'm not happy about this, Michel. You must make other arrangements for the return journey.

He shrugged. "If you feel it's necessary . . . "

"I do." Gina pushed past him and sat down. Jack grinned at Michel and took the seat beside her. Things were looking up.

"Aahh! What? Where am I?"

"It's okay, Gina," Jack patted her arm. "We just hit a pothole. I think."

Gina looked out the window. It was dawn and they were on a dirt track through the most barren land she had ever seen. Jack had opened a window, but the air coming in was even hotter and Gina felt she was covered with dust and dirt. "Where in the hell are we?"

"In the heart of the glorious Atlas mountains," Michel said proudly from his seat in front.

"But will we ever get out of them?" she muttered as the bus struggled up a hill. "How much further, Michel?"

"We're about halfway there."

There were several groans from the people within earshot.

Gina saw the worried expression on Bob's face. Thankfully his boss was still asleep. "Phone ahead, Michel, would you? Make sure there's a magnificent breakfast ready."

Michel frowned. "Phone?"

"You do have one, don't you?"

"*Mais non.* There is a house in about five miles. Maybe they'd have a phone."

Gina stared at him. "Maybe?"

He shook his head. "Probably not."

She sighed.

Michel smiled at her. "You must not worry, *mademoiselle.* Everything will be perfect. La Mamounia is the best hotel in the world."

"It'd better be."

Michel said something to the driver in rapid French. The driver gave a loud laugh.

Gina looked worriedly at Jack.

"I'm sure it'll be fine." He rubbed his cheek, making it even dirtier.

Gina shook her head and closed her eyes as the bus shuddered its way up another hill.

"Here we are!" Michel announced.

Gina opened her eyes as they pulled up in front of what could only be described as a palace.

Jack rubbed his eyes. "Wow, this is something else!"

Gina smiled in relief as the hushed tones around the bus made it clear that the delegates were equally impressed.

Michel shepherded them into reception, spoke quickly to the young man at the desk and then clapped his hands. "Ladies and gentlemen, I know you must be tired and hungry. If you would like to leave your luggage over here and give your passports to the receptionist, you will be checked in while you are having breakfast. Those of you who would like to freshen up first will find cloakrooms at the end of the hall."

There was a murmur of approval and Gina smiled gratefully at Michel. "Thank you so much. That makes everything a lot easier."

"Pas de problème, mademoiselle."

"Please. Call me Gina."

Jack grunted and pushed past the two of them.

Gina hurried off to the ladies' to wash off some of the dust. Ten minutes later, feeling slightly better she went into the restaurant. She gasped as her eyes took in the colourful scene. Breakfast was a buffet affair and chefs in snow-white aprons and hats served hot food from stainless steel dishes. A selection of fresh fruits graced another counter, the colours taking Gina's breath away. She walked slowly around, her mouth watering at the sights and smells. This was luxury indeed. La Mamounia seemed to have everything from muesli to smoked salmon and scrambled eggs! She stood back and watched happily as the hungry delegates piled their plates and made their way to the dining area, where the tables were laid with the best of linen and silverware. Waiters moved silently between the tables, serving tea, coffee and hot chocolate.

"This is more like it." One of the men winked at her as he passed.

Jack arrived over with a tray heaped with pancakes, bacon, sausages, fried eggs and a large glass of orange juice.

"Sure you've got enough there?" Gina said dryly.

He grinned happily. "For the moment."

Bob gave her the thumbs up behind his boss's back. They were both tucking into equally large helpings. Satisfied that everyone had been served, Gina helped herself to some pancakes, ladling a generous amount of syrup on the side of her plate, and she couldn't resist a chocolate muffin. It would go nicely with her *café au lait*.

Just after Jack went up for seconds – along with most of the other delegates – Michel arrived. "Everything is arranged, Gina."

She loved the way he pronounced her name. It sounded so exotic.

"The luggage has been taken up to the rooms," he continued, "and I will distribute the keys now. This is yours. I made sure to get you the best. It is a large room overlooking the pool. Especially beautiful when the sun is going down," he murmured looking into her eyes.

Gina smiled. He really was very good-looking. "That was very kind of you," she said formally, " but I would be happier if you looked after Bob Malley and David Hargreaves."

Michel scribbled the names in his notebook. "Consider it done. They are important, *non?*"

"They are to me. They're the ones who will report back to my boss on whether or not I did a good job."

"They will have only good things to say, I promise." He pulled up a chair and sat close to her, glancing over at where Jack stood filling his plate. "You two are together?"

"Yes. Oh, no! That is, we work together. That's all."

Michel smiled. "I am glad to hear it." He stood up as he saw Jack approach. "Maybe I could show you around later. When your friends are resting."

"That would be nice."

"So what's the schedule?" Jack asked loudly. He didn't like the way the two of them were whispering.

"Meet back here for lunch at twelve-thirty and then David Hargreaves – that's the man with the specs and red hair, Michel – will give the opening address. There are two presentations and then the delegates are free to do what they want until tonight."

"What's on this evening?"

"A traditional Berber night," Michel replied. "Excellent Moroccan cuisine and some belly-dancing. There are some beautiful girls, *monsieur*. I will introduce you."

Jack glared at him. "No, thanks."

Gina nudged him. "Oh, go on, Jack. Pamela's not here to look over your shoulder."

Jack was even more put out at Gina's eagerness for him to meet other women. He tucked into his croissants and didn't bother to reply.

Michel shrugged. "I will see you both later." He smiled at Gina and was gone.

"He's really nice, isn't he?" she said dreamily.

"You didn't say that when we were sitting on that smelly, clapped-out bus," Jack muttered.

"Well, that wasn't his fault. Anyway, it got us here in the end."

"Just about."

"Shall we go and have a look at the conference room?" Gina did a quick circuit of the room and when she was satisfied that everyone was happy she followed Jack out into the hallway

The conference facilities were excellent and even Jack pronounced himself satisfied. He checked the wires, the lighting and all the equipment while Gina went through each presentation. Bob would want to check them all before lunch and she wanted to make sure that everything was in order.

She turned off the screen and yawned. "Come on, Jack. Let's get some rest before lunch. I'm exhausted and I feel filthy."

"OK. Everything's working and I brought a spare microphone and laser pointer, just in case."

"Good man. I think this is going to be a success."

"Once there's plenty of free drink it will be."

"Yeah, I suppose none of them actually care about the conference. They're just here for the drink and the sun."

"They'll sleep through it all," Jack assured her.

"They'd better not! I put a lot of work into those screens!"

"As long as Bob and Hargreaves are happy, that's all that matters."

"I suppose. Right. I'm off to bed."

"I'm not that tired. Maybe I'll go walkabout."

"On your own?"

"Why not? I'll absorb some of the atmosphere, the culture."

"Well, I'm going to absorb some shut-eye. Seeya."

Jack looked wistfully after her. He'd imagined them exploring the *souks* together. Maybe even hand in hand. Still. There was plenty of time. He could go and investigate and then he'd know the best places to take her. With a lighter heart, Michel forgotten, he set off.

Gina woke in the darkened room, turned on the light and checked her watch. It was just gone eleven. Wonderful. She wasn't meeting Bob until twelve so there was time for another shower. She'd gasped when she'd first walked into her room. It was huge and luxurious and wonderfully cool. Doors opened out onto a large balcony that was designed in such a way that it was possible to sunbathe in total privacy. No need for any white bits or strap marks! A few people sat around the large pool on magnificent sun-loungers, while waiters weaved unobtrusively between them, delivering juices and bottled water. She reluctantly went back into her room. She had to get some sleep if she was to last the day. She looked around in satisfaction at her luxuriant surroundings. The drapes were wall to wall, with a blackout curtain to keep the sun's harsh rays at bay. The expensively tiled floor was almost covered with a richly patterned rug that her toes sank into. The bed was huge and the sheets a dazzling white. She slipped out of her clothes and headed for the bathroom. The bath was huge and round and a selection of bath oils in a variety of colours and scents was neatly displayed on a shelf beside it. A pile of fluffy white towels stood on a rack nearby and a voluminous white robe with a large M on the pocket was hanging on the back of the door. She slipped into the shower and gave a small shriek of pleasure when the strong spray hit her body. She twisted and turned letting the water massage all the aches out of her neck and shoulders. After a few minutes, she turned off the taps reluctantly, wrapped herself in a large towel and went to bed.

Now, three hours later, she looked longingly at the bath but she didn't have time for a long soak. She'd treat herself to that before she went out this evening. After another quick shower, she dried her hair, applied her make-up and put on a cream suit. The skirt was short – probably too short for Pamela's liking – but it was all very well Pamela criticising her clothes. She was tall and could carry a longer skirt. Gina was just too small and they made her look frumpy. She twirled in front of the full-length mirror, pleased with her reflection. A few hours in that wonderful sun and the white dress she'd brought should look great.

When she went downstairs, Bob and Jack were waiting for her. Both men did a double take.

"You look nice," Bob said admiringly. Jack just stared.

"I feel great. I had a lovely nap and a shower that almost took the skin off my back!"

He grinned. "The showers *are* great, aren't they? I was almost pinned to the wall! I keep meaning to get a decent one installed at home."

Gina made a face. "Ours is useless too. You need to

run around to get wet!" She turned to look at Jack, whose face and arms glowed with sunburn. "Were you sunbathing, Jack?"

"Nope, I was out sight-seeing. Wait till you see this city, Gina. It's amazing." Jack's dark eyes glowed with enthusiasm.

"Yeah?" She looked at him approvingly. He may have gone sightseeing but he'd left enough time to change into a pair of white jeans, a blue short-sleeved shirt and his cropped, golden head shone. There was a pleasant smell of aftershave too. Even Pamela would be impressed!

"You have to visit the square," he told her.

"Is that on the itinerary?" Bob consulted his notes.

Gina nodded. "Yes. Michel is bringing us around the *souk* tomorrow and then on to the square."

"The *Djemaa El Fna*." Michel stood in the doorway. "I am glad you like my city, *monsieur*."

"His name's Jack," Gina said. "And this is Bob."

Bob shook hands. "Thanks for looking after us, Michel. We're very pleased with everything so far."

"Your room is comfortable?"

"It's wonderful and David's – he's my boss – his is even better!"

Michel met Gina's eyes. "I am glad to hear it. If you need anything else, you have only to ask. I am here to look after you."

Jack snorted and switched on the screen.

Gina turned down the lights. "There's nothing new for you to see, Bob, other than your logo."

Bob took a seat halfway down the room. "The logo?"

166

Gina gave Jack the nod. "We thought we'd begin and end each presentation with your logo."

"Oh right." Bob didn't see what the big deal was. Their logo was just an L and an S intertwined. Quite boring really, though he'd never dream of saying so to old Hargreaves.

He sat back as a crescendo of music seemed to come at him from every angle of the room. It died down to a hush as two gold objects spun on to the screen in front of him. They danced about for a moment, before intertwining and then he realised that he was looking at the Lifesavers logo. "That's brilliant, Gina!"

She grinned triumphantly. It had taken a while to talk Pamela into using the animation but she had finally agreed when Gina assured her that the cost would be minimal and the effect would be stunning.

"Wait till David sees this!"

"You think he'll like it?" she asked anxiously.

"He has to. It makes the bloody thing look classy and, Lord knows, that's not easy!"

Jack guffawed.

Bob looked at him. "Another fan of our wonderful logo, eh?"

"Let's say it's a bit unimaginative," Jack said diplomatically.

Gina showed Bob the rest of the presentation and when he pronounced himself happy, he went off to find his boss. The MD wanted a quick rehearsal before lunch.

Gina held her breath as the older man picked up the remote control. When he pressed it, the logo flew up on the screen, paused for a few seconds and then faded away to reveal his first screen.

"Very fancy," was all he said.

"He's happy," Bob assured them later as they went into lunch.

"How can you tell?" Jack asked dryly.

"If he wasn't, you'd know all about it, believe me." He rolled his eyes dramatically before turning his attention to the buffet.

The presentations went off without a hitch. Jack said it was because everyone was stuffed after the wonderful lunch and they'd fallen asleep in the comfortable chairs.

"Well, Mr Hargreaves didn't complain," Gina retorted, "so it must have been a success."

As the delegates moved out into the gardens, she and Jack packed away all the equipment. "Fancy going sightseeing?" he said casually.

Gina, who'd seen Michel waiting outside, shook her head. "No, Jack. All I want to do is catch some rays and maybe go for a swim."

"Sounds good. The pool looks gorgeous."

"Well, I want to look over a few notes in my room first. Maybe I'll see you there later."

Jack watched her hurry away. The door hadn't fully closed behind her before he caught sight of Michel coming to meet her.

Gina agreed immediately when Michel suggested showing her the *souk* and the square and tried not think about Jack as she hurried to change into shorts and a T-shirt. Michel had assured her that bare arms and legs were fine. So there, Pamela! She looked around cautiously as she came back into reception but there was no sign of Jack. Michel held out his hand and together they went out to the waiting taxi.

Gina felt as if she were going to throw up. She clutched Michel's hand and wondered how much longer she could stand the smells, the noise and the claustrophobia.

Michel looked down in concern at her white face and the beads of sweat on her forehead. "Are you OK?"

"I'm a bit tired," she said with a apologetic smile. She could hardly tell him the truth!

"Maybe we've done enough for today. I'll take you to the square and get you a nice glass of mint tea."

"Lovely." Gina averted her eyes from the old man swatting flies off hunks of raw meat.

After taking a few twists and turns through the labyrinth of stalls, they were back out in the open. Gina gulped in the air. It was hot and dry, but at least it wasn't as smelly.

Michel led her towards the square. "There is a wonderful café over here. We will go upstairs and you will be able to see everything."

"Wonderful," Gina said, wishing she'd stayed by the pool. She let Michel's hand go while she rummaged for a tissue in her bag. When she looked up he was gone and a man was bearing down on her, grinning toothlessly with a large snake wrapped around his neck.

"Photo? Photo?" He went to put the snake around her neck.

Gina shrieked and ran. She looked frantically around for Michel but she couldn't see him in the crowd. An old woman came towards her offering water. She was tempted – her mouth was so dry – but mindful of Doug's warnings, she shook her head. She bent down to remove a stone that had got caught in her sandal and when she straightened up, a young boy was trying to shove a monkey into her arms. "Photo? Photo?"

"*Non! Non! Non!*" she screamed, running away. Strong arms grabbed her and held her. She screamed again.

"Gina. It's me! Michel. What's wrong?"

Gina burst into tears and fell into his arms. "Take me back to the hotel, Michel. Please. Please take me back."

"*Bien sûr.* Of course."

She huddled in the corner of the taxi, sniffing, aware that Michel was looking at her as if she were mad. Damn it, she'd really made a fool of herself, but she'd been so frightened. It was so loud and . . . and . . . foreign! And she didn't think she'd ever be able to forget the smells in the *souks*. That was one tour she was definitely going to back out of tomorrow! Bob and Michel would have to look after the delegates. Nothing would get her back in there. If she had her way, she wouldn't leave the hotel again until it was time to go home. But then there was the traditional night tonight. Her stomach lurched at the thought.

Michel was trying to distract her. "Wait till you

see the wonderful dancers tonight! And the food — delicious!"

Gina swallowed hard.

"The lamb is cooked in a tagine — a special earthenware dish — with different fruits. You will really enjoy it."

Gina thought of the man swatting away the flies and felt her stomach heave.

"Gina? Are you OK? You are very pale."

"I think it's the heat, Michel. And I'm really tired."

"Then you must sleep." He kissed her cheek and opened the door as the car stopped in front of the hotel.

Gina forced a smile. "Thank you, Michel. It's been . . . fun."

He bowed over her hand and smiled. "See you tonight, *chérie.*"

Gina hurried back to her room and sank down on to the bed. She kicked off her shoes and looked at the luxury and opulence that surrounded her. It made the last couple of hours seem like a bad dream. She felt a bit silly now, running like that. And screaming — my God, how she'd screamed! Completely over the top. But that place . . . she shivered as she thought of the *souk* with its low tarpaulin roof and narrow claustrophobic alleyways. She'd been completely overwhelmed by the noise, the smells and the heat. It was like she'd stepped into another world. She stood up and went into the bathroom. What she needed was a nice relaxing bath. She turned the taps, poured three different oils into the bath and inhaled deeply. Then she went back into the bedroom and helped herself to a generous glass of duty-free Drambuie. There was nothing to mix it with but she didn't care. She needed a drink. She undressed and carried her glass into the bathroom. It would be wonderful, she thought as she slid into the water, if she could get out of tonight's entertainment. It would be so much nicer if they could have dinner in the hotel restaurant. Just her and Jack. She wasn't even too keen on seeing Michel again. She didn't think she had the energy for the mating ritual after today's little episode. Whereas dinner with Jack would be relaxed, funny and uncomplicated. She sighed. There was no way she could do it, though. Even if Bob forgave her, Pamela would be livid when she found out. No, it looked as if a traditional night was on the cards. A traditional night with traditional food. Unless . . .

Chapter Fourteen

"Are you sure you don't want this, Gina?" Bob hesitated as he moved her food onto his already full plate.

"No, I'm not hungry," Gina replied truthfully. Not after the steak and chips followed by the creamy profiteroles that she'd had in her room a couple of hours ago.

"Do you want some of this, Jack?"

Jack held out his plate eagerly. "Lovely, Bob. You're so unadventurous, Gina. The food here is gorgeous."

Gina was about to say exactly what she thought about the food when she saw Michel making a beeline for her.

"Gina, *chérie*. You are not eating. Is your food all right?" His face was all concern.

"It's lovely, Michel. But I have a very small appetite."

Jack snorted and she kicked him.

"The appetite of a beautiful little bird." Michel kissed her hand.

"More like a ruddy great vulture," Jack muttered.

Gina gave him a dirty look and turned her back on him. She smiled flirtatiously at Michel. "Come and sit beside me, Michel," she invited. Now that she'd had a rest, two large Drambuies and a decent meal inside her, she was ready for anything. "I'd love to hear all about you."

Michel poured more wine into her glass and sat down very close to her.

Jack stood up. "Come on, Bob. Let's go and talk to the natives." He took his plate and made his way over to the belly-dancers, pausing on the way to get another pitcher of beer.

Bob followed him happily. David Hargreaves was already chatting up one of the dancers. If he could do it, then so could Bob!

The next morning Gina pulled back the curtains on a brilliant blue sky. There were no presentations today. Just a tour of the city followed by a final brainstorming session. Gina and Jack were free. Jack had tried to talk Gina into going, but she'd had quite enough of that.

"I'm having my breakfast in bed, Jack, and then I'm going to sit by the pool," she'd told him the night before.

"Well, maybe I'll join you." Jack hated the thought of sitting in the sun. He always burned no matter what factor sun lotion he used. But it would be well worth it if he got to spend the day with Gina.

Gina sighed. She didn't want Jack hanging around all day. She'd never score with Michel at this rate. She gave him a bright smile. "OK, Jack. I'll see you after lunch."

Jack frowned. "So late?"

"Oh, there's no chance of me surfacing before then! And when I do get up I might just catch some rays on my balcony." She grinned. "You know. Make sure I've no white bits."

Jack reddened as he thought of Gina naked on her balcony. "Oh, right. Well, I'll see you after lunch, so."

Gina now looked at the clock. Ten o'clock. Her breakfast should be here any minute. She put on the fluffy white bathrobe and went out onto the balcony. She scanned the gardens and the pool area in the hope of spotting Michel but he was nowhere in sight. He was probably busy around the hotel. He had two other groups to look after, he'd told her, and he also acted as tour guide a couple of times a week. She sighed in frustration. This was her last full day and she was hoping there'd be an opportunity for her and Michel to take up where they left off last night.

It had all been going so well. They'd had a wonderful evening. By the time Michel walked her back to her room, Gina's heart was thumping rapidly. He was kissing her thoroughly outside the door when the hotel manager walked around the corner.

"I'll try and drop back later," he'd whispered hurriedly before following the irate manager down the corridor. Gina could still hear the shouting after she'd closed the door. She'd put on a slinky little silk nightie, draped herself across the bed and waited. But, by four-thirty, she realised he probably wasn't coming. Changing into her baggy, cotton T-shirt, she curled up in the middle of the bed and fell asleep.

A knock on the door pulled her back to the present. Tightening the belt of her robe she opened the door.

"Good morning, *mademoiselle*."

"Good morning." Gina stood aside as the girl carried in a large tray and set it on the table by the window.

"*Bon appétit.*"

Gina handed her a couple of dirhams. "*Merci.*"

"*Merci beaucoup, mademoiselle.*" The waitress beamed at her and pocketed the coins.

Gina lifted the covers off the various dishes on the tray. Cornflakes, fresh orange juice, fluffy scrambled eggs, toast and pancakes. She sighed. How on earth was she going to get through this lot? It hadn't seemed so much when she'd ordered it last night. Just as she sat down there was another knock on the door. Shit! Michel!

"Just a minute!" She hurried over to the mirror. Fluffed up her hair, pinched her cheeks and loosened the top of her robe a little.

When she opened the door, Michel held out a single red rose. "Oh, *chérie*. I am so sorry I did not get back to you."

"That's OK, Michel." She smiled shyly and took the flower. "Thanks for the rose. Would you like to come in now?" She tried to sound casual, but her voice shook with anticipation.

"Alas, I cannot, *chérie*. I must bring a tour around the *souks*. But can I see you later tonight?"

Gina's face fell. Tonight was their last night and they were having a celebratory dinner. She couldn't possibly miss that. And then they were all going into the casino afterwards. "I have to work tonight, Michel. I wouldn't be able to slip away until quite late."

He kissed her hand. "I can wait." He pushed her gently into the room and took her in his arms, kicking the door shut behind him.

Gina wound her arms around his neck and kissed him back eagerly.

"Oh, Gina, you are so beautiful." He pushed the robe down off her shoulders and kissed her neck.

Gina cursed herself for changing back into her T-shirt.

Michel drew back and gazed down into her eyes. "I must go, *chérie*. Damned tourists!"

She grinned. "I'm a damn tourist, remember!"

"*Non, chérie*. You are my dearest Gina. My beautiful Gina." He kissed her deeply and then turned to leave. "Until tonight."

"Where will we meet?" Gina said breathlessly.

"I will wait for you in the garden."

"I'll get there as quickly as I can but it might not be until about eleven."

He gazed at her solemnly. "I will wait as long as it takes. You are worth waiting for, *chérie*."

Gina closed the door after him and skipped back to her chair. Suddenly, she was ravenous! She made up her mind to call Jack when she'd finished breakfast and arrange to spend the day with him. She could afford to be generous. She was walking on air. But whatever they did, it was an absolute must that she developed her tan.

That little white mini halter-dress was going to knock the socks off Michel!

Jack was amazed when he got the call from Gina. He'd watched her leave with Michel the night before and proceeded to get pissed with Bob. But maybe Michel had been given the elbow. Maybe he was in with a chance after all! She'd sounded in great form. Brilliant! He'd take her on the boat trip that he'd seen advertised in reception. It sounded like a nice day. A spot of fishing, some sunbathing on deck – he cringed at the thought but Gina would like it – and a slap-up lunch.

Gina had been a bit nervous when Jack told her his plans. She wasn't keen on boats and the thought of eating their weird food did nothing for her. Still, she'd get a great colour in the sea-breeze. She agreed to go and Jack rushed off to organise it.

"Glad you came?" Jack asked later that afternoon, as they lay side by side, sipping champagne in the hot sunshine.

"You bet." Gina stretched out langorously. "This is definitely the life!"

Jack looked at her curvy figure in the yellow bikini and had to agree. His neck and legs were burning, but he didn't care. It was worth it. It had been a great day and it wasn't over yet. After dinner this evening he planned to talk Gina into going dancing in the nightclub around the corner. And then – well, you never know. It would be the perfect end to the perfect day.

"Come on, lazybones," Gina stood up and stretched a hand down to him. "Let's go for a swim."

Jack took her hand. Yes, it was definitely turning out to be a perfect day.

Gina hummed as she got ready for dinner that evening. She'd had a wonderful time today with Jack. They'd joked, chatted about work and even done a bit of flirting. It had been great fun. And now once she got through the formal part of this evening, she had an evening of passion with Michel to look forward to. God, she felt hot just thinking about him! There was no doubt in her mind that they would end up in bed together. His eyes had said it all this morning and she couldn't wait. Hannah would probably say she should be playing it cool, but she didn't care. She'd led a ridiculously celibate life lately what with the mixed signals from Greg, and Mike Hamilton's lousy timing. It was about time she had some fun.

She put on a pair of lacy, white panties and sprayed perfume all over herself. She eyed herself critically in the full-length mirror. Except for the small white triangles caused by her bikini top, her skin was golden. Her face was a little red, but a small bit of foundation would sort that out. She quickly applied it, some mascara and some lip gloss and slipped the dress over her head. It clung to her boobs and then fell in soft folds to just above her knees. The gold sandals would set it off to perfection. She twirled in front of the mirror and frowned. Was it a bit too tarty? No, she decided. It was sexy. And tonight she definitely wanted to look sexy!

Jack whistled happily as he headed for the dining-room. He wore his best outfit – a white shirt and a pair of beige combats – and he'd splashed himself generously with aftershave. The whistle died on his lips when he entered the dining-room and saw Gina standing talking to Bob and David Hargreaves. The two of them were ogling her openly and Jack couldn't blame them. She looked amazing. The skimpy dress she was wearing left very little to the imagination, clinging to her in all the right places.

"Hiya, Jack! Come and join us," she called.

His heart flipped at her smile and he went over to join them. "Hello." He accepted the glass of wine she handed him.

"We've just been hearing all about your boat trip. Sounds like you had a better day than us."

Jack managed to tear his eyes away from Gina and grinned at Bob. "It was great," he agreed.

"You've got a bit of sunburn there," Hargreaves said gruffly. "A man with your colouring should have more sense."

"I feel fine," Jack lied. His skin was positively tingling, but he didn't care.

"You have a healthy glow, Jack. Don't mind him," Gina said when they left to take their seats.

"You look great, Gina." Jack looked down at her sparkling eyes, shiny mop of curls and golden breasts.

"Thanks, Jack. You look pretty cool yourself. Let's sit

down there." She pointed at two seats far away from the Lifesavers' MD. "I think we deserve an evening off."

"Sounds good to me." Jack followed her happily and pulled out her chair with a flourish.

"Why, thank you, kind sir!"

"You're welcome, my lady."

"I'll be expecting this kind of treatment back at the office, you know."

"Well, we'll have to see. If you're a good girl."

"Oh, I promise I'll be a very good girl," Gina said with a husky little laugh.

Jack blinked and tossed back his glass of wine. Things were definitely looking up!

Gina watched with pleasure as the delegates chatted happily. Doug would be proud of her. The business end of the trip had gone off without a hitch and everyone loved the hotel. Even the bus fiasco had become a talking point and there were several jokes doing the rounds about how CML was going to get them back to the airport. Camels seemed to be the most popular form of transport.

She held up her hand as Jack went to top up her glass. "I don't think I should, Jack. I feel a bit tiddly."

"So what? Sure haven't we finished work? Look at old Hargreaves. He's well on!"

Gina turned to look at the MD. He did look a bit the worse for wear. She laughed. "You'd imagine he'd have learned his lesson last night. I hope he doesn't start dancing again."

"As long as he doesn't strip!" Jack succeeded in filling her glass.

"I might do that," Gina fanned herself with her napkin. "It's so hot in here."

"Don't go getting my hopes up unless you mean it," Jack murmured.

Gina smacked his hand playfully. "Behave yourself, Jack Byrne! I think I'll go and freshen up. Won't be long." She made her way out to the bathroom, walking very carefully. The combination of wine and heels meant she had to concentrate really hard. Outside she checked her watch. It was ten-thirty and they hadn't even made it as far as the casino yet! She couldn't wait to see Michel. He'd wandered in and out of the dining-room all evening, casting her burning, meaningful looks. Maybe she could slip away now. The speeches were over and, as Jack had pointed out, David Hargreaves was pissed. She touched up her make-up, ran her fingers through her hair and made her way out to reception.

Michel came towards her, smiling broadly. "*Chérie!* How wonderful to see you."

"Hello, Michel. I think I may be able to get away now."

"But that is wonderful! Just let me have a word with the porter and I will join you in a few minutes."

"Don't be long," she whispered, her lips close to his.

Michel blinked. "I will be with you as soon as possible," he said, running his fingers across the smooth skin of her back.

Gina smiled and moved off down the hall, her hips swaying provocatively.

"Gina! There you are. I was worried."

"Jack!" Gina cast a quick look over her shoulder but thankfully Michel had disappeared.

"Are you OK?"

Gina smiled at the concern in his eyes. "Ah, Jack. You're so nice. I'm fine. Just a bit warm. I think I'll go and get some fresh air."

Jack's eyes twinkled. "I think that's a very good idea."

"You do?" Gina was sure he'd object to her deserting him. "OK. See you later."

"See you." He stood smiling as she moved away towards the French windows.

Gina stood on the porch straining to see into the garden but it was pitch dark. Holding on to the balustrade, she made her way in the general direction of the rose garden. She was sure there was a bench around here somewhere. She decided not to go too far. It would be terrible if Michel couldn't find her.

"Gina?"

"Over here," Gina whispered back, her heart racing.

The next thing she knew, he was behind her, kissing her neck. She tried to turn around but his arms held her firmly. She gave in to the sensual feel of his lips and tongue and leaned back against him.

His hands moved around to cup her breasts, while his tongue traced lines down her back.

She let her head fall back and groaned as his fingers

crept inside her dress and tweaked her nipples. Now his tongue was back at her ear and one hand left her breast to stroke her thigh.

Gina shuddered.

His hand moved up and she felt his fingers play around the edge of her panties.

"Oh, God, yes! Yes, Michel!"

The hand froze.

"Don't stop, Michel. What's wrong?"

"Sorry to disappoint you, Gina."

Gina swung around. "Jack?! What the hell are you doing here? What do you think you're playing at?" She pulled at her dress, glad the darkness hid her red, embarrassed face.

"Making an eejit of myself, by the look of things. I'll go and leave you to it. I'm sure lover-boy will be along in a minute." He disappeared into the darkness.

Gina sank down onto the grass. "Shit, shit, shit!"

"Gina? *Chérie?* Why are you sitting here in the dark talking to yourself? Have I kept you waiting? I'm so sorry."

He helped her up and pulled her into his arms but she pushed him away. "Actually, I've a bit of a headache. I'm going to have an early night."

"But in reception, you said you wished to meet me . . ."

Gina could just about make out the total confusion on Michel's face. She felt sorry for him but the mood had gone. "Sorry, Michel."

"Maybe I could come to your room and help distract you from the pain? Maybe give you a massage?" He kissed her neck, and trailed his fingers down her back.

Gina thought of Jack's hands doing the exact same thing only moments earlier and sighed. "No, Michel. I really need to be on my own. I'm sorry."

Michel watched her disappear into the darkness and pulled out his packet of Camels. *"Merde!* Bloody foreign women. They don't know what they want!"

Gina sat in her room, taking gulps of Drambuie. At times like this, she wished she smoked. How was she going to face Jack tomorrow? And what on earth did he think he was playing at anyway? Following her out to the garden like that. He must have thought she was really drunk. She shook her head and took another drink. No, Jack wasn't like that. He'd never take advantage. The real surprise had been the way he'd turned her on. Her cheeks reddened as she remembered the feel of his lips and his hands on her breasts and on her thigh . . . My God, if she hadn't called out Michel's name who knows how far it might have gone! How was she going to work with him after this?

She smiled nervously. "So you see, Jack, I'd had way too much to drink. I was on a high, what with the conference being such a success. And I was just having a bit of a flirt with Michel. You know how it is. When you're away from home . . ." She gave an embarrassed little laugh.

Jack dug his hands into his jeans. "Yeah, sure. I was fairly pissed myself, Gina. It wouldn't have happened otherwise. Sorry if I embarrassed you."

"That's OK. You know me. I don't embarrass easily. Let's put it behind us, yeah? Friends?"

"Sure. I'd better go and get the gear together."

"Right. Great. See you later." Gina watched him walk away. Bloody cheek! Was he saying he'd only come on to her 'cos he was drunk? She'd expected him to be angry with her or embarrassed, maybe even disappointed. Certainly not disinterested. For some reason she felt a bit deflated.

Chapter Fifteen

"Honestly, Mal, he looked like Mr Blobby! It was embarrassing enough when he started belly-dancing, but when he took off his shirt . . ." Gina rolled her eyes in dramatic disgust.

Malcolm roared with laughter. "Sounds like the kind of guy to avoid at parties."

"David Hargreaves is the kind of guy to avoid full stop," Jack assured him. "When he's sober he's a pompous prat who doesn't have a decent thing to say about anyone and when he's drunk, he becomes a total embarrassment."

"Well, it sounds like it was an interesting few days."

Gina reddened and kept her eyes averted from Jack's. "Yeah, but the food was awful, Mal."

"How would you know? You never even tried it!" Jack gave her a scathing look.

"Well, I'm sorry, I'm sure!" Gina retorted.

Mal looked from one red face to the other. By the looks of things something else had gone on in Marrakech that they weren't telling him about. "Well, I'm glad you had a good time," he said, ignoring the tension.

"Indeed," Pamela said from the doorway. "Was any work done?"

Jack grinned at her. "Sure. It all went off very smoothly, Pamela. Gina did a great job."

Gina shot him a grateful look and he smiled back before going off to get himself a coffee.

"I'm glad to hear it. If you're wrong I'm sure Lifesavers won't be long telling me." Pamela went into her office and closed the door.

"Ungrateful bitch," Gina muttered. "She could at least have said well done."

Malcolm polished his glasses. "She's probably a bit worried, Gina. Doug went into hospital yesterday."

"God, I totally forgot. When's the operation?"

"Tomorrow morning."

"Poor guy. So what else has been happening here, Mal? Where's Susie and Greg?"

"I haven't a clue where Greg is. He's out more often than he's in. And Susie's off sick."

Gina groaned. "Shit. Did she say what was wrong?"

"You'll have to ask Noreen. She took the call."

Noreen wasn't much help either.

"She didn't give a reason, Regina," she said with a disapproving sniff. "Very short with me, she was. She said she'll be back tomorrow. Apparently she has a doctor's certificate. I'll believe it when I see it."

Gina sighed and went back to her desk. She turned on the PC and checked her e-mail. Fifteen new messages. Bloody hell! She frowned when she saw there was one from David Hargreaves. As she opened it she saw it was copied to Pamela and Bob. Oh God.

Dear Gina

Just a note to thank you and Jack for a job well done. Already compliments have come in from many delegates and several have mentioned you by name. We at Lifesavers look forward to doing business with CML again.

David Hargreaves.

"Good God."

Jack came back in and looked at her warily. "What is it?"

"Read it for yourself."

Jack leaned over her shoulder and read the screen. "Crikey."

"She can't give out about us now, can she?" Gina said smugly.

"She certainly can't. Who'd have thought old man Hargreaves could be so nice."

Gina laughed. "He's probably nice to anyone who's seen him belly-dance!"

"Now that's cruel and cynical."

"But true," Gina said, glad that they were able to laugh and joke again. Maybe they'd be able to put Marrakech behind them after all.

Pamela called them in half-an-hour later. "You seem to have made quite an impression on Mr Hargreaves."

"He made quite an impression on us," Jack said straight-faced.

Gina studied her feet.

Pamela nodded. "Well done. Maybe you could take care of the Las Vegas job too, Gina."

Gina stared at her. No one but Doug had ever looked after DVD Advertising. "Don't you want to look after that one yourself?"

"I can't afford to be away a full week. I will if I have to – if you don't think you're up to it . . ."

Gina squared her shoulders. "Of course I am."

"Good. Well, I'll introduce you to Marian Hickey. She's their Marketing Director. If she's happy with you taking over, it's all yours."

"Great."

"Here's Douglas's DVD file. Go through it with a fine-tooth comb. Marian's a hard taskmaster with very high standards. You need to be prepared."

"I'll memorise every page," Gina promised.

"Jack? You'll need to liaise with a chap called Pete O'Neill. He's going to be organising the convention from their end and he wants to know everything about the technology we're using – and I mean everything."

Jack nodded. He was used to this. Usually these people knew nothing about computers or presentation software and he was able to lose them after a few minutes of technobabble. Then he could get on with his job in peace.

"Is Susie still out sick?"

Gina sighed. It had been too much to hope that Pamela hadn't noticed Susie's absence.

"Yes, but she'll be back tomorrow."

"Mmmn. Make sure she has a doctor's cert. I will not tolerate idlers."

"I'm sure it's genuine. She *is* pregnant," Jack protested.

"Don't remind me," Pamela said grimly. "OK, that's all. If you've any questions about DVD, ask Greg. He knows Marian quite well. They went to school or college together apparently."

"He doesn't appear to be here." Jack didn't see why Susie should be the only one getting a hard time for being absent.

Pamela frowned. "I noticed. OK. If there's nothing else?"

Gina and Jack left the office.

"God, I hope Susie has a good excuse," Gina said nervously. "Pamela's ready to hop on her."

"Susie's a good kid. If she's not here, then there's a good reason why not."

"I hope you're right, Jack."

* * *

Susie examined her face in the mirror. Her left eye was still swollen, almost closed, and the bruise was an angry purple colour. Her lip was healing well but the doctor had said she would probably be left with a scar. But she'd been more worried about the baby when her father had turned on her, his eyes filled with rage.

"Ye dirty little bitch! Ye whore!"

He'd slapped her hard across the face and she'd fallen back over little Trisha's trike. As she tried to stand up she saw his boot coming towards her stomach and instinctively folded into a ball in an attempt to protect the fragile life growing inside. The steel toe-cap caught the side of her face. He came at her again, this time catching her in the mouth. Susie felt the pain explode inside. He was drawing back to kick again when Florrie jumped on him and tried to drag him away.

"For the love of God, Christy, stop. Ye'll kill her!"

"Fuck her! I'd be doin' her a favour. Doin' us all a favour. Bringin' shame on the family. Bloody slut! Whore!"

The baby sat on the floor screaming and crying *"Mama, Mama!"* and Susie's two brothers looked on from the safety of the hall.

Christy threw Florrie off and spat on his daughter. "Yer not worth it. I wouldn't be bothered trying to teach ye a lesson. Your mother's let ye away with murder all yer life. Sure it's no wonder ye turned into a dirty little trollop. Get out of me house!"

"No, Christy!"

"She's not staying under me roof another night! Ye needn't think *we're* going to bring up the brat for ye. We've enough mouths to feed. Get out of me sight!"

Florrie nodded at Susie to go upstairs. "Calm down, Christy. I'll get you a drink."

Susie winced as she picked herself up off the floor. She could barely see and when she put up a hand to touch her face, it came away covered in blood. Dear Jesus, what had he done to her?

She stepped over Trish, still sitting in the middle of the floor, her thumb in her mouth, and tried to smile at the boys. Their faces were pale and shocked. "It's all right, lads. Nothing to worry about. Why don't ye go into the yard and play? Give Da time to calm down. Go on, now."

The boys ran off and Susie inched her way up the stairs, wincing as she became aware of the dull pain in her back. God, if he'd hurt the baby she'd kill him. She would! She'd take the bread knife and nothing would save him. She locked herself into the bathroom and turned on the cold tap. The water turned to red when she put her hand into the basin. She squinted at her reflection in the mirror. Her lip was bleeding and her left eye was cut and swollen. She rinsed her mouth, gingerly sliding her tongue around to check her teeth. They seemed to be intact. Her legs started to give way beneath her and she sat down unsteadily on the loo, pressing a wet towel against her eye.

There was a faint tap on the door. "Susie? Susie, love, are ye all right?" her mother whispered.

Susie stood up slowly and opened it.

Florrie stared at her daughter's swollen, bloodied face. "Oh, God love ye. We'll have to get you down to the doctor. But ye'll have to wait till Marie gets home. He'll lose the head altogether if I don't get him his tea."

"I think I need to go to hospital, Ma," Susie said, clutching her stomach. "I've got an awful pain down here."

Florrie looked over her shoulder worriedly. "I'm sure you're fine," she said with a nervous smile. "Sure I was always getting pains and aches when I was pregnant."

"Was that before or after he kicked ye?" Susie said viciously.

"Oh he never, Susie, I swear! And he didn't mean to hurt you either. He's just upset."

Susie shook her head in disgust.

Florrie looked away. "Stay here. I'll send Marie up when she gets in. Will I get ye a cup of tea?"

Tea. Florrie's answer to all problems. "No, Ma. Just leave me alone."

Florrie turned away, her shoulders slumped, resigned.

"Florrie! Where's me bloody tea?"

She jumped at her husband's voice. "Comin', love, comin'." She hurried down the stairs, her daughter forgotten.

Susie sank down on to the floor and rested her head against the side of the bath. Large silent tears started to roll down her cheeks. What was she going to do? Where was she going to go? Her da had meant it, she knew that. He would throw her out. Her ma might be able to put it off for a week or a month, but it would happen eventually. Even the money that she was bringing in wouldn't save her. She wiped her tears on her sleeve. But she'd only be able to afford the smallest bed-sit if she was to save any money for when the baby came. It was bound to be an expensive time. The sooner it was adopted the better for the poor child. Why would anyone want to be born into this bloody family? She doubled over as another pain gripped her. Maybe there wouldn't be a baby to worry about after all.

When Marie got home she took one look at her sister and phoned for a taxi. "The bastard," she said, drumming her fingers on the table while they waited. "I'll bloody kill him."

Susie said nothing. She was just glad that someone else was taking charge. Her head felt woozy and the ache in her stomach wouldn't go away.

"Come on, love. The taxi will be here in five minutes, let's get you outside. We'll go to the Beaumont."

Susie groaned at the thought of the long wait they'd have in the A & E of the large, busy hospital.

As it turned out, they didn't have to wait at all. Once Marie told them her sister was pregnant and had stomach pains, they brought her into a cubicle immediately.

The doctor smiled kindly at her. "You're fine, Susie. You just bruised some ribs when you, eh, fell over. That's what's causing the pain. The baby's fine. Take a look for yourself." He nodded at the image on the ultrasound machine.

Susie looked at Marie.

Her sister smiled. "Ye may as well, sis."

Susie held her hand even tighter and turned to look at the screen.

The doctor pointed at a dark patch. "That's the baby there. And see that flicker? See it?"

Susie nodded.

"That's the baby's heart beating away like a little steam engine."

Susie stared at him and then looked back at the screen. "Really?"

"Yep. Would you like a picture to take away with you?"

"I don't think she . . ."

Susie glared at her sister. "'Course I would," she said obstinately.

"Here you are."

Susie took the picture tentatively and studied it. This little blob was her baby.

"Now, once we've got your eye stitched up you can go."

"Are ye sure she's going to be OK?" Marie asked anxiously.

He nodded. "Maybe a bit of a headache for a few days, but she should be all right. There's no sign of concussion. If you feel dizzy or sick though, Susie, come back in or go to your GP. And you really should talk to the police."

Susie and Marie exchanged glances.

"It was an accident," Marie said quietly.

The doctor snorted. If he had a fiver for every 'accident' he'd tended he'd be a very rich man. Why did women put up with it? It was probably the husband, though Susie Clarke didn't look old enough to be married. He sighed. "Whatever you say, love. But you take care. We don't want any more . . . accidents now, do we? You were lucky this time."

"What are ye going to do?" Marie asked on the bus home. She couldn't afford another taxi.

"Dunno."

"Who's the father? Couldn't he help?"

Susie gave an embarrassed smile. "I don't even know

his surname or where he lives. It was just a one-night stand."

Marie stared out the window. "Maybe ye should think about, about . . ."

"I'm not getting rid of it," Susie hissed, aware of the curious looks from the oul one in the next seat.

"Did I say that?"

"Ye were going to!" Susie retorted.

Marie sighed. "Well, what *are* ye going to do? How will ye manage?"

Susie listened to her sister asking all the questions that she'd been asking herself. "I'll give it up for adoption," she said firmly. "It's the best thing."

"Yer right." Marie nodded her head vigorously.

"How do ye go about it?" Susie asked.

"Dunno. I'll find out if you like."

"Oh, would ye?"

Marie patted her sister's hand. "Yeah, sure."

"Ah, thanks, Marie. And thanks for coming with me today. I was so afraid . . ."

"Yer all right, Suz, both of ye. And don't worry about Da."

"He wants me out, Marie. And I think Ma does too. She's afraid of him."

Marie's mouth set in a determined line. "Well, you're not leaving. Not when yer like this. I'll threaten to go to the Guards. That'll shut him up."

"Ye wouldn't!"

Marie grinned. "Course not! But he doesn't know that."

"But what about when yer not there?" Susie said nervously. Marie worked as a hairdresser which meant late nights Thursdays and Fridays.

"Just keep out of his way, Susie. Keep out of the house as much as ye can. Stay in work late. Sure, don't ye work in a nice cosy office? And by the time ye get home he'll be gone to the pub. And by the time he gets back ye'll be in bed and gone again in the morning before he gets up. Sure we could tell him ye'd moved out and he'd probably believe it!"

Susie giggled and then yelped at the pain in her lip. Thank God for Marie. She made it sound as if everything would be all right. "I won't be able to go back to work looking like this." She put a hand up to her swollen face."

"Sure the cert covers ye until Thursday. Yer face will be grand by then. In the meantime, stay in yer room and let Ma drown ye in tea. It'll make her feel better."

"Thanks, Marie. I don't know what I'd do without ye."

"Ah go on," Marie said, embarrassed. "Sure wouldn't ye do the same for me?"

When they got home, she pushed Susie towards the stairs and went in to confront her father, but he'd already gone out.

"Is she all right?" her mother asked anxiously.

"Just about," Marie said grimly. *No thanks to you,* she added to herself.

"I'll bring her a cup of tea."

"Oh, for God's sake, Ma. Is that all ye can do? Why

don't ye stand up to him? He could have killed her and the baby."

Florrie shook her head. "Ah, no, love. He'd never do that! He was just upset. Yer father's very set in his ways. He doesn't believe in sex outside marriage."

"And that's an excuse, is it?"

Florrie wrung her hands together and looked at her eldest daughter pleadingly. "I'm tellin' ye. He didn't know what he was doing. It was just an accident."

Marie relented. It wasn't her ma's fault after all. "OK, Ma. If ye say so. But there better be no more accidents or he's going to have one himself. I mean it." She stood up and went upstairs to check on her sister, leaving her mother sitting at the kitchen table, muttering and shaking her head.

Chapter Sixteen

Doug's eyelids drooped as he began to feel the effects of the pre-med. It was the first time he'd shut his eyes in days. Though he felt bone-tired he just couldn't sleep. Every time he closed his eyes his brain went into overdrive. They'd offered him sleeping tablets but he'd refused. The thoughts of losing control didn't appeal to him. Even Kelly Matthews hadn't been able to distract him. He'd been reading *The Times* yesterday when the beautiful blonde nurse put her head around the door.

"It is you!" she said rushing over to him and enveloping him in a big hug. " I couldn't believe it when I saw your name on the list."

"Kelly! How are you? I forgot you worked here."

She sat up on the side of the bed. "I'll be assisting in your operation. Head theatre nurse now, you know."

"Congratulations." Doug thought of all the things those slender fingers had done to him in the past and now she'd have his heart in her hands too! Not many women had managed that, he thought wryly.

"We'll have to get together again when you're better," she was saying, with a playful smile. "It's been far too long. I could show you my bedside manner."

Doug looked at the luscious lips, the inviting eyes and the large tits bursting out of her uniform and wondered why he didn't feel remotely interested. "That would be nice," he said politely.

"Now, I don't want you to worry about a thing, Doug. You're getting cut by the best, I promise you. You'll be back to yourself in no time." She paused as she heard voices outside. " I'd better go. The sister-in-charge is a narky cow. I don't want to give her an excuse to report me. I'll see you tomorrow. Good luck, Doug."

He felt himself drifting now. He'd seen Kelly when they'd wheeled him in. She looked more professional in her greens and with her hair tucked under a hat. She'd smiled and given a little wave before disappearing into the next room. Doug hadn't seen Grimes, but he'd heard the surgeon's booming voice. Well, that was a relief. At least some student wasn't going to be cutting him open. He opened his eyes as they lifted him over onto the table.

"It's OK, Mr Hamilton. It will be over before you know it. Now if you just breathe in . . ."

Surprisingly his last thoughts were of Pamela and her pale, anxious face when she'd left last night. He wondered idly if she actually loved him.

* * *

Pamela looked at the clock. Douglas should be in theatre by now. The operation was to take about five hours. Then he'd be in recovery for an hour before they moved him to intensive care. They said she could see him then. Just for a few minutes. But Pamela wasn't sure she wanted to. She'd seen her father after his operation ten years ago and the memory of him hooked up to all those tubes and machines was still vivid. And he'd only had his gall bladder removed. A simple operation. Nothing like what Douglas was going through. Don't think like that, she admonished herself. He'll be fine. It's a common enough operation. Everyone knew someone who'd had a bypass. It was almost a status symbol. And Douglas was such a fit man.

"Are you all right, Pamela?"

Greg had been standing in the doorway for several minutes and she hadn't even noticed him.

She smiled at her brother-in-law. So like Douglas in some ways, but so different in others. "I'm fine."

"If you hear anything . . ."

"I'll let you know."

"Thanks. And if you want anything, or if you want to get out of here, I'll mind the shop."

"Thanks, Greg."

He nodded and left. She watched as he went back to his desk. He wasn't all bad. Just irresponsible. He'd never really grown up. But then Douglas had probably grown up enough for them both. He was a man who took his responsibilities very seriously. Probably because he'd lost his father at such an early age. Pamela had liked that side of him. He hadn't shown it to her immediately. All she'd seen was a handsome, suave businessman who enjoyed the good life. It had taken a while for her to discover the determined, serious young man underneath. Dependable, her mother had called him and she was right. Pamela knew she'd never have to worry about her security as long as Douglas was around. The house was theirs – he'd paid off the mortgage as soon as it was feasible – and there were several policies on both their lives and their health. He had savings in several different institutions and his stockbroker had made some successful investments on his behalf. No, Pamela would never have to worry about money. Faithfulness was a different matter. She sighed, surprised at how much it still hurt. Douglas had had his first fling when they'd been married only a year. And it was the first of many. She always knew when he was playing around. He'd bring an extra shirt to the office, go through his aftershave and deodorants a lot more quickly and suddenly have an awful lot of evening meetings. She told herself it wasn't important. He was an attractive man who loved sex and she'd never been enough for him. It wasn't that she didn't like him making love to her, she did. But once or twice a week was quite enough. She knew her lack of interest frustrated him and so when he sought satisfaction elsewhere, she turned a blind eye. She was confident that his affairs were never serious. It was purely a physical release. She didn't have to worry about him running off with another woman. He wasn't stupid. He loved his life and she believed he loved her too in his own way. He was proud of her and the life she'd created for him. He would never do anything to jeopardise it. He had been behaving a bit funny lately, but then that was because of the heart attack. He'd got a fright. As soon as he was over the operation, things would be back to normal. And then Greg would go back to his own weird life, Gina would stop being starry-eyed and they'd be able to get rid of that sullen, wretched girl. Her *and* her baby.

"Any news?" Jack asked.

Greg shook his head. "No. Nothing yet."

Gina was glad that Jack had finally broken the uncomfortable silence. The place had been like a morgue all morning. "Surely he should be out by now."

Malcolm shook his head. "It's a long operation. They have to open the rib cage, stop the heart . . ."

Greg held up his hand. "Yes, thanks, Mal. I don't think we need a blow-by-blow description."

Malcolm shrugged.

"Is *she* OK?" Gina nodded towards Pamela's office.

"Seems to be, but it's hard to tell with Pammy," Greg replied.

The phone rang in Pamela's office and they all turned.

"No, Marjorie, no news yet," they heard her say.

"I don't know how she does it. I'd have to be there. Waiting outside the door. How can she work knowing what he's going through?"

Greg smiled at her. "Not everyone's as caring as you, Gina. Our Pamela is a bit – let's say cold."

Jack frowned. He didn't particularly like the woman but it seemed a bit disloyal of her brother-in-law to talk about her like this to her staff. "Just because she doesn't wear her heart on her sleeve doesn't mean she doesn't have feelings."

Gina rolled her eyes. It wasn't like Jack to jump to Pamela's defence. It was just jealousy that had him playing Sir Galahad. "I still don't see how she can just carry on as normal," she insisted.

With that Pamela's door opened. "I'm going out – and no, there's no news. If anyone wants me, I'm on the mobile."

She breezed past them and Jack raised an eyebrow at Gina.

Noreen jumped to her feet as Pamela walked into reception. "Mrs Lloyd-Hamilton. Any news?"

"No, Noreen."

"Oh. Do you want me to . . . do anything?"

Pamela deliberately misunderstood. "Just finish those letters. I'll be on the mobile."

Pamela sat in her car, staring at the phone in her hand. She knew that if she rang they'd tell her he was out of surgery. And she knew they'd tell her she could visit. She looked at the people walking their dogs in the park opposite and wondered what would happen if she didn't ring. If she didn't visit tonight. Doug wouldn't know she was there anyway. It would be morning before he really came to. Even then, he'd probably be too weak to hold a proper conversation. She'd only be in the way. She switched off her mobile and started the car.

* * *

"Hi, Doug. How do you feel?"

Doug opened his eyes and tried to focus. Pamela, no, Kelly. "Not too bad. Where's Pamela?"

"Pamela? Oh. Your wife. I'll go and check."

Doug lifted his head and looked down. Instead of the large bandage he had expected to see, a narrow plaster covered the wound, running from his breastbone to his stomach. Not very dramatic at all. He looked up as Kelly came back alone. "She's not here yet."

"Oh." He licked his lips.

Kelly held a glass to his mouth and he took a sip. "Thanks," he said hoarsely.

"She's probably held up in traffic. You know what the Rock Road is like." Kelly smiled kindly.

"Yes."

"I've got to go now. Another one lined up for the knife. I'll drop in before I go off duty."

"Thanks, Kelly."

She patted his hand and moved quietly past the other beds.

Doug closed his eyes. It was nearly twenty-four hours since his operation and his wife hadn't been in to see him. There must be something wrong.

He rang the bell. "Nurse, I want to make a phone call," he whispered.

"Now, Mr Hamilton, that's not a good idea . . ."

"I want to make a call and I want to make it now. You can get me a phone or I'll go and find one."

The nurse looked at the fixed set of his jaw and sighed. "OK."

"Noreen? It's Doug. Yes, yes, I'm fine, put me through to Pamela, will you? No? Then where is she? No. No, well she must be on her way. Thanks, Noreen. Bye bye."

"It's not like Mrs Lloyd-Hamilton, Regina. If she's not going to be in she always phones. Always."

Gina looked at Noreen's agitated expression. "I'm sure she's fine, Noreen. This isn't exactly the easiest time for her. She probably had a terrible night – what with all the worry."

Noreen nodded. "You're right, Regina. And if she got one of her headaches then she'll have turned off the mobile. But poor Mr Hamilton is so worried and that can't be good for him in his condition. I'll keep trying The Sycamores."

"How's that, Mrs Lloyd-Hamilton?"

Pamela gazed absently at the hairdresser in the mirror. "Pardon? Oh, sorry, Raymonde, it's wonderful as always."

When she paid the receptionist, she took her mobile out of her bag, stared at it and then shoved it hurriedly back in. She walked briskly across to Grafton Street. She badly needed new shoes. She had nothing suitable to go with the John Rocha suit she'd bought last week.

Doug handed the phone back to the nurse. "Bloody mobiles. My wife's is always on the blink."

She nodded sympathetically and left him to listen to the clicks and bleeps of the machines around him. Where the hell was she? How could she desert him at a time like this? They weren't exactly love's young dream but they'd always been there for each other. They'd worked through every crisis together. Mind you, any crisis they'd had to face so far had been work-related. Doug couldn't remember anything of a personal nature. Then there was Pamela's phobia of hospitals, but God, surely she could overcome that? He was her husband, for God's sake!

Pamela walked out of the shop with two shopping bags in her hand, headed for the car and turned on the phone. She couldn't put it off any longer. The traffic was atrocious but for once she welcomed it. The phone rang almost immediately.

"Yes? Oh, hello Noreen. Everything's fine, but my mobile's been out of order. Yes, I can't believe that it broke down at a time like this. Yes, I'm on my way there now. Is there anything else? Good, well you can call me if you need me. Yes, yes I'll tell him. Bye-bye, Noreen."

Pamela sighed when she finally managed to get away from her secretary. Sometimes Noreen's devotion to Douglas was rather tiring. When she got to the clinic a Volvo pulled out of a space in front of the entrance. She drove reluctantly into the spot. It looked like she couldn't put this off any longer. She enquired at reception and they sent her straight up to ICU. She was hovering outside the door when a nurse came out. "Can I help you? Who are you looking for?"

"Mr Hamilton. Douglas Hamilton."

"Oh, Doug. Yes, he's just inside the door. You'll see a big improvement in him since last night. "

"Will I?"

"Oh, yes. All those machines can be quite frightening but they do their job."

"Yes."

"Well, I won't keep you. I'm sure he's dying to see you."

Pamela pushed open the door.

"Pamela! God, I was getting worried about you. Is everything all right?"

Pamela stared at her husband. God, he looked terrible! So pale and small, dwarfed by the machines around the bed.

Doug saw her shocked expression. "Don't worry about these. They're just keeping me alive," he joked.

"I brought you these."

Doug raised an eyebrow at the large bag of grapes. He made no move to take them. "Thank you."

She put them on the locker and perched awkwardly on the edge of a chair.

"So where have you been?"

"I'm sorry, dear, but I got one of my headaches. You know how they affect me. All I could do was take to my bed and disconnect the phone."

"Poor you," he said dryly.

"Oh, I'm OK now. How are you, more to the point? You look well."

Doug wondered had he actually woken up yet. This was a strangely surreal conversation to be having with his wife. He'd just had a serious operation to solve a life-threatening problem and she was acting as if he'd just had a tooth pulled. "I'm doing OK. Are you sure you are?"

She gave a little laugh. "Oh yes. You know my headaches. Hell one day, gone the next."

"I wasn't referring to your headache."

She looked away.

"Is this upsetting you, Pam? Were you afraid I might . . . die?"

"No, of course not, silly."

"Pam, talk to me."

"Really, Douglas. You're being ridiculous. Of course I was worried, but Mr Grimes is an excellent surgeon. He performs thousands of these operations a year. I knew you were in safe hands."

"Yes, I was."

"And you'll be out in a few days, then we can take a nice holiday. What about Nice? You like it there. Mind you, maybe Mr Grimes wouldn't approve of you gambling. The excitement might be too much."

Her laugh sounded slightly strained to them both.

"Or we could just go somewhere like Drumoland Castle. That would be more restful. You could play some golf, or do a spot of fishing."

"Maybe. How's work? Did everything go OK in Marrakech?" He'd already asked her about the Lifesavers conference but somehow it seemed necessary to get her talking about normal, everyday topics.

"Yes, I told you it did. Now stop worrying about work. I have it all under control."

"I'm sure you do."

"Well, I'd better go. I don't want to tire you out."

Doug stared at her. "Already?"

"The nurse told me not to stay long," she lied.

"Oh. I see."

"I'll come back tomorrow. Is there anything you'd like me to bring?"

"No. Well, maybe some Häagen-Dazs. My throat is sore from the tube."

"Poor darling." She kissed his forehead. "Now you get some rest. I'll see you tomorrow."

"Bye, Pamela." He closed his eyes when she'd left. He felt so tired now. Tired and lonely.

Pamela sat in the car clutching the steering wheel. He'd looked so feeble lying there. Feeble. It wasn't a word she'd have ever associated with Douglas. He was such a strong, vibrant man. A man in control. A leader. But not now. He was weak and fragile and it made her feel – afraid. Afraid for their world. Their safe, strong little world. Suddenly it didn't seem secure any more. *Pull yourself together, Pamela. The man's just gone through major surgery.* In a couple of weeks he would be fine. And in a couple of months he'd be back at work and it

would be like all of this never happened. She smiled.
He'd probably be back a lot sooner. Knowing Douglas,
he'd be on the phone to work within a couple of days.
He'd be driving her nuts trying to run things from
home. Nothing would keep Douglas Hamilton down
for long. Everything would be back to normal in no
time. The worst was over. She started the engine and
swung the car out on to the Rock Road.

Chapter Seventeen

"So what was the hotel like?" Hannah asked after they'd finally secured a seat in the crowded bar of The Old Stand. It was nice to be in Dublin.

Gina swallowed a handful of peanuts. "Fantastic, Hannah. Out of this world. It would have been a really nice break if I hadn't had to go outside."

Hannah laughed. "You're a terrible wimp."

"I know." Gina was shamefaced.

"I like my comfort too," Hannah told her, "but I'd still love to experience the exotic *souks*."

"Smelly *souks*, more like."

"Be reasonable, Gina. If they're selling food in that heat there's bound to be smells and flies."

"Maybe, but I don't have to 'experience' them, do I? No, thank you very much. I would have been quite happy if the hotel was my only experience."

Hannah shook her head. Exotic to Gina was a beach in Ibiza and chilli sauce on her burger! "What about the trip through the mountains?" she persisted. "*That* must have been interesting."

Gina put her head on one side. "Interesting? Hot and dusty is the way I remember it. The bus was about a hundred years old and the air-conditioning was noisy and useless."

Hannah laughed. "Well, that's what can happen when you go off the beaten track. So, any romance?"

Gina flushed.

"That says it all. Come on. Give."

"It was nothing, honest. A bit of a fling with the courier, but it didn't get very far."

"You little hussy!"

Gina laughed. "Oh well, you know what they say. All work and no play makes Jack . . ." Her voice faded away and her cheeks reddened.

"A dull boy." Hannah finished the saying. "So tell me about him."

"Who?"

"The courier, of course. What was his name? Francois or Jean, I suppose."

"Michel."

"Ah, Michel! He sounds gorgeous."

Gina giggled. "Nutter! He was, though. Dark eyes, dark hair, tall, charming."

"And was he any good?" Hannah winked lewdly.

"Dunno. It didn't get that far." She shot Hannah a look. "At least not with Michel."

Hannah looked at her curiously. "What does that mean?"

"Nothing."

214

"Gina Barrett! Tell me everything this instant!"

"OK, but you've got to promise not to tell anybody – not even Fergal."

"Cross my heart," Hannah said and leaned forward expectantly.

Gina filled her in on the dreaded night in the garden at La Mamounia.

"My God," Hannah said when she finished. "It's like something out of a Barbara Cartland novel! So, what happens now?"

Gina shrugged. "Nothing. There's a bit of atmosphere between us . . ."

"I'll bet!"

"But I'm sure we can put it behind us."

"Why would you want to do that?" Hannah said with a sly grin.

"What?"

"Why put it behind you? By the sound of it our Jack is quite something. Why don't you go out with him properly?"

Gina stared at her as if she'd lost her senses. "Go on a date with Jack Byrne?"

"Yeah, why not?"

"But I don't even fancy him!"

"After that little session in the gardens, I wouldn't be so sure."

"But I didn't know it was him," Gina pointed out. "Now can we please forget all about it, Hannah? First it was Mike Ford. Now it's Jack Byrne! Who are you going to try and fix me up with next?"

Hannah grinned. "Well, there's old Ned. You know the one who's a permanent fixture in the corner of Horan's bar? Apparently he's loaded."

Gina threw a handful of peanuts at her. "Enough! The sooner I get away from you the better! Vegas, here I come."

"Yeah. Just you and Jack. Very cosy."

"Me, Jack and fifty advertising people," Gina corrected, though she *was* a bit nervous about the trip. Were things going to be very awkward between them? She'd have to be careful not to drink too much. And stay away from him in the evenings. It was a pity, really. They'd always got on so well. Gina felt more comfortable with Jack than any other guy she'd ever known. It would be a shame if she lost that friendship.

Hannah saw her woebegone expression and changed the subject. "You better not bring too much money. I lost a fortune the last time. Well, fifty quid."

"I probably won't gamble at all. I'm not really into it."

"Believe me, you will be. It's hard to resist the atmosphere. And you always think the next bet is going to be 'the one'. Some people lose serious money. I remember seeing a man sitting on the steps of Caesar's Palace crying."

"That's crazy. I don't know how anyone can take risks like that. The most I've ever gambled is a fiver on the Grand National. Anyway, enough about me. How's London? How's Fergal?"

"OK."

Gina watched the smile fade from her friend's face. "What's wrong? You're not fighting, are you?"

"No, well, yes, oh, I don't know."

"Well, make up your mind. What's the problem?"

"He's been offered a job in Dublin. MD of a large brokerage."

"And is he taking it?"

"He wants to, but only if I agree to come with him."

"And you don't want to."

"You know how hard I've worked to get on in this job, Gina. Now I've finally been promoted, I'm earning a ludicrous amount of money. He can't expect me to throw all of that away."

"And if you don't come?"

"He won't take the job and I'll feel lousy."

"Would he not consider commuting?"

Hannah stared at her. "From London to Dublin? Every day?"

"Why not? Lots of people do it. The fares are dirt cheap and it's only fifty minutes. Where's the brokerage?"

"Down the road from CML."

"Oh. Well, the traffic would be bad coming in from the airport but probably no worse than what he's dealing with at the moment."

"Yes, but that's *without* a plane trip," Hannah reminded her. "He'd need to be up at the crack of dawn to fly to Dublin every morning. No, it would never work."

"So what *are* you going to do?"

"I've no idea. Oh, let's talk about something else. Have you heard from Mike Ford?"

Gina looked at her suspiciously. "What makes you ask that?"

"I met him down home a few weeks ago. He said he was coming to Dublin and he'd look you up."

"Or you told him to look me up."

Hannah's eyes twinkled. "I only said I was sure you'd be happy to see him."

"You're an interfering woman, Kennedy. Anyway, you're little plan didn't work. His visit coincided with Marrakech."

"Dammit."

"I'm not really sure I'm interested any more, to be honest. I'm sort of seeing someone else."

"My God! You are living an exciting life these days! Chatting up foreigners. Making love to Jack. Who else is there?"

"It's Greg, Doug's brother."

Hannah's face fell. "Greg Hamilton? You're not serious?"

"And why not?" Gina said coolly. She was getting sick of people's attitude towards Greg.

"Because he's a waster, Gina. Oh, come on. Look at the way he treated you last year."

"What are you talking about? I didn't go out with him last year."

"No, but you wanted to! You were always going on about him. He obviously led you on. I wouldn't trust him an inch. And after all, look at his brother. Hardly the most monogamous character."

"We don't know that," Gina said defensively.

"Oh yes we do."

Gina stared at her.

Hannah sighed. "He went out with a girl I know. Last summer."

"You're kidding."

"Nope. I don't think it was that serious. She's a good-looking girl. Very independent. Enjoys the good life."

"No better man than Doug to show her a good time," Gina said glumly. She'd had her suspicions that Doug did a little more than flirt but this was still a bit of a shock.

Hannah brushed her hair back from her face with a slender hand. "Do you think the wife knows what he's like?"

"Hard to know."

"What's she like?" Though Hannah had met Doug a couple of times when she'd visited Gina's local, she'd never met Pamela.

"Beautiful, clever, a great manager and a cold bitch."

"In that case I don't blame him playing around."

"Hannah!"

"Well, I don't." She shrugged. Doug Hamilton was a very attractive man who obviously loved women. If he was married to such a cold character it was only natural that he'd need to find comfort elsewhere. She wouldn't mind comforting him herself.

"You fancy him, don't you?" Gina accused. "What about poor Fergal?"

Hannah rolled her eyes. "Oh, for goodness sake, Gina! There's nothing wrong with looking at the menu and 'poor Fergal' does just fine."

"Anyway, don't judge Greg by Doug's behaviour."

"No?"

"No. He's really nice, Hannah. Honestly."

"Then why don't you introduce me? We could go out as a foursome. Bring him home some weekend and I'll bring Fergal."

Gina looked away slightly embarrassed. "It's a bit early for that. We've only been out once."

"And when was that?"

"Before I went to Morocco."

"But that was ages ago!"

"Only three weeks," Gina said defensively. "And what with Doug's operation, well I'm sure he's had a lot on his plate."

Hannah shook her head. "And you call that going out with someone? Give me a break."

"I wish you'd give *me* a break," Gina retorted. "I thought this was supposed to be a fun girls' night out, not the Spanish Inquisition!"

"OK, sorry. I'll get another round and then we really must go for something to eat. I'm starving."

"Fine." Gina was relieved. Hannah always made her feel like a doormat and it wasn't true. She didn't let men walk all over her. She just wasn't as aggressive as Hannah. That wasn't such a bad thing, was it? OK, she'd been silly the time she'd agreed to iron Mark's shirts. Even Tim thought she was nuts for doing that – especially as she wouldn't do his. Hannah had hugged her when she'd finally broken up with him: 'Congratulations, kid. That's the best decision you've made in a long time.'

Gina hadn't been quite sure how to take that remark.

Hannah had made it clear from the beginning what she thought of Mark. In fact Hannah hadn't liked *any* of the men Gina had gone out with. Strange really, because Gina got on well with all of Hannah's boyfriends – and there had been a lot of them.

Hannah arrived back with their drinks. "Here we are. So did Mike say he'd call again? How did you leave things?"

Gina sighed. Maybe she should have stayed in with a good book. "He said he'd give me a call the next time he's in Dublin."

"Let's go home tomorrow," Hannah said suddenly.

"What?"

"Yeah, we could go to Horan's tomorrow night. I'm sure he'd be there."

"You want to drive all the way to Kilkenny on the off-chance Mike Ford might be in Horan's? Are you nuts? Talk about making me look desperate."

"He won't know that's the only reason we're there, will he?" Hannah pointed out. Driving to Kilkenny wasn't such a big deal to her. She spent most of her life in cars or planes.

"No, I'm not going and that's final, Hannah."

"OK, OK, keep your hair on. You do like him, though, don't you?"

"He's all right. But I've told you, it's Greg I'm interested in."

"Right."

"Don't say it like that."

"Like what?" Hannah asked innocently.

Gina shook her head. Her friend would never

change. It was quite annoying. Especially as she was probably right. Gina had been furious this afternoon when Greg had wished everyone a nice weekend and sauntered out of the office. He had definitely been avoiding her. Oh, he still paid her compliments and chatted to her in the office, but that was it. Not as much as a mention of another date.

"Let's go to Captain America's. I fancy a burger," she said innocently.

"And maybe we'll bump into Greg," Hannah said mildly, well aware of her friend's motives.

Gina scowled. "I'm warning you, Hannah."

"What? What did I say?" Hannah knew when she'd gone too far. Better to change the subject before Gina hit her. "How's your new helper working out?"

"Good question. She was out sick for a few days and when she finally came in, her face was all bruised."

"Oh yeah? Poor kid."

"Mmnn. There was some cock-and-bull story about falling over but I think someone thumped her. She's not the most chatty individual, but when she came in that day she just sat at her desk with her head down and hardly said a word."

"And did you ask her about it?"

Gina shook her head. "Susie isn't the kind of girl who likes to confide. Especially in me."

"Why don't you take her out to lunch some day? It might be easier for her to open up outside the office."

Gina laughed. "I'm the last person she'd open up to. Anyway, she knows where I am if she wants to talk."

Hannah looked at her shrewdly. "You don't like her."

"She's not easy to like. She's sullen, suspicious and downright rude sometimes."

"Well, if someone knocked me around, I'd be suspicious too. Does she live with a boyfriend?"

"No, with her folks."

"It must be the father so."

"No! How could a man hit his own daughter? His *pregnant* daughter at that!" Gina thought of her own gentle father.

"She's pregnant? Oh well, that will be it then. She must have told him. Or he found out and bam!" Hannah pounded her fist into her hand.

Gina stared at her. It hadn't occurred to her that Susie's parents mightn't know about the baby. But then, she hadn't exactly given it a lot of thought. She'd stopped even asking how Susie was because her replies were so defensive. She felt a pang of guilt. Maybe she should try and talk to her on Monday.

* * *

"You OK?"

Susie jumped at Malcolm's voice.

"Sorry, didn't mean to startle you. I just came back for my jacket. You're working late for a Friday night, aren't you? I would have thought a young girl like you would have been off gallivanting."

"Looking like this?" Susie's face was now an interesting shade of purple and there was a jagged scar across her lip.

Mal sat down beside her. "It doesn't look so bad. I hope the other guy looks worse."

Susie looked away. "It was an accident . . ."

"Of course. I think I'll make myself a coffee. Would you like one?"

Susie looked at him suspiciously. "I thought ye just came back for your jacket?"

"Yeah, well the traffic's crazy. I'd be better off hanging around here for a while. Unless of course you don't want me to?"

"No. Sorry, I didn't mean . . ."

"So am I making the coffee or are you?"

Susie smiled. She was glad she'd watched Gina using the machine. She'd only ever drunk instant before she joined CML. "I just made some, but it's only decaf."

"Ah, looking after junior," Mal said approvingly. "Good for you. Decaf will be fine. We should all switch really. This office is wired to the moon most of the time."

Susie giggled and went out to get him a cup.

"So what are you working on?"

"Nothing," she admitted. "I'm just not too keen on going home."

"Oh?"

"It's me da. He's not too impressed about the baby."

"I see." Mal's face was grim. So Mr Clarke was responsible for her accident. "So what are you going to do? You can't stay here all night every night."

"Oh, I don't. Just another hour or so and he'll be gone to the pub by the time I get home."

"But you should be getting plenty of rest." Mal remembered how exhausted Caroline had been when she was pregnant. She was always complaining.

"But I am resting." Susie sat back down and swung her legs on to a chair. "Look, feet up! Oh!" She clutched her stomach.

"What is it? What's wrong?" Mal's face was full of concern.

Susie smiled as realisation dawned. "The baby moved."

"Really! Oh, wow! Can I . . . would you mind?"

"Sure," Susie said shyly. "Just here."

Mal put his hand where she showed him and waited.

"Nope, he must have gone back asleep." He laughed at the disappointment on her face. "Don't worry. In a few weeks you'll be sick of being kicked senseless. My daughter Rachel had a kick like a mule. We went to see *Speed* one night, and at one of the romantic bits, Caroline let out this almighty yell. We were nearly thrown out!"

Susie giggled.

Malcolm smiled. "You're a tough little nut, aren't you?"

Susie rubbed her bruised forehead. "Dunno about that."

"He did that to you, didn't he? Your dad?"

She looked at him, her eyes suspiciously bright. "He says I'm a whore."

"Don't mind the old bastard! I'm sorry. I know he's your father, but he's talking a load of crap."

Susie smiled through her tears. "No, yer right. He is an oul bastard." She caressed her stomach. "But he didn't get the baby and that's all that matters."

Mal looked at her worriedly. "Not this time. You really should leave home, Susie."

"I know but I don't have the money. Another couple of months and I should have enough for a deposit on a flat."

"Is there no one you could move in with? Flats are expensive."

She shook her head. She'd never had a best friend, not really, and Marie was saving to get married to Paddy. "No. No one."

Mal looked at her miserable expression. "Ah well, you're probably better off. You don't have to worry about anyone else's snoring or smelly socks."

Susie giggled again. He was really nice. Not the nerd she'd thought he was at all. And he always seemed to be making her laugh.

"Well, I'd better go." Mal stood up and put on his jacket. "Caroline will be wondering what on earth's happened to me."

"Oh. Well, bye then and . . . thanks."

"Oh, for nothing."

"Mal, ye won't say anything to the others, will ye?"

He put his finger to his lips. "My lips are sealed. But promise you'll come to me if you need to talk . . . or anything."

"I promise."

"Good. Cheerio, then. Have a nice weekend."

"Seeya." Susie sighed as she watched him go. It must be nice to have someone waiting for you. Someone wondering where you were, worried. No one had ever worried about her, not even her ma. She didn't have time, what with the smaller kids. Susie and Marie had been expected to look after themselves and they had.

But, Susie reminded herself, Marie was looking after her now. Sure wasn't she checking out all the adoption details? *And* she'd stood up to their da and made sure he hadn't thrown her out. Susie cheered up at the thought. She looked at her watch. It would take about an hour to get home if she left now. It was cutting it a bit fine, but Da should have left for the pub by then and she was so tired. She picked up her bag and her coat, said goodnight to the security man and began the short walk to the Dart station.

Chapter Eighteen

"Douglas? Did you hear what I said?" Pamela asked her husband impatiently.

Doug looked up absently. "Sorry?"

"You haven't been listening to a word I've said. The club dinner is on this evening and we need to be there by eight."

"I'm not going."

"What do you mean, you're not going? We always go. You're on the committee for God's sake."

"I'm going to see Mother."

Pamela clenched her pen tightly. "Well, you can do that now and still be back in plenty of time."

Doug looked at her steadily. "I'm not going, Pamela, and that is that. You go."

"How can I possibly go on my own?" she said angrily.

He shrugged. "Do what you like."

"I'll tell them you're not well. It's the only reasonable excuse at such short notice." She flounced off, stabbing the number into the phone as she went. "Jane, darling?

It's Pamela. I'm afraid we can't make it this evening. Poor Douglas is feeling just a tiny bit under the weather. Yes, he's marvellous considering. Just gets a teensy bit tired now and again."

Doug gave a wry smile. This was the nearest thing to sympathy he got from Pamela. The kind she faked in front of their friends. He stood up and looked out of the window. It was a beautiful evening, nice enough for him to walk to Ranelagh. He still wasn't allowed to drive and usually he took taxis wherever he wanted to go. But today he felt like walking. Anyway, he was supposed to take plenty of exercise. All part of his rehabilitation. His mother would be very impressed. She thought it was hilarious that he and Pamela drove everywhere.

"You'd think you were both invalids. Your father and I used to cycle and walk everywhere, you know. He only got the car the year before he died. We used to cycle out to Howth sometimes and buy fresh fish for supper."

They sounded like halcyon days to Doug. Simpler. His parents hadn't been rich but they'd seemed idyllically happy with each other and their small family. He felt a pang of envy as he walked up through Herbert Park. He had a beautiful wife, a successful business, a wonderful home in one of the most prestigious areas of Dublin but somehow his life seemed empty. Up until a couple of months ago, he'd been very happy with his lot. He'd enjoyed life – lived it to the full. And yet now, now it was different. He'd come face to face with his own mortality and everything had changed. Pamela was losing patience with him. She'd tried to talk to him about work a number of times but he just couldn't summon up any interest. He'd even called Kelly Matthews and invited her out for lunch, but he'd found his mind drifting while she talked. They'd gone back to her flat, but though Doug had fondled and kissed her large breasts appreciatively, he found that was all he could do. Kelly used every trick in her vast repertoire but to no avail.

"I'm afraid little Dougie doesn't want to come out to play, today," he said apologetically.

"It could be the medication," Kelly had said kindly, buttoning her blouse. "It affects some men like that."

Doug chuckled. Maybe he'd lost it. Maybe he'd need to get some Viagra to get him going again. Well, Pamela wouldn't care if he was impotent. In fact, it would probably suit her better that way. After all, he'd arrived home from hospital to find all his things had been moved into the guestroom.

"I thought you might be better in here," Pamela had said, slightly nervously. "I don't want to disturb you when I'm going out in the morning."

"Very considerate," he said dryly.

She looked at him sharply.

"No, really, Pamela. You've been wonderful. What with looking after the business and everything."

She visibly relaxed. "Oh, that's OK. You know I enjoy it. And the most important thing is for you to take things easy and make a full recovery."

That had been three weeks ago and it was clear that Pamela thought he should have recovered by now. At least enough to resume their hectic social life. Though she hadn't suggested that he move back into their room.

He turned into the square and crossed the road to his family home. His mood lightened as he climbed the steps. This had always been a happy home thanks to his mother and her bravery after his father died. She had made sure that her children had wanted for nothing, especially love. He sometimes thought Janet and Greg were oblivious to how hard life had been for her. She had been such a young widow, but to his knowledge, she'd never looked at another man. No one could measure up to Charles Hamilton.

Doug let himself in. "Mother? It's me, Doug."

"In here, darling."

He went into the large sitting-room, with its soft, floral décor and kissed his mother's cheek before sitting down in the chair opposite. "How are you?" He studied her carefully. There was colour in her cheeks and her eyes were bright. She looked so much better than last week.

"I'm fine, dear. More to the point, how are you?"

Doug had finally told her about his operation, realising that he couldn't keep up the pretence any longer. He needed to talk. And he found he'd been able to tell her things that he couldn't say to Pamela. "Fine, fine. A little out of breath. I walked, you know."

"All the way from Ballsbridge?" Her voice was teasing.

"Yes, it was tough going. Any chance of a cup of tea?"

She stood up slowly and reached for her stick.

Doug sprang to his feet. "Oh, no, I'll get it. I thought Betty was here."

"Not today. Her grandson is making his Holy Communion. But she left the fridge full and baked soda bread and scones. Silly woman. You'd think she was feeding an army."

Doug followed her out to the kitchen and sniffed the wonderful aroma of fresh bread. "She probably knew I was coming." He took down the breadboard and cut four thick slices.

Sheila smiled. "Well, there's obviously nothing wrong with your appetite." She made the tea and put two mugs on a tray along with a jug of milk, butter, the fresh bread and some scones.

"Any jam?"

"The cupboard over your head."

Doug carried the tray back into the living-room.

"So when are you going back to work?" Sheila sat down and laid her stick against the wall.

Doug buttered a slice of bread and bit into it with relish. "No rush," he said cheerfully when he'd swallowed.

Sheila frowned. "Surely Pamela needs you?"

"She's managing fine without me. Everything's going like clockwork."

"But aren't you bored?"

"Not really. I'm doing a lot of reading. I'm finally getting to read books I've had for years. I've just finished *The Satanic Verses*. I must give it to you. It's very interesting."

"I'm not sure it's my kind of book," she said dryly.

He chuckled. "Maybe not. No, I'm quite enjoying

watching the world go by for a change. Do you know what I mean?"

Sheila didn't. Through illness – first arthritis, then angina – she'd been forced to sit back for years now and she had never got used to it. She'd always been active – she had to be, bringing up three young children on her own. When her health had started to fail, the frustration of taking things easy was what she found hardest. She wasn't afraid of death. She was ready for that when her time came. It was just this incessant waiting. She studied her son. He didn't look his forty-two years. He could easily pass for thirty-five. His skin was clear and his eyes were bright and full of life. He was thinner now, and his jeans hung on him but he wouldn't be long filling out again the way he was wolfing down that bread.

"I'm not sure I do, Douglas," she said finally. "I'd much prefer to be in the middle of things than sitting on the sideline watching the world pass me by."

He reached over and squeezed her hand. "Poor thing. You've had a rough time, haven't you?"

"We all have our crosses to bear. I live a comfortable life, I've three wonderful children, I can't complain."

"Have you heard from the other two at all?" Doug moved on to the scones.

Sheila's face lit up. "Janet phoned last night. She's pregnant again."

"That's wonderful! Is she OK? How far along is she?"

His sister had had three miscarriages already.

"Well, that's the really good news, nearly six months."

"Six months! She left it late enough to tell us."

"It's understandable. She wanted to get past the danger point before she told anyone. The longest she'd managed to go before was four months, so this is looking really good."

"I'm delighted for her. She deserves it. They both do. Bill must be over the moon."

Doug could imagine the happiness the stocky, jovial Canadian must be feeling. He'd longed for a family, they both had. He sighed. A family had never been part of his plans and it was probably too late now. Anyway, Pamela would never agree to ruin her figure.

Sheila saw the sad smile. "You'd make a great father, you know."

Doug looked startled. "Me? Crikey, no. I'm much too selfish."

"You'd change. Once you've held your own child in your arms, you realise you would give your life for him."

He smiled at her tenderly. "Not everyone is as great a mother as you, though I'm sure Janet will be."

Sheila watched him sadly. It was such a pity Douglas had never had children. But somehow she'd guessed that's the way it would be. He'd always been more interested in money and success than in raising a family. And Pamela had been the same. She feared that's why he'd really married her. She was a trophy wife. And just as ambitious. There didn't seem to be much room for love in such a relationship. In fact, partnership was probably a better word to describe it.

"A penny for them."

"Oh, I was just thinking that finally one of my children is going to make me a grandmother."

He grinned. "Oh, I don't know. Greg probably already has!"

"Douglas!" She looked at him, shocked, but there was a twinkle in her eye. "How's he getting on in CML? I haven't seen him in ages. He seems to be working long hours."

"Really?" Douglas thought of the lambasting Pamela had been giving his brother only that morning.

"He's never in the office, he breaks appointments, he's a bloody waste of time," she'd said angrily.

For Pamela to curse, she must be very annoyed with him indeed.

Doug smiled at his mother. She didn't need to know any of this. "I haven't been in the office, Mother, so I don't know. I'll call him." *And tell him to get his ass in gear and go and see his mother.* "More tea?"

Sheila shook her head. "No, I'm sick of the stuff. A small sherry would be nice, though."

"*Tch-tch.* It's only six-thirty."

She arched an eyebrow.

"Very well, but I'd better join you. I don't like the idea of you drinking alone. Turning into a geriatric lush."

"Who are you calling geriatric?"

"Sorry, Mother. Now where do you keep the brandy?"

* * *

Pamela sat in the conservatory, sipping a glass of Chablis, one slender foot tapping the wooden floor impatiently.

She'd been so sure he'd come home and tell her he'd changed his mind. But it was now eight o'clock and there was no sign of him. She didn't know why he didn't just move in with his bloody mother. Why he didn't retire and have done with it. It was true that there was still a few weeks of his convalescence left, but he was fine. Pamela hadn't expected him to be quite so robust so quickly. The only time he showed any sign of having been through major surgery, was when he tried to lift something heavy. Other than that, he was as good as new. As Pamela watched the rapid improvement, she thought, with some relief, that they'd be able to do without the services of Greg Hamilton soon. But Douglas showed no interest at all in CML and anytime she asked him about coming back to work, he prevaricated. It was so unlike him. She'd been delighted to see him walk into the office last week but had been extremely irritated to learn that he'd only come in to meet Jack for a drink. So it looked like she would be holding the fort while Jack and Gina went to Las Vegas. And she would have to cope with Greg's tardiness. And deal with Susie Clarke. If it wasn't for the normality of Malcolm and Noreen she'd go completely mad! Maybe she could persuade Douglas to go to Las Vegas. Then at least she'd have Gina in the office. She'd talk to him about it later. That was sure to appeal to him. He'd never be able to resist the temptation. She went to have a look in the freezer. She'd defrost a couple of steaks and open a bottle of St Emilion. That would put him in the right frame of mind.

Douglas walked into the house and smelled the food. Damn, who the hell was here now? He slipped past the living-room and went into the kitchen and stopped short at the sight of his wife in an apron studying a cookery book. "What on earth are you doing?"

Pamela looked up and smiled. "Oh, hello. Well, if we're not going out I thought I should make us something to eat. Is steak OK?"

"Lovely," he said, still staring.

"I was going to make a sauce to go with it, but it looks terribly difficult."

"Don't worry about it. I'll mix up some Bisto."

"No, no, I'll do it. You pour yourself a glass of wine and go and relax."

"Are you sure?"

"Yes, no problem."

He gave her another puzzled look and went into the dining-room.

"I thought we'd eat in the living-room," she called after him. "It's cosier."

He went into the living-room. Two armchairs were pulled up in front of a low table, set with silverware, napkins and two large crystal glasses. "Very nice."

He picked up the wine that she'd left to breathe on the sideboard, sniffed appreciatively and poured. He carried a glass out to her, tipping a drop of it into the gravy she was making before handing it to her. "Adds a bit of bite," he said with a wink.

Doug was just pouring himself a second glass when she carried in the tray. "I'll take that."

"No, you won't. You know you're not supposed to be

lifting anything heavy. Now eat up. I hope everything's OK."

The steak was a little overcooked for Doug's liking. The new potatoes were a bit hard and the asparagus slightly cold, but Doug munched happily and praised her loudly. "It's absolutely lovely, darling. We should do this more often."

"Only if you plan to do the cooking," she said, returning his smile.

Doug sipped his wine and gazed happily at his wife. This is what had been missing from their lives. These intimate moments. Just the two of them. For the last few years it seemed they were always going out or entertaining. On the rare occasion that they were free, he would be playing squash or she attending a jazz-ballet class. They never spent any quality time together.

"How is your mother?"

"Better than I've seen her in a long time. And there's some good news for a change. Janet's pregnant again."

"Oh, yes?" The smile was frozen on Pamela's face.

"Yes, and it looks like she may make it all the way this time."

"I'm happy for her," she said quietly, her head bent over her meal.

"Mother sends her love, by the way. She says it's been ages since she saw you."

"Well, things are so busy in the office. I haven't seen my own parents in weeks."

He looked concerned. "You're managing all right, aren't you?"

Pamela smiled bravely. "Yes, yes of course. Though I miss having you to bounce things off."

"Greg's not much use, is he?"

Pamela wasn't going to criticise his brother again. That wasn't the way to win him over. "He just doesn't know the business that well. And he's an academic through and through."

"And lazy."

Pamela shrugged her delicate shoulders.

"Maybe we should get you more help. Someone more qualified."

"Oh, I don't think there's any need for that. You'll be back soon."

Doug said nothing.

"I was thinking. Maybe you should do the Las Vegas trip after all. It would be a nice break for you."

"I don't know . . ."

"It would be a great help. There's so much for Gina to do here."

He looked startled. "Oh, go *instead* of Gina? Oh, no, I don't think so. I'm not familiar with the details . . ."

"It would take no time at all to bring you up to speed."

"No, Pamela. It's out of the question." He pushed his plate away and drained his glass.

Pamela's mouth set into a grim line. "Fine. It was just an idea. Forget it." She stood up and walked out of the room.

Doug slumped back in his chair. So much for their cosy evening together.

Chapter Nineteen

"Is Jack gone?"

"Yep. All clear. Now what's the plan?" Malcolm leaned back in his chair.

Gina perched on the side of his desk. She felt very uncomfortable about having anything to do with this birthday party. But Jack was thirty and she'd got caught up in the arrangements long before the Marrakech incident. My God, she thought wryly. That sounded like the title of a Robert Ludlum book! She turned her attention back to Malcolm who was looking at her expectantly. "Well, we're going to send him to Jury's, supposedly to set up for a presentation, and when he arrives, hey presto, we all jump out and shout surprise!"

"What about the invitations?"

"Nora's taking care of family and old friends and stuff and I've been told to make sure all his workmates are there." Gina was glad the big day was on Friday. She was weary of dealing with Jack's sister. A forceful woman to say the least.

"I think you should bring him to the hotel, Gina," she'd said firmly.

"But he always sets up the gear on his own. It will just make him suspicious if I tag along."

"But what if he doesn't turn up?" Nora asked anxiously.

"He'll turn up," Gina assured her. "He's never let the side down yet."

"But he might decide to go early – or worse, he might decide to get up early the next morning and do it."

Gina looked at her agitated expression and realised it would be a lot easier to give in. "OK, I'll go with him. I'll concoct some story to make sure we arrive bang on eight o'clock."

"Oh, that's wonderful, Gina. I'll be able to relax now."

Gina sincerely doubted it.

"So, Susie, looking forward to the party?" Mal said, conscious that Gina was actively excluding the girl.

"I'm not going," she muttered.

"Oh, but you must! It's the first real social occasion we've had since you joined CML. Now, you don't want to insult us, do you?"

Susie frowned. "No. It's just that . . ."

"You're coming," Mal said firmly. "Is Pamela going to join us?" he asked Gina.

"I think Doug has press-ganged her into it. But she probably won't stay long."

"Just as well. She'd only put a damper on things and I don't think Jack will be too devastated if she has a pressing engagement elsewhere."

"He mightn't, but I think Doug will. He's taking the whole thing very seriously. He told me the company would treble whatever I manage to collect for the present."

"Blimey! That's not like the boss we know and love! So how much do you want?"

"I thought ten pound from each of us and maybe just five from Susie – after all she's new and hardly knows him," Gina explained.

Susie stuck her chin out stubbornly. "I'll give what everyone else is giving. I'm not mean."

Gina looked at the two angry red spots on the girl's cheeks. "I was only saying – "

"I know what ye were saying, but I'll pay me share." She rummaged in her baggy jeans, pulled out two crumpled fivers and threw them on Gina's desk.

"Right, well, thanks." Gina threw Mal an exasperated look.

"So Doug will be there, will he?" Mal carried on as if nothing had happened.

"Yeah."

"When is he coming back to work?"

"I don't know. It must be soon. It's been ages since the operation."

"And then Greg will be leaving us." Mal watched for a reaction. Jack had told him what had happened in Marrakech and Mal thought that even if Gina hadn't realised it was Jack she was cavorting with, she certainly hadn't been pining over Greg!

"I suppose." Gina looked forlornly at the back of

Greg's head through the glass of Pamela's office. She still couldn't understand what had gone wrong. They'd had a lovely night out – at least she'd enjoyed it – but he hadn't asked her out since. It must be because she wouldn't go to bed with him. What other reason could there be?

"And once you've sorted out that problem, I want you to concentrate on the First Finance conference."

"What about DVD?" Greg asked lightly.

Pamela looked at him suspiciously. "Gina is taking care of that."

"Is that really such a good idea, Pammy? She's a bit raw to take on such a big job on her own. I could always go along and keep an eye on things."

"Could you?" Pamela said dryly.

"Yes. I get on very well with Marian Hickey, as you know," Greg said, warming to his theme. "I'm sure she'd be a lot happier if I were running things."

"No doubt, but I need you here." The last thing Pamela needed was Greg taking one of their best customers to bed and then dumping her.

Greg looked at her sullenly. "You still think I'm after Gina, don't you? I told Doug I'd keep my distance and I have. I'm sure I've broken the poor little thing's heart."

"I'm sure."

"Oh come on, Pammy, everything's under control here. I'd be much more use to you in Vegas."

Spending the company money, I don't think so. "It's all decided, Greg. Gina and Jack are going to Las Vegas and you are organising the banking conference in Limerick."

He scowled. "Great."

Pamela stood up. "Fine. I'm glad that's sorted. Now I really must go. I'm having lunch with your brother."

"When is he coming back?"

She closed her handbag with a decisive click. "Soon. Now I must go. I'll give him your love, shall I?"

She breezed out of the office and made her way down to Baggot Street where she turned right. She crossed the bridge, barely noticing the swans or the people stretched out on the bank eating sandwiches, and walked on up past the bank and across to the small, cosy restaurant in the basement of Longfield's Hotel.

Doug stood up as she came in and kissed the proffered cheek.

Pamela waved at a couple of people before turning her attention to her husband. "Hello, darling. How did it go?" She sat back as the waiter placed the large linen napkin in her lap.

"OK. Nothing new, really. I got lectured on my lifestyle and diet. Blah, blah, blah."

"But you have been careful, Douglas. Haven't you? I've warned Irene to cut down on the fat in your food." She looked at the bottle of wine on the table. It was half empty already.

He smiled at her. "I know, dear. I told them I was living an exemplary life. I think they just like to make their point." He looked longingly at the duck in the rich red wine sauce on the menu. He'd better go for the poached fish.

"So, are you allowed to return to work yet?"

"They've left it up to me."

Pamela looked up from her menu. "And?"

"I think I need a bit more time, Pamela."

Pamela bit her lip. How much more bloody time? Exactly how long more was she supposed to carry CML alone? She gave him a tight smile. "Can you give me some idea?"

"Oh, for God's sake," he started impatiently.

"Well, are we talking a week, a month, a year?" she hissed. "Be fair, Douglas. I need *something* a little more definite."

He sighed. She was right. He was being unreasonable. "I'm sorry, darling. I know this is difficult for you."

"It certainly is," she said stiffly.

"Look, Grimes suggested I see a counsellor."

"A counsellor? What on earth for?"

"To talk through the whole experience. Apparently an operation as serious as this can have psychological effects."

"Well really . . ."

"I know. I was a bit sceptical too, but it might be nice to talk to someone."

Pamela concentrated on the plate of food in front of her so he wouldn't see the hurt in her eyes. "You've got me to talk to, haven't you? Going to a counsellor seems a bit silly."

Doug looked at her sadly. Yes, it would seem silly to her. "You're right, dear. It would probably be a complete waste of time."

"Of course it would. I've told you, Douglas. What

you need – what we both need – is a holiday. We could go now. Before the Las Vegas job and while your brother is still with us."

"Maybe," Doug said doubtfully. He would jump at the chance of a quiet break somewhere remote. Somewhere where he and Pamela could talk. Where he could tell her how frightened he had been. Explain to her how he'd had to confront his own mortality. But he couldn't imagine them ever having such a frank conversation. She would balk at the thoughts of such an intimate exchange.

Pamela watched him carefully. "We could rent a little cottage somewhere. Turn off our mobile phones for a week, switch off from the office, switch off from life."

He looked up in surprise. "Really? You wouldn't mind?"

"Of course not, Douglas. You're not the only one who needs a break. I don't think you realise quite how stressful this has all been for me."

Doug reached over and squeezed her hand gratefully. Maybe he'd misjudged her. Maybe she did care about him.

"I mean, it's no joke running a business on your own."

The light went out of his eyes and he took a mouthful of wine. "No."

"So what do you think? Will I book something?"

"I'll think about it."

Pamela sighed impatiently. The man couldn't seem to make up his mind about anything these days. Well, to hell with him. She would go to a health farm on her own for a few days. CML would just have to manage without her. And maybe that was the push Douglas needed.

Doug returned to the office with his wife. "Just to say hello," he explained.

Pamela left him to it and went into her office, closing the door with an angry click.

When he finally escaped from Noreen he went into the main office. "Hi, Greg. How's it going?"

His younger brother gave him a lazy smile. "Not bad, and what about you, you useless layabout? When are you going to start earning your keep again?"

"Oh, I don't know if I'll bother." Doug sat in Jack's place and winked at Gina. "I'm quite enjoying being a kept man."

He swung around to face Susie. "So, Miss Clarke. How are you getting on?"

"OK," Susie mumbled.

"Settling in all right? Is everyone treating you OK?"

Susie thought of the way his wife practically ignored her, his brother constantly made smart comments about her clothes and Gina talked to her as if she was thick. "Yeah. Fine."

"Good, good. Is Jack about?"

"No. He's at a meeting in IBM."

"In that case, Gina, you can tell me all about this party. What are we buying him? Have you decided?"

"We thought a TV. The one he has is ancient."

"That's a good idea. Have you enough money for a decent one?"

Gina flushed. "Well, I've got forty pounds, and if you give me a hundred and twenty . . ."

"You won't get a decent one for that. I'll give you two hundred."

Greg stared at his brother.

Gina beamed at him. "That's very generous, Doug. Thanks."

Doug waved away her thanks. "No problem. I'll come with you to choose it."

"Oh. There's no need for you to go to all that trouble."

"No trouble at all. How about tomorrow night? It's late-night shopping, isn't it?"

"It is," Mal confirmed, well used to being dragged around the shops by Caroline of a Thursday.

"Right. I'll pick you up here at six, Gina. See you guys on Friday night." And he was gone.

Gina stared after him.

"Don't you like the idea of going shopping with my big brother, Gina?" Greg said shrewdly.

"Of course not. I mean yes. I mean, well, I don't want him to tire himself," she finished lamely.

"I'm sure he'll cope," Greg said dryly. He wondered if Doug was after Gina for himself. Maybe that's why he'd been warned off. Pammy baby wouldn't like that at all. Greg made a mental note to keep an eye on his brother *and* his pretty little employee. Gina seemed very uncomfortable at the suggestion of the shopping trip.

"Susie? Are you sure about this ten pound? No one expects it, honestly."

Gina had decided to give it one more go after everyone else had left. She'd tried to talk to Susie a few times about her 'accident' but the girl had clammed up completely. Now she was looking at Gina, an expression of total animosity on her face.

"I'm not broke, ye know. I wish ye'd stop treating me like a charity case."

Gina looked horrified. "I'm not, Susie, honest. It's just that you're not on a huge salary and what with the baby coming, I know it can't be easy."

"I'm managing just fine," Susie lied. "And I'll pay me way like everyone else. Why don't ye mind yer own business and stop sticking yer nose into mine?"

Gina felt her cheeks redden and choked back an angry retort. What an ungrateful little bitch! Why bother even trying to talk to the girl? If Pamela wanted to get rid of her at the end of her probation it wouldn't bother Gina in the least. Not after this. She was about to leave when the phone rang. She put down her bag with a sigh. "CML, hello?"

"Gina?"

"Yes?"

"Hi. Mike Ford here."

Gina sank back into her chair, a smile on her face. "Oh, Mike. Hi. How are you?"

"Fine, fine. Listen, I can't really talk but I just wanted to tell you, to ask you that is. . ."

"Yes?" Gina's smile got broader. He sounded nervous.

"Well, I'll be in Dublin on Friday. I know it's short notice but I'd love to see you."

"Friday! Oh, Mike, I can't."

"Yes, I suppose it was unlikely you'd be free."

"It's just that I'm helping to arrange a party for a friend. I couldn't possibly get out of it."

"Sure. Not to worry. Look, I have to go. Can I call you again?"

"I'd like that. Sorry about Friday."

"Don't worry about it. Take care, Gina."

"Bye." Gina hung up the phone with a sigh. Maybe she should have brought him along to the party but with Greg there *and* Jack . . . no. Better to keep Mike Ford well away from CML.

Susie lumbered off to the Dart station, still furious. She'd been mortified when Gina had as much as said that she wouldn't be able to afford ten pounds. And in front of Mal too! The fact that she was right had nothing to do with it. She got on the train and sat fuming as she thought of her humiliation. She was still going over the whole sorry business in her head when she walked up the garden path and straight into her father who was just coming out of the house. She put her head down and tried to slip past him but he planted himself firmly in her way.

"And where the hell do ye think yer going?"

"Oh, Da. I'm tired. Leave me alone, will ye?"

"Leave me alone?" He prodded her chest with his finger. "Leave me alone? Oh, I'll leave ye alone all right. No problem. I'll leave ye alone. I told ye to get out of this house. Did ye think I was joking?" He continued to prod her chest with every word.

Susie caught the smell of drink and began to feel frightened. "No, Da, no. Sorry. I'll leave tomorrow. I promise."

"Ye promise!" He spat on the path in front of her. "A lot yer promises are worth, ye little tart!"

"Honest, Da. I mean it. I'll go tomorrow."

"Ye'll go all right. Ye'll go tonight. Ye'll go now." He grabbed her lapels and pulled her face up close to his. "Ye've got ten minutes to get yer stuff and get out. If ye leave anything, I'll burn it. Do ye hear me? Ten minutes."

Susie pulled herself free and stumbled into the hallway, her face white. Her mother was standing there, her cheeks wet with tears. "I'll help ye pack, love," she said, blowing her nose noisily.

Susie stared at her with frightened eyes. "But where am I going to go, Ma?"

"Anywhere is safer than here," her mother said firmly and for the first time Susie noticed the bruises on her mother's arm.

"Come with me, Ma," she said urgently. "Take the kids and come with me."

Florrie Clarke gave a thin smile. "Don't be silly, love. Me place is here. Now come on. Let's get a bag packed for ye. Don't worry about the rest of yer stuff. I won't let him touch it. I'll keep it safe until ye find a place."

Susie realised there was no talking to her and climbed the staircase tiredly. She shoved a few clothes into her backpack and sat down on the bed she'd shared with Marie for the last eight years. The tears ran down her cheeks as she looked around the shabby room with its

251

threadbare carpet, cheap duvet and thin curtains. It might not be a palace but it was home and she was terrified at the thought of leaving it. Her only options – as she'd given her last tenner to Gina – were a hostel or the office. Maybe if she rang her old teacher, she'd take her in. Chrissie O'Malley had always been nice to her. But God, it was a bit much asking her for a bed! She was practically a stranger. No, she'd go back to the office tonight and try and organise something more permanent tomorrow. She checked her watch. It was eight o'clock and the security man would lock the place up at ten. She scribbled a note to Marie telling her she'd call the salon tomorrow and let her know where she was staying. Hoisting her backpack across her shoulders she took one last look around and went downstairs.

Her mother was waiting in the hall. "He's asleep in the chair," she whispered. "Will I make ye some tea before ye go?"

Susie shook her head.

"Will ye be all right, love? Call me, won't ye? Let me know?"

Susie nodded, not trusting herself to speak. She gave her mother a quick hug and left without a backward glance.

Chapter Twenty

"Mr Hamilton? This is Joe Gavin from Century Development"

Doug rubbed his eyes and looked at the clock. It was two am. "Who?"

"Joe, from upstairs? I think you may have had a break-in at the office."

Doug was awake now. Joe Gavin. Yes. The little pixie of a man from upstairs. "Break-in? Why do you say that? The alarm can't have gone off. The police would have notified me."

"I realise that, but I definitely heard noises and I'm sure I saw a light. I thought you'd want to know."

"Thanks, Joe. Very decent of you. I'll check it out."

"Sure, what are neighbours for? I'm sure you'd do the same for me."

"Yes. Right. Well, thanks again. I'd better get in there."

"If you need any back-up, give me a shout. I'm still here."

Doug grinned at the thought of the skinny little man

coming down to take on a couple of beefy burglars. "That's very kind. I'll give you a shout if I need you."

Pamela appeared in the doorway as he pulled a sweatshirt over his head. "Did I hear the phone?"

"Joe Gavin heard noises in our office. I'm just going in to check things out."

"Well, be careful." She yawned and went back to her room.

"Don't you worry about me," Doug muttered as her door closed. "I'll be fine."

It took less than five minutes to get to the office along the deserted streets. Doug got out of the car and looked up at the building. There was a light on upstairs, but CML was in darkness. He rubbed his eyes wearily. He'd probably been dragged from his bed because of a bloody cat or something. He opened the main door and then rummaged for the key to CML. The door swung open and he flicked the light switch.

"What? Oh! Doug!"

A bulky figure unfolded itself from the soft leather sofa. Susie's tousled blonde head and frightened eyes appeared from under a duffle coat.

"Susie? What the hell are you doing here?"

"I . . . I'd nowhere else to go," she stammered.

"What?"

"Me da. He's kicked me out."

Doug sighed heavily. Why had he ever agreed to hire this misfit? "What are you talking about, Susie?" He sat down heavily in the chair opposite.

Susie pulled her coat closer around her. "When he found out about the baby, he – well, he told me to get out. And then tonight, well he was a bit drunk and . . ."

Doug's eyes narrowed. "He didn't hurt you, did he?"

"Nah, not this time."

"This time?"

Susie flushed and looked down at her lime-green nails. "He lost the head a bit when I first told him."

"He hit you?"

She nodded, still not looking at him. God, but she was unlucky. How had he known she was here? Why did *he* have to bloody find her? She was definitely out on her ear now. He probably thought she was making the whole thing up. Probably thought she was here to rob the place.

"I could do with a cup of tea. Want one?"

Susie looked up, startled. "OK."

Doug went into the kitchen, put on the kettle and rummaged in the press for Pamela's tea bags.

Susie followed him in. "I didn't think ye drank tea."

"I do at this hour. I'd like to get *some* sleep tonight."

"Sorry," she said sheepishly. "How did ye know I was here?"

"The chap upstairs heard you. He thought you were a burglar."

"I'm not, honest," she said hotly.

Doug looked amused. "It's OK, Susie. I think if you were going to rob me, you'd do it at a more civilised hour. So how did you get in?"

She watched him pour boiling water into two mugs.

"I slipped in earlier when the security man was on his rounds and I hid in the ladies' until he had locked up."

"Very enterprising." He took the tea bags out, added milk and handed her a mug.

"Ta."

He led the way into his office and sat down, gesturing her to sit opposite. "So what now?"

"I suppose ye want me to leave," she mumbled, turning the mug round and round in her hands.

"Well, you can hardly sleep here on a regular basis."

"It was just tonight, honest. I didn't have anywhere else to go." She lifted her chin and looked at him defiantly. "Are ye going to sack me?"

"Why would I do that? You're doing your job. No, your problem is – how shall I put this – of a more personal nature."

"I'll find somewhere tomorrow. First thing."

"Aren't you in work first thing?"

"Well, yeah but . . ."

"And how much money have you got?"

"Enough." Susie thought of the fifty-three pound in her savings account.

"Really?"

She nodded, keeping her eyes on the mug in her hand.

"Look, Susie, let's be honest here, shall we? It's three o'clock in the morning. I'm tired and I'm sure you are too." He looked at the dark circles under her eyes and her chalk-white cheeks. "What *exactly* have you got planned?"

Susie's eyes filled up. "Nuthin'."

"And you're strapped for cash?"

She nodded, sniffing loudly.

He patted her hand awkwardly. "Right. Now you've told me, we can put our heads together and do something about it, can't we?"

Susie stared at him. Why was he being so nice to her? What was he after? She looked into his eyes but saw nothing but kindness. Her tears overflowed and she let out an almighty wail.

Doug looked startled. It was the last thing he'd expected from a tough cookie like Susie. "There, now. No need for tears. We'll get you sorted. I'm sure there are places for people like you." He waved his hand vaguely. He'd never given much thought to the plight of unmarried mothers before.

"Thanks." She blew her nose noisily into a disintegrating tissue.

"For the moment, I think you better come home with me. We'll figure out something more permanent tomorrow. After a few hours, much needed, sleep."

Susie's mouth dropped open and her eyes were out on stalks. "Home with *you?*"

"Yes. That's best."

"But Pamela . . ."

He grimaced. He'd forgotten about his wife. Pamela would go berserk! He smiled grimly at Susie. "Don't you worry about a thing. Pamela will be happy to have you."

Happy to see me at the bottom of the Liffey, more like, Susie thought. Even Gina had never been to The

Sycamores. She knew that, because there was an article in *VIP* about the house only last week and Gina had been glued to it.

"Are ye sure . . ."

"Of course," Doug said brusquely, beginning to get slightly irritated at the suggestion he couldn't invite who he wanted to his own home. "Get your things. It's late."

Susie picked up her backpack and went out to the car while Doug locked up.

"Get in, then," he said impatiently, striding around to the driver's side. He drove in silence, annoyed with Susie for putting him in this position and annoyed at the thought of Pamela's reaction. She could barely stand having Susie in the office, never mind in her own home. He screeched to a halt at a red light. Why the hell was he worrying what she thought? It was his house too. The lights changed, and he moved off quickly, swinging the car around the corner and into the long driveway. He pulled up with a flourish outside the front door. "Right, here we are," he said, forcing a light note into his voice. He turned to Susie who sat rigid in her seat, her fingernails digging into the soft leather, her face white.

"Susie?"

She stumbled out of the car and hung on to the bonnet, not trusting her legs to hold her up.

"Are you OK?"

"Just a bit sick," she said faintly.

Doug looked at his watch and laughed. "A bit early for morning sickness, isn't it?"

"It's never too early or too late for morning sickness," she said morosely.

"And my driving didn't help? Sorry."

Susie shrugged, her face red.

He grinned. "Come on, then. Let's get you settled."

Susie turned towards the front door, but stopped when she realised he was walking briskly towards the garage. Bloody hell! Surely he didn't expect her to kip in there. But Doug walked on past the garage and around the side of the building. She hurried after him. When she turned the corner, she noticed a staircase and Doug was standing at the top of it, trying each of his keys in a panelled door.

Susie made her way slowly up the stairs and reached the top just as he threw open the door with a flourish.

"It's a while since I've been in here, so I don't know what state it's in. Irene's supposed to keep it clean. Where the hell is the light switch? Ah, here we are!"

He flicked a switch and Susie blinked as the room was flooded with light. When she got used to the brightness, she looked around at what appeared to be a very modern, very spacious flat. No, not a flat. You couldn't call anything this glamorous a flat. It was an apartment. "Crikey!" she breathed.

Doug grinned. "It's not bad, is it? Beats the office."

"Who lives here?"

"No one," Doug said as he walked into the kitchen area and opened a few cupboards. "Good woman, Irene. She's left in coffee, tea and long-life milk, so you're OK for a cuppa. No. The people who used to own the place had a nanny and this is where she lived. Pamela thought it would come in handy if we had guests, or if our parents came to stay. *Which they never had,* he reflected now. *Had they ever been invited?*

"It's fantastic," Susie said, walking from the white fitted kitchen, to the small dining-room where a pine table and four chairs sat in front of a large window. She peered out, but it was too dark to see anything.

"It looks out on the gardens," Doug said helpfully, moving into the sitting-room and throwing open another door. "This is the bedroom. There should be – yes, there we are – plenty of bedclothes. I'm afraid the bed isn't made up."

"That's OK. It won't take me a minute." Susie fingered one of the white lace-trimmed sheets. "Are ye sure it's OK for me to use these?"

"Oh, for God's sake, Susie, isn't that what they're for?" Doug said irritably.

"Sorry."

"The bathroom's through here."

Susie followed him into a room that was as big as the bedroom she shared with Marie. Had shared with Marie, she corrected herself. God, wait till her sister saw this place. But she wouldn't, Susie realised, coming back to earth with a bump. She'd be out of here tomorrow. Probably first thing, if Pamela had anything to do with it.

Doug rummaged in the airing cupboard. "There. I've turned on the immersion heater. There should be plenty of hot water by morning."

"Thanks."

"That's OK. Look, you won't have a chance to find somewhere else until the weekend so you'd better stay here till then. Right. I'll be off. See you tomorrow. Oh, here's the key and there's a dead bolt on the front door. Be sure and lock it after me."

"Right. And Doug? Thanks. Thanks a million."

He waved and was gone. She locked the door after him and turned to inspect her new home. "Don't get used to it," she told herself wryly. "In a couple of days ye'll be in a crummy bedsit."

She went into the bedroom and picked up the duvet. It was incredibly soft – must be feathers, she thought. She put on the lacy cover and the matching pillowcase on one of the equally soft pillows. Her bed made, she went back out to the kitchen and made more tea. She shouldn't really have any more to drink. God knows, since she'd become pregnant she'd spent enough time in the loo! It was really late and she knew she should go straight to bed but it seemed a shame to waste her time in this gorgeous place. She took her tea – in a china mug, no less – back into the sitting-room. There was a comfortable sofa covered in a soft floral material, a TV, a stereo and a telephone. She picked up the remote control, switched on the TV and flicked until she found a music station. Then she kicked off her platform shoes and sank back on to the sofa. She might as well enjoy the luxury while it lasted.

* * *

Pamela swung the car around and headed for the gate. As she inched out onto the road she had to brake hard to avoid hitting a pedestrian. The girl jumped back and threw her a dirty look that quickly turned to an embarrassed smile. Susie Clarke! What on earth was she doing here? Pamela pressed a button and her window lowered silently. "What are you doing here, Susie? A bit far from home, aren't we?"

Susie's face got redder and she looked down at her bump. "I stayed here last night."

"What was that?" Pamela asked irritably, turning down the radio. My, the girl mumbled. How disastrous if she ever answered CML's phones.

"I stayed here last night," Susie said again, slightly defiantly.

A frown puckered Pamela's perfect features. "Where? And, more to the point, why?"

"Me da threw me out and I slept in the office and Doug came in and found me and he brought me here." This all came out in a bit of a rush.

Pamela looked doubtful. "Mr Hamilton brought you *here?*"

Susie nodded. "I slept over the garage."

"I see. Well, we'll talk about this later. You'd better get a move on or you'll be late for work. I'd give you a lift but I've an urgent meeting in Blackrock."

"Mrs Hamilton – Pamela?"

Pamela stopped the car again with an exaggerated sigh. "Yes?"

"Which way is it?"

"Up to the top of the road, turn left, through two sets of lights and left again."

"Ta," Susie said, but Pamela had already sped off in the opposite direction.

Pamela crashed the gears as she sped down the Rock Road. What in God's name had Douglas been thinking of? Bringing that girl to The Sycamores! Sometimes she thought they'd made a mistake and operated on his head instead of his heart. His behaviour was definitely that of a man who'd had a frontal lobotomy. She took a few slow, deep breaths in an attempt to control the anger building up inside and phoned home. It rang a few times before a very sleepy Doug finally answered.

"Hello?"

"What's going on, Douglas? I almost ran Susie Clarke down in our driveway. She says you brought her home last night."

"I did."

His matter-of-fact reply made Pamela even angrier. "And are you going to tell me why?" Her voice was like ice.

"Not right now, no. I'm very tired. I'll fill you in this evening."

"But . . ." Pamela started and then hit the steering wheel violently when she realised he'd already hung up. "Bastard! How dare you hang up on me?" She swung the car into the outside lane, narrowly missing a Mazda, and put her foot down. Well, damn him! She wasn't going to put up with this. Hadn't she been there for him throughout his ordeal? Hadn't she taken the reins of CML and carried on successfully? Wasn't she willing to forego a holiday in a far-off place and go to some remote, cold part of Ireland? She had been the perfect wife, no one could say otherwise. Well that was it. She was going to put herself first for a change. She dialled the office. "Noreen? Will you call that health farm in Wicklow for me? See if they have a vacancy for this weekend. No. On second thoughts, see if they can take me for the full week. Yes, Noreen, that's what I said. Good. See you later."

CML could look after itself for a week. And if a crisis came up, Douglas could deal with it. He needed to be brought out of his malaise. And he needed to be kept occupied or God knows what other waifs and strays he'd bring home.

* * *

Doug put on his bathrobe and went downstairs. He couldn't get back to sleep after Pamela's call so he decided he might as well have some breakfast. Irene was in the kitchen cleaning the worktops and singing slightly off-key.

"Good morning, Irene."

"How are you, Mr Hamilton?"

"Tired." He sat down at the kitchen table and picked up the newspaper.

Irene looked at him, concerned. "You do look a bit peaky. Maybe you should stay in bed today. You mustn't do too much too soon."

"I wish you'd tell my wife that," he muttered under his breath. Out loud he said, "I'm fine, Irene. Maybe I'll have a nap later. Right now what I'd really like to do is read the paper and enjoy some of your marvellous bacon and eggs."

Irene frowned. "Mrs Hamilton said you wouldn't be eating a full breakfast any more."

He gritted his teeth. "Don't you mind Mrs Hamilton, Irene. How could one of your gorgeous fry-ups do me any harm?"

Irene blushed and patted her hair. "Well, my Billy says I do put up the best breakfast in the country."

"And he's right. I'm glad he realises how lucky he is."

Irene bustled off, happy, and started to unload bacon, black and white pudding, sausages and two eggs from the fridge. "I'll poach the eggs, if you like. That would be healthier."

Doug wagged his finger at her. "Don't you dare. And I hope there's some white bread in the house. I can't abide that brown stuff Pamela insists on eating."

Irene laughed. "I picked up a fresh loaf on my way in."

"You're a treasure." Doug gave her a broad smile before turning his attention to the newspaper. In the old days he would have turned to the business pages first, but now he read the paper from cover to cover, pausing only to refill his cup. "Oh, by the way, Irene. We have a guest staying in the flat."

"Oh, yes?" Irene's eyebrows shot up.

"Yeah. A girl from work needed a place to crash for a

couple of days. Will you look after her for me, Irene? Stock up the fridge, change the towels, that sort of thing?"

"Of course." Irene eyed him curiously over the pan of sizzling bacon.

In all the time she'd been working for the Hamiltons, no one had ever stayed in that flat. Irene had been tempted to stay over herself a couple of times when Billy was away on one of his long-haul trips – they'd never have known – but something had held her back. Pamela had made it very clear that she wanted a daily and not a live-in housekeeper. It was an awful waste having that lovely flat lying idle. She gave it a good clean once a month but, to her knowledge, Mr and Mrs Hamilton never went near the place. Irene had smuggled her daughter, Sissy, in one time when they were away to have a look at the famous Sycamores and Sissy had immediately fallen in love with the flat. "Couldn't ye talk to them, Ma? I'm sure they'd be glad of the rent."

After much nagging from her daughter, Irene finally broached the subject with Pamela.

"Have you ever thought of renting out that little flat over the garage, Mrs Hamilton?"

"No," Pamela had replied, not even looking up from the magazine she was reading.

Irene tried again. "It's a lovely little place. You'd get a good rent."

Pamela looked at her in amusement. "I don't think that we're quite so destitute that we have to take strangers into our home."

"But if they weren't strangers . . ."

Pamela lowered her magazine. "Is there something you want to ask me, Irene?"

"Well, it's just that my Sissy is looking for a place – you know teenagers these days, they can't wait to leave home – and if she was here, well, it would put my mind at rest."

"It's out of the question, I'm afraid," Pamela said frostily and went back to her magazine.

Irene had hurried back to the kitchen, mortified. Lady Muck! Sometimes she could be a right snotty cow. There was no need to be so short with her. Irene deserved some respect.

She turned the sausages and looked over at her boss. If it wasn't for him, she'd probably have walked out long ago. But he was nice. Always asked after her Billy *and* the kids. Yes, a lovely man. How he'd married that stuck-up bitch was beyond her. Maybe when this girl left the flat, she'd approach him about letting Sissy move in. That was it. That's what she'd do. She transferred the breakfast to a large plate and set it down in front of him.

Doug eyed the greasy food and imagined his arteries hardening in protest. He beamed at Irene. "Looks great, Irene. What would I do without you?"

Chapter Twenty-one

"For God's sake, Susie. I asked you to have that presentation finished this morning. It's five o'clock and you're telling me it's *still* not ready?" Gina glared at the girl who stared mutinously at the screen in front of her.

"I told ye, I keep getting errors on the hard disk. I've had to re-boot loads of times. There's something wrong with this machine. It's not my fault."

"It was working perfectly well at nine o'clock this morning. But then you weren't here at nine o'clock, were you?"

Jack looked at Gina's flushed, angry face. She was going a bit over the top. This was the first morning Susie had been late since she'd joined CML. And the number of times she came in early and stayed late more than made up for one lapse.

"Let me take a look," he said easily. "This machine *has* been giving a lot of trouble."

Susie smiled gratefully.

"You're wrong, Jack," Gina said with an icy glare. "Mal's machine was the one that was acting up."

"No, this one was too," he said cheerfully.

She flounced back to her desk.

Not doing yourself any favours there, Jack old boy, he thought ruefully. Susie moved out of the way and he sat down in front of the machine.

Gina tried to read the DVD file but she couldn't concentrate. She was furious with Jack. She thought things were OK between them now. But why was he siding with Susie and undermining her authority? And when she thought of all the work she'd put into organising his surprise party! Not to mention putting up with that sister of his. And *now*, she had to go shopping with Doug. She looked at the two of them chatting easily and felt very hard done by indeed. But if she was honest it was the imminent arrival of her boss that really had her in bad humour. The thought of spending the evening with him made her very nervous. But Susie's late arrival this morning and Marian Hickey's coolness on the phone when she'd heard the presentation wasn't ready, hadn't helped. Now the final straw was Jack jumping to Susie's defence.

"Evening, everybody." Doug marched in, with Noreen fluttering at his side.

Jack looked up and grinned at his boss. "Howaya, Doug. Are you here to buy me a pint?"

"I'm not, no. Just dropped in to collect something and then I've got an appointment in town." He winked at Gina.

"Pity."

"I'll go for a pint with you." Malcolm stood up and put his jacket on. Gina had warned him to get Jack out of the way.

"I'll just finish up here." Jack turned back to the PC.

"You can't," Gina said hastily. "Susie has to finish some work for me tonight." Gina looked pointedly at the other girl.

"What? Oh, yeah, that's right. Sorry, Jack. Could ye leave it till morning?"

Jack shrugged. None of the women in this office knew what they wanted. "Sure. Well, Mal, we may as well go for that drink. My services don't seem to be needed here."

"Bye, lads." Doug watched them leave, accepted the cup of coffee from Noreen and sat down in Jack's chair. "Are you ready to go, Gina?"

"Just give me a minute." She hurried out to the ladies'.

Doug waited until she was out of earshot before turning to Susie. "How are you? Did you get any sleep at all?"

"Yeah. Thanks. Eh . . . I met Pamela this morning. I don't think she was too pleased."

"She was just surprised, that's all," Doug said smoothly. He'd managed to avoid talking to his wife all day. He knew exactly how she was going to react to having Susie Clarke under her roof and he didn't want to hear it.

"Well, I'm very grateful and I promise I'll be out of your hair as soon as I can."

270

"If money's a problem, we could let you have an advance on your salary if you like."

"Ah, that'd be mega!" Susie said, her eyes lighting up.

Doug grinned. She wasn't a bad kid. Just a bit rough round the edges. "OK, then. I'll have a word with Malcolm. It'll be just between the three of us. And it might be better, Susie, if you didn't tell the others you're staying at The Sycamores."

"I haven't. I wouldn't," she said fervently. He'd put a roof over her head and she wasn't going to do anything to upset him.

"Good." It was one thing bringing her home but Pamela would never forgive him if everyone knew about it.

Gina stood in the doorway, fascinated at the sight of her boss and her junior in such deep conversation. What on earth could they have to talk about? There was no way Doug could fancy her. Maybe he was asking her about work. But it seemed a more personal exchange than that.

She coughed discreetly before re-entering the room. "I'm ready."

Doug stood up immediately. "Then let's hit the shops. Will we see you at the party tomorrow night, Susie?"

"Eh, I'm not sure."

"Oh, you should come. It's sure to be a laugh. You'll enjoy yourself, won't she, Gina?"

Gina busied herself with her jacket. "Sure."

Susie saw the look on Gina's face. *She doesn't want me*

to come, the bitch. She stuck her chin out defiantly. "I'll come, so."

Doug grinned. "That's the spirit! See you there. Come on, then, Gina. Let's go and get this present."

Gina followed him out of the office, not bothering to say goodbye to Susie. She stood patiently in reception while Doug assured Noreen that he was getting better and promised her a dance at the party. Finally they were able to leave and Gina climbed into the comfortable passenger seat.

"Are you happy with Susie?" Doug pulled out into traffic and headed into the city.

Gina gave him a sidelong glance. "Pretty much. She's had some good ideas. Her attitude could be better, though."

"In what way?"

"She's very . . . prickly. Keeps to herself most of the time. I'm surprised she agreed to come to the party. She hasn't socialised with us at all so far. Even at lunchtime she goes off on her own."

"Well, she's going through a tough time at the moment. It can't be easy being nineteen and pregnant."

Gina sighed. What did this girl have that made all the men in her office so sympathetic? Even Doug! Gina couldn't understand it. She was getting to dislike the girl more every day. "I suppose," she said finally, realising Doug was waiting for some kind of response. She was sorely tempted to tell him that she was late in this morning and that, because of her, Marian Hickey was on the war path. Now that would piss him off! He wouldn't be so magnanimous then.

"What shop shall we go to?" she said, anxious to change the conversation. She was sick to the teeth of Ms Clarke.

"Brown Thomas, I suppose."

Gina cringed. The best shop in Dublin was hardly the place to get a bargain-basement TV. And that was all they could afford – even with Doug's generous contribution.

"You don't agree?" Doug raised his eyebrows, not used to having his decisions questioned.

"Well, I thought we might get better value in one of the bigger electrical places."

"Like where?"

"Power City? Dixons?"

"OK, then. Where are they?" Doug wasn't familiar with either establishment. Pamela did most of her shopping on Grafton Street and he only went along when he absolutely had to.

"There's a Dixons in Tallaght and Blanchardstown and there's a Power City in Finglas and Sallynoggin."

Doug sighed in frustration. "You might have mentioned this before, Gina." They were sitting in heavy traffic on Stephen's Green.

"Sorry," she said meekly.

"There's a Sony Centre not far from here, we'll go there."

"Don't you think . . ."

"We'll go there," he said firmly.

"Fine," Gina said glumly. A decent-sized Sony TV would cost a fortune. She'd thought they'd just get one of the cheaper brands.

Ten minutes later, Doug parked on a double-yellow line outside the shop and they went inside. As Gina had suspected, the hi-tech models were a lot more expensive. After looking unhappily at the only television within their price range, Doug threw his credit card down on the desk. "We'll take that one." He pointed at a more expensive model.

"But we don't have enough. . ."

"I'll pay the difference," he said gruffly, annoyed that Gina had been right. He leaned against the counter wearily while the assistant processed his payment and then they went back to the car, Doug carrying the large box.

Gina looked at him worriedly. He was breathing heavily and he was very pale. "Are you OK?"

"Fine, fine." He dumped the TV in the boot and climbed into the driver's seat. "Shit!" he said when he spotted the paper fluttering underneath his windscreen wiper – a bloody parking ticket! These days it was usually a warning saying your car would be clamped within the hour. That always worked out fine if you were quick. Just his bloody luck that a bored copper had been passing instead.

Gina watched nervously as he snatched the ticket off the windscreen, scrunched it into a ball and tossed it into the back seat.

"I need a drink," he said moodily. "Let's get out of the city, it's too bloody hot. How about taking a run out to Blackrock?"

"The traffic would be terrible and, eh, I'm going out later," Gina invented.

"Then we'll go to O'Dwyers. At least parking shouldn't be a problem there. What time are you going out?"

"What? Oh. Nine."

"Good, plenty of time. I'll have you back to your car by eight. Is that OK?"

"Fine." Gina smiled weakly, afraid to refuse. Not given his current mood.

The traffic had eased a lot and within fifteen minutes they were sitting at the bar. Doug took a long drink from his pint.

"Are you OK?" Gina thought he was still quite pale.

"Fine. It's just lifting things makes me a bit breathless."

She nodded sympathetically. "I'm sure that's natural. When will you be coming back to work?"

Doug sighed. He was fed up with people asking him that. "I'm not sure yet. So where are you going tonight? Is it a heavy date?"

Gina reddened. She hated lying. She was just no good at it. And she always went red. "No, just a drink with a couple of friends."

"Pity. I was going to suggest we go for a bite to eat." He wasn't looking forward to facing Pamela. The longer he kept out of her way, the better.

"Sorry, but I can't let them down."

"Of course not. It was just an idea. So do you think Jack will like his present?"

"He'll be over the moon. It's exactly what he'd go for himself – if he could afford it."

"It was a bit pricey," Doug said ruefully. "Let's keep that just between us, shall we?"

"No problem." *You mean keep it from Pamela,* Gina thought to herself. Ms Lloyd-Hamilton would be horrified at her husband spending that kind of money on one of the staff.

"Are you looking forward to the DVD junket?"

"Oh, yes! I've never been to the States, never mind Las Vegas."

"It's an experience," he said dryly.

"The last time someone said that to me it was about Marrakech and that was an experience I could have done without."

"Really? Why?"

Gina told him all about the trip and about the antics of the Lifesavers Managing Director. She left out her little interlude with Jack.

Doug wiped his eyes when she'd finished. "I didn't think old Hargreaves had it in him! I'm sorry I missed it now."

"It was good *craic*," she admitted with a smile. She couldn't believe she was sitting here chatting to Doug like this. And what's more, she was enjoying herself. She was sorely tempted to come clean about her non-existent engagement and go to dinner with him. As it was she'd probably end up in front of the telly with a pizza. Again.

"Las Vegas will be fun too," Doug was saying. "But very different. If anything the place is too perfect."

"That'll suit me just fine. I was born to live in luxury."

"Then you should be very happy. The hotels are amazing."

"That's what I like to hear!"

"How are you getting along with Marian?"

Gina pulled a face. "All right up until today."

"Oh?" Doug frowned.

Shit, why did you have to say that, Gina? "Oh, nothing to worry about," she said lightly. "But I had to put back a meeting. The presentation isn't ready yet."

"There's still plenty of time."

Gina stared at him. She'd expected a lecture on customer satisfaction, but he didn't seem bothered at all. "We're only about a day behind, Doug. I won't let you down."

"I know you won't, Gina. Don't worry so much. Life's too short."

Gina almost choked on her beer. "Have you found religion or something?"

Doug gave a short laugh. "I suppose my priorities have changed a bit. A brush with death has that effect." He signalled the barman for another round.

"I can imagine."

"So have I changed for better or worse?" His eyes twinkled at her.

She drained her glass and wondered how honest she should be. "Well, I find you a lot easier to talk to," she said finally.

"Oh? Was I such an ogre in the past?"

"No, it's just . . ."

"What?"

"I don't think we should go down this road."

"Oh, come on, Gina. You can't keep me in suspense like this."

"Well, you've always made me . . . nervous."

Doug laughed. "Really? In what way?"

Gina scowled. "You're not taking this seriously."

"Sorry. I promise not to laugh any more. Now tell me how I make you nervous."

"Your comments." Gina fidgeted with her glass and wished she'd kept her big mouth shut.

"About your work?"

She blushed. "No. About my personal life and my appearance."

"Sorry?" His expression was as innocent as a child's.

"Oh, Come off it, Doug! You know exactly what I mean! You comment on my legs, my clothes. You always sit too close. You lean over me at any excuse. It's practically sexual abuse!"

Doug nearly choked on his drink. "Jeez, Gina! You're overreacting a bit, aren't you?"

She glared at him, in full stride now. "No, I'm not. It's very intimidating if you must know, and I've gone out of my way to avoid being alone with you." She sat staring at him, horrified, knowing she'd gone too far. He looked totally shocked.

Doug finally found his voice. "You're serious! I had no idea, Gina. You must believe that. It was never intended as anything more than a bit of fun. I'll be honest, you're a very attractive girl but I would never come on to someone who works for me." He shook his head in disbelief. "I feel like some kind of sick pervert!"

"Oh, you're not that! But, well, you do play around, don't you?" *Shut up, Gina! Shut up!* If she kept this up she'd definitely be down the job centre first thing in the morning.

Doug's mouth curved into a smile. "What makes you say that?"

She sighed. "It's a small town, Doug."

There was a flicker of alarm in his eyes. "Oh?"

"My friend, Hannah, says you went out with one of her friends last summer."

"Ah, that must have been the lovely Jean. I remember her. Great legs."

Gina snorted in disgust. "How can you be so casual about it? You were unfaithful."

"Then you believe in marriage, Gina?"

"Of course I do. I certainly wouldn't bother getting hitched if I didn't plan on being faithful."

"It's not always so black and white. What do *you* know about me, about Pamela, about our marriage?" he said bitterly, draining his glass.

The reality of the situation hit her like a douse of cold water. "Absolutely nothing. You're quite right. Sorry."

"An apology!" His lips twitched. "I'm impressed!"

"I should go."

"Oh, don't. We both know you're not meeting anyone."

"Of course I am . . ."

"I thought we were being honest, Gina."

She gave a lame grin. "OK, I'm not."

"You were just afraid of being alone with me."

"Eh . . . yeah."

He sighed. "That makes me feel awful."

"Sorry, but, well, it's OK now. We've cleared the air and I know you didn't mean to make me feel like that."

"That's a relief. So what about it? Do you fancy going for a Chinese with your lecherous but extremely repentant boss?"

"I'd love to."

He laughed as he put on his jacket. "And when I think that I was warning Greg to leave you alone."

"You did what?" Gina stared at him. God, no wonder Greg had dropped her like a hot potato! But maybe that meant he still fancied her.

Doug sighed at the dreamy look in her eyes. "Oh, don't tell me you've fallen for him? He's not worth it, you know."

"That's not very loyal of you," she chided. "Anyway, I think I'm old enough to choose my own boyfriends."

"Of course you are," he said meekly. Lord, she really had it bad. But then most women were taken in by his brother. He'd never understood why.

"So please don't talk to your brother about me again," she said sternly.

"I won't."

"Thank you."

"*Now,* can we go and eat?"

"Certainly," she said primly and led the way out of the pub.

Chapter Twenty-two

"Thank God yer all right, Susie. I've been going up the walls worrying about ye. When I got home last night, Mam was sitting in our room crying. I thought the oul' bastard had killed ye!"

"Howaya, Marie." Susie turned down the television and clutched the phone to her ear. The noise of the salon in the background was deafening.

"It took ages to get any sense out of her," Marie continued.

"There's a surprise," Susie said bitterly.

"Ah, don't blame her, Suz. It's not her fault."

"No?"

"No, she's afraid of him."

"She should have left him years ago. How could she stand by and watch him attack her daughter?"

"But she did *try* to stop him," Marie reminded her gently.

"Yeah."

They were both silent for a moment.

"I can't believe yer living in Ballsbridge. There's posh!"

Susie giggled. "It's amazing. Ye should see this place."

"It's a pity ye can't stay there."

"No chance of that. Doug might let me but Pamela would have a fit."

"Well, if ye like I'll make a few calls for ye. I got the *Evening Herald* and there's a few possibilities. I suppose ye want somewhere near work?"

"Yeah. God, yer great, Marie. I never even thought of buying a paper."

"Don't worry about it. I rang Barnardo's too. Ye know? About the adoption?"

"Oh."

"They were real nice. They're sending me some leaflets."

"Yer a star."

"They'd like to see ye. Have a chat."

"Ah, there's no rush." Susie didn't want to think about all that yet. "I need to sort out somewhere to live first. Can I ask one more favour?"

"As long as it's not a loan."

Susie laughed. "No, it's just my next visit to the hospital is on Monday. Will ye come?"

Marie hesitated. "Would ye not ask Ma?"

"No." Susie said flatly.

Marie sighed. "All right then. I'll come. Look, I have to go. Joanne is giving me bulls looks. I'll call ye if I find a flat."

"Thanks, Marie." Susie put down the phone and

picked up a cracker. Even now, five months into her pregnancy, she still couldn't face much food. "I must be the only woman alive who loses weight when she's pregnant," she grumbled miserably, taking a bite.

She was dozing in front of *Coronation Street* when the doorbell rang. She went outside, rubbing her eyes, and slid back the deadbolt.

"Good evening, Susie."

Pamela stood on the top step, elegant in a navy silk cocktail dress, her hair loose around her shoulders. Susie stared at her. "Hiya."

"May I come in?" Pamela didn't wait for a reply. She brushed past her and went into the living-room.

Susie watched her looking around. *Probably checking to see if I've stolen anything,* she thought bitterly.

Pamela eyed the magazines, the glass of Coke and the packet of crackers on the coffee-table. "You seem to have made yourself at home."

"I won't be here much longer. I'm looking for a place of me own."

Pamela swung around to face her. "Good. Because I want you out of here on Saturday. Is that clear?"

Susie nodded silently. What had she done to make this woman hate her so much?

Pamela smiled, but her eyes were hard. "We were happy to help in your hour of need, of course, but it's just not possible as a long-term arrangement. You understand that, don't you?"

"Sure."

"Good. Well, I'm glad we've had this little chat. See

you in the morning. I'm afraid I won't be able to offer you a lift. I have a hair appointment first thing."

"That's OK."

"I'll say goodnight then. Oh, and Susie," she paused to move the Coke further in on the table. "Do be careful of my glasses. They're Waterford Crystal, you know."

"Sorry."

"Goodnight then." And Pamela left, leaving a cloud of expensive perfume in her wake.

Susie shut the door. Well, it was pretty clear who wore the pants in that household. Any dreams Susie had of staying on a bit longer had been knocked right on the head. She sat back down on the sofa, took a sip of Coke and started to giggle. "What are ye like, Susie! Drinking out of Waterford glass, no less! Yer really goin' up in the world!"

Pamela marched back to the house, her blood boiling. She'd been trying to get hold of Douglas all day to get an explanation and seeing that little madam lolling about in her beautiful flat had really added fuel to the fire. What on earth did he think he was doing bringing her into their home? Pamela would have coped better with a mangy dog. She went inside and tried his mobile again, but it was still turned off. She'd tried the office earlier.

"Noreen, do you know where Douglas might be? We seem to have got our wires crossed and his mobile is out of action again."

"He went shopping with Regina for Jack's birthday present, Mrs Lloyd-Hamilton."

"Of course, silly me, I'd forgotten. Thank you, Noreen. See you tomorrow." Pamela had banged down the phone. He brought one employee home, he took another shopping. It seemed he was the perfect gentleman to everyone except his wife. What was going on? He'd never treated her like this before. They were supposed to be going to John and Sophie's for drinks in half an hour but it didn't look as if he was planning to turn up.

She paced the room worriedly. Douglas had done a lot of hurtful things in the course of their marriage but he'd always been courteous and kind. Now, not only was he standing her up but he didn't even have the decency to call. Pamela's eyes filled up, the hurt overtaking her anger. This behaviour couldn't continue. She wouldn't stand for it.

She marched up to her room and started to pack a bag. Noreen had booked her a room in the elite health farm she visited twice a year and she couldn't wait to get there. Her shoulders and neck were tight with stress. Douglas Hamilton had a lot to answer for. She sat down in front of the dressing-table and looked at herself critically in the mirror. Despite the perfect make-up, she could clearly see lines around her eyes and mouth that hadn't been there before. She frowned and then quickly smoothed out her expression again. No point in making things worse. Her blue eyes were faded and tired. Her long, heavy dark hair seemed to have lost some of its lustre. She looked every one of her thirty-eight years. She definitely needed this break. She looked at the tiny travel clock in front of her. Ten o'clock. They wouldn't be going anywhere tonight. She removed her make-up and took off her dress. Slipping on a white satin caftan she went down to the living-room to wait for her husband.

Gina took another mouthful of wine – dribbling some of it down her chin – and leaned across the table to look intently into Doug's face. "But you can't love her, can you? She's an awful cow."

Doug felt slightly annoyed through the haze of drink. And something else too. Sad. That was it. He felt sad. "Pamela's not so bad. She's just not comfortable with many people. She's a very private person." He topped up their glasses.

Gina snorted. "Well, if she's so great why do you play around?"

"I suppose I'm just that kind of guy. It's no reflection on Pamela."

Gina raised her eyebrows.

"How about some dessert?" Doug asked.

"Oh, yes please!" Gina said, easily distracted. She needed a fix of chocolate.

Doug called for the menus.

Gina looked at it in disgust. "Lychees! How can they call that dessert?"

"What about some ice cream?"

"Do you have chocolate ice cream?" she asked the waiter, hopefully.

"Yes, madam."

"Fine. I'll have a large dish of that."

"And you, sir?"

"Just coffee and bring two brandies."

286

Gina sighed resignedly. "I'm going to die tomorrow."

Doug smiled. "Eat, drink and be merry, for tomorrow we die," he quipped.

"Is that your new philofos . . . phylopos . . . motto?"

He thought for a moment. "I suppose it is."

The waiter brought their drinks and her ice cream and Doug watched as she cleaned the dish out in seconds. It was nice to see a woman eat with such relish. Pamela never did. She was so fond of calorie-counting that Doug sometimes expected her to bring a calculator with her when they were eating out. It was ridiculous. If anything, she was too thin.

Gina pushed the dish away and downed her brandy in a gulp.

"I've enjoyed this evening, Gina. And I'm glad we've, eh, straightened things out."

"Me too." She smiled into his eyes. He really was gorgeous. Not as gorgeous as Greg, but still . . .

"You've got gorgeous eyes," she murmured.

He smiled. "Do I?"

"You know you do. Modest you ain't."

"I'm a total reprobate as far as you're concerned!"

"Not total. You've improved a lot since your, your . . ."

"Bang?" he suggested.

She giggled.

"Well, I was going to say since your heart-attack actually."

"Very funny."

"Seriously, though." She stared deeply into his eyes. "You really have changed. You're softer."

"If you're planning on asking for a salary increase, forget it," he warned.

Gina giggled. "Oh, well. It was worth a try."

"I think we'd better be making tracks."

"No, why?"

"Well, we're the only ones left in the restaurant and the waiter keeps yawning."

Gina peered at her watch. "Oh, I'd no idea it was so late!" She stood up unsteadily and Doug put an arm out to steady her. She leaned back against him. "Thank you, kind sir."

He looked down at the dark eyes and inviting lips. She really was a very sexy woman. "You're welcome."

They left the restaurant arm in arm and strolled down to the taxi rank.

"I hope my poor little car will be all right. That's the second time this week I've left her outside the office."

"Turning into a lush are we, Ms Barrett?"

"No, just falling in with bad company," she said smiling up into his face.

Doug drew her to him and kissed her very gently on the lips.

Gina responded eagerly, sliding a hand up around his neck. His tongue explored her mouth. Gentle, teasing.

"Oh, Greg," she breathed, huskily.

Doug's head snapped back.

"Oh, don't stop." She tried to pull his head back down to hers.

"I don't think that's such a good idea, Gina," he said, taking her arm and frogmarching her down the road. "And

I certainly don't fancy being a stand-in for my brother."

"What?" Gina looked up at him, slightly dazed. "What's wrong, Doug? Did I do something wrong?"

He gave her a quick peck on the cheek before pushing her gently into the back of a taxi. "Not a thing, my sweet. Sleep well."

He turned and started the short walk to The Sycamores. "You're really too old for this kind of carry-on, Hamilton. So much for your policy about employees." His mind turned to Pamela. And he sighed at the thought of the inevitable confrontation. But at least he wouldn't have to deal with her tonight.

"Douglas? Where on earth have you been? And why was your mobile switched off? How was I supposed to get hold of you if there was anything wrong?"

He looked down into his wife's angry face. "It's not my mother, is it?"

"No, your precious mother is fine," she said bitterly. "It's a pity you don't show the same concern for me."

Doug massaged the bridge of his nose. "Not now, Pamela. I'm tired."

"Yes, *now*, Douglas. And I don't care *how* tired you are!"

Doug passed a weary hand across his eyes and crossed to the drinks cabinet.

"You look like you've had quite enough already," she snapped.

"Do I, darling?" He poured an even larger measure.

Pamela glared at him. "Well? Are you going to tell me what's going on? I think you owe me an explanation."

"Do I? Well, Gina and I went to get Jack's birthday present – we got him a lovely TV, by the way – and then we were hungry so we went for a bite to eat."

Pamela tapped her foot angrily. "You know what I'm talking about, Douglas. Why has Susie Clarke set up residence in our flat?"

Doug smiled wryly. She wasn't even interested that he'd been out all evening with another woman. But then she'd never cared what he did or who he did it with as long as it didn't disrupt her little world. "She needed somewhere to stay. What should I have done? Let her sleep on the streets?"

"She's got to go. I want her out of The Sycamores and out of CML."

"Oh, for God's sake! Her father threw her out and she'd nowhere else to go."

"I don't care," Pamela said wildly. For some reason she knew she had to get Susie Clarke out of their lives. "She's obviously not going to work out. Her attitude and appearance are all wrong for CML."

"From the wrong side of the tracks, is that it, Pamela?" Doug said grimly.

She ignored his sarcasm. "She's leaving tomorrow, Douglas."

"No, Pamela, she is not," he said very quietly. "She's a good worker. As for the flat, I've told her she can stay as long as she wants and I've no intention of going back on my word."

Pamela stared at him, white-faced. "You've told her she can stay under my roof without even discussing it with me?"

Doug drained his glass. "It's my roof too, Pamela. Please don't forget that. Now I'm going to bed. Goodnight."

Pamela sank down into a chair, pulling her caftan tightly around her. She felt cold and her hands were shaking. With fear. Douglas had never talked to her like that before. And all because of that little nobody. As Pamela thought of her swanning around the flat, flaunting her swollen belly like a trophy, her anger returned. The girl hadn't mentioned that Douglas had told her she could stay. Maybe he hadn't. Maybe it was all a bluff and Susie really did plan to leave on Saturday. If not, Pamela would just have to persuade her to. There was no way that girl was staying at The Sycamores. Pamela massaged her temples and thanked God that she was heading for the health farm the following day. Douglas would just have to cope if a crisis arose. And she'd no doubt that one would.

Chapter Twenty-three

Susie shifted uncomfortably on the hard chair and sipped her juice. This was a real pain, in every sense of the word. She'd been moved twice already by Jack's sister.

"He might be able to see you when he comes in, dear. Oh, no, not there, pet. I'm saving that table for Mum and Dad." And Nora Byrne would bustle off again to annoy someone else.

Finally, Malcolm took pity on her and asked her to sit with him and his wife. Now there was a snob, if ever there was one! When Mal had introduced them, she'd looked Susie up and down, given her a limp handshake and ignored her ever since. In fact the only one Caroline Patterson had shown any interest in was Doug. She was all over *him* like a rash. Susie watched Mal from under her lashes to see if it bothered him, but he didn't seem to notice his wife's blatant flirting. Now Mal was off talking to Noreen, and Susie and Caroline sat in silence. Bloody great party this was. Susie pulled at the baggy drawstring trousers Marie had got her in the Penney's sale. They'd probably have looked all right if they weren't sticking to her as everything seemed to these days. She was always hot. And these bloody chairs hadn't been built with pregnant women in mind. She stood up to go to the loo.

"Oh, no, dear, don't go *now!* He'll be here any minute."

Susie scowled at Nora and sat down again. If it wasn't for Jack she'd have gone home ages ago. Noreen had hardly said two words to her since she'd come in. And Doug wasn't too chatty either. But she'd contributed her ten quid for Jack's present so she had as much of a right to be here as anyone else!

Nora hushed everyone and switched off the light. The door opened.

"Surprise!"

Pamela blinked as the lights came on and everyone jumped up. "Only me," she said with an apologetic smile.

"Oh, Mrs Lloyd-Hamilton! We thought you were Jack." Nora bustled forward and took Pamela's arm. "Come right this way. I've saved you a nice table. Your husband's already here."

Pamela looked at the other woman. She was sure they'd never met before, but from her colouring she deduced it must be Jack's sister. "You're very kind. Hello, darling." She smiled at Douglas and proffered a cheek for his kiss.

Doug frowned. This wasn't what he'd expected after last night's little tiff. "Hello, darling. You look lovely."

Nora beamed at them both. "I better get back in position. They should be here any minute."

"Can I get you a drink? Wine? G & T?" Doug asked when they were alone.

"No, I'm not staying," Pamela said coldly, dropping the pretence.

"Oh, for God's sake Pamela, you have to stay. How's it going to look? Where are you going anyway?"

"I'm going to the health farm. I need a rest. This has been a very stressful time for me."

While it's been a walk in the park for me, Doug thought dryly. "So you'll be back on Monday?" he said aloud.

"No. Next weekend."

"What? But you can't! What about the DVD job?"

"You're the one who wanted me to give Gina more responsibility. Well, that's what I'm doing."

"There's responsibility and there's throwing her in at the deep end," Doug said through gritted teeth. He knew Pamela was only doing this to get back at him. She could be really bloody-minded sometimes. "I don't think it's a good idea," he said forcing his voice to remain level.

"Don't you? Oh. What a pity. Well, it's organised now. I'm just here to wish Jack a happy birthday and then I'm on my way. Where on earth is he, anyway?"

* * *

Gina looked at her watch again. "Oh for God's sake, Jack, leave it."

"But I won't be able to connect up the screen." Jack continued to rummage through the large box under his desk.

"You can go back tomorrow morning and do it. I'm going to be late."

"It's my birthday tomorrow," he protested. "And you want me to work?"

"It will take you all of five minutes," she said, grabbing his arm and steering him out of the office.

"Where are you going anyway?" he said glumly. It was a real pain to see Gina dressed up to the nines knowing she was probably rushing off to meet another bloke.

"A party."

"Could I tag along? I could pick up a six-pack." He looked at her hopefully.

"Afraid not, Jack. It's not that kind of party."

"Oh? What kind is it, then?"

"It's a family occasion." *Well, that wasn't a lie now, was it?* Gina put the key in the ignition and pulled hurriedly out into traffic.

"Oh. I'm going to one of them tomorrow night." Jack looked morosely out of the window. Not only was he not going out tonight but he had to spend his birthday at his sister's, eating overcooked food and getting dirty looks if he drank more than two beers.

"That will be nice." Gina smothered a giggle. She swung the car into Jury's carpark and nudged up against a cone to park.

"You can't leave it here," Jack protested. She was a scary driver at the best of times.

"I'll move it when we've unloaded the gear. Come on."

"Well, open the boot then."

"No. Let's find the room first. Then we can come back for the equipment." She'd rehearsed that line a few times today. He could hardly arrive into his party weighed down with gear!

"OK." Jack followed her inside and down a long corridor. "Shouldn't we just ask at reception?"

"Nah. I know where I'm going."

"But you said we had to find the room." He looked puzzled.

"Did I? Ah, here we are." She pulled open the door and stood back to let Jack go in first.

"Where's the bloody light switch? I can't see a thing."

"Surprise!"

The light went on and everyone started throwing streamers at him. Jack blinked.

"What the hell . . ."

"Happy birthday to you. Happy birthday to you . . ." Nora led the singing and shoved her brother into the centre of the room.

Susie mimed the words, Pamela planted a smile on her face and Doug and Mal sang along heartily. *"Happy birthday, dear Jack, happy birthday to you."*

"For he's a jolly good fellow," started Mal enthusiastically, ignoring his wife's scathing look.

When the singing stopped, everyone clapped and the DJ turned up the volume.

Gina shoved a pint into Jack's hand and kissed his cheek. "Happy birthday, Jack."

Jack looked around him in amazement. "Mam, Dad, Gary, Jim – Jim Clancy! I haven't seen you in years!"

A stout man with carrot-red hair shook his hand. "How's it going, Jack? You know me – never miss a party. Especially one with such good-looking women. Who's *she?*" He nodded towards Pamela.

Jack followed his gaze and laughed. "Way out of your league, Jim. Anyway, since when were you into older women?"

"I'm into women, full stop. Excuse me a sec, will ye, mate? There's a pretty little blonde at the bar."

Jack watched his friend leave. God, he hadn't changed a bit!

"Hello, love. Having a good time?"

Jack returned his mother's kiss. "Yes, Mam. Thanks. Did you organise all of this?"

"No, I have to say, most of it's down to your sister. And that nice girl you work with."

"Gina?" Jack looked at her, surprised.

"That's the one. Gina. She's lovely, isn't she? Does she have a boyfriend?"

"Mam!"

"Just asking."

"Happy birthday, Jack." Doug came over and Jack's mother excused herself.

"Did you know about this?" Jack asked.

"Of course."

"Well, you kept it pretty quiet, I'll give you that. How are you feeling these days, Doug?"

"I'm fine. Why don't you go and talk to Gina? She looks like she might need rescuing. Who's that she's with, anyway?"

Jack grinned. "My sister, Nora."

"Oh. Sorry."

"That's OK. She can be a little overbearing." He crossed the room to his sister and the girl he fancied so much. "I believe I have you guys to thank or throttle for this bash."

Nora hugged her brother. "You're welcome! Oh, look! It's Aunty Doris! *Cooeee* . . . Aunty!" Nora hurried away.

"Thanks, Gina," Jack hugged her tightly.

Gina pushed him away, laughing nervously. "Ah, sure I'd do the same for Pamela."

"Thanks a lot."

"Don't look now, but she's heading this way," Gina murmured.

"Jack, dear! Happy birthday!" Pamela made as if to kiss his cheek, but didn't quite make contact. "I'm afraid I can't stay. *Noblesse oblige* and all that." She gave a little laugh. "Now you have a wonderful time and make sure that my husband goes home at a reasonable hour. I don't want him falling into bad company again." This was accompanied by a cool glance at Gina.

Gina flushed and took a gulp of lager.

"'No bless who? And what was all that about bad company?" Jack asked, a confused look on his face.

"No idea. Who cares anyway? Let's dance." Gina grabbed his arm and dragged him out onto the dance floor. As Jack spun her around she caught Doug's eye and he winked at her. She pretended she hadn't seen him, beamed at Jack and danced like a maniac.

She'd had a ferocious hangover when she woke up

that morning. It had been only six, when, clutching her head, she'd stumbled into the kitchen in search of Alka-Seltzer. She'd sat at the table, sipping it – she couldn't gulp, her stomach was too fragile – and piecing together the events of the previous evening. And then she'd remembered. "Jeez, Gina, you kissed him! You kissed the boss! First Jack, now Doug – why not go after Mal and make it a hat-trick!" She racked her brain trying to remember exactly what had happened. She was pretty sure she'd gone home in a taxi – alone. Thank God for that, at least. But she remembered there had definitely been a passionate clinch outside the Chinese. But had he kissed her? That wouldn't be quite so bad. But no, she remembered with a groan, he'd been the one to pull away first. Oh, Lord! What must he think of her? And did he now think he was on to a good thing? Did he see her as a new candidate to add to his harem?

She came back to the present as the song ended and the DJ announced a break.

A disappointed Jack led her off the dance floor. "What will you have to drink, Gina?"

"Just a glass of lager, thanks."

"Right. Well, you go and keep Doug company and I'll get the drinks."

"No!"

Jack stared at her.

She smiled brightly. "No, no. What am I thinking of? You're the birthday boy! I'll get the drinks."

"OK. Thanks." He gave her another funny look before going over to join Doug.

"Hiya, gorgeous."

Gina nearly jumped out of her skin, but relaxed when she saw Greg at her side. His voice was so like his brother's. "Oh, hi, Greg," she said absently.

Greg frowned. "How about a dance?"

"I'm getting Jack a drink. Maybe later." She made her way over to Jack and Doug, willing her hands not to shake.

Greg sipped his pint thoughtfully. Was he right about Doug and Gina? She definitely seemed to have cooled towards him. Or maybe she was just playing hard to get. He grinned. That wouldn't last long. He turned his attention to a striking blonde standing at the bar, an unlit cigarette in her hand.

"Allow me," he said with his most devastating smile.

Gina handed Doug his drink, cursing inwardly as she felt the colour flood her cheeks.

"Hello, Gina. You're looking well." Doug took his pint and smiled into her eyes.

Gina looked away. *Was he laughing at her?*

"Did you get home OK last night?" he asked politely.

She spluttered into her drink. "Eh . . . well . . . eh . . ." *Why did he have to mention last night? There was no reason to tell anyone.*

"What's this? What were you two up to?" Jack smiled expectantly.

Doug saw the look of panic on her face and took pity on her. He really shouldn't make fun of her like this. If anything, he should be apologising to the poor girl. He gave her what he hoped was a reassuring smile. "After we picked up your birthday present, I dragged Gina off for a meal. You were very good to take pity on an old man, Gina. I'm sure you could have been doing something much more interesting."

"Not – not at all," she stammered. "I enjoyed myself."

"Me too."

Gina relaxed.

"What's this about a present?" Jack interrupted. "I don't see any present."

"Here you are, Jack," Mal was standing behind him with Noreen and Susie at his side and a large box in his arms. "From your comrades in arms," he said setting the box carefully at Jack's feet.

"Ah, thanks, lads. Let me guess – it's a razor."

"No, that's what Pamela wanted to buy you, though," Doug quipped.

"Where *is* Mrs Lloyd-Hamilton?" Noreen asked looking around.

"Oh, she had to leave," Doug said casually. "She's going away for a few days."

Mal gave Gina and Susie the thumbs-up behind Doug's back and the girls exchanged grins.

Jack tore off the paper, his eyes widening when he saw the Sony name. "Crikey, lads. This is great! Thanks."

"Glad you like it, Jack. Happy birthday." Doug lifted his drink in a toast.

"Happy birthday, Jack," they chorused.

Nora came rushing over. "Sorry, people. We need the Birthday Boy. It's time to bring out the cake."

Jack grinned at Gina. "Well, that'll be a nice surprise."

Nora led him off and Gina groaned inwardly as she realised she was next to Mal's wife. "Hi, Caroline. You look well."

Caroline smiled thinly. "I've a dreadful headache."

"Oh dear. I think I have some paracetamol." Gina rummaged in her bag. She'd forgotten what a moan Mal's wife was.

"They wouldn't be strong enough," Caroline said dismissively. "A lie-down in a darkened room is the only solution."

Gina caught Susie's eye and pretended to shove her fingers down her throat.

Susie smothered a giggle and tried to turn it into a cough.

Caroline looked at her suspiciously before turning to her husband. "Malcolm?"

Mal broke off his conversation with Doug and Noreen. "What's up?"

Caroline held her hand to her head dramatically. "We really must go. I've a dreadful headache."

"But the party's only starting!" Mal protested.

Caroline looked at him reproachfully. "You don't want it to get worse, do you? You know how sick I'll be if I don't lie down immediately."

Mal sighed. It was strange the way Caroline only seemed to get headaches when they were out with his friends. "OK, then. Just wait until Jack has cut the cake. I don't want to leave without saying goodbye."

Gina smiled at him sympathetically. "Well, I'll see you, guys. I need a top-up. Hope your headache gets better, Caroline. Coming, Susie?"

Susie jumped up, grateful to get away from Caroline. Even if it was with Gina. "Yeah, right. Seeya, Mal, Caroline."

"Night, girls. Enjoy yourselves," Mal called wistfully as they hurried away.

Gina led the way to the bar, managing to circumvent Doug, Greg and Noreen on the way. "What are you having?" she asked Susie.

"Just a shandy, please."

Gina smiled at her. "She's a right misery-guts, isn't she? Were you stuck with her for long?"

"Since I got here," Susie said grimly. "Poor Mal. How does he put up with her?"

"God knows. I think he must be a saint." Gina paid the barman.

Susie giggled and the girls exchanged a conspiratorial smile.

Gina's face lit up. "Oh, listen! M People! Let's dance."

"I dunno . . ." Susie looked down at her bump.

"Oh, come on. I'm sure the baby will love it!"

Leaving their glasses on a table near the dance floor, they pushed their way into the crowd.

Greg stood watching. What an odd-looking pair! Gina, small and gorgeous, in a red, silky dress that clung to every curve. And Susie looking larger than life in a voluminous yellow shirt and baggy trousers.

Doug came over to join him. "Still interested in Gina, then?"

"I certainly am, brother. The question is, are you?"

A flicker of alarm crossed Doug's face, but he forced himself to stay cool. "Don't be ridiculous! She's just a kid!"

Greg smiled lazily. "You think so? I'd say she's a very sexy little lady."

Doug was about to warn his brother off when he remembered his promise to Gina. "Have you been to see Mother?" he asked instead.

"I gave her a call on Monday."

"Jeez, Greg! It wouldn't kill you to drop in occasionally. You only live five minutes away!"

"Give it a rest, Doug. I'll drop in over the weekend." Greg finished his drink. "It's your round."

"It usually is," Doug said dryly, signalling the barman.

Jack watched Susie and Gina dance, only half listening to what Jim and Gary were saying. Gina looked particularly gorgeous tonight. She caught his eye and waved. He waved back. Maybe he *should* ask her out. The music slowed down and the lights dimmed. The girls walked back to their table.

"Excuse me, lads." Jack put down his pint and made a beeline for Gina but his progress across the room was slow – that was the problem with being the guest of honour – and by the time he got to Gina's table, Greg was leading her on to the floor.

Susie smiled sympathetically.

Jack paused in front of her, embarrassed. "Hiya, Susie. Want to dance?"

"It's not me ye wanted to dance with."

"Course it is. Come on, now. You can't turn me down. It's my birthday!"

"Right so," Susie agreed laughing.

Jack led her onto the floor, well away from where Greg and Gina were smooching.

Susie liked the way he held her. So carefully – as if he might hurt her. And he was so tall. He made her feel small – no mean feat at the moment!

"Thanks for coming tonight, Susie. I know this probably isn't your kind of thing."

"I'm enjoying meself, Jack," she said and realised she meant it. She was having a good laugh with Gina – now there was a turn up for the books – and Mal had been as nice as ever. Caroline had practically ignored her but that was OK 'cos she'd ignored everyone else too! All in all, it was the best night out she'd had in ages. And now here she was dancing with this gorgeous fella. OK, she was his second choice, but still . . .

"The smoke isn't bothering you, is it?" Jack looked down at her, his dark eyes full of concern.

"Not at all. I'm grand."

"I'm not going to smoke in the office any more, Susie, I just want you to know that. I'm not actually supposed to anyway," he added with a grin. "Pamela goes mad. But Mal told me it would be bad for you and the baby so I'll nip outside from now on if I need a fix."

Susie stared at him. "That's really nice of ye, Jack. Though I'm sure a little bit of smoke won't hurt the baby."

Jack shook his head firmly. "Ah, no. We can't be putting you at risk. And Gina says you're still getting sick so the smoke probably upsets you anyway."

"Well, it does a bit," she admitted. God, even Gina was concerned about her. "Thanks, Jack. Yer very thoughtful."

He beamed down at her. "Not at all."

Doug came up and tapped him on the shoulder. Jack bowed to Susie and stood back to let Doug take over. Gina watched curiously over Greg's shoulder.

"So, Susie, are you having fun?" Doug smiled at her.

"Yeah, grand." Susie stared up at him and wondered if she was dreaming. Why did someone like Doug Hamilton want to dance with her? It wasn't long before she got her answer.

"I've been thinking," he said. "There's no point in you looking for a flat at this stage. If you stay at The Sycamores, you'll be near work and we'll be able to keep an eye on you."

"But – but Pamela . . ."

"Thinks it's a great idea," he assured her.

Susie wrinkled her nose. *Yeah, and I'm Cindy bleeding Crawford!* He obviously didn't know about their little chat the other night. And she certainly wasn't going to tell him. God, this was complicated. And if she wanted to hang on to her job she had to handle it right. "I don't think it would work," she said finally.

"You have somewhere else to go?" he asked her, eyebrows raised.

"Well, no . . ."

"There you are then. Anyway, you probably couldn't

afford a decent place." He laughed. "Not on what we're paying you!"

"I'm not sure I can afford yer flat either," Susie pointed out. He hadn't mentioned money yet.

"Oh." Doug looked flummoxed. He hadn't even thought about rent. What would be a reasonable figure? He hadn't the remotest idea! "I tell you what. I've let my study and the library at home get into an awful state since I got sick. Why don't you sort it out for me and we'll call it quits?"

Susie looked at him warily. Work in The Sycamores, with Pamela wandering around the place. Very cosy! "I don't think so . . ."

"Oh, come on. You'd be doing me a favour."

Susie chewed on her lip. He was right. She really couldn't afford anywhere else. And she was pretty sure she could handle Pamela and her nasty little jibes. Well, she could avoid her anyway. "And that's it? I don't pay ye anything?" she asked.

"Well, you can pay your own phone bill." Doug wasn't going to finance her calling her pals in Australia!

"That's fair," Susie said slowly. She pulled away from him and stuck out her hand. "OK. Ye've got a deal."

"So why don't we get out of here?" Greg urged. "Go somewhere quieter? Gina?"

"Sorry?" Gina said absently. Why on earth were Susie and Doug shaking hands?

"Have you heard a word I said?" Greg said irritably. She was taking this act a bit too far for his liking.

Gina panicked when she saw the cross look on his face. Here he was finally paying her a bit of attention and she was going to screw it all up. "Of course I have! But I can't leave yet, Greg. It's Jack's birthday. It wouldn't be right."

"I'm sure he won't even notice," Greg said dismissively.

Gina hesitated. She knew Jack would be hurt if she left. But she didn't want to upset Greg either. She sighed. "I'd better not."

"I need a drink," Greg said moodily and headed for the bar.

Gina hurried after him. "Let me get it, Greg. To make it up to you."

Greg rewarded her with a small smile. "Well, OK, then."

Gina smiled, relieved, and rummaged in her bag for her purse.

Jack watched the two of them. They were standing so close and she was smiling up into his face. She'd never looked at him like that. Probably never would either.

"Another pint, Jack?" Doug came up and slapped him on the back.

"I don't think so," he muttered.

"Of course you will! It's your night. You can have anything you want!"

Jack watched Greg's hand caress Gina's bare back. "I don't know about that," he said grimly, "but I will have a Jameson. And make it a large one."

Chapter Twenty-four

"Doug? It's Mal. Sorry to disturb you, but we have a bit of a problem."

"I'm sure it's nothing you can't handle, Malcolm," Doug said, his attention still on the *Crossaire* crossword in *The Irish Times*.

"I really think you need to be involved here, Doug," Mal said firmly.

Doug put down the paper with a sigh. He knew he shouldn't have answered the phone. "What is it, Mal?"

"It's a bit . . . delicate. I'd prefer to discuss it in person."

Doug checked his watch. It was nearly eleven-thirty. He brightened. "Tell you what, Mal. Let's discuss it over lunch. I'll meet you in The Langkawi at one."

"Fine. I'll see you then, Doug. Thanks." Mal put down the phone, shaking his head. Any excuse for an outing, that was Doug these days. He didn't seem remotely interested in what went on in the office. Still, at least he'd agreed to meet. Otherwise Mal would have had to get

Noreen to contact Pamela on her health farm. And he was hoping he wouldn't have to involve her at all.

He looked down at the sheet of paper in front of him, and ran his eye down the column of figures one more time.

"Want a coffee, Mal?" Susie stood smiling down at him.

"No, thanks," he said quite shortly, keeping his head down.

Susie frowned. Mal was in very bad form today. She wondered if she had done something to annoy him but they had very little to do with each other – except for when Mal had organised her advance. Maybe that was it. Maybe he didn't approve. Oh, well, sod him!

Mal watched her surreptitiously as she made fresh coffee. He was pretty sure she hadn't done it, but there was a niggling doubt. He was one hundred per cent sure of Gina, Noreen and Jack. Greg? Well, he was a different story. Mal almost hoped it *was* him. He drew his calculator towards him one more time, hoping against hope he'd made a mistake.

"Fancy going to the pub for lunch, Mal?" Jack asked him at twelve-thirty.

"No, sorry, Jack. I have to go out."

"Fair enough."

"I'll come." Gina stood up. "What about you, Susie?"

Susie grinned. "Yeah, why not? Mind you, I probably won't be able to eat anything!"

"Poor you," Gina said sympathetically. "I couldn't

handle that at all." They'd been getting on like a house on fire since the party.

"Ah, ye get used to it. And it's a great way to lose weight!"

Mal watched as the three of them left, laughing. Susie certainly wasn't acting guilty. But Doug would be convinced it was her. He was hardly likely to suspect his own brother.

"How much?" Doug asked quietly, turning his knife over and over.

Mal sighed. "Three hundred pounds."

"And you're absolutely sure."

"Yes," Mal said for the third time to Doug and the umpteenth time to himself.

The waiter came over and they quickly gave their order. Doug ordered a bottle of the house white wine.

"I need a drink," he said grimly when they were alone again.

"You're not the only one." Mal had been feeling quite depressed since he'd discovered there was money missing.

"OK. Tell me everything. From the beginning."

"It was Monday evening when I first noticed it. I hadn't had to go to the petty cash box until then."

"And when was the last time you'd opened it?"

"Friday lunch-time. I asked Susie to get some stamps when she was down at the shops."

Doug frowned. "OK. Go on."

"Well, like I say, I didn't open it again until last night.

There had been six twenty-pound notes, three fifty-pound notes and three tenners. And some small change, but that was still there."

"Very decent of our burglar to leave us something!" Doug paused as the waiter poured the wine.

"The lock was fine," Mal continued when they were alone again. "I checked that. I just don't know how it happened."

"Did you leave it opened and unattended at any stage?"

"Of course not," Mal said, affronted that his boss should even suggest such a thing.

Doug passed a weary hand across his eyes. "Sorry, Mal. I know how careful you are. Who else has a key?"

"You and Pamela."

"Noreen doesn't have a spare tucked away somewhere?" Doug knew she had copies of most of the keys in CML.

Mal shook his head. "Definitely not."

Doug took his keys out of his pocket. "Well, if I have one, it should be here." He started to scan the heavy bunch of keys.

"That's it." Mal pointed at a short, thick one.

"Right, and I haven't been near the office all weekend so there's no way anyone could have used my key to open it."

"And Pamela probably keeps hers on her key-ring too and she hasn't been in since Friday."

"So someone must have got hold of your key, Mal."

Mal shook his head in frustration. He'd been over

this again and again. "There's no way, Doug. I always keep my keys on my belt."

"Well, have you any *other* explanation?" Doug said impatiently. Why the hell wasn't Pamela here to deal with this?

"No," Mal admitted.

"So who do you suspect?" Doug asked as their starters were put down in front of them.

"I don't know."

"Oh, come on, Mal. Don't give me that."

"Well, there's a new lad working in security."

"Yeah?"

"And then there's . . ."

"Yes?" Doug prompted.

"Susie," Mal said dismally.

"I don't believe it," Doug said dismissively.

Mal looked surprised. He was sure Doug would have had Susie at the top of his list. "Well, she's new. And she's hard-up and her dad's giving her a rough time over the baby so she needs to move out."

"She already has," Doug said quietly.

Mal put down his knife and fork and stared at his boss. "Excuse me?"

"She's staying at The Sycamores."

"What! How on earth . . ."

"It's a long story." Doug filled Mal in on the night he'd found Susie sleeping on the couch in reception. "So you see," he said finally, "she doesn't have money worries any more. As well as having the advance we gave her, she now has a flat rent-free."

"Pamela must love that," Mal said without thinking.

Doug smiled wryly. "Let's say I'm not exactly flavour of the month."

"So Susie's in the clear," Mal said, relieved.

"I'd say so. But where does that leave us? What about this security guy?"

Mal shook his head. "I don't think so. I made some discreet enquiries. He hasn't been on a shift on his own yet."

"And he'd still need access to a key," Doug agreed. "Jeez, Mal, we have to get to the bottom of this. We can't carry on with a thief in our midst."

"We could set a trap," Mal said half-heartedly. Doug hadn't mentioned his brother – and he certainly wasn't going to – but Greg would have no problem getting his hands on either Doug or Pamela's keys.

"That's not a bad idea. But first I think we need to interview everyone."

Mal took his glasses off and polished them absently. "Do we have to?"

"Well, they have to be told what's going on and the thief knows you know the money is gone. Maybe he'll give himself away in an interview."

"But everyone else is going to feel . . . victimised." Confrontation was not Mal's forte. Even an argument with Caroline left him shaking.

"Tough," Doug said brusquely. "We have to get to the bottom of this. I've no time for ego-massaging. The innocent have nothing to worry about."

Mal ate his satay chicken and said nothing.

"We'll start first thing this afternoon. Is everyone in?"

"Yeah – though I'm not sure about Greg."

Doug paused, his fork halfway to his mouth. He'd forgotten about his brother. His face clouded over. Yes, he'd forgotten all about his easy-going, spendthrift, constantly broke brother. But he was quite sure Malcolm hadn't. He watched him polish off his starter. Mal was a decent guy and he wasn't dumb. "Have you considered him?" he asked quietly.

Mal shrugged.

"Come on, Mal. You must have."

"He's new too," Mal said uncomfortably, "but he's hardly likely to steal from his own brother!"

"No, he'd usually just ask." A look of pure relief crossed Doug's face. Greg had come to him on many an occasion for a 'loan'. And these 'loans' were rarely repaid, but Doug kept doling out the cash anyway. If Pamela knew, she'd kill him. Doug tucked into his duck with gusto, his appetite restored.

"So we have a crime with no suspects," Mal said lightly, but he wasn't convinced of Greg's innocence.

"We'll get to the bottom of it, don't you worry. I want it all sorted before Pamela gets back." He just knew that she'd fire Susie and ask questions later and he wasn't going to let her do it. The poor kid had enough to contend with.

When they got back, everyone was present – Greg included. Doug stood in the middle of the room, his face sombre. "I'm afraid I have some rather distressing news. An amount of money has gone missing from the petty-cash box. Now it's not pleasant to think that there is a thief in our midst but that would seem to be the case. Malcolm and I wish to talk to each of you this afternoon to see if we can shed some light on this mystery. It would make it easier if we had your total co-operation. I would like to clear up this matter quickly and quietly – and I'd prefer not to have to involve the police."

Noreen gave a small gasp before looking pointedly at Susie.

Gina looked from Mal to Doug in disbelief. "Surely it's a mistake? A miscalculation?"

"I'm afraid not," Mal said gravely.

Doug looked around the shocked faces and clapped his hands together. "Right. Well, Noreen, we'll start with you. The sooner we get started, the better."

Doug held the door and Noreen preceded him into his office, her mouth set in a disapproving line. Mal gathered up his papers and followed them.

When the door closed, Gina sank back into her chair and threw her pen across the desk. "I don't believe this."

"Why not? These things happen," Greg said with a sly look at Susie.

Susie glowered at him. She knew he thought it was her. They probably all did. Certainly Noreen did. She'd made that very obvious.

"Not here they don't, Greg," Gina said, her face sad. "Not here."

Mal took his glasses off and massaged the bridge of his nose. "We're not getting very far, are we? Apart from Noreen's thinly veiled implications about Susie – which were completely unsubstantiated – we're no nearer an answer."

"We'll get the thief, Mal." Doug stood up and opened the door. "Susie? Could you come in now? And Gina, be a love and get us three coffees."

"Sure." Gina jumped up as Susie went into Doug's office.

Doug shuffled papers and made small talk until Gina had delivered the coffee and left. Then he looked straight into Susie's eyes, his expression solemn but his voice kind. "OK, Susie, you know what this is about."

"I didn't do it!" she burst out.

"We're not saying you did," he said gently. "We're just trying to piece together everyone's movements on Friday and Monday. Then maybe we can figure out what happened."

She looked at him suspiciously. "What do ye want to know?"

Malcolm took a sip of his coffee and cleared his throat. "Well, Susie, remember when I asked you to get the stamps on Friday?"

"Yeah, what about it?"

"Do you remember who was in the room when I opened the box?"

Susie went red. "Just me and you. Everyone else was at lunch."

Doug scribbled something down on the pad in front of him. "And did you see what was in the box?"

"No . . . oh, I dunno. There were some twenty-pound notes. Mal gave me twenty-five quid and I brought back ten pence change."

"That's right," Mal confirmed, with a small reassuring smile. "And do you remember where I got the key?"

"From there." She pointed at the ring on his belt.

"OK. Now did you see anyone else near the box that day?"

"Nah. Sure yer the only one with a key and no one could get anywhere near that. Ye always wear your keys on yer belt. I can hear ye coming for miles!"

Doug smiled. "And what about Monday? Did you see anyone near the box then?"

"Nope." She stared sullenly into her mug. This was all bullshit. They were asking all these questions but she knew they'd just blame her in the end.

Doug stood up. "OK, Susie. I think that's all for now."

She looked up in surprise. "That's it?"

"Yes. Thanks for your help."

Susie went back to her desk, ignoring Greg's smarmy grin.

"She made one very good point," Doug was saying.

"What's that?"

"Whenever you walk you jangle. Those keys are always on your belt. However the thief got into the box, it wasn't using your key."

"I did tell you that," Mal said, slightly peeved. He

was extremely careful when it came to security and the only time those keys came off his belt was in the car or at home.

"You did." Doug smiled apologetically. "Right. We'd better talk to Greg."

"Would you prefer me to go?"

Doug shook his head. "Not at all. He's a member of staff like all the rest. He's not getting special treatment."

When Greg came in, he slouched down into the chair, stretched his legs out, and put his arms behind his head. "I don't know why you're bothering with all this, Doug. It's obvious who the thief is."

"It is?" Doug said, his face grim.

"Oh, come on. It has to be that little scrubber, Susie Clarke."

Mal's face went an angry red. He hated ignorant assholes like Greg Hamilton who judged people because of their accent, or their clothes or their address. Susie was worth ten of this waster! "Why does it have to be?" he ground out.

"She needs the money. She's poor. She's always hanging around the office in the evenings."

"Did you see her hanging around on Friday evening?" Doug asked as Mal's face get redder.

"Well, no, but I've seen her stay back lots of other times."

"And where do you think she got the key?"

"Pamela's office," Greg said without hesitation. "Pamela keeps all her keys in the vase on her desk. Everyone knows that."

"I didn't," Doug said, his eyes narrowing.

"Me neither," Mal agreed.

"Then you're not very observant," Greg said, completely unfazed by the accusatory looks coming from both men.

"And how do you know the key to the petty-cash box is there?" Doug asked.

"I don't," Greg said studying the print on Doug's wall, his voice bored. "But I'd take a bet on it."

Mal nodded to Doug and left the office. He found the key to Pamela's office on his belt and let himself in. It only took a few seconds to locate the vase Greg was talking about. Mal emptied it out on the desk. There were three keys. A spare one to her office, one for her filing cabinet and one for the petty-cash box. Silly bloody woman! Thank God she didn't have a key to the safe! Mal went back into Doug's office and threw the key down on the desk.

Greg smiled. "I should have put money on that one."

Doug scowled at him. "Right, Greg. You can go."

"Good. I hope you're going to deal with the little bitch quickly, and leave the rest of us in peace."

Doug stood up and opened the door. "Thank you, Greg." He shut it firmly after his brother had sauntered out.

Mal was sitting at the desk, his face grim. "This doesn't prove it was Susie, you know. It means it could have been absolutely anybody."

"I realise that, Mal. Calm down."

"But how did they get *into* Pamela's office?"

"Sorry?"

"Well, she's been keeping it locked lately." Mal didn't mention that she'd only adopted this practice since Greg had joined them.

"I see. So it wasn't open at all on Monday?"

"Nope. Definitely not. In fact one of the cleaners was complaining to me that she was never able to get in to dust."

"The plot thickens." Doug yawned and looked at his watch. It was five-thirty. He hadn't spent this long in the office in months. "I think we'll call it a day, Mal. Let's sleep on it. Maybe something will occur to one of us. I'll call you in the morning."

"Fine by me," Mal agreed wearily. He felt positively sick and had done since the moment he'd realised the money was missing. And then having to haul in the staff – his friends – and question them. Days didn't get much worse than this. "Seeya, Doug." He went out to his desk, picked up his jacket and headed for the door. He felt as if all the eyes in the room were on him. "Seeya tomorrow," he said over his shoulder.

No one answered.

Chapter Twenty-five

Susie was helping herself to a bottle of water from the fridge when a plump, middle-aged woman came bustling in.

"Are you the lass staying in the flat, then?" Irene looked her up and down, her eyes widening when they rested on Susie's bump.

"That's right." Susie headed for the back door.

"I'm Irene Rooney. The housekeeper."

"Right."

Irene bristled. Cheeky little madam! She could at least introduce herself! "I'd be obliged if you'd ask before you go taking things."

"Doug said I should make myself at home."

"*Mr* Hamilton is very kind, but like I say, I'm the one who has to keep the fridge stocked."

"Sorry," Susie said over her shoulder and carried on into the garden. The last thing she needed was that oul biddy having a go at her. She went down to the bottom of the garden and settled herself under the tree nearest the stream. At least it was cooler down here. It was just her luck that Dublin was hit by a heat wave when she was heavily pregnant – "heavily" being the word. She was only twenty-eight weeks but she was huge already. She took a long drink from the bottle and thought back over the afternoon. The atmosphere in the office was awful. And she was sure everyone thought she'd taken the money. Noreen and Greg did anyway. But Mal had just looked sad. God, she hoped *he* didn't think she was guilty, that would be awful. For some reason it was important what Mal thought of her. And Doug too. He'd been so nice – oh, God, why was she worried *what* they thought? She hadn't *done* anything!

"Lovely down here, isn't it?"

She looked up to see Doug standing over her, his jacket slung over one shoulder.

"Yeah," she said, refusing to return his warm smile. God, he really was a fine thing. For an oul fella.

"Sorry about the inquisition earlier, but it had to be done."

She shrugged.

"Mind if I join you?" He sat down beside her and rolled up his sleeves before she could object. "How's baby?"

"Active." she smiled reluctantly, as her child kicked enthusiastically.

"Really? What does it feel like?" Doug asked curiously. He'd never been around a pregnant woman before.

Susie thought about it. "It's kind of hard to explain.

Like at the beginning, it's a fluttering sort of feeling. Now, though, it's more like a bloody football match!"

Doug laughed. "Must be a boy, so."

"Definitely. No girl would cause this much hassle." Susie stroked her bump affectionately. She hadn't expected to feel anything for this baby. It wasn't as if she'd loved the father. But since the first time she'd felt it move, it had suddenly become very real. It was no longer just a problem. It was a baby. *Her* baby. And it scared the hell out of her. Not just the thoughts of labour – though she was terrified of that – but what would come later. Handing him – for it was definitely a boy – over to strangers. How could she do it?

"This would be a great garden for kids," Doug was saying.

Susie nodded. "Sure. Until they fell into the river."

He laughed again. "Never thought of that. But it could be cordoned off. Imagine playing hide and seek? There'd be loads of places to hide. And a boy would be spoiled for choice if he wanted to do a spot of climbing."

"So are ye going to have kids?" she asked curiously. She was sure Pamela must be too old.

"No, no," he said, slightly embarrassed. "I don't think we're cut out for it."

"Pity." Susie looked at the beautiful garden and then back at the large elegant house. It would be a great home for a kid. Mind you, Pamela probably wouldn't let him budge out of his cot in case he made a mess! Susie looked at her boss. He was staring absently into the water, obviously miles away.

"I'd better get to work. That study won't clear itself."
She started to scramble up.

"Oh, leave it for tonight, Susie. It's too damn hot.
Let's stay out here for a while. Tell me about yourself."

Susie sat down again. What the hell was she supposed
to say? Tell him about the tiny home she came from on
the north-side? Or the fact that the only holiday she'd
ever been on was a day-trip to Bray? Or maybe he'd like
to hear about her da. Or her mouse of a mother. "There's
nothing to tell," she said finally, her face sullen.

"Then talk to me about the future. What are your
dreams?" Doug wasn't going to be put off by her
negative tone.

Susie shook her head. Was he thick or just bloody-
minded? "Before or after I get thrown out of me job and
home for something I didn't do?" she said angrily.

"Did you take the money?" Doug said quietly.

"No, I bloody well didn't! I told ye!"

"Fine. I believe you. Now, let's say no more about it.
How about some food?"

Susie looked confused. "Well, I was just going to
make something . . ."

"Oh, yeah, what?"

She looked down. "Egg and chips."

"My favourite! Come on. We'll use my kitchen.
There's more room and the chips would just stink up
your flat."

"Well, OK. But ye better help. I'm no skivvy." She
followed him into the kitchen, shaking her head. This
man was a total space cadet! He ate out in the swankiest

of restaurants and now he wanted to share egg and chips with her! What was he on?

"I'll peel the potatoes," he said, rooting in a drawer for the potato-peeler.

She watched guiltily as he pulled the drawer to bits. *God, Susie, ye've an awful nerve! The man's putting ye up in a gorgeous flat for nothing and yer complaining about making him a plate of chips!* "It's OK. I'll do it."

Doug brandished the peeler triumphantly. "No. I wouldn't hear of it. Can't have a woman in your condition overdoing it."

Susie laughed. "I don't think peeling a few spuds would kill me."

"Nevertheless. I said I would help and I will. You can cook them, though. I always burn chips and I can never manage to get my egg nice and runny."

"Oh, it *has* to be runny or ye can't dip your chips in it!" Susie said, shocked.

"Exactly! And the bread has to be white."

"And really fresh." Susie plugged in the deep-fat-fryer and rooted in the cupboards for a frying-pan.

"Oh, that's a must," Doug agreed. "And it has to be butter. None of this low-fat shit!"

"Yeah. I hate that stuff."

Doug pointed the potato-peeler at her. "Ms Clarke. You know your food! I would go as far as to say you're an expert!"

Susie giggled. "Ye haven't tasted it yet. Oh, God. How does this bloody thing work?" She stared at the gleaming range with all its knobs and dials.

"Haven't a clue," Doug said cheerfully. "But I think if you turn on this, and then . . ." He twisted a couple of knobs. Nothing happened.

Susie caught sight of the power switch on the wall. "Maybe if we put this on, it might help."

Doug swatted her with a tea-cloth. "You see, I told you you were an expert!"

They put the meal together with much laughing and joking. Susie was thoroughly enjoying herself which was really funny 'cos only a couple of hours ago she'd been sure she was going to get the sack! *And* she felt hungry. Another bloody miracle!

Doug drank lager and Susie tea, while they both wolfed down the dinner.

Doug smiled as he watched Susie make a chip butty. He'd quite enjoyed himself tonight. And that was pretty amazing considering the day he'd had. He looked around at the state of the kitchen. Irene would blow a fuse if she saw it! But he'd clean it up himself later.

Susie licked her lips. "That was gorgeous." It was the first meal she'd enjoyed in months. Usually either she didn't want to eat at all or, when she did, by the time it was cooked the smell put her right off. Except for the occasional chicken curry from the takeaway – for some reason that went down OK – she'd lived on crackers.

"It certainly was. You're a good cook."

"It was only egg and chips," she said, her face red. If she didn't know any better she'd think he was chatting her up!

"Ah, but it's the way you cooked them. Lovely runny

eggs! How can the doctors expect me to give all that up?"

"Why do they want ye to do that? Yer OK now, aren't ye?"

"Yeah, but I'm supposed to keep to a healthy diet. Lots of fruit and veg, lean meat, no fats . . ."

"What's the point of living?" Susie said in disgust.

Doug gave a wry smile. "You have a point."

"Oh, sorry. I didn't mean . . ." Susie cursed silently. *Put your foot in it as usual, Susie.*

Doug smiled at her bent head. "That's all right. I prefer a bit of plain speaking. Too many people are walking on eggshells around me – excuse the pun! It's pissing me off, to be honest."

"It's only 'cos they care. Ye should count yerself lucky."

Doug realised that from her point of view he probably had it made. He must seem completely ungrateful and selfish to her. And he was really. Look at what she was facing. Childbirth at nineteen. No one to look after her or be with her. The prospect of giving away the child. A violent father . . . Lord, he had it easy by comparison. He stood up and put their dishes in the sink. "Let's do something."

"Like what?" Susie looked suspicious.

"How about a game of chess?"

Susie stared at him. "Dunno how to play."

"I'll teach you." Doug was all enthusiasm now.

She looked worried. This could turn into a really boring evening. "Nah, thanks. I think I'd prefer a bath. And *The Bill* is on tonight. That's if yer sure ye don't want me to work."

"No, that's OK. You get on. I'll clear up. And thanks for dinner."

She smiled shyly and let herself out the back door.

Doug shoved the dishes into the dishwasher, gave the table a quick wipe and went back out into the garden. It was still warm, though the sun was almost gone. He walked down to the water and sat down under the tree where he'd found Susie. It had always been his favourite spot. All you could hear was the gush of water, the rustle of the trees and the woodpigeons calling mournfully to each other. He watched a Coke can being carried downstream and mused over the last couple of hours. He'd never have believed that he could spend time in this girl's company and actually enjoy it. But she was funny and entertaining and she seemed so vulnerable when she talked about the baby. And when she attacked him and her eyes flashed angrily . . . all he felt was admiration. She was quite a girl. Very mature for her age. But then she'd had to grow up quickly. She'd been through a lot. He was convinced she had nothing to do with the theft. Susie might be a little rough round the edges, but she was no thief. So who was?

He skimmed a stone across the water and went through all the possible candidates. It could well be one of the cleaning staff. They would have had plenty of opportunity to take Pamela's key and copy it. Then they just had to wait for an opportunity to use it. Simple. He could not accept that it was any one of his staff. Greg was the only one who'd be capable of it, but Doug was pretty sure of his brother's innocence. It would be too much like hard work when all he ever had to do was hold out his hand. Doug flung another stone into the water and stood up. It was his fault that his brother was so irresponsible. He'd made life too easy for Greg. Overdid the surrogate father bit. And Greg had made the most of it. On the odd occasion that Doug stood firm and said no, Greg would go to their mother. And after a lecture, she'd give in too. Between them they'd enabled Greg to lead a wonderful life and do the minimum amount of work.

Doug made his way back to the house, his head down and his hands deep in his pockets. He had to admit to some responsibility for his brother's attitude. Another failure. Because that was what his marriage was, he realised. A failure. He went into the small sitting-room, switched on the stereo – Van Morrison's voice filled the room – and flung himself on to the sofa. He'd been lying to himself for months now, but there was no denying it any more. Something was very wrong in his marriage. The thing was, he wasn't quite sure what it was or when it had happened – or had it always been like this? Was it, in fact, he who'd changed like Gina said? They never talked any more. Except about work. Pamela always wanted to talk about work. CML was her life. He'd been so proud of her when they'd first set up the company. She'd worked so hard, even at weekends, and their social life had been put on hold. Doug realised now – it had been the happiest time of their marriage. They'd stumble into the flat each evening, exhausted, have a takeaway, a bottle of wine and then make love on the large, overstuffed sofa. Pamela had never been a passionate woman, but he'd always found her aloofness quite sexy and she had a beautiful body. Just looking at her naked was enough to get Doug excited. And with his other little . . . diversions, he was more than satisfied. But now their love-life was almost non-existent. And it wasn't just because of his heart attack, though that's what Pamela had implied. It had been on the decline long before that. In fact, except for the sympathy screw the night before he went in for the operation, they hadn't had sex in months. He hadn't really noticed because he'd met this sexy little redhead in Annabel's with the most amazing tits . . .

Anyway, the point was – he finished his beer and went out to get another – there were some real problems in his marriage. Pamela was more interested in the house and the business than in him. In fact, sometimes he got the impression that he was an irritant. Something to be tolerated. He wasn't at all sure where they were headed any more. Was their life always going to be a round of dinners and cocktail parties? Is that the way Pamela wanted it in five years? Ten years? Wasn't it all just a little bit shallow? They needed to talk and re-evaluate things. It was time. And it was time they decided for certain that they didn't want children.

He scrunched up the can in his hand, feeling decidedly depressed. His thoughts turned back to Susie Clarke. A young girl alone and afraid but, he realised, he envied her. Because she had something more precious than anything in his life. And she was probably going to give it away. He wondered if he had a child what it would be like. What his son would be like. Would he like sport? Or music? Would he end up as a banker, a plumber, or maybe even – he laughed – a rock star? Would he look like Pamela or would he be a Hamilton through and through?

Or would it be a little girl? Doug smiled. A little girl would be nice. He could see her now. A little girl with enormous blue eyes – they were bound to be blue – clutching a large teddy bear. Her sweet heart-shaped face surrounded by a mass of blonde curls. Her laugh infectious, her mouth permanently turned up in a smile that would show off a row of perfect tiny white teeth. Her mother's grace and style. Doug tried to picture Pamela cuddling their little girl. Bandaging up cuts and bruises. Nursing her when she was sick. Reading her bedtime stories. . . but the dream faded. Doug just couldn't imagine his wife doing any of those things. She wouldn't be interested. She'd agreed easily when he'd told her that he had no interest in raising a family. That was when he'd first proposed. He had wanted to lay his cards on the table. Make sure then that they both wanted the same things. His goal had been to turn CML into the number one conference management company in the country. There was no place for children in his plans. He'd thought it strange, even then, that Pamela had agreed so readily. Didn't all women have a maternal streak? And even if she agreed then, surely she'd had second thoughts over the years? But if she had, she'd never mentioned it and she'd shown no interest in their friends' children. But didn't all women want kids at some stage? Didn't they love to get in a huddle and talk about the difficult births, stretch marks and sleepless nights? Well, not Pamela. And that had suited him just fine. Until he was lying in a hospital bed waiting to be carved up, that is. Then he'd started to wonder. What if this was it? What if he died on the table, what was his legacy? What did he have to show for his forty-two years on this mortal coil? His business? Was that it? No heir, no son to carry on his name. No one to look up into his face trustingly as he taught them to swim or ride a bike. No one to love him unconditionally.

Susie would be nuts to throw it all away. And he didn't believe she wanted to. He'd seen the look on her face when the baby had kicked. She'd been transformed, her hand going instinctively to caress the little foot that had struck out with such strength and determination. It would be a shame if she went through with this adoption. He was sure she'd regret it for the rest of her life. And there was no need for it. She had a roof over her head. She had a job – and he'd guarantee her that it would be waiting for her when she was ready to come back, whatever Pamela said. That bit was easy. She was a hard worker and very talented. Much more artistic than Gina, and that was saying something. And, she was definitely honest. She'd had nothing to do with the theft; he'd stake his life on it. No, she was a good kid and he was going to look after her. She needed support at a time like this. The sister seemed to be there for her, but she needed a man in her life too. He smiled. Maybe he could be a surrogate dad again. Just for a while. Just till she was able to stand on her own two feet. And then, well then he'd have to figure out what to do about his own life. But he wouldn't worry about that for the moment. No. For the moment he'd concentrate on taking care of Susie. Susie and her baby.

Chapter Twenty-six

Gina took one last look in the mirror and sat down to put on her highest heels. Why did she always date such tall men? Greg Hamilton made her feel even shorter than usual. She barely came up to his chest. Standing up again, she teetered out of her bedroom and down the hall to the little kitchen.

Tim looked up from his sweet and sour chicken. "What are you all done up for?"

"I've a date."

"Oh, yeah? With Mike Ford?"

Gina shook her head impatiently. "No! What do you know about Mike Ford? What makes you say that?"

Tim grinned. "Touched a nerve, have I? Mum mentioned he was back and Hannah told me he was interested in you."

Gina sighed. The Kilkenny grapevine. "When did you see Hannah?"

"Saturday night in Horan's. That bloke Fergal's a nice

guy. The four of us went down to that new little wine bar. So is it?"

"What?" Gina looked at him distractedly.

"Is it Mike Ford you're going out with?"

"No, it isn't."

"So who is it?"

"Never you mind. But make sure and clean up here when you're finished. I might bring him home for coffee."

"Coffee, eh?" Tim winked. "Wait till Grainne hears this."

"Oh, is she coming over?"

"Yeah, she said she'd drop by after her classes. She should be here any minute."

Gina looked guilty. She'd better get out quick. Grainne was studying accountancy at night and Tim had told her that Gina was going to night classes too. Now, whenever they met, Grainne bombarded her with questions about the course. The problem was Gina hadn't been there in three weeks. Not since the night Doug had announced there'd been a robbery. Greg had suggested they go for a drink and of course, she'd agreed.

"But only a quick one," she'd said firmly. "My class starts at seven." But she never made it to class that night. Or the next night when Greg had taken her to a movie. Or the next week either when they'd gone to see a play. Gina had managed to keep this from Tim so far. She usually went to her classes straight from work, so he hadn't realised she'd missed any. And, of course – being a guy – he hadn't noticed that she came home in different clothes than she'd gone to work in that morning. Or that she was flushed, or that her eyes sparkled. So, she'd got away with it. So far. But if Tim did find out he'd give her a terrible lecture about the wasted fees – paid for with their dad's hard-earned money. She promised herself that she'd go back next week. And Fiona would give her notes for the nights she'd missed. Fiona Sweeney was a good mate and they'd covered for each other before. It was impossible for Gina to feel too guilty. She was in love and she'd give up anything to be with Greg. She was positively walking on air. She stared dreamily into space as she thought of their last night together. It was their third date and when Greg suggested they go back to his place, she'd agreed immediately. His flat had been exactly what she expected. Smart, sophisticated – not at all like her shabby, basic little home. Greg hadn't bothered with the pretence of coffee. As soon as they got in the door he'd taken her in his arms and kissed her. Then he took her hand and led her into the bedroom – Gina had never seen such a big bed! He turned on the stereo very low and started to take her clothes off, very slowly. First her blouse . . .

"Maybe we'll stay in to meet this new boyfriend of yours," Tim was saying casually.

Gina jumped. "What?"

"I said maybe Grainne and I will stay in and meet your boyfriend."

"No!" Gina was banking on having Greg to herself for at least an hour so that they could continue where they left off in his flat. "No, not yet, Tim," she said more reasonably. "Please? We need to get to know each other."

"OK, then. I wanted to see the new James Bond film anyway."

"Thanks." She flashed him a grateful smile.

"I hope his intentions are strictly honourable," Tim said, only half joking.

"*God, I hope not!*" Gina muttered to herself. "Got to go."

"Isn't he picking you up?" Tim frowned.

Gina saw his disapproving look. He was so old-fashioned. "He wanted to," she assured him quickly, "but I told him I'd meet him at the restaurant."

"Oh. OK. Have a good time. Be careful."

"Yeah, I will. Seeya." Gina shut the door and ran down the stairs, heaving a sigh of relief. The last thing she needed was the third degree from Tim. He would have been very unimpressed if he knew that Gina was actually meeting Greg in The Pizza Hut. Tim Barrett was like his dad. He believed that a guy should always collect a girl *and* drop her home. She jumped into the car and sped off into town. Greg hated being kept waiting. Having said that, he was the one who'd been late each time they met. And Gina would be sitting there like a lemon, trying to ignore the curious stares from guys at the bar. That's why she'd said she'd meet him in The Pizza Hut tonight. It wasn't as bad as a pub. She didn't feel quite as conspicuous. Gina hated to be kept waiting, but she hadn't said so to Greg. She knew it was pathetic but she couldn't help herself. She'd forgive him anything. Once his mouth was on hers and his magic fingers started to touch her in all the right places, everything else was forgotten. She was like a drug-addict these days. Or maybe a sex-addict would be more accurate. She'd sit in the pub or restaurant, nodding politely as he talked about the wonders of Thailand or the problems he was having with his motorbike, and dream of the moment when he'd take her in his arms. Then she would give herself up to the amazing sensations that ran through her body as he touched, kissed and licked her.

She sighed, trying to concentrate on finding a parking space. It was bloody difficult for her to concentrate on anything these days. She'd never experienced such passion. Well except for . . . she shook her head as the memory of 'That Night in Marrakech' surfaced. That was different. It had been down to too much wine and a romantic setting. It was immaterial that it had been Jack. It wouldn't have mattered who the man was. It had been nothing more than lust. Whereas this – this just had to be love. Never had she known such overwhelming sensuality. Morning, noon and night all she thought about was Greg. Seeing Greg. Kissing Greg. Sex with Greg. It didn't help that his desk was only a few feet away from hers. Every so often he would look up from his work and catch her watching him. He'd smile that lazy, gorgeous smile of his and she'd start to feel hot all over.

Gina hopped out of the car and ran up the road to the restaurant. She was almost ten minutes late – he was sure to be there. She pushed the door open and scanned the busy restaurant, looking for his blond head.

"Gina! Hey! Over here!"

Gina whirled around, a broad smile on her face and stopped short when she saw Jack. "Oh. Hi."

"You remember Gary, don't you, Gina?"

Gina smiled at Jack's friend who was staring at her with his mouth open. "Sure. How are you, Gary?"

"Eh, eh, umm, fine."

Jack grinned. Gina usually had that effect on his mates. "Are you on your own?" he asked her.

"Eh, no, I'm meeting someone."

"Hello, darling. Sorry for keeping you." Greg strolled in and slipped a possessive arm around Gina. "Hello there, Jack."

"Hi," Jack mumbled, the smile leaving his face.

"Come on, Gina, let's eat. I'm ravenous."

Gina smiled apologetically. "OK. Seeya, Jack. Nice to see you again, Gary."

Gary stared after her. "God, she's gorgeous."

Jack grunted.

"Weren't you going to ask her out?" Gary said, still ogling her.

"Unless my eyes just deceived me, she's already seeing someone," said Jack sarcastically.

"It mightn't be serious."

Jack turned around in time to see Greg lean across the table and kiss Gina hard on the lips. "You think not?" he said grimly.

"Well, maybe it is," Gary conceded.

"So, gorgeous. Have you missed me?" Greg took her hand and licked the palm.

Gina shivered. "Don't be silly. I only saw you in work a couple of hours ago."

"Hours? It feels like weeks! But I'm glad you went home and changed into that!"

Gina blushed. "You like it?" He should do, the white silk shirt and black suede trousers had cost enough!

"Like it? You look sensational! I want to ravish you right here and now."

Gina's dark eyes were full of longing. "Sounds good to me," she murmured.

Greg laughed. "Patience, my sweet. Man cannot live on love alone. Now what are we going to eat?" He picked up the menu and stuck his head in it.

Gina tried to concentrate on the menu but it wasn't food she was hungry for.

Greg glanced at the bowed head of shiny, chestnut-coloured curls and grinned. God, she was gagging for it! Quite a little sex-pot. Inexperienced though, but then that made it more interesting. He was able to introduce her to a whole host of new experiences and teach her how to make him happy too. She glanced at him across her menu now, her brown eyes full of longing and passion. "Want to get a take-out instead?" he asked softly.

Gina nodded, not trusting herself to speak.

Within ten minutes, they were heading out the door, carrying their pizza box.

"Goodnight, guys," Greg called to Jack, cheerfully. "Got to rush," he added with a lewd wink.

Gina gave a quick, embarrassed wave and was gone.

"Wonder where they're off to?" Gary said absently.

Jack glared at him. "Evening Mass, of course."

Gary looked surprised. "Oh. That's nice."

Jack shook his head and ordered another beer.

* * *

"Oh, Greg," Gina said breathlessly.

Greg rolled over and stretched his arms back behind his head, his smile smug. "We aim to please," he murmured.

"Oh and you do." she said fervently, heading for the bathroom on shaky legs.

"How about a drink?" he asked when she returned.

Gina looked nervously at the clock. "Sure, but let's have it in the living-room. Tim will be home soon."

"Ah, yes. Big brother. I'm looking forward to meeting him."

Gina pulled on her trousers. "Come on, then. Get dressed. I'll get the drinks." She hurried out to the kitchen, pausing to check her hair in the hall mirror, and praying that Greg would get a move on. The last thing she needed was for Tim to see a naked man in her bedroom. She found the corkscrew and opened a bottle of red, splashing the wine into two glasses and setting them down on the coffee table in front of the sofa. Then she turned on the stereo. Right. That looked a bit better.

"Greg?" she called. "I have your drink ready."

Greg wandered in with his shirt open. Gina watched him anxiously. "Button up, Greg," she pleaded.

He sat down beside her and started to button his shirt. "Too much temptation for you?"

She laughed nervously. "Yeah. I've been thinking. Why don't you come down to Kilkenny with me next weekend? Hannah's going to be there – you'd like Hannah."

"Yeah? Maybe some other time, honey."

"OK." *Don't push it, Gina. Don't rush him.*

The front door banged loudly – Tim and Gina always gave each other a warning – and Tim strode into the living-room. "Evening all." He walked over to Greg with his hand outstretched. "Tim Barrett."

Greg reached up to shake Tim's hand. "Greg Hamilton."

"Would you like some wine, Tim?" Gina asked, as her brother sized Greg up.

He plonked himself down in an armchair. "Yeah, why not? So, Greg. You're working for CML now."

"Just helping out until Doug's back on his feet again."

"Right. How is he?"

"Not bad at all."

"That's good. Bad business about this robbery, eh? I'm sure that's the last thing he needed."

"Yes but he's handling it all wrong, if you ask me. It needs to be dealt with quickly. It's important to send out a message to people that this sort of thing won't be tolerated."

Gina overheard him as she returned with Tim's wine. "You mean Doug knows who did it?" she asked, surprised. She hadn't heard a word.

Greg gave her a patronising smile. "Well, isn't it

obvious? Susie Clarke took the money. Who else would it be?"

"And what evidence is there?" Tim asked, seeing the horrified look on Gina's face.

"Oh, she had the opportunity – she's always hanging around the office in the evenings – and she needs the money."

"That hardly makes her a robber, Greg!" Gina protested.

He smiled at her. "You think the best of everyone, Gina. But it has to be her. Everyone else has been ruled out."

Gina sipped her wine silently. She didn't believe it was Susie. In fact she was sure it wasn't. The barriers had come down between the two girls on the night of Jack's party and a strong friendship was beginning to blossom. And while Susie still had a bit of a chip on her shoulder, Gina knew that she wasn't a criminal. But she didn't want to argue with Greg over it. Especially in front of her brother. "I still don't believe it," she muttered finally.

Greg shrugged. "I'd better go. Thanks for an amazing evening, Gina." He leaned across and kissed her deeply, his hand on her thigh.

Gina flushed. Even though she was nearly twenty-nine, she still didn't like to parade her sex life in front of her brother. She stood up. "I'll see you out."

"Bye, Tim. Nice to meet you."

"Yeah, you too," Tim replied, none too enthusiastically.

After a long kiss goodnight, Gina came back into the living-room. "Well? What do you think?"

Tim drained his glass and stood up. "Not a lot. I thought you and Susie were friends."

"We are!"

"You didn't exactly jump to her defence though, did you? I'm off to bed. 'Night."

Gina flopped back down on the sofa and finished her wine. Tim was right, she thought miserably. She'd let Susie down. But dammit, her relationship with Greg was too new and too important to mess around with. Damn Tim. He just didn't like Greg. But she did and that's all that mattered. She switched off the light, went into her room and threw herself down on the bed, snuggling into the pillow and inhaling deeply. It smelled of Greg. She smiled as she relived their lovemaking. God, he made her crazy! She'd never experienced such wild sex. It was amazing, frantic, urgent. It was no wonder she found it hard to keep her eyes open in work these days! Mind you, it would be nice just to have a cuddle in front of the telly sometimes. Or to curl up afterwards and talk. Or to fall asleep in each other's arms. But that wasn't Greg's style. Everything was fast, urgent and passionate. And then he immediately got dressed, or turned over and went to sleep.

"Don't be so greedy," Gina admonished herself. "He's sex on legs. What more do you want?"

Chapter Twenty-seven

Pamela parked her car and let herself into the house. She checked the mail on the hall table – two bills, an invitation and a thank-you card – and went in search of Douglas. The sitting-room was empty and she moved down the hall to his study. She heard the noise from the computer as she approached. He seemed to spend all his time in here since she'd got back from the health farm. "Douglas? Have you . . . oh, it's you." A veil of hostility fell across Pamela's face.

Susie looked up from her work. "Hiya."

"Where's my husband?"

"He went out to get something to eat."

Pamela frowned. "He's gone to dinner? He never mentioned a dinner engagement."

Susie grinned. "Nah. He's just gone to pick up some burgers and chips."

"I see." Pamela turned to leave.

"I'm sure there'll be enough to go around if yer hungry."

"I'd rather eat dog food," Pamela said coldly and turned on her heel.

"It was made for ye, ye snobby bitch," Susie muttered to her receding back.

Pamela went upstairs and ran a bath, sprinkling several drops of lavender in the water. She needed something to calm her. The benefits from the health farm had worn off almost the moment she'd arrived home. It was bad enough having the girl staying here, but now Susie seemed to spend most evenings closeted with Douglas in the study. The situation was positively insufferable. She went into her bedroom and undressed, hanging her suit up carefully. She removed her make-up and went back into the bathroom, closing the door and locking it. She'd been sure Susie would have left weeks ago. Both The Sycamores and CML. The money that had mysteriously disappeared from the petty-cash box should have taken care of that. But her plan had backfired. Not only had Doug never even suspected Susie, he'd been furious and suspicious when Pamela told him that she'd taken it.

"Why the hell didn't you tell Malcolm what you were doing?" he'd said angrily.

"He wasn't there. It was on Friday night. After I left Jack's party, I realised that I had absolutely no cash. So I borrowed some. I don't see why you're making such an issue of it. I *am* a director after all."

Doug had scowled at her. "I'm making an issue of it because we thought one of the staff had stolen that money and we interviewed – or should I say interrogated – each of them."

Pamela flicked through the newspaper. "So? It will keep them on their toes." She pretended a nonchalance she didn't feel. The idea had been that Douglas would be angry with Susie, not with her. And he was supposed to have missed her while she was away. Welcomed her back with open arms. Apologised for his funny behaviour.

"For God's sake, Pamela, someone could have been falsely accused because of your thoughtlessness."

"Well, they weren't and now the mystery is solved."

"As for keeping your keys in a vase, that's really stupid!" he'd told her, angrily.

"Is it? Well, I'm sorry I'm doing such a lousy job of running your company while you stay at home and play with your new toy. Maybe if I wasn't so overworked I wouldn't make these mistakes." She threw down the paper and ran upstairs, sobbing as she went.

Douglas had run after her and apologised, Pamela remembered now, as she sank into the hot scented water. But he still hadn't relented on the Susie Clarke issue. He was adamant that she was here to stay. At least until the baby was born. And now he had her working in the house. Working! That was a laugh! They seemed to spend all of their time chatting, messing about on the computer or raiding the fridge. If it wasn't for the fact that Susie was plain and as big as a house, Pamela would suspect them of having an affair. But it was worse than that. Douglas seemed to think that Susie was his responsibility. He was like a schoolboy looking after an injured bird and he was fiercely protective whenever Pamela made any derogatory comments about the girl.

She felt a shiver of fear run down her back. She tried not to speculate as to why her husband was so interested in Susie Clarke. She was afraid she already knew. She gave herself a mental shake. Don't think about it. At least now he was talking about returning to work. That would keep him occupied and maybe he'd be more like himself once he got back into a daily routine.

Pamela's concern had been so great she'd gone to see Sheila Hamilton.

Armed with a large bouquet of white lilies she'd dropped in to see her mother-in-law one lunchtime.

"Thank you, dear," Sheila had said, taking the lilies and handing them to Betty. "Would you put these in the other room, Betty? Their perfume is a little too strong for me."

Bitch, Pamela thought, smiling sweetly. Her mother-in-law had never liked her. She sat down on the sofa in the old-fashioned living-room. "How are you, Sheila? You look marvellous."

"I can't complain." Sheila watched the other woman and wondered why she'd come.

"Great news about Janet," Pamela said to break the awkward silence. "She must be very happy."

"She'll be happy when she holds the child in her arms and not before. Douglas tells me you've a girl in CML that's due about the same time."

"Yes," Pamela said dismissively. The last person she wanted to discuss was Susie Clarke. She glanced surreptitiously at her watch.

"Are you in a hurry?"

"No, well, yes. Oh, I'm sorry, Sheila." Pamela pushed a tendril of hair distractedly from her face. "I do have a meeting in town but I needed to talk to you. About Douglas."

Sheila's face creased in worry. "What's wrong? Is there a problem with his health again? But he looks so well."

"No, nothing to worry about there," Pamela reassured her. "It's his mind I'm concerned about."

"What do you mean?"

"Well, the doctor told him weeks ago that he could return to work, but he's showing absolutely no interest in the company at all. I went away for a few days, hoping that he might jump in and take over, but apart from taking care of a . . . minor crisis, he stayed away. I just don't understand it. It's so out of character."

Sheila Hamilton watched her daughter-in-law as she talked. She did seem genuinely worried. And Sheila had to admit that she shared some of Pamela's concerns. "He does seem happy to leave the business to you," she agreed, "but then all of this has been quite a shock. I expect it takes more time to recover mentally than physically."

Pamela looked sad. "Of course you're right. I just think he'd recover much faster if he had the distraction of work. There's a conference in Las Vegas next week. I suggested he go on that, I thought it might be good way to ease him back in."

"Very sensible. What did he say?"

"Oh, he was happy to go, but not to work."

Sheila frowned. This certainly wasn't like Douglas.

He'd always had a firm grip on the reins of CML. "Would you like me to talk to him?" she said, knowing that this was exactly what Pamela wanted.

Pamela's face lit up. "Would you, Sheila? I'm sure he'd listen to you."

"I'm not going to try and talk him into anything," Sheila said firmly. "He's old enough to make his own decisions."

"Yes, well I'd be happy if he could manage to make even one decision at the moment," Pamela said, a steely note creeping into her voice.

Sheila smiled wryly. She'd wondered how long it would be before Pamela let the mask slip. "He'll probably drop over during the week. I'll talk to him then."

Pamela stood up and smoothed down the skirt of her expensive suit. "Thank you, Sheila. I do appreciate this."

"He's my son, Pamela. A mother will do anything to help her child."

Pamela gave her a tight smile. "Of course. I'll find my own way out. Bye bye."

Sheila didn't stand up and Betty came bustling in when she heard the front door close. "Is she gone already? I was going to make some tea."

"Pamela doesn't have time to have tea with the likes of you and me, Betty."

"I suppose she must be busy," Betty replied, plumping up some cushions and running a finger along the sideboard, checking for dust.

"Yes, I suppose she must." Sheila sighed. Maybe she was just a little too harsh on Pamela. The last few months couldn't have been easy for her. But though Sheila felt sympathy for her she still couldn't warm to the woman. She was just too false. Sheila knew that it must have killed her to come here and ask for help, so she must be worried. Whether she was worried about Douglas or the business Sheila didn't like to dwell on. She'd always hoped that in her own weird, complicated way, Pamela loved Douglas. To think otherwise was too depressing.

Pamela soaped her arms and legs and then massaged them with a loofah. Going to see Sheila had paid off though she never did find out what his mother had said to him. He still refused to head the DVD conference but he had promised to return to work the following month. And hopefully that meant he'd have less time to spend with Susie Clarke.

"Susie? I'm back," Doug called as he went straight through to the kitchen and set the bag of food on the table.

Susie followed him in and filled the kettle. "Pamela's home. I told her you'd gone for burgers but she said she didn't want any." Susie didn't think it was a good idea to tell Doug her exact words.

Doug laughed. "No. Pamela's a lot more health-conscious than I am. Where is she?"

"Dunno."

"I'll just go and say hello."

"Do you want some tea?" Susie called after him.

"No, I'll have a beer." Doug went into the sitting-room and when he found it empty, ran upstairs. Pamela wasn't in the bedroom either so he knocked on the door of her bathroom. "Pamela?"

"Yes?"

He tried the handle and frowned. Since when had she started locking doors in their own home? "Everything OK? I wasn't expecting you home yet."

"Evidently," she said sarcastically.

Doug sighed. "Have you eaten?" he asked patiently.

"No."

"Well there's some salad and smoked salmon in the fridge and a nice bottle of chablis to wash it down."

"I'm not hungry," she said curtly. "I think I'll go straight to bed."

"Fine. Suit yourself," Doug retorted and went back downstairs.

Pamela felt a pang of guilt. He was really trying but, damn him, why should she go down and pretend everything was OK? They hardly made a cosy threesome.

Susie put a plate of food down in front of him and a cold beer beside it. "There ye go. I'm sure yer doctor would approve!"

Doug laughed. "Let's not think about him." He took a bite out of his burger but, thanks to Pamela, he'd lost his appetite. Why did she have to be so bloody-minded? Since he'd told her Susie was staying she'd built up an icy wall between them that he couldn't penetrate. She'd softened when he'd told her he was coming back to work, but her good mood hadn't lasted long. And she was just impossible when Susie was around. What *had* she got against the poor girl?

Susie ate her food in silence, sensing his mood. Pamela obviously wasn't talking to him again and there were no prizes for guessing why. As long as Susie stayed at The Sycamores there was going to be trouble. And though she didn't like the woman she didn't want to cause any trouble for Doug. He'd been so good to her. But at the same time, she couldn't afford to leave. Not now. She was thirty-four weeks pregnant, as big as a house and so damned tired all the time. The thought of having to find somewhere else to live at this late stage depressed her. And the way this little fella was kicking, she was convinced he was going to come early. She smiled wryly. He obviously couldn't wait to get into the world. Silly little bugger. If he knew better he'd stay where he was!

Doug noticed the smile. "What's funny?"

"Ah, just wondering about this little man." She patted her stomach. "Ye know the kind of thing. What's he going to be like? Will the poor kid look like me?"

"He'd be very lucky if he looked like you. You're very pretty. And clever too," Doug said seriously. He'd noticed as they'd got to know each other better, how she was always putting herself down. All the make-up and garish clothes were a protective layer. "Have you thought any more about what you're going to do?" he asked gently. He knew that Marie had been trying to persuade her to see a counsellor about the adoption, but Susie kept making excuses. Doug knew it was because she wanted to keep the baby.

"What's there to think about?" Susie said carelessly and carried her plate to the sink.

"You don't have to do it, you know."

She whirled around to face him, her eyes angry. "And what would you know?"

"Tell me why you decided to have the baby adopted in the first place," he said, ignoring her flash of temper.

"Why?" she said mutinously. "What good will that do?"

"Just tell me," he said patiently.

"I'd no way of looking after it, that's why!" she said.

"Exactly!" he said triumphantly. "Whereas now you have a good job and a home."

"For the moment," she said quietly.

Doug went over and took her hands in his. "Look at me, Susie."

She looked up into his face reluctantly.

"Your job is secure. I've told you that. And it's not because I feel sorry for you, it's because you're bloody good. I see a very bright future for you."

Susie filled with pride at his words, but forced herself to be realistic. "But the flat . . ."

Doug sighed. "I won't kid you, Susie. I can't offer you the flat as a long-term solution, but it's yours until you can afford a place of your own. A place that's suitable for bringing up a child."

Susie looked at him. She wanted to believe him. She

wanted to believe it was all possible but it wasn't. She pulled her hands away. "You make it sound so bloody easy!" she said angrily.

"Isn't it?"

"No. No, it isn't! So, I have a job. Great. But who minds the kid when I'm out at work?"

Doug shrugged. "Well, there's your mother . . ."

"Her! I wouldn't trust her with a dog!" She spat the words out in disgust. "If she couldn't protect her own daughter, what hope would there be for a bastard grandchild?"

Doug was shocked by her bitterness. "There are crèches . . ."

"Oh yeah," she agreed, "and they cost money. And what about the cost of a cot and a pram, and clothes and toys? And babies get sick, ye know. What about doctors' bills?" She was close to tears now. What was it he'd said? *Have you thought about what you're going to do?* Dear Jesus, she'd thought of nothing else! She fell asleep every night and woke up every morning wondering if there was any way, any way at all, she could keep this baby. She looked at Doug leaning against the kitchen table, his expression downcast. He was a good man but he hadn't a clue what it was like to live in her world. "I'm off to bed," she said quietly.

"I'm sorry if I upset you, Susie. I was only trying to help. But I'm afraid I'm a bloody fool who knows nothing about bringing up children."

Susie gulped back the tears and gave him a tremulous smile. "Ye meant well. 'Night."

Doug sat down and put his head in his hands. He had meant well but he'd just talked a load of bullshit. Now he felt a total fool. What must she think of him? He'd over-simplified everything. Applied his business mind to a subject that was both sensitive and complicated and one he knew nothing about. Talk about dumb. And here she was, a young girl with a poor education, who'd thought the whole sorry mess through. Who'd accepted her limited options. Who'd faced the harsh realities. It was a huge burden for such young shoulders and the more he saw her carry it, her head held high, the more his admiration grew.

Chapter Twenty-eight

"Gina? You've done a wonderful job and I'll be telling Mrs Lloyd-Hamilton so too." Marian Hickey held out her hand.

Gina flushed with pleasure as she shook it. Praise from a tough cookie like Marian meant a lot. "I've enjoyed every moment," she said truthfully.

"Not half as much as the rest of the gang," Marian said dryly, looking around the packed casino.

"I haven't seen any of them in ages." Gina raised her voice. She was still gobsmacked by the incredible noise of the slot machines and the crowd. All the casinos were garish and flamboyant and the waitresses, wearing lashings of make-up and skimpy uniforms, patrolled the rooms calling *'Cocktails?'* in high-pitched, squeaky voices.

"I believe most of them are around the roulette table," Marian was saying.

"I hope they don't lose too much."

"Not our problem, Gina. They're big and ugly

enough to look after themselves. Now I think it's time we had some fun." She shoved a bundle of chips into Gina's hand. "Just my way of saying thank you."

"Oh, Marian!" Gina stared at the chips. It was at least a hundred dollars. "Where shall we try first?" She looked around excitedly.

Marian shook her head. "Sorry, kid, you're on your own. I'm off to try my luck with your colleague."

Gina looked at her astounded. "Jack?"

"Yeah. Best-looking guy in the place. A bit rough and ready but that's how I like my men. Wish me luck!"

She pushed her way into the crowd and left Gina standing staring after her. Marian fancied Jack? But she must be nearly ten years older than him. And Jack was so, well, so, unworldly. What would a shark like Marian Hickey see in him? Gina shrugged and wandered off in the other direction. She hoped fervently that Jack would let her down gently. She was a customer after all. Gina paused at a large table surrounded by people. Gerry Kelly, Marian's right-hand man, was among them. She squeezed in beside him to see what was going on. As she did a hush descended round the table and a large man, wearing a cowboy hat, blew on a pair of dice, whispered something and threw them down the table.

"Six," the croupier announced and there was a loud cheer.

"Way to go, Buddy!" A man clapped Cowboy Hat on the back.

"What's happening?" Gina asked Gerry.

"Oh, hi, Gina. We're winning, that's what." He

grinned broadly and pulled another pile of chips towards him.

A hush fell as Cowboy Hat blew on the dice and threw them once more. They landed just in front of Gina.

"Seven." The croupier called and there were loud groans from around the table.

"What's wrong?"

"When it's a seven, the house wins everything."

"Oh." Gina watched as the croupier raked all the chips off the table, including a sizeable amount of Cowboy Hat's. The man shrugged, picked up his two remaining chips and left the table without a word. "Did he lose much?" Gina asked.

"A few hundred," Gerry replied vaguely.

"Crikey." This was much too heavy for Gina's liking.

The croupier offered Gerry three sets of dice. He hesitated then selected a pair.

"Why do you get to throw?" Gina asked.

Gerry glared at her. "Gina, will you shut up?"

"Sorry," she said meekly.

Gerry crossed himself and threw the dice.

"Three," the croupier announced and there was a murmur of approval. The croupier gave more chips to five of the players, Gerry included.

Gina looked confused. "I don't understand. A three is less so how come you win?"

Gerry gritted his teeth. "I'd be happy to explain it all to you sometime, Gina. Just not now, OK? Now please go away."

Gina shrugged and moved on. Some people were so touchy! She paused beside two Chinese women playing 21. Now this was more her sort of game. She sat down beside them and the croupier smiled at her.

"Evening, Ma'am. Minimum bet five hundred dollars."

Gina gasped "What!"

The other women stared at her coldly.

"You'll find tables with lower odds on the other side of the room," the croupier said kindly.

"Thanks," Gina stood up and hurried away, mortified. It was then she noticed that a lot of the men in this part of the room were in dinner jackets and the ladies wore evening gowns. Back at the slots, everyone had been dressed casually. "Time to get back into your depth, Gina," she muttered to herself. True enough, the tables across the way had a minimum bet of two dollars. "That's more like it." She was heading for one of the card tables when she spotted Jack's fair head. Better warn him about Marian, she decided. She made her way over and sat down on the stool beside him. "How's it going?"

Jack grinned and indicated the large pile of chips in front of him. "Not bad."

Gina's eyes widened. "How much is there?"

"About eighty dollars. I only had ten when I sat down."

"That's brilliant! Is it hard?"

"Nah. Have a go."

Gina handed the croupier a ten-dollar chip and received twenty fifty-cent chips back. She looked confused. "If the minimum bet's two dollars, why is she giving me fifty-cent chips?"

"Because you can split your bet," Jack explained. "You just need to have a *total* of two dollars on the table."

"Oh! So I get four bets for two dollars?"

"If you like."

Gina put her chips on seven, twelve, fourteen and twenty.

"No more bets," the croupier said as she popped the ball into the spinning wheel.

When the ball finally came to rest, Gina couldn't see the number as the wheel was still spinning.

"Ten black," the croupier called.

"Oh." Gina watched disappointed as her chips were taken away. Then she saw another pile being shoved towards Jack. "Jack! You won!" she squealed.

"Yep," he said with a grin.

"What's your secret?"

"Well, you see, you put your chips on single numbers. That's great if they win. You'll get big money. But your odds are better if you bet on a colour, or on an odd or even number. Just watch for a while and you'll see."

"Nah. I'd prefer to try my hand at 21. I just came over to warn you."

Jack frowned. "Warn me about what?"

"Marian's after you."

"Why, what have I done?"

"Not a thing. It's your body she's after."

A broad grin spread across Jack's face. "Oh yeah?"

Gina stared at him. "You're not seriously interested?"

"And why not? She's a good-looking woman."

"But she's so much older than you!"

"Yeah, and experienced as well, no doubt." He grinned from ear to ear.

Gina looked at him in disgust. "God, you're all the same!"

"What's wrong, Gina? You're not jealous, are you?"

"Don't be ridiculous!" she spluttered. "I'm off to play 21. You're welcome to each other!"

She took a seat at the nearest card table and set the chips down in front of her.

"Howdy, li'l girl," the man next to her said with a friendly smile.

"Hi," Gina muttered, barely looking at him.

"Are you ready to play, ma'am?" the croupier asked.

"Yeah. Deal me in."

Twenty minutes later and fifteen dollars poorer, Gina left the table. She headed towards the slot machines, stopping on the way to exchange her chips for a bucket of quarters. Maybe this was more in her league. She ordered another drink from a passing waitress and sat down in front of a large machine. "And I'm not moving until I win something," she said, getting a funny look from the little old lady sitting beside her.

She fed coins into the machine for over an hour but it swallowed all her money hungrily, occasionally throwing back a couple of quarters to keep her interested. It didn't help that the machines on either side of her coughed up copious amounts of coins every few minutes. The little old lady had two full buckets at this stage. Gina sneaked a look at her and wondered if she was cheating.

While she played, she drank. A lot. The cocktail waitress in her gaudy uniform always seemed to be at her side. When the last quarter disappeared with a disappointing clunk, she stood up unsteadily and looked around for a familiar face. A couple of delegates were standing at a machine nearby. As she made her way over to them, a loud siren went off and she looked around in time to see the old lady scooping up bucketfuls of coins from *her* machine.

"Well, of all the nerve! Look at that old witch! That's my money! I've poured a small fortune into it and now she's got it all!"

Liam Johnson laughed. "You win some, you lose some, Gina."

"But I haven't w*on* anything!" she complained.

"Maybe you're lucky in love." Don Healy slipped a sweaty hand around her waist.

Gina looked at the overweight Lothario, old enough to be her father. "Not if you're all that's on offer," she murmured in disgust.

"What was that?" He hugged her tighter to him.

"Nothing." She said grimly. *He's a customer, Gina. Remember that.*

"Wow! Look at Madame Hickey in action." Liam distracted Don long enough for Gina to extricate herself from his clutches.

She followed his gaze and gasped when she saw

Marian Hickey wrapped around a man on the dance floor. It was Jack Byrne. "What on earth is Jack up to? He must be drunk!"

"Why? She's a fine-looking woman," Liam said.

"Yeah. I wouldn't mind some of that," Don agreed.

You wouldn't mind a blow-up doll, Gina thought.

"Not jealous, are you, Gina?" Liam grinned at her.

"Of course not! It's just not very professional."

"If you're feeling left out, I could comfort you." Don made another grab for her and she managed to side-step him. "Thanks, Don, but actually I'm more interested in women." She sauntered off leaving the two of them staring after her open-mouthed.

She realised that word would have spread around the whole gang by morning but did it really matter? It wasn't as if she were interested in anyone here. Her eyes were drawn back to the dance floor, where Jack and Marian were smooching, his hands moving up and down her bare back. She remembered the feel of those fingers. She took a gulp of her drink. Oh, if only Greg were here. That's all that was wrong with her. She was missing Greg. She ignored the little voice in her head that reminded her that she'd been in Nevada four days and this was the first time she'd actually thought about the man. She looked enviously at the the two fair heads so close together . . . "Oh, stop it, Gina, for God's sake! You're just lonely and drunk." She looked at the glass in her hand. She'd absolutely no idea of how much she'd had to drink, but judging from the way the room kept tilting it was a lot. She turned her back on the lovebirds and made her way unsteadily towards the coffee bar where she ordered a double expresso. As she choked the strong liquid down her throat she started to feel a bit better. When she'd had another cup, she'd go to the ladies', tidy herself up and try her hand at roulette again. And she'd steer clear of cocktails for the rest of the evening. She watched a couple at the next table, gazing into each other's eyes, their hands entwined and her spirits plummeted again. She stood up abruptly and staggered off to the ladies'. There was only so much romance she could take. Other people's, that is.

"Hi, Gina." Marian emerged from a stall as Gina tried to apply some lipstick with a shaky hand.

"Hi." Gina paused in her efforts but was too drunk and depressed to summon up a fake smile.

"Have you had any luck?" Marian opened another button on her blouse, arranging the collar so that a good inch of lacy camisole was on display.

"None. How about you?" Gina forced herself to ask. *She's the customer. She's the customer.*

"Oh, I've struck gold," Marian replied, with a dirty laugh. "Maybe you should follow my lead. Forget gambling. Go find a man instead."

"No thanks. I'm not into one-night stands." Gina took a deep breath and waited for the bolt of lightning to strike. "And anyway, I have someone waiting for me back home."

"You don't mean Greg Hamilton?" Marian said incredulously.

"How did you know?"

"Oh, Jack mentioned you were seeing him, but it's not serious, is it?"

"Why do you say that?" Gina said defensively. Why the hell did everyone stick their noses into her love life?

"Because nothing with Greg ever is, sweetheart."

Gina flicked her hair over her face and began to brush with a vengeance. "What would you know?" she said rudely. *She might be the customer but there was only so much a body could take!*

Marian smiled grimly. "Plenty. Greg's broken more hearts than you've had hot dinners. Don't get me wrong, he's a nice guy and great in bed –"

Gina head jerked up.

"– But you shouldn't take him too seriously. Just enjoy the ride – oops, forgive the pun – while it lasts."

"Did you go out with him?" Gina asked, her voice barely a whisper.

Marian laughed. "I wouldn't say that, exactly. Let's say we 'connected' a few times. Had a bit of fun. It's the only way to play it with Greg, believe me."

"He's different with me," Gina protested.

Marian gave her a pitying look. "Sure, honey."

Gina felt the tears prick her eyes. Dammit, she wasn't going to cry in front of this bitch! "I've got to go," she said, flinging her hairbrush and make-up into her bag and practically running out the door.

"Where's the fire?" Jack asked as she crashed into him.

"Leave me alone, damn you!" Gina said angrily. "And when you're whispering sweet nothings into your girlfriend's ear, leave my life out of it, OK?" And she stormed off.

"What on earth did you say to Gina?" he demanded when Marian joined him.

"Oh, I just told her a few home truths about our friend Greg. Why?"

"She just gave me a right earful."

Marian linked her arm through his. "She'll be OK. Believe me, I've done her a favour."

Jack let her lead him back to the bar. "Tell me about him," he said when he'd got their drinks.

"Who, Greg? Well, he's penniless, totally unreliable, irresistible and great in the sack."

Jack winced. "If he hurts her, I'll kill him."

Marian raised an eyebrow. "I'm sure she's well able to fight her own battles. She certainly wouldn't thank you for interfering."

"But if he's just stringing her along, using her . . ."

Marian sighed. She was getting bored with the subject of Gina Barrett's love life. She'd much prefer to discuss Jack and Marian. Preferably in her room and in a horizontal position. She put a hand on his thigh and stroked it gently. "Maybe I'm wrong," she said placatingly. "Maybe he's really serious this time. She is a lovely girl. Now come on. I want to dance."

Jack shook her off and stood up. ""No. I'd better go check on her."

"Oh, for heaven's sake," Marian said irritably.

"I'm sorry, Marian. But she's a friend."

"Fine. But don't expect me to be waiting for you when you get back."

"I'd be amazed if you were," Jack said dryly and walked away.

"Who is it?" Gina called from under her pillow.

"It's me. Jack."

"Go away."

"Oh, come on, Gina. Let me in." He hammered on the door again.

Gina sighed and went to open the door. "What do you want?" She turned her back on him and went to sit on the bed.

He closed the door and came to sit beside her. "Marian told me what she said."

"Had a good laugh at me, have you?"

"No, of course not. You know me better than that. I just came to see if you were OK."

She smiled brightly. "I'm fine. That cow's just jealous. She obviously fancies Greg herself."

"I'm sure you're right," Jack said kindly and Gina burst into tears.

"Oh, don't cry, love." He gathered her into his arms and stroked her hair.

"What's wrong with me, Jack? Why doesn't anyone want me?"

Jack swallowed hard. "There's nothing wrong with you. You're lovely."

"But I always seem to pick the bad guys."

"Sssh." He rocked her in his arms as she bawled

loudly and soaked his shirt. She started to calm down but Jack continued to hold her.

Gina snuggled into his chest. She could feel one of his hands in her hair while the other caressed her neck. She felt a shiver of pleasure run through her and closed her eyes.

"Are you OK now?" Jack pulled back a little so he could look down into her face.

Gina looked up into his eyes. He was so kind, so gentle. "Yes," she whispered, her eyes moving to his lips. She reached up her hand and touched his cheek.

Jack grabbed it in his. He looked at her mouth, moist and red, felt the softness of her hand, saw the look in her eyes . . . she was drunk. He couldn't do this. He stood up suddenly, his face red.

"I should go."

"Please don't," she said softly.

"I have to."

"But you don't want to, do you?" she smiled coyly.

"No, dammit, I don't, Gina. But I don't want you like this either. I don't want to be used as a comforter when one of the other men in your life let you down!"

"But I . . ." Gina reached up to take his hand but he pulled it away.

Jack looked down at her, his eyes sad. "Go to bed, Gina. You've had a lot to drink and you'd regret it in the morning. Let's just forget this ever happened." *Again,* he thought miserably to himself.

Gina watched the door close behind him. When was she ever going to learn that it wasn't a good idea to make the first move? And what the hell was wrong with her anyway? Why did everyone reject her? Even Doug – a married man nearly old enough to be her father – had been the one to pull away! Maybe she *should* consider becoming a lesbian. It couldn't make life any more complicated than it already was! She slumped back on the bed, pulled a pillow over her head and was comatose in seconds.

Chapter Twenty-nine

Susie groaned and turned over, trying to find a more comfortable position. It was useless. Between her bump, the cramp in her leg and indigestion, there was no way she was going to get back to sleep. Maybe some hot milk would help. She eased herself out of bed, found her slippers and put on her dressing-gown. It was only the beginning of September but already there was a sharpness in the night air. The kitchen was even colder and she shivered as she took the milk carton from the fridge. As she poured it into a mug she gagged at the smell and threw it into the sink in disgust. It must be at least a week old. But then she rarely used the kitchen, having most of her meals either in town with Marie or over at the big house with Doug.

She peeked out the window at the clear, dry night. She could always nip across and get some milk. It was two-thirty but Doug's car wasn't in the driveway so the alarm wouldn't be set and Pamela would have gone to bed hours ago. She never went near the kitchen if

Pamela or Irene was about. Both women made it very clear that she didn't belong here. In fact, Irene was an even bigger snob than Lady Muck. "And she's no better than me," Susie muttered to herself. She got her key and went over to the house.

The light was on in the kitchen but that wasn't unusual. Susie chuckled as she opened the door. Electricity bills weren't a problem in The Sycamores. Not like they were in the Clarke household. The smile froze on Susie's face as she saw the figure sitting at the kitchen table shovelling the remains of Irene's chocolate gateaux down her throat.

Susie watched Pamela, mesmerised. She wasn't even using a spoon. Her hands were covered in cake though, as Susie watched, she paused to lick them thoroughly, before taking a gulp from the bottle of wine beside her. Susie gasped and Pamela whirled round.

"What the hell do you want? Are you spying on me?"

"No! Of course not! I just came over for some milk. Sorry."

Pamela eyed her suspiciously. "Milk? Well, go on then. Get it and get the hell out of here."

Susie went to the fridge, casting surreptitious looks at her dishevelled boss. Susie had never seen her like this before. She doubted if anyone had – even Doug! Her hair hung in a tangled mess around her shoulders. There was chocolate on the front of her kaftan and her eyes were bloodshot.

"What are you looking at?" Pamela barked, making Susie jump.

"Nuthin'. Are ye . . . all right?" Susie stood with the carton of milk in her hand not sure what to do.

"Why wouldn't I be? I had one of my headaches earlier and didn't eat dinner. I just felt a bit peckish. That's allowed, isn't it? This *is* still my kitchen."

"Yeah, sure. I feel like piggin' out meself sometimes."

Pamela glared at her. "I am not 'pigging out' as you so charmingly put it. I'm just having a snack." She took another slug of wine from the bottle and wiped her mouth on her sleeve.

Susie wondered if she was actually still in bed and this was all just some weird dream. She was dying to get back to the safety and sanity of her little flat but she wasn't sure Pamela should be left alone. "Do ye want me to stay?"

Pamela struggled to focus on the girl. "Stay? Stay? Oh no, Susie. I want you to go. I've wanted you to go for months."

"But Doug said . . ."

"But Doug said," Pamela mimicked. "Douglas has quite obviously lost his mind. If it wasn't for that damn heart attack you'd never have got one foot inside our door. The man isn't himself. And he's getting worse, thanks to you. The sooner you and your brat are out of here the better. You've ruined my marriage but I'm going to get it back, I tell you. I'm going to get *him* back."

Susie gaped at her. Pamela's voice was hysterical and there was a wild look in her eyes. "No, yer wrong, Pamela. Doug loves ye." As she said it, Susie realised it was true. The reason Doug was so miserable at the moment was *because* he loved Pamela. She tentatively put a hand on Pamela's shoulder but was pushed roughly away.

"Oh, please, don't pity me! The last thing I need is to be pitied by a little slut like you!"

Susie shrank back as if she'd been hit, her face white. "You've no right to talk to me like that," she said her voice trembling.

Pamela laughed harshly and pulled the bottle towards her. "It seems I've no rights at all these days. Not even in my own home."

"I'll go." Susie moved slowly towards the door.

"Don't get my hopes up," Pamela said bitterly.

* * *

"I should be going." Mal looked at his watch. It was almost two! He hadn't been out this late since before Rachel was born and even then it was only because Caroline liked clubbing. Malcolm had never been one for late nights.

"I suppose," Doug agreed as he studied the girl at the bar with the breasts spilling out over her very tight top.

"Caroline will be wondering where I've got to."

"Pamela won't have noticed."

Mal looked at him. "Are things that bad?" He wasn't into deep conversations, and as far as he could remember, he and Doug had never discussed their private lives before. But Doug had changed. Mal wondered, if *he* had a heart attack, how Caroline would react.

"They could be better," Doug said lightly. "Susie's presence doesn't help."

"No, it wouldn't."

"She's a great kid, you know that, Mal? I don't know what Pamela has against her."

Mal shook his head. "Women. Don't even bother trying to understand them."

"You're right, Mal. You're right. Though Susie's different. You have to admire her. What she's going through. I just wish she'd forget all about this adoption business."

Mal frowned. "You haven't said that, have you?"

"Well, I've told her she doesn't have to worry about her job. And that she can stay in the flat until she can afford something better."

Mal sighed.

"What?"

"I know you mean well, Doug, but the easier you make it for Susie to keep the baby, the guiltier she's going to feel if she decides to give it up. And it's all very well talking about the financial aspects. They are a big part of it. But bringing up a kid on your own is bloody hard work. You can take it for me that the first few months of Rachel's life were far from easy and that was with two of us sharing the load."

"Are you saying I don't know what I'm talking about?" Doug said with a wry grin.

"You haven't a clue!" Mal chuckled.

"But I know she wants it," Doug insisted.

"Maybe she does. But if you ask me she's being damn sensible about all this. She's thinking of the baby, not herself."

"I really admire her," Doug said seriously.

Mal frowned. "You're not, eh . . ."

Doug's eyes narrowed. "What?"

Mal sighed. "She's been through enough, Doug. Don't add her to your harem."

Doug looked at him in disgust. "What do you take me for? Jesus, she's young enough to be my daughter!"

"Yeah, well you've gone out with a few of them before," Mal reminded him.

"That was different. I didn't know them. It was only a bit of fun. Susie's different."

"Yeah, she is," Mal agreed. "It's funny really. Here she is alone, poor and wanting to keep the baby despite everything and here am I, settled, comfortable and with a wife who won't even consider another child."

"I didn't know," Doug said quietly.

"Why would you? We don't usually get into these kinds of discussions often, do we?"

Doug drained his glass and tried to catch the barman's eye. "True. What is it about men that they can only talk about the important things when they're plastered?"

"We're wimps," Mal said gloomily. "We think if we don't talk about our problems, they'll go away."

Doug laughed and ordered another round of drinks. "And has Caroline said she definitely doesn't want another baby?"

"Not in so many words, but she keeps making excuses why now is not a good time. Except it hasn't been a good time for the last two years. And now she's started this evening course."

"Oh yeah? What in?"

"Art. Total bloody waste of time and money, if you ask me. She hasn't brought home a single painting yet. Still, it gets her out of the house a couple of nights a week and she seems happier."

"And if she's happier, life's a lot easier for you."

"Exactly." Mal watched the well-endowed girl squeeze past Doug on her way to the ladies', licking her lips as she went.

Doug smiled absently at her and turned back to Mal. "I wish I could send Pamela on a course. But I think it's going to take a bit more than that."

"So what exactly is the problem?" Mal asked settling back in his seat. Caroline was going to kill him for rolling in so late. Another hour wouldn't make much difference.

Doug frowned. "I'm not really sure but she's been behaving very oddly since my operation. Or else I have."

"You have," Mal confirmed.

Doug looked at him in surprise. "That's what Gina said. But isn't that only natural? I mean I could have died!"

Mal nodded solemnly. "You could have."

"And, well, it just makes you wonder, Mal. What's the point of it all? The business, the worry, the constant pressure."

"I think that's called life. It's the same for everyone."

"Yeah, but surely it's up to us how we handle it. I don't think I'll ever let work bother me again. Pamela comes home spouting about budgets and deadlines and all I can think is, so what?"

"Have you told her this?"

"I've tried, well, maybe not. Since Susie moved in she hardly talks to me at all."

Mal stared glumly into his pint. "Caroline doesn't talk to me either. She talks *at* me. *Take the bins out. The grass needs cutting. I need money to get Rachel new shoes.*" Rachel seemed to go through a lot of shoes, Mal thought absently.

"I thought you guys were happy." Doug didn't understand why, but Mal did appear to be happy with the woman.

"We're the same as most couples, I suppose. We've just got into a rut."

"Not a great advertisement for marriage, are we?" Doug said gloomily.

"Well, at least I've got Rachel."

Doug stared moodily into his glass. "Yeah. It must be great to have a kid. I've only just realised that."

"It's not too late," Mal pointed out.

Doug shook his head. "Pamela wouldn't be interested."

"She might surprise you."

"And hell might freeze over."

"Well, this may sound a bit radical, Doug, but if you want children and she doesn't, get out now while you still can."

Doug lowered his pint and stared at his accountant. "What?"

Mal looked at him as steadily as he could, given his inebriated state. "Rachel can be a spoiled little bitch –

Caroline gives in to her far too much – but I'd do anything for her. She's my life. If Pamela won't give you a child, find someone who will."

Doug stared into his pint.

Mal suddenly felt very sober. This conversation was getting way too serious for this hour of night. He picked up his jacket. "I think it's time I hit the road. Goodnight, Doug."

"'Night, Mal."

* * *

Hannah stared miserably into her coffee. She'd finally done it, so why didn't she feel better? Instead of feeling relieved she felt unsure, nervous even.

"Hannah?"

She looked up when she heard her name and smiled at the man looking down at her. "Mike Ford! What the hell are you doing in a restaurant in the middle of Soho?"

"I've just finished dinner with my solicitor. I was just on my way to the gents' . . ."

"Don't let me stop you," Hannah said, laughing.

He looked at the vacant seat opposite her. "Are you on your own?"

"I am now," she said dryly.

He raised an eyebrow.

She sighed. "It's a long story."

"In that case let me visit the gents' and I'll buy you a drink when I get back and you can tell me all about it."

"Why not?" Hannah said, surprising herself. She wasn't feeling very sociable at the moment. But Mike was easy to talk to and he'd help her forget what a lousy evening it had been so far.

* * *

Gina tried to concentrate on the film but her mind was wandering.

"Do you want another drink?" Jack mouthed.

She shook her head, glad to have the protection of her headphones, and pretended interest in the screen in front of her. They were only halfway through the flight and sitting so close to Jack was making her uncomfortable. They'd hardly spoken since the night in her room. Lord, that was only two nights ago. It seemed like a lifetime. A lifetime of embarrassment and misery. And trying to avoid both Jack *and* Marian Hickey wasn't easy. Marian had come over to her at breakfast the following morning.

"Hope I didn't upset you last night, honey."

Gina's fake smile mirrored Marian's. "Not at all."

"Did Jack find you?"

Gina bent her head over her breakfast. "Yes, but I told him he was overreacting."

Marian lit a cigarette and inhaled deeply. "That's exactly what I said. He fusses about you a lot, doesn't he? Is there some kind of history between you two?" Her voice was casual but her eyes were sharp.

Gina forced a laugh. "Lord, no!"

Marian smiled warmly. "Oh, good. He's very shy isn't he?"

"Yes, I suppose he is," Gina agreed.

"Well, I can be patient." Marian assured her.

But as far as Gina could see, Marian's patience hadn't helped. Jack had avoided her like the plague and Marian was furious that they weren't sitting together for the long flight home.

"For God's sake, Gina, don't put me anywhere near that woman," Jack had whispered urgently at the check-in desk.

"She just asked me to," Gina had hissed back. "And she *is* the customer, Jack."

"I don't give a damn. Pamela can sack me if she wants, but I can't take eleven hours of her. She's like a Praying Mantis!"

Gina re-arranged the seating. It wasn't really a problem. She'd been allocated two courtesy upgrades to first class so Marian and her assistant manager were the obvious candidates. Marian had tried to bully Gerry into swapping with Jack, but Gerry just reclined his seat and started to snore. But Gina hadn't planned on Jack ending up beside her. Still, she knew she couldn't make a big deal out of it. She had to play it cool. That's what he was doing. He hadn't mentioned the other night at all and he'd been relaxed and normal with her. Which just infuriated Gina even more and made her feel a total fool. And as for Greg. Hannah had been right about him. She was going to give him the elbow as soon as she got home. Bloody men! She'd had a bellyful.

Chapter Thirty

Marie Clarke stared at the phone. "Who?"

"Doug Hamilton. Susie's boss."

"Oh, yeah, howaya. There's nothing wrong with Susie, is there? She's nowhere near her time yet."

"No, no, she's fine. I just wondered if we could have a chat, Marie. About Susie. Maybe we could meet?"

"Eh, yeah, I suppose."

"How about tomorrow night?"

"I have to work till nine."

"You're in Henry Street, aren't you?"

"Yeah." God, he knew an awful lot about her!

"Well, is there anywhere around there we could meet for a coffee?" Doug didn't frequent the north side of the city that often.

"There's Bewley's," Marie suggested.

"Fine. See you there at nine-thirty?"

"OK."

"That's great. See you then, Marie."

* * *

Doug watched the girl walk into the restaurant and stop to look around her. But that couldn't be Susie's sister. She was very slim, quite plainly dressed in skin-tight black jeans and a cropped black top. And her dark blonde hair looked natural. Still, it must be her, he realised, as she walked towards him, a nervous smile on her face. And then he grinned as he caught a flash of her fluorescent nail varnish. It was Susie's sister all right!

Marie had no problem identifying Douglas Hamilton. He was just as gorgeous as Susie had said. A bit like Robert Redford but younger.

Doug stood up. "Marie?"

She reddened at the curious stares from the other tables when he held a chair for her. "Ta . . . thanks."

"I wasn't sure what you'd like so I just ordered a pot of coffee and some scones," he said apologetically.

"That's grand."

"Thank you for meeting me. I hope you don't think I'm sticking my nose into what is really a family matter."

"Don't worry about it. I'm the only one in the family who's really interested."

Doug looked shocked. "But surely your mother . . ."

"Ah, yeah, she asks after our Susie all the time. But she's afraid to do any more than that."

"And your father?" he asked gently.

Marie gave a resigned shrug. "He's the same as ever. But he goes mad if we even mention Susie."

"Can't you get a barring order? There must be something you can do?"

Marie gawped at him. "Oh, we'd never do anything like that! He's me da! Ye have to understand, Mr Hamilton. He's not a bad man. Not really. It was just bad timing for poor Susie. He'd had a few jars and, as far as he was concerned, she'd brought shame on him and the family."

Doug said nothing. He couldn't begin to understand the logic of a family who accepted such behaviour but it was none of his business. Susie was his only concern. The coffee arrived and Doug poured. "I'm a bit concerned about Susie," he said as she stirred milk and sugar into her cup. "Do you think she wants this baby?"

"I'm not sure. I think she's a bit broody all right but at the same time she always had her heart set on getting a good job. She isn't a bit like me. I can't wait to settle down with my Paddy and have kids."

Doug smiled. "Have you been together long?"

Marie sighed. "Three years. Sometimes I don't think we'll ever be able to afford to get married. Paddy wants us to move in together but I want to wait."

"I'm sure your father would prefer that," Doug said dryly.

Marie laughed. "Yer right there."

"Well, the main reason I asked you here, Marie, was to see if we could put our heads together and figure out the best way to help Susie. A colleague of mine has already pointed out the error of my ways because I've been encouraging Susie to keep the baby. He says I'm putting her under pressure and she'll feel even more guilty if she gives it up."

Marie sighed. "I'm sure ye mean well but I think yer friend's right. A baby would ruin her life. No man wants ye when ye have a kid. Our street is full of girls like her, wheeling their prams up and down to the shopping centre and the dole office. I'd hate her to end up like that. With only a kid for company."

Doug sighed. "So what do you think we should do?"

Marie shook her head. "I wish I knew. I talk to the adoption agency every couple of weeks, just to keep in touch like. I've tried to get Susie to visit them but she keeps putting me off."

"I see. Well, I've told her that her job is safe and that she doesn't have to move out of the flat until she can afford somewhere decent."

Marie sipped her coffee. "If she does decide to keep it, she'll get single mother benefits, maybe even a council house or flat. I'll ring the Social Welfare and see what the story is."

Doug nodded approvingly. It looked like Susie wasn't the only member of the Clarke family with brains. "Good idea. And I'll talk to Malcolm, our accountant. I'm sure she'd be entitled to some tax breaks as well. I suppose there's nothing more we can do at this stage. And I don't think we should mention any of this to Susie for the moment. Your sister's a very independent young lady. I don't think she'd be too impressed with us trying to organise her life for her. In fact I don't think we should even tell her we've met."

"God, no, she'd bleedin' kill me!"

Doug laughed.

"But I still think she'd be better off getting the baby adopted, Mr Hamilton, honest I do."

"Well, maybe you're right, Marie. But let's agree that neither of us will try to influence her one way or the other. We need to be there for her whatever she decides. Both of us."

Marie looked at him curiously. "Ye don't mind me saying, Mr Hamilton, but yer showing an awful lot of interest in me sister. I mean yer only her boss. And ye've only been that for a few months."

Doug thought about what Mal had said. "I assure you my intentions are honourable, Marie. I just feel sorry for her."

Marie reddened. "I didn't mean to insult ye."

"You didn't. I'm glad someone is looking out for her."

"Well, yer very kind. She's lucky to have ye."

"Well, I'm lucky to have her, too. Your sister happens to be very good at her job."

Marie's eyes widened. "Really?"

"Really. She has a great future ahead of her."

Marie looked doubtful. "I hope so."

* * *

"Thank you, ladies. Same time next week."

Pamela walked over to the bar and picked up her towel. The jazz-ballet session had been strenuous but it had taken her mind off her problems. Briefly.

"Coming for a coffee?" Marjorie asked as usual, leading the way to the changing rooms.

"How about something stronger?" Pamela said lightly.

Marjorie looked surprised. "Sure. The Horseshoe?"

Pamela shook her head as she began to peel off her leotard. She didn't feel very sociable and The Horseshoe Bar in The Shelbourne Hotel would be full of acquaintances. "No. Let's go somewhere quiet."

Now Marjorie was really curious. Pamela wanted to go somewhere quiet? Anna would be astounded when she told her this! She was always saying – quite bitchily – that Pamela only went out to be seen.

"If she's not in the social columns at least once a month she goes into a panic," she'd assured Marjorie and Sophie.

Marjorie had tut-tutted but couldn't help agreeing. Pamela certainly didn't go out for the food or drink. She usually just nibbled on a salad and rarely drank anything stronger than a spritzer.

No, Pamela's aim was undoubtedly to be the centre of attention. She seemed to have a very high opinion of herself and thought everyone else should too. Marjorie sometimes wondered why she bothered with the woman – they could hardly be called friends – still, she enjoyed being seen with Pamela and it was always fun to hear gossip about the glitterati of Dublin society. Pamela knew everyone and all their secrets and she was less than kind when she passed on the gory details.

"See the woman in the black Armani?" she'd murmured to Marjorie in Brown Thomas only the other day. "Celia Marshall. She's supposed to be just back from a skiing holiday but she was in Los Angeles getting a face job."

"No!"

"Yes. Just in time for her fiftieth birthday party." Pamela gave a harsh laugh. "At least that's what she's admitting to."

"Are you going?" Marjorie asked.

"Of course. We're old friends." She raised her voice and waved. "Celia, darling?"

And that was Pamela.

"Let's go to The Mercantile," Marjorie suggested now. It was a place her daughter went from time to time so it was unlikely they'd bump into any of their own crowd.

"Fine." Pamela headed for the showers.

"Same again?" Marjorie asked warily.

Pamela drained her glass and nodded.

Marjorie waved to a lounge girl. "A gin and tonic and a mineral water, please."

"Oh, come on, Marjorie. Have a drink."

"No, really, I won't. I'm driving."

"That never stopped you before," Pamela said nastily.

"Well, maybe just one more. Two gin and tonics." She smiled at the waitress. She was annoyed that Pamela had talked to her like that in front of the girl. She should just walk out. But if she did, she'd never find out why Pamela Lloyd-Hamilton was in such a state. And she definitely was upset. Three gin and tonics! It was unheard of!

"How's Douglas?" she asked.

Pamela put her head on one side as if considering the question. "How is Douglas? That's a good question. Let me see."

The waitress put their drinks in front of them and Marjorie threw ten pounds at her, waving away the change.

"Physically he's fine," Pamela continued. "Mentally . . ." She shrugged and took a large mouthful of her drink.

"What do you mean?" Marjorie asked anxiously. She was very fond of Doug. Often wondered how such a nice man had ended up with such a cold woman.

"He's been behaving very strangely," Pamela said, darkly.

"Oh, yes?" Marjorie didn't want to appear too eager to hear the details. She might scare Pamela off.

"Hanging around with some strange people."

Marjorie looked mystified. Was he into drugs? Gun-running? "Is he in trouble?" she whispered.

Pamela laughed harshly. "He will be."

"And these people? Are they dangerous?" Marjorie was on the edge of her seat now.

"Not to me," Pamela assured her, knocking back her drink and waving wildly at the lounge girl for another. "I'm going to win."

"Win?"

"Damn right. I've come this far. I'm not going to let some little tart ruin everything."

"Oh." Marjorie began to understand. Doug was seeing someone. And it must be serious. The others hadn't seemed to bother Pamela. Marjorie sighed wistfully. She wouldn't have minded . . .

"I'll take care of her. Who does she think she is, anyway?"

Marjorie tried to hush her as a couple of people turned to stare but Pamela was in full flight.

"Coming into my home. Acting as if she owns the place."

Marjorie gasped. Doug had moved one of his mistresses into The Sycamores! This was unbelievable.

"Who is it, dear? Anyone I know?" Marjorie quickly gave the waitress their order – a double for Pamela.

"Just a silly little bitch from the office. With a voice that would shatter glass."

"I'm so sorry, Pamela. I don't know what to say. It's been a very difficult time for you both, what with the operation and everything. Maybe Doug is having some kind of mid-life crisis."

"Hah! I'll give him a real crisis to worry about! I won't have it, Marjorie! I tell you, I won't tolerate it any longer."

"Of course you're right, dear. Maybe you should move out for a little while. You could come and stay with us. Jim wouldn't mind." Jim would go spare but she'd deal with that later.

"Why should I?" Pamela was slurring badly at this stage. "She should move out. And he can go too if he likes."

"Don't be too hasty, Pamela. You and Doug have been together a long time and I'm sure you've come through other . . . delicate situations."

"Delicate sishuasions? What a nice way of putting it, Marj. You mean I've put up with his women?"

Marjorie reddened, conscious of several curious heads turned their way. "Well . . . I . . ."

"This ish different. You don't understand. He's different. And I'm damned if I'm putting up with it any more. She's got to go. Now. Tonight." Pamela stood up and wobbled precariously. She put out a hand to steady herself. "That baby will not be born in my house! Now, you must excuse me, Marj. I think I'm going to be sick."

Marjorie watched, open-mouthed, as Pamela weaved her way towards the ladies'. Then she fumbled in her bag for her mobile and punched in a number. "Anna? Anna, it's Marjorie. You're never going to believe this . . ."

Chapter Thirty-one

Gina pushed the pasta around her plate and wondered what Greg was doing. He hadn't called all week. His reaction when she'd tackled him about Marian Hickey hadn't been at all what she expected. She'd hoped for a denial, or at least an apology. But instead he'd been amused. And then irritated.

"Marian and I go back a long way. We haven't seen each other for a while. But what difference does it make? You're being terribly possessive, Gina. It's not very attractive."

Gina was floored. Shouldn't he be telling her that Marian didn't matter to him? That she'd exaggerated their relationship? Shouldn't he be promising undying love and showering her with flowers and chocolates? Gina should have dumped him there and then but when he started to run his fingers up and down her thigh and told her she was being silly, all thoughts of telling him to take a hike went straight out of her head.

"Gina? Are you listening to me?" Hannah looked in

frustration at the dreamy expression on her friend's face. She'd been trying to organise a girls' night out for weeks, and now that she'd finally managed to pry Gina away from Greg, she was sitting here like a lovesick teenager, in a world of her own.

"Course I am!" Gina looked offended.

"Yeah, right. Well, I'm really glad I flew all the way from London for such a riveting evening," Hannah said sarcastically. "You're great company. I just wish you'd let me get a word in edgeways!"

"Ah, don't be like that, Hannah. I've got a lot on my mind."

"And I don't?" Hannah said irritably.

"Yeah, you do too. But you and Fergal will come through this. You've always got back together in the past."

Hannah threw up her hands in frustration. "You see? You haven't been listening! We've split up, Gina. It's over. Kaput. Finished."

Gina looked startled. "Really?"

"Really." Hannah sighed and drank some more wine.

Gina dragged her mind away from Greg. This was serious. "And . . . how do you feel about it?"

Hannah shrugged. "Sad, I suppose. We've been together a long time. But it's been on the cards for a while now."

"Was it because he wanted you to move to Dublin?"

"That didn't help," Hannah admitted. "He never took my job seriously. It wasn't as important as his. In hindsight I see he was a major sexist."

"Fergal? No!"

"Oh, yes. He definitely thought a woman's place was in the kitchen or bedroom."

Gina couldn't believe it. Fergal had seemed the ideal millennium man. Supportive, understanding . . ." So how's he taking this?"

"Not well," Hannah said glumly, "but he'll get over it. No doubt he'll find someone who'd love to live in the shadow of a man. But it won't be Hannah Kennedy!"

Gina looked at her friend in admiration. She was so sure of what she wanted. And she didn't let anyone make a fool of her. *The way Greg's making a fool of you.* Gina sighed. If only she could be as strong. But once she let a man into her life all they had to do was say jump and she'd say how high? She was pathetic.

Hannah looked at her mournful expression. "So tell me all about it."

"About what?" Gina said innocently.

"About why your face is as long as a wet weekend. About why you look as if someone shot your dog. Come on. Out with it. Tell Aunty Hannah."

Gina sighed. "Oh, I don't know, Hannah. I suppose I'd just prefer it if Greg was a little more . . . a little less . . ." She shook her head in frustration.

"You want him to be totally nuts about you and completely oblivious to all other women?"

"Yes! That's it!"

"Don't hold your breath, honey."

"Now, why do you say that? He's got to fall in love with someone. Why shouldn't it be me?"

"Guys like Greg only fall in love with themselves," Hannah said dryly.

"You hardly know him!" Gina protested.

"I know the type. Oh, come on, Gina, you know he's not for you. I don't think you even want him. You just want him to want you."

"Now you're talking rubbish," Gina said hotly. "I was devastated when I heard about him and Marian."

"Only because you were disgusted that he was interested in another woman. Come on, Gina. Be honest with yourself. You always go for his type. Guys that treat you like dirt. Maybe there's a reason for that," she mused, almost to herself. "Maybe you don't actually *want* a serious relationship."

"Now you're being ridiculous," Gina scoffed. "I've been after a man since I could walk!"

"Well, you're after the wrong ones, then. Maybe I should set you up on a blind date. I'm sure I could pick the perfect guy for you."

"No way!"

"I could do better than you've done so far," Hannah assured her.

"Yeah, well, maybe. But I'm not giving up on Greg just yet. I can't, Hannah. I mean, he's gorgeous and he's great in bed and he's funny. If only . . ." she trailed away.

"He called when he said he would? Turned up on time?" Hannah finished for her.

"Something like that," Gina agreed miserably.

"What about Mike Ford?" Hannah asked lightly.

"What about him?"

"Have you been talking to him recently?"

"He called just before I went to Las Vegas. It's unbelievable. Any time he's phoned there's always been a reason why I can't meet him. I'm sure he thinks I'm just not interested."

"And are you?" Hannah watched her closely.

"Oh, I don't know, Hannah. He's a nice enough guy. Maybe that's the problem." Gina looked miserably into her wine glass. "Maybe he's just too nice for me."

"Umm. Maybe. I think he's kind of cute."

"Then you go out with him!"

Hannah smiled. "I might just do that."

"Oh shit, no!"

Hannah looked startled. "Well, if you don't want me to . . ."

"No not you! Over there. It's Mal's wife," Gina hissed.

Hannah looked over her shoulder at the dark-haired woman deep in conversation with a man at a corner table. "So?"

"Well, it's not Mal she's with, is it, idiot?!"

Hannah sat up and took another peek. "Don't jump to conclusions, Gina. I see. It might just be her brother, or cousin or something."

"Do you look at your brother like that?" Gina said caustically.

"Well, no, but even if he isn't related. There's nothing wrong with going out for a meal with another man. It could be completely innocent."

"Maybe you're right – oh my God!" Gina watched

horrified as Caroline slipped a stockinged foot out of her shoe and slid it up the man's leg.

"What? What?" Hannah urged.

Gina watched, mesmerised, as the man's hand came down to stroke Caroline's leg.

"Gina?" Hannah craned her head around to see what was going on. "Crikey!"

"The bitch," Gina hissed. "How could she? Poor Mal!"

"For God's sake, don't tell him."

"Why not? He deserves to know," Gina said stubbornly.

"He won't thank you," Hannah promised her. "I mean, what are you going to say? 'Mornin' Mal, nice day. Oh, by the way. I saw your wife canoodling with another man last night'?"

Gina glared at the couple. "But I hate to see her getting away with this."

"Maybe it's more innocent than it seems."

"Oh, come on! Look at them now! His tongue must be halfway down her throat! How can they carry on like that in public?"

"I still think you should keep your mouth shut. And if you go and tell Mal you'll have caused a lot of heartache for nothing."

Gina continued to watch the pair, who were completely oblivious to the world. "He's not even good-looking."

"He's a bit scruffy all right."

"And he's a lot older than Mal too. Silly cow. I never did like the woman. Mal would be better off without her."

"That's his decision, not yours. I'm telling you, Gina.

Keep your nose out if you know what's good for you."

"OK, OK. But I'm not letting her off the hook completely." Gina winked at her friend and strolled down the room towards the ladies' and right past Caroline's table. "Hi, Caroline," she said casually and kept walking.

Caroline jumped away from the man as if she'd been burned, her eyes widening in panic. "Eh, hi."

By the time Gina came out of the loo they had left.

"You've never seen anyone move so fast," Hannah told her with a chuckle.

"Which proves I'm right," Gina retorted.

"Maybe the scare of seeing you will be enough to make her come to her senses."

"Maybe," Gina said but somehow she doubted it.

"Oh, forget about her, Gina. Let's have some dessert. I'm in the mood for something disgustingly fattening."

* * *

"Susie, ye have to do something soon. There's arrangements to be made."

"Ah, Marie, leave me alone. Me back is aching and me eyes are closing in me head. I don't need ye hassling me too."

Marie looked at her worriedly. Susie did look terrible. Her face was very pale – it said it all that she hadn't even bothered to put any make-up on. "Maybe we should go up to the hospital. Let them have a look at ye."

"I'll be OK," Susie assured her and shoved another cushion behind her back. "I just need a rest."

Marie looked out the window. Pamela's BMW was outside. "How's Lady Muck?"

"Ah, she has me pestered. 'Come to tea, Susie. Have dinner with us, Susie. Would ye like me to massage yer feet for ye, Susie?'"

Marie laughed. "Ye big eejit, ye. Have ye caught her having any more midnight binges?" Susie had told Marie all about Pamela's strange behaviour.

"Nah, but then I keep clear of the place when she's there or if that oul biddy Irene's about." She winced in pain. The cushion wasn't helping at all.

"Are ye sure yer all right?"

"Yeah. Now go to work. Ye'll be late."

"Well, all right. But promise ye'll call me later."

"I will. Seeya."

"And Susie? Think about the adoption, won't ye? The longer ye leave it the harder it will be."

"Yeah, right. I will."

Marie patted her arm awkwardly and let herself out of the flat.

Susie stared absently at the TV. The more she thought about the baby the more confused she got. At night when the cramp in her leg kept her awake and she felt sorry for herself, she was sure that she wanted the baby adopted. She wanted to feel normal again. She wanted her body back – even if it was a shapeless lump of lard. But when she woke in the morning and felt him begin to stir inside her, she'd stroke her bump lovingly and talk to him. She'd tell him about his Aunty Marie, about his silly old granny, about his Aunty Trish who was young enough to be his playmate, about his uncles who'd teach him how to play football. She even told him about his cantankerous oul granda!

Susie sighed when she heard a tap on the door. No doubt that would be Doug. Him and Marie seemed to be running a bloody shift. She heaved herself up off the sofa.

Doug stood on the doorstep, a covered plate in his hand. "Irene thought you might fancy some shepherd's pie."

Susie looked at him in disbelief. "Is there crushed glass in it?"

Doug laughed. "Ah, now don't be like that. Irene isn't so bad."

"No?" Susie took the plate and stood back to let him in.

"No. She's just a bit nosy."

"If you say so," Susie said dryly. She hadn't told Doug about the digs and smart comments that Irene shot at her anytime they bumped into each other. Which Susie made sure wasn't often –

'Still here then? You've got a cosy little number and no mistake, dear.' The woman would give her a thin smile.

Or 'Poor Mr Hamilton isn't himself at all. Still, I'm sure he'll be better soon and then things will get back to normal around here.'

Meaning he'll send me packing, Susie interpreted. She wondered what Doug would think if she told him about these little gems. But she wouldn't. He'd enough on his plate trying to keep Pamela happy.

She took the lid off and sniffed appreciatively. She might

be a nasty oul one, but at least Irene could cook! Susie slid the plate into the microwave. "Do ye want some?"

"Already had two platefuls," Doug said cheerfully, sitting down at the kitchen table. "But I'd love a coffee. I saw Marie leave. How is she?"

"Driving me mad."

"Oh? Why is that?"

"She keeps trying to tell me what to do. Like someone else not a million miles from here."

"I don't know what you mean," he said, the picture of innocence.

"Course ye don't." She put a cup of instant in front of him and poured a glass of milk for herself. When she looked up, Doug was staring at her.

"What? What are ye staring at?"

"You look different."

Susie flushed. "No make-up," she mumbled, taking the plate from the microwave and sitting down opposite him.

"That's it!" He smiled broadly at her. "The natural look suits you."

Susie shot him a dirty look.

"No, honest. I mean it. You don't need all that stuff. You have a cute little nose and lovely eyes."

"Ah, go on." Susie shovelled some pie down her throat to cover her embarrassment.

Doug smiled. "And you're very pretty when you blush."

"Will ye shut up, for God's sake! I'm a mess. Now, if ye can't talk sense, go away and let me eat me dinner."

"There's a way to talk to your boss!"

"I'm not in work now," she said cheekily.

"All right, then. There's a way to talk to your landlord!"

She grinned. "OK. Ye've got me there."

Doug watched her eat. "So have you thought any more about it? The adoption?"

Susie threw down her fork. "Ah, for God's sake! Not again! Of course I bloody have! What do ye take me for?"

"Sorry," he said meekly.

Susie sighed. It was hard to be annoyed with the man. He'd been so nice to her. And it was great that he was so interested. "That's all right. But it's a bit much, Doug. You're pulling me one way, Marie's pulling me the other. It's driving me nuts."

"Sorry. That's exactly what we *didn't* want to do."

Susie's ears pricked up. "What's that? Have you two been discussing me?"

Doug sighed. He'd warned Marie to keep her mouth shut and now he'd let the cat out of the bag. "We're just worried about you," he said gently.

"Well, there's no need. I can take care of meself."

Doug looked at the defiant look in her eyes. Even after all these months she still got stroppy if she thought anyone was pitying her. "Ah, cut it out, Susie," he said, sounding irritated.

She gaped at him. "What?"

"You heard me! All your sister and I are trying to do is help. Look out for you. Now it's fine if you want to tell me to go away and mind my own business but that girl deserves nothing but your thanks. She's been great."

Susie sat looking down at her hands. "I suppose," she mumbled.

"There's no 'suppose' about it. She's been a great sister to you. It's about time you realised that."

"I do!"

"Right. Good. Well, I'll leave you to it." He stood up and headed for the door.

"Ah, Doug, don't go. I'm sorry."

He turned to look at her.

"Please? Sit down and finish your coffee." Her eyes pleaded with him.

"No," he said bluntly. "It's a bloody awful cup of coffee. But if you have a beer or a glass of wine I might be persuaded." He plonked himself back in the chair and grinned at her.

Susie looked at him suspiciously as she took a beer from the fridge. "You missed yer calling, ye know that? Ye should have been a bloody actor."

"Well, my mother always said I had the looks for the job," he agreed.

"That's not what I meant and ye know it."

"Oh, I think you did!"

Susie swiped him with the tea-towel. "Don't push it, boss!"

* * *

Pamela looked at the clock. It was over an hour since she'd watched Doug make his way across the drive to the flat. What on earth did he talk to the girl about? What was the attraction? *You know the attraction, Pamela,* a little voice inside reminded her. She poured herself a glass of wine. Just a small one. She'd been very careful of her alcohol intake since that dreadful night with Marjorie. She couldn't believe she'd let herself go like that and it was even more worrying that she still couldn't remember exactly what she'd said. She hadn't gone to her ballet class last week and had avoided Marjorie's calls. The woman would be positively triumphant that Pamela Lloyd-Hamilton had been a little worse for wear and revealed some family secrets. Pamela sipped her wine and wondered exactly what she *had* revealed. She remembered complaining about Doug and there had been something about Susie too. She put her drink down on the coffee-table. That's what came of losing control. It just wasn't worth it. At least – she took the glass up again – not in public. She looked at the clock and felt the tears start to prick the back of her eyes. How could Douglas prefer to sit over there with that little tart when she was here waiting for him? She remembered the evening they'd sat at this very table and had a cosy dinner. Then she remembered how the evening had ended and drained her glass. She refilled it before going out to the kitchen to check out the fridge.

Chapter Thirty-two

"Are we going out or not?" Gina finally asked.

"Oh! Great goal! What?" Greg didn't turn around. "Yeah, in a while. This is nearly over. Come and sit down."

Gina sighed, brushed some crisps off the sofa and sat down beside him. She watched irritably as he absent-mindedly kicked the coffee-table, and wondered why she was still going out with him. She knew she should finish it, but she always lost courage at the last minute. And what with her end-of-course exams and everything she just hadn't got a chance. It wasn't as if she saw that much of him outside of work. Greg seemed to live a very busy life. The bastard was probably screwing half the women in town!

They were supposed to be going out for a meal tonight but when she'd arrived he was sitting watching the match in a pair of dirty jeans and a moth-eaten jumper that even her dad wouldn't be seen dead in. She watched him raise the can to his lips – those gorgeous lips – and realised that she was able to look at him completely objectively now. He was like a gorgeous, spoilt little boy. And he would never grow up. Even the sex wasn't as good anymore. Oh, his technique was as good as ever but that was the problem. It was all technique with Greg. There was no love, no romance. Just sex. And Gina wanted more. She stood up.

"Oh, get me another can while you're up, will you, Gee?"

And she hated it when he called her Gee. "Get it yourself." She pulled on her jacket.

"What? Where are you going?" He asked, his eyes still on the screen.

"Home."

He looked up at her. "Oh, come on, hon. Don't get all narky on me."

"I'm not," she said, through gritted teeth. He always made it look as if she was the one being childish. Huh! That was a laugh! She walked to the door.

"OK, then. If you're going to be like that. I'll call you." He turned back to the match.

"Don't bother, Greg!"

"You see! You are narky!" He grinned triumphantly and jumped up out of the chair. "OK. You win. I'll get my coat."

Gina took a deep breath and looked him straight in the eye. "There's no need, Greg. I don't want to go out with you. Not tonight. Not tomorrow night, not even next week. It's time we called it a day."

Greg looked mystified. He crossed the room and

cupped her face in his hands. "But we're having fun, sweetheart. Aren't we?" He bent his head and kissed her.

Gina didn't respond.

He pulled back and looked into her face. "So that's it?" he said with a sad smile.

"Yeah, Greg, that's it. But it's been fun. See you at work." And she walked out of his flat, closing the door firmly behind her.

She was shaking as she stumbled out to the car. Now that was worthy of Hannah! Cool, calm, controlled. *Good girl, Gina. Nice one!* It would have been better if Greg had run after her and begged her to stay. Grovelled at her feet. But that was never going to happen. And she wasn't going to hang around waiting. She'd wasted enough time on the guy. She started the car and swung out on to the road, a smile breaking on her face. She wondered if anyone would still be in the pub. She felt like celebrating. Celebrating the new Gina. Bye-bye doormat, hello to the new, cool, sophisticated model. Hannah would be so proud of her. OK, it had taken her a few weeks to finally end it but she'd done it now. *She'd* done it. *She'd* dumped Greg Hamilton. God, it felt good!

"Another drink, Susie?"

"Ah, no thanks, Mal. There's only so much of this stuff I can take." She took another sip of her non-alcoholic beer and dreamed of the day when she'd be able to order a bacardi and coke. A large one.

"What about you, Doug?"

"Yeah, thanks, Mal." Doug knew he'd had more than enough already but what the hell?

"Jack?"

Jack gave him the thumbs up. "Cheers, mate. Same again."

Mal beamed at them all and headed for the bar.

"He's really chuffed with himself, isn't he?" Susie said.

"Yeah. Good luck to him. Mal's the best," Jack replied.

"He is," Doug agreed. "Where's Gina tonight?"

"Probably out with your brother," Jack said grimly.

Doug grinned. "Jealous, Jack?"

"'Course not! I'm going for a leak."

"I think ye touched a raw nerve there," Susie said as he strode off, shoulders hunched.

"Don't I know it. He's had a crush on Gina for as long as I can remember. I don't know why he's never done anything about it."

"Do ye think Gina and Greg are serious?" Susie hoped not, for Gina's sake. Greg might be Doug's brother but he was still a scumbag.

"I don't think Greg is serious about anything or anyone."

"Poor Gina. Still, he finishes up next week, doesn't he? Maybe out of sight will be out of mind."

"Let's hope so." Doug sighed. Greg leaving meant his return to work. And he wasn't at all sure he wanted to.

Mal arrived back with the drinks. "Here we are. Sure I can't get you something, Susie?"

"No, yer all right, Mal. Thanks."

Mal noticed her rubbing the small of her back. "Hang in there, kid. It won't be long now. When's the big day?"

"Six weeks," Susie said with a weak smile.

"Nervous?"

"A bit." She liked the way Mal talked to her about her pregnancy. It wasn't the way that Doug and Marie did. It was, well, normal. He talked to her about her blood pressure and the cramps that attacked at night – Caroline had got them too – and he told her about the birth in a funny way so it didn't seem quite as frightening.

"The nurses were more worried about me than Caroline. I was positively grey. Finally one said to me: 'If you're going to faint do it over there. I don't want to be tripping over you!'"

Susie had laughed. As usual Mal had made her feel like every other pregnant woman. Not a single girl, having a baby alone and planning to give it away. That's why she often drifted towards him in the pub. For a start it got her away from Doug. He couldn't seem to talk about anything else these days. Gina was OK too. She hardly ever mentioned the baby. But then she was so caught up in her love life she didn't have time. And Jack was grand.

He treated her like a piece of her mother's china. "Are you too hot? Would you like me to open a window?" when they were in work. "Can I get you something at the shops?" At lunchtime when she was too tired to go as far as the door. And "Is the smoke bothering you?" he'd ask five minutes after they got into the pub. Yeah,

Jack was great. Gina must be blind. Susie would be chuffed if a fine thing like Jack fancied *her.*

"What's going on here? No one told me there was a party." Gina flopped down beside Susie. "Your round, is it, Jack? I'll have a beer, thanks very much."

Jack grinned. So she wasn't out with Lover Boy after all. "I'm on my way."

"Howaya, Gina. I thought ye were going out with Greg tonight." Susie moved her coat to give Gina more room.

"Thanks. No, there was a change of plan. I'll fill you in later," she murmured before smiling over at Doug. "So what's going on? And what on earth are you doing here, Mal? Like it's a bit sad on your day off. Have you nothing better to do?"

"He came in to share his good news," Doug said.

"Oh yes?" Gina looked at him. Doug looked as if he'd been boozing for hours. His eyes were glassy and his cheeks were flushed.

"Caroline's pregnant," Mal told her proudly.

Gina's eyes widened. "You're kidding?" She took the lager Jack was holding out to her and took a large gulp.

"No. She told me today. Cheers," he said, oblivious to the shocked look on Gina's face.

Susie nudged Gina hard. "Well, aren't ye going to congratulate him?"

"Yeah, yes, of course. Congrats, Mal." She stood up to hug him. "I'm really delighted for you."

"Thanks, Gina."

"Would I be imagining things or were you a little less

411

than enthusiastic in your congratulations?" Doug asked her later.

Gina looked aound nervously but the others were deep in conversation. "Oh, Doug, It's terrible!"

"What is?"

"Poor, Mal. It's not fair."

Doug pulled her into a corner. "Gina, for God's sake, what is it?"

She took a deep breath. "A few weeks ago, Hannah and I were in *Pasta Pasta* and we saw Caroline."

"Yes?"

"She was with a guy, Doug."

"Oh, well, maybe . . ."

Gina held up her hand. "No, don't. Don't tell me it might have been innocent. I know what I saw."

"Bloody hell!"

"Do you think I should tell him?"

"No! God, no! He'd be destroyed."

"But that baby might be . . ."

Doug groaned. "It doesn't bear thinking about."

"Hey, you two, what are you looking so serious about? This is a celebration!" Mal staggered over and put an arm around each of them. "I'm so happy, guys. So happy."

Gina met Doug's eyes. "We're happy for you too, Mal."

"So what's the story about Greg?" Susie asked when she finally got Gina alone.

"I dumped him."

"Ye didn't?" Susie looked at her amazed.

Gina grinned. "I did. Oh, Susie, it was brilliant!"

"I'm delighted for ye."

"You never liked him either, did you?"

Susie shook her head. "Well, it's hard to like someone that treats ye like dirt. *And* he tried to make out that I'd stolen that money."

"Well, everyone knows now that you didn't," Gina said reassuringly. " Oh, I'm sorry, Susie. I didn't realise he bothered you so much. You always seem to handle things so well."

Susie shrugged. "I can deal with his kind but it doesn't mean I like it. But Jack always stuck up for me. And Mal too."

"Poor Mal," Gina said.

Susie frowned. "Why 'poor Mal'? He's going to be a da again. He's delighted."

"But *is* he the father?" Gina muttered, her tongue loosened by four lagers.

Susie put down her drink. "What are ye saying, Gina?"

Gina shook her head. "Nothing. Don't mind me. I shouldn't have said anything."

"Ah, come on! Ye can't say something like that and leave me hangin'. Ye said 'Is he the father?' Are ye saying he mightn't be? That the wife's playing around?"

Gina studied her hands.

"Ah, no, that's it, isn't it? She's putting it about. Isn't she, Gina?"

Gina glanced over at Mal and nodded. "But for God's sake don't tell anyone."

"I won't tell a soul," Susie promised. "The cow! I never did take to her."

"Me neither. She always had airs and graces. I don't know why. She was brought up in a corporation scheme."

"And what's wrong with that?" Susie pretended to be annoyed.

"Nothing, but it obviously bothers her. She tells everyone she's from Chapelizod when she's really from Ballyfermot."

"Silly bitch."

"Who?" Mal appeared beside them. "Who's a silly bish?"

"Pamela, of course," Susie said quickly.

"Ah, she's not so bad." He swayed precariously. "I love everybody tonight, girls. I'm going to be a daddy again!"

They watched him weave his way back to the lads.

"God, that was close," Gina said with a sigh of relief.

"He's too pissed to hear anything at the moment," Susie assured her.

"You're right. Maybe it's time we put him in a taxi."

Susie yawned. "Well, I'm going home anyway. I wonder if Doug's ready to leave." She wandered off leaving Gina looking puzzled.

"So what were you and Susie whispering about?" Jack asked.

Gina shrugged. "Ah, nothing much."

"Go away out of that. The two of you were very serious altogether. What's going on?"

"Seeya, everybody. Thanks for everything!" Mal waved vaguely around him and nearly fell over a stool.

Doug caught hold of him. "Come on, mate. I'll give you a hand."

Mal laughed. "Ah, sure you're not much better than me!"

"Well, then, we'll hold each other up then."

Gina waited until they were out the door before turning back to Jack. "I'll tell you but you've got to promise to keep your mouth shut."

Jack held his hand up. "Scout's honour."

It was half an hour later before Susie and Doug climbed into a taxi. They could easily have walked but Doug insisted it was too far for her and, given the pain in her back, she didn't put up much of a fight. For a change.

"Poor Mal," Susie said

"Why?" Doug asked innocently.

"It's OK, Doug. I know. Gina told me."

"Ah, for God's sake! I told her to keep her mouth shut."

"Don't blame Gina," she said loyally. "I kind of wheedled it out of her."

"Well, don't tell anyone else."

"Of course not! But don't you think someone should tell him?"

"No, I do not," Doug said emphatically.

"But he has a right to know . . ."

"Susie, I'm warning you. You're the very one who complains about me and Marie interfering in *your* life."

"That's different," she said stubbornly.

"Please leave it," Doug said wearily. He had too much alcohol inside him to deal with this now.

"OK." Susie stared out the window. *But it's not fair. He's so nice. Someone should tell him the truth. He shouldn't be stuck with another man's child.* "Poor Mal."

"I can't believe it," Jack said as he walked Gina to her car.

"It's true. I saw them with my own eyes. They were all over each other! And in the middle of a restaurant."

"Bloody hell! She must have been sick as a parrot when she saw you."

"I damn well hope so. Hannah said they practically ran out of the restaurant." She stopped to get her coat and brolly out of her car . "Sorry little car. Got to leave you here again or Mister Policeman will fight with me."

Jack took her arm and steered her towards the taxi-rank. "You're losing it, Barrett."

"Ah, leave me alone. I have to have something to love."

"What about gorgeous Greg?" Jack tried to sound casual.

"Oh, that's over."

"Yeah? Sorry to hear that." *Yes! Yes! Yes!*

"Are you?" Gina looked at him from under her lashes.

"No, not really. He's a complete asshole."

She giggled. "He is a bit."

Jack smiled happily. "Well, I'm glad you've come to your senses at last."

"By the way. Why did Doug and Susie share a taxi?"

"'Cos she lives with him."

Gina stopped dead in her tracks and stared at him. "What!?"

"Oh, not *with* him. He's letting her use the flat at The Sycamores."

"Susie never told me! How come you know?"

"I overheard them talking but I think it's all a bit hush-hush."

"How the hell did he get Pamela to agree to that?"

"God knows."

"Crikey. There's a turn-up for the books."

"Don't say anything, Gina," he warned her. "If they'd wanted us to know they'd have told us, so keep your mouth shut."

"That goes for you too," Gina retorted. "Don't go telling anyone about Caroline."

"Of course I won't! Poor Mal."

Chapter Thirty-three

It was just after ten on Sunday morning, when Pamela walked into the kitchen. As she'd hoped, she had the place to herself. Douglas was probably out for his walk – he did at least five miles a day now – and Susie rarely came near the house when he wasn't there. Pamela was glad to have some time alone. When Douglas was here he could hardly go for ten minutes without mentioning Susie Clarke or that damn baby. Pamela wasn't sure how much more of it she could take. She took the orange juice out of the fridge and put on a large pot of coffee. When she'd poured the juice and found her china mug she settled down to read the papers that Doug had left strewn across the table.

She flicked quickly through the news and business pages pausing only to collect the coffee pot and her vitamins and then she turned to savour the social columns. Thanks to Douglas she hadn't appeared in any of them for a while. He still refused most of their invitations, only attending functions that would help the business. They'd missed some important social events but there was no way Pamela would go alone. That would give rise to all sorts of unsavoury and speculative gossip. She sighed as she studied pictures of some of her acquaintances at a recent charity lunch. She missed going to these things and being the centre of attention. She was always photographed and she loved to listen to all the bitchy gossip – which politician had recently been spotted in a gay night club in drag – what lady had pawned all her jewellery to pay off her gambling debts and was now wearing paste imitations. Pamela reached for one of the tabloids and flicked until she found the most vicious columnist of them all. Her favourite. There was always a blend of truth and fiction and she liked trying to guess which was which. Not a difficult task as she knew most of the people concerned. Douglas despised these columns and laughed at her for reading them. When they were out, he steered clear of the social journalists and their photographers, much to Pamela's concern.

"You have to play along, dear. It's expected," she'd often said to him. "If they ever get anything on you they'll show no mercy."

Douglas just laughed. "Let them do their worst. I've no time for that kind of journalism. I'm sure they make most of the stuff up."

"Not always, darling. Remember Jeremy." Jeremy Hally had been a well respected solicitor until a gossip columnist hinted that he had a penchant for child pornography. Pamela had been present at a function in

The Westbury when his wife, after imbibing of the free punch, slapped him in the face and hurled abuse at him. They'd separated soon after and he'd left the country.

Pamela relaxed, sipped her coffee and drank in all the articles until a small piece at the bottom of the page caught her eye.

Which major name in the world of conference management and husband of Dublin 4 socialite has not only played away but brought home the prize too! Rumour has it that he's soon to be a father, and the mother of his child has taken up residence in the family home. Now isn't that cosy! My mother always used to say 'you should never do it on your own doorstep'. Probably a bit late for that piece of advice! Tut-tut!

Pamela dropped the paper and the pages fluttered to the floor. "Oh my God!" How and where had this story surfaced? Even the CML staff didn't know Susie was staying with them – Douglas had promised her that. But maybe someone had spotted Susie coming and going and put two and two together and come up with five. Could it be Irene? Would their trusty housekeeper do such a thing? Pamela dismissed the possibility almost as soon as it entered her head. They paid her too well. She'd never risk losing this job. So who could have done it? Who had access to this kind of information? She paced the room wringing her hands anxiously. How on earth could such a story have come about unless . . .

She sank down into the nearest chair, not trusting her legs. "Marjorie," she breathed. That dreadful night. She couldn't remember quite what she'd said but Susie had definitely come into it. Oh, God, this was awful! It meant the story had come from a reliable source and it was only a matter of time before the other papers took it up and dug even deeper. She rocked back and forward on the chair. Her palms were clammy and her mouth dry. She paused every so often to re-read the piece. Maybe people wouldn't realise it was them . . . "Don't be ridiculous you stupid, stupid, woman! Who else could it be?" She jumped up and resumed her pacing, pummelling her fist into her hand. It would be clear to everyone – well everyone that mattered – that the article was about Douglas. She wondered had he seen it – but of course he wouldn't have. He never read these pages. She'd have to tell him. She jumped as the front door banged.

Doug strode into the kitchen, picked up a mug and helped himself to coffee. "Morning. Did you see the news?"

Pamela gripped the edge of a chair for support. "News?"

Doug smacked the front page of the *Independent.* "This! They're talking about increasing the VAT rate. Bloody ridiculous! Bloody government must be giving themselves another pay rise. The next time I see Bert – "

"Stop, Douglas, please. There's something I have to tell you."

Doug looked at her white, pinched expression and put the paper down. "What is it, love? What's wrong?"

Pamela swallowed hard. She couldn't remember the last time he'd called her 'love'. "I'm afraid there's another piece of news in the paper that concerns us."

Doug picked up *The Independent* again.

"No, not in there." She picked up the tabloid and handed it to him. "In here."

"Oh, Pamela, you know I'm not interested in this rubbish!"

"Douglas, please! Just read it. The boxed piece at the end."

She walked to the window and stood looking out at the garden. The autumn wind was whipping the russet leaves around like snowflakes. They looked as if they were dancing, she thought idly. She wrung her hands and waited for the explosion. And she hadn't told him the worst of it yet. Or maybe he didn't need to know . . .

Her thoughts were interrupted by a loud guffaw from her husband.

"Is this what's bothering you? Oh, for goodness sake, Pamela!"

"But – but they're ruining your good name. *Our* name. I'll be a laughing stock. We won't be able to show our faces . . ."

"Oh, don't be so bloody melodramatic!"

"Well, shouldn't we sue or something? For defamation of character or libel or something?"

"That would only make things worse. It would just draw more attention to us. Better just to let the whole thing blow over. Mind you, Susie's not going to be impressed. Me the father of her child!" He laughed again.

Pamela looked at him, astounded. "Is that all you're worried about? What Susie thinks?"

"She *is* the one that's being vilified. And me."

"And what about me?"

"You come off as the injured party. What are you worried about?"

"I come off as the fool! Honestly, Douglas. Sometimes I think you've lost your mind! How can I hold my head up in public after this?"

"Oh, stop overreacting, Pamela, and have another coffee." He pushed the pot towards her and picked up the article again. "I'd love to know how they got hold of this."

Pamela said nothing.

Doug looked at her bent head and noticed she was nibbling on a nail. A habit she'd broken years ago. He sighed. "Pamela? Is there something else?"

She glanced at him from under her lashes. There was no point in trying to keep it from him. He was bound to hear something sooner or later. One of their 'dear friends' would make sure of it. "It may have been something I said to Marjorie."

Doug gave a wry smile. "*May* have?"

"We went for a drink one evening after dance class. I had a bit more than usual and I told her that we weren't getting on very well."

"Go on," Doug said quietly, his eyes not leaving her face.

"Well, I know I mentioned Susie in less than flattering terms but . . ."

"But you can't remember exactly what you said," he finished for her.

"No," she admitted.

"You must have had quite a skinful."

"It's not like I do it that often," she retorted.

"Thank God for that. Well, we can safely assume that whatever you said Marjorie passed on to everyone we know."

"But I can't believe she'd tell the press."

"I'm sure she didn't. But somewhere along the line someone else did. The only thing we can do is brazen it out." He went out to the hall and came back with the phone.

"Who are you calling?"

"My mother," he said as he punched in the number.

"Your mother? What on earth for!"

He held up his hand. "Mother? Hi, how are you? Good. Listen, get your glad rags on – we're taking you to lunch. No, I'll explain everything later. Pick you up about twelve-thirty? Good. See you then."

Pamela stared at him. "We're in the middle of a crisis and you want to bring your mother out to lunch. Where are we going? The local chip-shop?" she asked sarcastically.

"No, The Herbert Park." He replied as he dialled their number. "Hello? Yes, Douglas Hamilton here. Could I book a table for three for lunch at one o'clock? Lovely. Thank you. Goodbye."

"Are you mad? Half of our friends will be there!"

"Which is exactly why we're going."

"No, we're bloody not! You can take your mother. I'm staying here." She turned on her heel and headed for the door but Doug was there before her.

"Now, listen to me, Pamela," he said, holding her firmly by the shoulders. "You are going to do exactly as I say. Do you understand?"

Pamela said nothing. He had that look in his eye. The one that said 'don't mess with me'.

"Now go upstairs and put on your most expensive, eye-catching outfit and be sure to pile on the war paint — you're a bit pale — and the jewellery. You're going to walk in there on my arm with your head held high and you're going to laugh and chat and act as if nothing has happened."

Doug felt a moment of pity. She looked positively distraught. It didn't bother him what people thought of him but it meant a great deal to Pamela. "Come on, honey. It's going to be fine. Trust me. When our friends see us behaving normally, Mother in tow, they'll dismiss the whole thing as rubbish."

"You'd better be right," she said coldly. "I'll kill you if this is a disaster."

"Let's not forget who got us into this mess," Doug reminded her quietly.

She pushed past him and went upstairs.

Doug sighed. This was all a bit embarrassing but the thoughts of the drama ahead had got his adrenaline going. And it would take his mind off Mal.

He was amazed at how jealous he'd felt when he'd heard Mal was going to be a father again. But when Gina told him about Caroline's antics all he felt was pity for the man. He wondered if Mal would stand by her if he knew about the affair. And if he did, would he look at the child growing up and wonder? Doug wasn't sure how he'd react in the same position. His first instinct would be to throw her out – which he realised was pretty hypocritical given his track record. But this was different. There was a child involved. Quite possibly another man's child. And then there was the other kid to think about. Mal was probably better off in ignorance. The fact that Caroline had told him she was pregnant suggested she intended to stay with him. Maybe the baby *was* his. Maybe Gina had got it all wrong. Or maybe Caroline had called a halt before it went too far.

"Maybe, maybe, maybe," Doug muttered to himself as he followed Pamela upstairs. It was time he got into costume too. He put on his best suit, a flashy silk tie and a yellow shirt. And after splashing on some aftershave he smiled at himself in the mirror. "Let the play begin."

"Mr Hamilton! Good to see you again."

"Hello, David. How are you?" Doug said loudly as they walked through the reception of The Herbert Park Hotel.

"Fine, thank you. Are you joining us for lunch today?"

"We are indeed."

"Then why don't you take a seat in the lounge and I'll send in some menus?"

"Thank you." Doug stood back and let Pamela and Sheila precede him. "And, David?" he said when they were out of earshot. "A nice . . . prominent table, if you know what I mean."

The other man gave a discreet nod. "Consider it done."

"G &T's all round?" Doug asked as he joined the ladies.

Pamela merely nodded.

"A dry sherry for me, darling," his mother replied before turning her attention to Pamela. The poor girl looked positively terrified. "You're looking very lovely today, my dear. That colour really suits you. Maroon, isn't it?"

"Mulberry," Pamela murmured.

"Lovely." Sheila smiled encouragingly. She felt quite sorry for her daughter-in-law. She had been very silly but getting trashed by the tabloids was a high price to pay for such a minor indiscretion.

Douglas beamed from one to the other. "I'm a lucky man to be having lunch with two such beautiful women."

Pamela took her drink from the waiter and drained half of it.

"Take it easy, darling," Doug murmured. "We don't want any slip-ups, do we?"

Pamela glowered at him and took another gulp.

"You'd better start looking a bit more cheerful or everyone's going to believe that story." Doug was smiling, but his voice was steely.

"Sorry, darling." Pamela said with a false smile.

"That's better," Sheila said cheerfully. "I'm sure it will

be all forgotten in a couple of days, Pamela. You mustn't let it get you down. It's that poor little girl I feel sorry for."

Pamela sighed. Great! Another one to add to Susie's fan club! "Yes, poor girl," she said flatly.

Doug looked up sharply, but she smiled innocently back at him. "OK, darling?"

He smiled back. "Fine, darling."

Sheila looked at them and wondered how their marriage had lasted this long.

"Pamela! Douglas! What a lovely surprise!"

Doug rose to his feet. "Anna! How lovely to see you." He kissed her cheek. "You look lovely. Jeff, good to see you." Doug shook the man's hand firmly.

Pamela stood up to exchange kisses. "Hello, darlings, how are you?"

"Fine, Pamela, and may I say how gorgeous you're looking today?"

Pamela gave a tinkly laugh. "You may, but your wife might not approve! Have you met Sheila Hamilton, Douglas's mother?"

"No! Pleased to meet you, Mrs Hamilton." Jeff shook her hand. "You don't look old enough to be Doug's mother."

"Now *you* I like," Sheila replied and they all laughed.

"Let me get you a drink," Doug said, drawing up more chairs. "In fact, I have an even better idea. Why don't you join us for lunch?"

Pamela stared at him.

"What a marvellous idea!" Anna sat down immediately.

"And you can tell me all your news, Pamela. I haven't seen you in ages."

"Lovely," Pamela said, her face pale beneath the make-up.

"Marjorie was saying you've missed your dance classes the last couple of weeks," Anna said casually.

Pamela looked dumbstruck.

Doug came to her rescue. "The poor darling's had the most awful flu. But of course she still insisted on going into work. An amazing lady, my wife." He leaned over and kissed Pamela's cheek.

Pamela gave him a grateful smile. "It was only a cold. But I did feel too tired for class. It's so energetic. You should try it some time, Anna. I'm sure you'd get a lot out of it. " She smiled at the woman, her eyes flickering to the skirt that fitted just a little too snugly around her hips.

Doug suppressed a grin at the outraged expression on Anna's face. He could relax now. Pamela was back on form.

"Why the hell did you ask them to join us?" Pamela hissed as they walked back to the car.

Doug smiled. "What's wrong with you? It couldn't have worked out better. It showed them and everyone in the room that we weren't bothered by that piece of garbage. And with the way Anna gossips, everyone else will have heard about this in less than twenty-four hours."

"I did think it went rather well," Sheila agreed gently.

"Well, my nerves are shattered and I've the most awful headache. Drop me home first. I need to lie down."

Doug looked apologetically at his mother.

"You still have to apologise to Susie," he said when they were in the car.

"Apologise? Have you taken leave of your senses?"

"You've tarnished the reputation of an innocent young girl. It's the least you can do," he said, barely managing to keep his temper in check. His mother didn't need to listen to all this.

"If she was so innocent she wouldn't be in the state she's in now!" Pamela retorted.

Doug pulled up outside the hall door with a screech of brakes. "That's enough, Pamela! We'll talk later."

"Goodbye, Sheila." Pamela gave her mother-in-law a grim smile, glared at her husband and slammed the door after her.

"Sorry, mother," Doug said, his voice tired as he drove on towards Ranelagh.

"There's no need to apologise to me, dear. I'm your mother. But you're right. Someone has to apologise to that poor girl."

"Yeah." Doug thought briefly about going to the pub after he'd dropped his mother home. Facing Susie was not going to be fun.

Chapter Thirty-four

Susie looked down at the newspaper spread out on the coffee-table. Pamela would do her nut when she saw this.

"God, I hope she doesn't think it's true!" Susie said aloud. "She couldn't. Me and Doug? No way!" She laughed at the thought and felt a bit better. But what would her ma and da think? Or would they realise it was her? Marie would know but she wouldn't believe it. And she wouldn't say anything. She knew how to keep her mouth shut. And what about Mal and Jack and Susie? They'd definitely think it was weird that she'd been living at The Sycamores and said nothing. She groaned as she imagined Noreen's reaction. She'd be horrified to think of her saintly lord and master shacked up with the likes of Susie. Though Susie doubted Noreen read the *Society Secrets* column.

This would mean Pamela would want her out of the flat immediately. And she doubted if even Doug would be able to save her this time. And ye couldn't really blame Pamela. It must be awful. Knowing that everyone thinks your husband's been messing around. Getting pitying looks – Susie knew all about them – and everyone gossiping behind yer back. They'd be talking about Susie too, but she was a nobody. They'd be wondering about the girl Doug got pregnant. They wouldn't know her name and they wouldn't care. Once she wasn't from their circle. And if anyone ever saw them side-by-side they'd know in a second that the rumours weren't true. Even though he was old enough to be her father, no one would ever believe that Doug would be interested in someone like her. She let her head fall back on the cushion and wondered if any man would ever be interested in her again. Interested in something more than a quick romp in the back of a car.

"Susie? Susie are you in there?"

Susie opened her eyes.

"Susie? It's Doug! Are you all right?"

Susie pulled herself up off the sofa and groaned at the crick in her neck. "Coming," she called and stumbled towards the door.

"Hi," she said rubbing her eyes.

"God, I was worried about you!"

"I fell asleep."

Doug followed her back into the living-room. "Sorry for waking you but I have to talk to you."

She noticed the strained look on his face. "Ye've seen it then?"

Doug looked at the newspaper on the table and sighed. "I was coming to tell you about it. I'm so sorry, Susie."

"Ah, sure it's not yer fault." She sat down and gestured for him to do the same.

Doug stood awkwardly in front of her. "No."

"How's Pamela taking it?"

"She's upset. Hasn't she been over to see you?"

Susie laughed. "God, no."

Doug sat down. "Well, she should have. Look, Susie, there's something you don't know."

Her smile faded at the serious look on his face. "What?"

"It's Pamela's fault that this charming little piece appeared in the paper."

"What? Sure, how could it be?"

"She had a few drinks too many with a friend one night and she was moaning about me. Unfortunately she also seems to have mentioned you and the fact that you're pregnant."

Susie stared at him, trying to take in what he was saying. "But she doesn't think you and me . . ."

"No, of course not," he said hastily.

"And if she was only letting off steam to a friend. Sure we all do that."

Doug laughed. "Well, our friends aren't really 'friends', if you know what I mean. The woman in question isn't a bad sort but she's a bit of a gossip. And Pamela. Well, Pamela is news," he said, slightly embarrassed. "She's always appearing in these kinds of columns but for the right reasons. It's a newspaper's dream to get something on one of their whiter-than-white socialites."

"But she didn't *do* anything."

"No, but something was done *to* her and that's news."

Susie sighed. She should be annoyed with Pamela but she kind of felt sorry for her. Imagine telling your most personal problems to someone who wasn't even a real friend. "So, what do we do now?"

Doug sat down, relieved she was taking it so well. "Nothing."

Susie stared at him. "But shouldn't we put people straight? They think I'm yer bit on the side. That I'm having yer baby!"

"Not that many people will realise it's us," he lied.

"Everyone in work will know! The companies ye do business with will know."

Doug looked at her helplessly. He could get his solicitor to force an apology from the paper but that would just draw more attention to them. "I'm not sure there's anything I can do, Susie."

"Then I'll have to move out," she said firmly.

"There's no need for that . . ."

"Of course there is!" Susie stood up with difficulty and started to pace, rubbing the small of her back. The pain seemed to get worse every day. "What are the gang in work going to think? We kept it a secret that I was staying at yer house so that looks funny for a start. And it's no secret that you and Pamela aren't exactly hitting it off lately."

"They're our friends, Susie," Doug said gently. "They'll believe what we tell them. And Malcolm knew you were staying here. I told him ages ago."

"Really?" Susie leaned heavily against the window-sill, trying to get some relief from the pain.

"Yes, and he knows there's nothing funny going on. He gave me quite a lecture too."

Susie looked at him curiously. "What about?"

Doug reddened. "He wanted to make sure my intentions were strictly honourable."

Susie giggled.

Doug smiled. "He's very fond of you, Susie. In fact everyone is. You've become a part of the team."

Susie felt a warm glow spread through her. Part of the team. She'd never been a part of anything before. Never even had any close friends. There was a gang she used to go drinking and dancing with, but they were only out for a bit of *craic*. Nothing serious. It was weird that the people she'd thought were from a different world now saw her as one of them. Weird but nice.

"Noreen and Greg don't think that." They still treated her like shit but she wouldn't say as much to Doug.

Doug sighed. "Noreen is . . . set in her ways."

"A snob ye mean," she retorted.

He gave an embarrassed smile. "Maybe. And as for Greg. I'm sorry if he's been unfriendly. He doesn't always take the time to get to know people."

Susie said nothing. Greg was his brother after all. She wouldn't like it if he slagged off Marie.

"So what do you say? Will we just ride this out? Keep our heads down?"

"What does Pamela think?"

"She feels the same as you."

"Then maybe the three of us should be making the decision." She put on her slippers and threw a heavy cardigan around her shoulders. "Let's go."

Doug looked alarmed. "Now?"

"Well, we need to agree what we're going to say. I mean we're all in work tomorrow. We have to get our story straight."

"I suppose we do," Doug agreed, surprised at the way she was taking control of the situation.

"Right then." Susie led the way across to the main house, letting herself into the kitchen.

Doug shut the door on the cold winter's evening. "She's probably lying down. She had a headache. I'll go get her. Why don't you help yourself to some of the chocolate cake in the fridge?"

Susie put on some coffee and boiled a kettle to make tea. Then she went to the fridge but there was no chocolate cake. *No prizes for guessing what happened to that.* She wondered if Pamela had one of those eating diseases. She certainly seemed to do all her eating alone. She only ever seemed to nibble her food when anyone else was around. Susie was beginning to think she'd imagined that crazy night when Pamela was stuffing her face and drinking like a fish.

Doug came back down. "She's just coming," he said but his face was grim. "So, where's the cake?"

"There isn't any."

"Of course there is!" Doug went to the fridge. "That's strange."

Susie sighed. Didn't he have any idea? How could ye

live in the same house as someone and not know what they were up to? Susie was wondering if she should say something when Pamela walked in.

"I hope you've made some tea. My head is positively hopping."

"That's what you get for drinking on an empty stomach," Doug said coldly.

"What else do you expect?" she retorted. "Making me sit through lunch as if everything was rosy in the garden! I've never been so stressed."

"Where's the damn cake?" Doug asked, still staring into the fridge.

Pamela's eyes flickered from him to Susie. "I threw it out. The cream had gone sour."

"It was fine this morning," he said evenly.

"Are you calling me a liar?" she said her voice shrill.

"Of course not!" Doug got some biscuits instead and sat down. It was best not to hypothesise on what had happened to the cake. There was enough to deal with at the moment.

Pamela poured herself some tea, ignoring the empty cup in front of Susie. "So what is this about?"

Doug glared at her and poured Susie a cup. "You know what it's about, Pamela. That damn article. Susie has pointed out, quite rightly, that we have to face the people in work tomorrow and that we should be giving the same response to any questions."

"If any of my staff question me about my personal life, they'll be told to mind their own business!" Pamela retorted.

"Which would definitely fuel the speculation that there's some substance to the story. Is that what you want?"

Pamela stared into her cup. "What do you suggest?" she asked finally.

Doug took a deep breath. "I suggest that we all go into work in the same car. That we smile broadly as we walk through the door. And have a staff lunch in somewhere like Roly's."

Susie looked at him in admiration. That would definitely kill the story. Well, it would if . . .

"My God, that's your answer to everything, isn't it? There's a recession, let's have a party. The company's going under, let's have a drink and forget about it. Everyone thinks I'm having a fling, let's do lunch! You make me sick!"

Doug recoiled at the look of hatred on her face. " I just want to show the staff and anyone else that knows us that we are one big happy family. And that my only interest in Susie is as an employee and a tenant."

"Tenants pay for their accommodation," Pamela pointed out.

Doug jumped up, knocking his chair to the ground. "Enough! Do you hear me? I've had enough of your smart comments, Pamela!"

She jumped as he shoved his face into hers.

"Do I have to remind you yet again who got us into this mess?"

"You did! The day you brought *her* into this house!" she screamed back.

Susie sat staring at the pair of them and tears welled up in her eyes.

"Don't start all that again," Doug warned his wife. "You're like a broken record."

Susie stood up and inched her way towards the door. She was nearly out before Doug noticed her. "Susie! Where are you going? Come back here."

"I don't think I should be here . . ."

Pamela gave a hysterical laugh. "So you keep saying, Susie. So why don't you go?"

"Pamela!" Doug's face was thunderous as he saw the tears spill over onto Susie's cheeks. "Apologise at once!"

"Go to hell!"

"Pamela, I'm warning you . . ."

She stood up to face him. "What, Douglas? What are you warning me of? You've gone against all my wishes bringing her here. You spend all your time with her. You refuse to go anywhere with me. What else can you possibly do to me?"

She slammed out of the room leaving Doug and Susie staring after her.

"I think I'd better go." Susie mopped at her eyes with a tissue.

"Yes. OK then. Sorry, Susie. Look, she doesn't mean it. She's just upset."

Susie tried to smile but couldn't quite pull it off. She stumbled out into the garden as quickly as her bulk would allow.

Doug stood in the middle of the room, staring out into the hall. "What the hell just happened?" he muttered. He thought briefly about going after Pamela but there was no point in continuing the row. It was better to let her calm down. She'd see the sense of his plan in the morning. It was the most practical thing to do. He wandered to the drinks cabinet and poured himself a very large brandy.

Pamela lay trembling on her bed, tears flowing silently down her cheeks. She willed Douglas to follow her. To take her in his arms and tell her it was OK. To choose her above Susie. But she waited and waited and he didn't come. After about an hour, she heard the front door slam and the sound of his car. So that was it. He'd gone out. Had he taken Susie with him? Or was he gone to meet one of his girlfriends? To have a few drinks and drown his sorrows. To cry on someone's shoulder about how his wife didn't understand him. But he was wrong. She understood him. She understood him only too well. She went down to the kitchen, poured herself a glass of wine and peered into the freezer. A pity she'd finished all the cake. She'd just have to eat ice cream.

Susie rang home and prayed that Marie would pick up.

"Hello?" Her father's gruff voice echoed down the line.

She hung up and pulled her cardigan closer around her. What was she going to do? Four weeks to go before the baby was due and it looked like she might be out on the street soon. She wondered if Gina would put her up but then remembered that she shared a tiny flat with her brother. Jack's place was even smaller and as for Malcolm, well, living with Caroline would be as bad as living with Pamela! Except it would never happen because Caroline wouldn't let it. And Mal wouldn't be able to stand up to her the way Doug stood up to Pamela. No, if she was thrown out she'd have to go into one of these women's refuges. She'd a vague idea that they were really for abused wives but they were hardly going to refuse a heavily pregnant girl. The worry and tiredness started to catch up with her and she felt her eyes start to close. It was only seven o'clock but she wasn't going to sleep on this damn sofa again. She switched off the lights and went into the bedroom and was asleep within minutes of her head touching the pillow.

Doug was fixing himself some Alka-Seltzer when Pamela breezed into the kitchen.

"Good morning," she said and poured herself a glass of orange juice.

"Good morning." Doug looked up in surprise. He hadn't expected such civility. Not after last night's performance. He felt a surge of admiration and pride as he noticed her beautifully coiffed hair, her trim figure in the black suit and cerise top and the perfectly applied make-up. "You look lovely," he said honestly.

"Thank you." She acknowledged the compliment with a small smile. "I've been thinking about your plan for today and it does seem like the best course of action."

"Oh. Right. Good."

"Perhaps you'd like to give Susie a call and tell her

we'll be leaving in about twenty minutes?" She looked at the slim Cartier watch on her wrist.

"Sure." He went out to the phone in the hall.

Pamela closed her eyes and prayed that she could get through the day without falling apart. And without taking a drink. Her head was hopping and she quickly swallowed a couple of paracetemol before Doug returned.

"She'll meet us outside," he said brightly, striding back into the room.

Pamela nodded. "I'll wait for you in the sitting-room."

Susie pulled on a canary-yellow sweatshirt, piled on the make-up and added the largest earrings she could find. She needed all her armour today. The thoughts of facing the gang made her nervous but it was the drive into work with Pamela and Doug really scared her.

Doug gasped when she came out to meet him. She hadn't been wearing as much make-up lately and she'd looked so much more approachable. But today she looked scarier than ever. Still, it might be a good thing today. No one would ever believe she was his mistress. He smiled and she smiled back nervously.

"It's going to be just fine," he said reassuringly as he held the door for her.

"I hope you're right," she murmured as Pamela came towards them.

Pamela felt a physical pain run through her when she saw them whispering together. Probably talking about her. She straightened her shoulders and took some deep breaths. "Shall we go?" She slipped into the passenger seat without even acknowledging Susie.

It was a bit of an anticlimax when they arrived at the office. Susie, despite her bump, practically jumped out of the car, anxious to get away from the suffocating atmosphere. Doug and Pamela followed at a more dignified pace. But when they pushed through the double doors of CML, Noreen wasn't at her desk, Mal wasn't in yet and Jack and Gina were having a lively debate about a presentation that was flickering on the screen in front of them.

"Hi," Jack said casually before turning back to the screen.

Gina smiled. "Welcome back, Doug."

"Thank you, Gina. It's good to be here," Doug lied with a broad smile.

"Where's Noreen?" Pamela asked, as she carefully folded her silk scarf.

Jack grinned. "Gone out to get some of Doug's special coffee."

"And a surprise cake," Gina added.

Doug raised an eyebrow. "Well, I'd better look surprised then."

"Gina, Jack, would you be free for lunch today?" Pamela asked.

They looked at each other. "Eh, yeah," Jack said doubtfully.

"Good. I thought we'd have a small celebration to welcome Douglas back."

Jack gaped at her.

"Great idea," Gina said quickly.

"Good. Maybe you'd check if Malcolm is available? When he finally gets in." Pamela smiled at everyone and walked into her office.

Doug stared after her. She should get an Oscar for that one. "So what are you guys working on?" he asked, pulling up a chair.

"We're just looking at the presentation Susie did for PL Pharmaceuticals."

Susie's head jerked up and Gina gave her a reassuring smile.

"It's really good stuff!" Jack said enthusiastically.

Susie glowed. "Really?"

"Really.".

They took Doug through the presentation screen by screen and Pamela watched through the glass wall. She'd planned on bringing Douglas through the books and the business plan for the rest of the year. But as usual, he preferred to be somewhere else. With someone else.

When eventually Doug left them, Gina turned to Susie. "Nice weekend?"

"Yes, thanks." Susie concentrated on the screen.

"Got a lift in with Pamela and Doug, eh? Have you moved or something?"

Susie sighed and turned around to face Gina. "You know I have, Gina. Me da threw me out when he found out about the baby."

"Oh, God, I'm sorry, Susie, I didn't know."

"And Doug and Pamela offered to put me up 'cos I couldn't afford a place of me own."

"That was very nice of Doug . . . them."

"Yeah, it was. And then some sleaze-bag goes and turns it into something dirty and splashes it all over the papers."

"Hardly splashes." Jack pulled the newspaper from under some files. "It's only a few lines."

Susie glared at him. "It's not funny. How would ye like people to say those kind of things about *you?*"

"Sorry," Jack said meekly.

"How's Pamela taking it? I thought she'd have killed you or him by now."

"Or maybe even both of you," Jack added.

Susie was glad Doug had gone over all this on the drive in. "She's upset of course but she knows it's not true. Why would she blame us?"

Mal opened the door and strolled in. "Morning everybody. Lovely morning."

"It's pissing rain, Mal," Jack pointed out.

"Is it?" Mal whistled as he hung up his wet coat.

"You haven't heard, have you?" Gina hissed.

"Ah, Gina! Do ye have to go on about it." Susie groaned.

"Sorry."

"Heard about what?" Mal looked at them expectantly.

Susie shoved the paper in front of him. "It's a piece about Doug and me and it's all lies, do ye hear?"

Malcolm read it and then looked up at Susie, his eyes full of sympathy behind his steamed-up glasses. "Oh, Susie, this is terrible! Poor you. But don't let it get to you. You have Baby to think of." He perched on the side of her desk and put an arm around her shoulders. "Doug is well known in the city and he's always getting photographed or talked about. These sort of characters," he smacked his hand against the picture of the journalist, "are always trying to make a story out of nothing. It will all be forgotten before you know it."

Susie smiled gratefully.

"Mal's right, Susie," Gina smiled brightly. *Now why hadn't she said that?*

"Absolutely!" Jack agreed. "And no one ever believes this stuff anyway."

"Thanks guys," Susie murmured. They really weren't such a bad bunch.

Noreen bustled in with a cake box. "Jack? May I borrow your matches," she whispered, looking furtively at Doug's door. "And there's a card on my desk, everyone. If you would all sign it?"

They all stood up.

"Oh, one at a time please!" Noreen hissed in frustration. "We want to surprise him, don't we?"

They dutifully signed the card and trooped into Doug's office, Noreen proudly leading the way, cake in hand. Pamela followed reluctantly.

"Welcome back, Mr Hamilton. It hasn't been the same without you."

Doug saw the look on Pamela's face. "I'm sure you're exaggerating, Noreen."

"Not at all," she insisted. "We've missed you a great deal."

They crowded around as Doug cut the cake and Pamela slipped quietly away.

Chapter Thirty-five

"And they took you all out to lunch?" Tim asked.

"The whole gang of us," Gina confirmed as she turned out of the lane. "It was great *craic*. Pamela was a bit quiet but then she's never exactly chatty."

"Pamela. That's Doug's wife?" Grainne asked, trying to keep up with the story from the back of the car.

"That's right."

"Was Greg there?" Tim asked casually.

"Nope. He's left now that Doug is back."

"Oh? And what about you two?"

"That's over."

"Well, thank God for that!" her brother said.

"Tim!" Grainne admonished. "That's not very nice."

Gina grinned. "Ah, you're all right, Grainne. I'm used to him. You were never exactly Greg's biggest fan, were you, Tim?"

"No," he agreed. "Especially when he started to chat up my girlfriend."

"He didn't!" Gina said scandalised.

"He did."

"Oh, Tim, you promised you wouldn't say anything!" Grainne protested, mortified.

"It doesn't make any difference now. She's dumped him. Or did he dump you?" He frowned.

Gina laughed. "Relax. I dumped him."

"Good on you, Gina. He wasn't good enough for you," Grainne assured her, delighted that Gina had finally seen sense.

The guy had given her the creeps that night in the flat. Tim and Gina were only in the kitchen when he'd slid across the sofa and put his hand on her thigh.

"Why don't you and I meet up somewhere later for a little drink?" he'd said in that sleazy voice of his.

She'd been completely unprepared. Shocked that anyone could be that two-faced. "I don't think so," she'd said coldly, shoving his hand off her leg and going out to the kitchen to join the others. Tim had been furious but she'd warned him to keep his mouth shut.

"You'll only hurt your sister. Say nothing, I'm warning you, Tim. Anyway. It won't last."

Tim smiled at her affectionately as Gina parked outside Horan's. "My clever girlfriend."

"I'm looking forward to tonight," Gina said as they crossed the car-park.

"Me too," Grainne agreed. "Isn't it wonderful to be finally finished with those night classes?"

"It certainly is. I wouldn't mind but mine were a complete waste of time now that I've got my promotion," Gina admitted.

"For God's sake don't tell Dad that," Tim warned her.

"Of course not! Anyway, I'll be happy to have a piece of paper saying I'm qualified at something. Mind you, I better wait for the exam results before I count my chickens!" Gina led the way into the smoky lounge. "I wonder if Hannah's here yet?"

"There she is." Tim pointed down to the far corner.

"Where?" Gina craned her neck.

The crowd parted long enough for Gina to catch a glimpse of Hannah sitting very close to a man, his hand on her leg.

"Fergal!" She followed Tim, a broad smile on her face.

"Hi, guys," Tim said, pulling up stools for himself and the girls.

"Howaya, Tim!" Mike Ford stood up from his position beside Hannah and grinned. "Grainne, how's it going? Oh, Gina. Hi." His smile froze.

"Hi," Gina said faintly, trying to keep the smile on her face.

Hannah smiled and moved up on the bench they were sitting on. "Come and sit here, Gina, so we can have a chat."

Gina obediently squeezed in beside her.

"I'll get the drinks in," Mike said. "A lager, Gina?"

"Yes thanks, Mike."

"No, I'll get these," Tim protested, following him to the bar.

Grainne looked at the two girls sitting silently side by side. "I'm just nipping out to the ladies'."

"You don't mind, do you, Gina?" Hannah said in her usual direct manner.

"I don't *think* I do," she said honestly. "I don't really fancy him any more. It's just, well, a bit of a shock. I thought you and Fergal would get back together."

Hannah shook her head impatiently. "I told you that was over."

"Yeah, you did. I'm sorry. I haven't been much of a friend lately, have I?"

"We all get led astray by assholes from time to time," Hannah replied with a grin.

"Well, I'm back on the straight and narrow now," Gina said firmly. "Not an asshole in sight. In fact no man in sight at all," she added glumly.

"Sometimes the right one is under our noses all along," Hannah looked dreamily at Mike.

"Maybe. Look I think I'll head home. I feel a bit of a gooseberry here."

"Don't be ridiculous! I told Mike I was coming here to meet *you*. He just tagged along. He can get lost if you're uncomfortable."

Gina smiled. "Really?"

Hannah grinned back. "Really. We're mates, aren't we?"

"Yeah."

"So will I tell him to push off?"

"Ah, no. If you don't mind, then I don't either."

"Good girl!"

"Here we are, ladies." Mike put their drinks down in front of them and sat down. "So, Gina, is any of this gossip about Doug Hamilton actually true?"

* * *

"Well, darling? Have things settled down?" Sheila Hamilton watched her son push his salad around the plate.

"Yes, I suppose so. Except Pamela's hardly talking to me. But then that's a relief after some of the ear-bashings I've been getting recently."

"Don't be too hard on her, dear. No woman likes to think she's being laughed at and Pamela's position in society is very important to her."

"But why, Mother? Why in God's name does she care what these people think of her? They don't give a damn about us!"

Sheila sighed. She didn't think her son would thank her for reminding him that these people had once been just as important to him. "Why don't you take her out tonight, Douglas?" she suggested. "Somewhere nice. Just the two of you."

"On a Saturday night? I'd never get a table at this late stage."

"Then cook her a meal," Sheila suggested.

Doug laughed. "I don't think that would be really the way to win her around. Unless . . ." He grinned at her. "You've just given me a great idea, Mother." He flicked through his diary and then punched a number into his phone. "Liz? Hi, Doug Hamilton here. Liz, I know it's ridiculously short notice but is there any chance you could rustle up a dinner for two for tonight?"

* * *

"Oh, you poor thing! Do you feel awful?"

Caroline sat back on the side of the bath and wiped her mouth with a piece of toilet-paper.

Malcolm knocked again. "Caroline? Honey?"

"I'll be out in a minute," she said irritably.

"I'll go and put the kettle on. A nice cup of tea and a biscuit will help."

Caroline listened to his footsteps on the stairs and closed her eyes. If only he wasn't so bloody nice. That's what made it really hard. That's what made her feel guilty. "You've got to tell him," she muttered to herself as she went back into the bedroom.

"Mummy?" Rachel tottered in and climbed up on the bed beside her. "Can we go and play on the swings?"

"Don't be silly, darling. It's raining."

"But I want to." Rachel's expression was mutinous.

"Rachel, leave your mother alone," Mal said coming into the room with a tray. "If you're a good girl I'll bring you to Nana's later."

"Goody! Nana! And we'll have tea and cake?"

Mal smiled. "Probably. Now go and watch *The Teletubbies*."

Rachel ran off, singing *'eh-oh!'* as she went.

Caroline smiled. "Thanks."

Mal handed her a cup of tea. "No problem. Mam will be thrilled to see her. You take it easy today."

"It's just she's just got so much energy . . ."

"And she's spoiled rotten," Mal added. "A little brother or sister is exactly what she needs."

"Mal, there's something I need to say . . ." She was interrupted by the phone.

Mal stretched across the bed and took up the receiver. "Hello? Oh, yes, hang on."

"It's Teacher." He handed Caroline the phone with a broad wink. "Making sure you've done your homework."

She stared at the phone, her cheeks reddening. "Hello, Dick? Hi. Yes. Yes, I'll be there. See you then. Bye-bye."

"What was that all about?" Mal asked, munching on a biscuit.

"Dick's organising an outing to an exhibition tomorrow."

"That's nice."

"You don't mind?"

"No. Go and enjoy yourself, love. Sure, isn't Rachel going to a party?" Mal secretly relished the thought of being able to enjoy the football in peace.

"Yes. That's right."

"Well, there you go then. Right, I'll go and check on Rachel. Why don't you have another snooze?"

"Malcolm?"

"Yes?" He turned in the doorway and smiled.

"Oh, nothing. Maybe I will have another little sleep."

"You do that."

He closed the door gently and Caroline lay back on the pillows with a sigh. She was going to have to tell him. How come Gina Barrett hadn't said anything? It would have done Caroline a favour! She was fed up with this creeping around. It had been exciting at first. Meeting Dick at secret locations had made her feel alive and very sexy. But now she was pregnant it was time to put things on a more settled footing. And it was time she told Malcolm she was leaving. He was going to take it very hard. Losing her and Rachel was one thing but losing the new baby too . . . And then he'd realise that it probably wasn't his baby after all. Caroline's eyes filled up as she remembered how happy he'd been when she'd told him she was pregnant. She should never have said anything really. She should have just left. Taken Rachel and moved in with Dick. She wiped away the tears. No point in thinking about that now. She'd handled things very badly. But she'd sort it all out. She'd tell him tonight and then when she met Dick tomorrow they'd make their plans. He would be so thrilled when she told him he was going to be a father!

* * *

Doug was setting the table in the living-room when Pamela arrived home soaked and laden down with shopping-bags.

"What's going on?" Pamela looked at the little table drawn up in front of the fire. Set the way she'd set it that night. It seemed like years ago now.

"I thought we'd have a little dinner-party. For two." He came over and helped her out of her wet coat.

"I'm not sure I'm in the mood," she said coldly.

He took her hands, his eyes pleading. "Please, Pamela. It's been an awful week. Can't we put it behind us?"

Pamela studied his face. He seemed sincere. She smiled warily. "Let me go and change."

"Sure. There's no rush."

"What are we having?" she asked warily. Doug's cooking tended towards basic.

"I'm not sure yet," he said cheerfully and steered her towards the staircase. "Now, you go on and leave everything to me."

He strode off towards the kitchen whistling and Pamela, went upstairs a small smile playing around her lips. Maybe. Just maybe.

Doug opened the cartons that Liz had dropped off and inspected her list of instructions. The starter was cold so all he had to do was put it on plates and slice the bread. And she'd prepared confit of duck for the main course which just needed thirty minutes in the oven to finish it off. The vegetables would only take minutes in the microwave. "God bless you, Liz Connolly!" Doug said, grinning as he opened the wine to breathe. There was tiramisu in the fridge for dessert but Pamela probably wouldn't eat it. And anyway, he was hoping for a different type of dessert altogether!

As Pamela undressed, she wondered what this was all about. Did he really want a romantic evening or was he trying to soften her up so that she'd apologise to Susie Clarke? She hoped fervently it was the former. They hadn't spent an evening together in months and she couldn't believe how much she missed him. She'd always taken his company for granted. They'd been married so long and he was always there. Just like part of the furniture. Reliable. Dependable. A constant in her life.

But in the last few months she'd begun to wonder if her rock was about to crumble. Douglas had changed. He laughed at her social life and her friends, forgetting that they used to be his friends too. He spent more and more time with Jack and Gina and less and less time with her. And – the real bone of contention – he'd become totally obsessed with Susie Clarke. And it wasn't because he fancied her, Pamela thought as she brushed her long hair till it shone. She sincerely hoped that tonight would see a return of the old Douglas Hamilton. And maybe he'd be interested in moving back into their room. Pamela was surprised at how much she missed their sex life. Yet another thing that she'd taken for granted.

"Hello, beautiful," Doug said softly when she returned in a long black skirt and a white, cowl-necked top. Her hair hung loose around her shoulders. He went over and touched it lovingly. "It's a long time since I've seen you wear your hair like that."

"I didn't feel like putting it up," she said carelessly. She didn't want him thinking that she'd left it loose for him. Even though it was true.

Doug sensed she was uncomfortable. Pamela had always been a bit funny about intimacy. "I'll just go and check on dinner," he said loudly. "I've poured you some wine. Why don't you sit down and relax?"

Pamela took up her glass and walked to the fireplace. The room looked cosy and welcoming. Just as she'd designed it to. They used to sit in here all the time reading the newspapers in companionable silence. But not recently. Now, Pamela usually kept to her room and Doug stayed cooped up in his study with his CDs or with Susie.

"It's coming on nicely even if I do say so myself." Doug came back in and picked up his glass. He raised it in a toast. "To reconciliation?"

Pamela inclined her head and raised her glass. "To reconciliation," she murmured.

He smiled. "Good. I'm glad. I've been wanting to talk to you."

Pamela wondered if the topic of conversation was going to be their marriage, their company or good old Susie Clarke.

"But first let's enjoy our meal." He put down his glass and went outside.

When he returned with the fish cakes and home-made brown bread, Pamela smiled. "Do I see the hand of Liz Connolly in this?"

"Well, I didn't want to poison you," Doug admitted.

"Thank God for that. I was afraid I was going to have to choke down your spaghetti bolognese."

"My spag bol is very good," he protested.

Pamela nodded. "It *was*. When we were young and didn't know any better."

"That's not very kind." Doug tucked into his fish. "Anyway. Your cooking isn't up to much either."

"Which is why I employ Irene," Pamela pointed out.

"Fair point," he acknowledged with a smile.

"Are you glad to be back at work?" she asked politely. They'd hardly spoken all week so she didn't know and hadn't really cared how he was getting on.

He shrugged. "I'm not sure. I don't get the same kick out of it that I used to."

"It's business. It's not supposed to be entertaining," she said matter-of-factly.

"True. But I can't help wondering if I should be doing something else with my life."

Pamela wasn't sure she wanted to hear what was coming next. "What is this? A mid-life crisis?" she joked.

He smiled sadly. "Maybe. Haven't you ever wanted to . . . do something else." He studied her closely.

Pamela concentrated on her fish. "No. I'm quite happy as I am."

"Really? Are you sure?" he persisted.

She glanced up nervously. "Yes. Yes, I am."

He sighed and drank his wine.

"What's for our main course?" she asked, hoping to bring back the lighthearted atmosphere.

"Duck," he muttered. "I'll go and get it."

Pamela watched him leave. This was worse than she'd thought.

He returned with the food.

She smiled. "Thank you. This looks lovely."

They ate in silence and Pamela's mind raced trying to find something to distract her husband from his morose mood. And then it came to her. "We should branch out," she said at last.

"Sorry?"

"You were saying? About not getting a kick out of things any more? Well maybe it's time for CML to move into a new area."

"Like what?" Doug said gloomily.

"Well, I don't know. You're the ideas man. Maybe something to do with the Internet. That's where the future is, isn't it?"

Doug looked at her, a spark of interest in his eyes. "The Internet," he said thoughtfully.

"Oh, sorry. I didn't mean to interrupt." Susie stood awkwardly in the doorway.

"Then why did you?" Pamela said sharply.

"Sorry," Susie said again. "But there's a leak in me roof and it's right over the bed."

Doug put down his napkin and stood up. "I'll come and take a look."

Susie walked back out into the hall.

"Oh, for God's sake, Douglas!" Pamela hissed.

"Sorry, darling. I'll be as quick as I can."

"But what can you possibly do? Just call a plumber."

"But I need to be able to explain to a plumber what the problem is," he said gently. "It won't take long. You finish your meal, darling." He dropped a kiss on the top of her head. "I'll be back in time for dessert."

"Great," Pamela muttered throwing down her knife and fork as the door closed behind them. "Thank you, Susie. Thank you for ruining things yet again."

Chapter Thirty-six

"I'm sorry, Doug. I didn't mean to spoil yer evening."
Susie held the ladder while Doug poked around in the
attic.

Doug had a feeling she'd definitely spoiled his evening.
Still, it wasn't her fault. "Don't be silly," he called, with a
cheerfulness he didn't feel. "It isn't your fault. And I
could hardly let a pregnant woman sleep in a wet bed,
now could I?"

Susie giggled. "I wouldn't be able to tell if me waters
broke."

"Exactly!" He climbed back down. "OK. That seems
to have solved the problem for the moment but I'll need
to get someone in tomorrow to do a proper job on that
roof. Especially if this bloody weather continues."

Susie looked at the rain lashing against the window.
"It's miserable out. And look at ye! Yer soaked!"

Doug touched his damp hair. "No problem. I'd
better get back. Will you be OK now?"

"Fine. And thanks, Doug. And I'm . . ."

He held up his hand. "If you say you're sorry again, I'll strangle you."

She grinned. "OK. Well, goodnight then. I hope yer dinner isn't spoiled."

"A couple of minutes in the microwave and it will be fine," he assured her. But he couldn't say the same about Pamela. He was in trouble again. He ran the few feet across the driveway and let himself in the front door, shaking the rain off like a dog.

Pamela stopped halfway up the stairs and turned to look at him.

"Where are you going?" he asked pulling off his wet jacket.

"To bed."

"Oh, come on, Pamela. Don't be like that! We were having a nice evening, weren't we?"

"Yes. We were. Until Ms Clarke called and you jumped. As usual."

"Oh, Pamela! What could I do? It's pissing rain out and there was a bloody great leak in her roof. I had to do something."

Pamela gave him a funny look. "Of course you did. Douglas Hamilton to the rescue. Every time."

"What's that supposed to mean?"

"I think you know." She continued up the stairs.

"Pamela, please! I said I wanted to talk."

"I'm afraid it will have to wait. Like I did. For, let me see." She paused and counted on her fingers. "Yes, an hour and a half, Douglas. An hour and a half while you were off playing handyman with your little friend! My God, you

461

may as well be having an affair! You spend enough time with her!" Her voice was shrill and slightly hysterical and she was swaying ominously on the stairs.

Doug started up towards her. "Be careful, Pamela! And please calm down."

"Calm down!" she screeched. "How dare you tell me what to do!"

He reached out to her but she shoved him away and he suddenly realised that she was quite drunk. "Come on. Let's get you to bed." He put his arm around her.

She pushed him away again and drew herself up. "I am quite capable of getting there on my own, thank you very much," she said haughtily. "You save your good deeds for Susie."

Doug stood and watched her unsteady progress to her room and then went back downstairs, feeling very depressed. He looked sadly at the cosy little scene he'd set only a few hours earlier. He'd hoped for a very different outcome. He blew out the candles and carried his plate of congealing duck and the empty bottles out to the kitchen. He scraped the duck into the bin and then went back in to pour himself a large brandy. It looked like Pamela had been at this too. Since when had she become a drinker? First the episode with Marjorie. Now this. She had always been so temperate with both food and wine. She admonished him when he had a little too much to drink. So what had changed? There was no doubt she was unhappy. Was it all because of Susie? He threw back the brandy and refilled his glass. How could someone as poised and successful as Pamela feel threatened by a pregnant teenager? He switched off the lights in the sitting-room and carried his glass into the study. He put on some music, plugged in his headphones and settled back in the big leather chair. At least in here there was some solitude and peace.

It was only moments after Doug left when Susie felt the first pain. She decided a bath was probably the best thing. She didn't feel that bad – it was like a period pain – but she'd heard that that's often what the beginning of labour felt like. But it couldn't be that – there were nearly two weeks to go! It was all the standing around with Doug that had caused this nagging ache. And she'd got quite wet and cold when she'd gone over to the house. The bath would relax her, warm her. Maybe it would even help her to sleep. The last few nights hadn't been great. It didn't help that her macho son kept kicking her in the ribs. She fondled her bump and smiled. He was an active little fella, that was for sure. He was going to keep her busy. *Only if you're planning to keep him, Susie,* a little voice said.

"No. No, I can't," she said, lowering herself carefully into the bath. "Trust me, little fella. Yer better off without me. We'll find you a nice mammy with lots of money who'll spoil ye rotten." She watched him move about – he loved the water – and wondered how long it would be before she saw him. And how long she'd be allowed to keep him. She felt sick at the thought of him being taken out of her arms. "But what else can I do?" she said desperately, the tears rolling down her cheeks. "Oh, baby! What else can I do?"

* * *

Jack put the drinks on the table and sat back down beside Gina. "Are you really bothered about going to this party? 'Cos the barman says it's getting very nasty outside."

Gina pointed at the TV. "I know. There's flooding all over Dublin. And the Dodder has overflowed its banks. Doug's place will be flooded."

"Probably. So what will we do?"

Gina settled herself more comfortably and put her feet up on a stool. "Let's stay here. It's warm, dry. There's plenty of food and drink. What more could we want?"

"Suits me." Jack grinned happily. He'd been chuffed when Gina had agreed to come to the party with him but this was even better! He'd have her all to himself for the whole evening.

* * *

Malcolm stumbled out to the car and fumbled for his keys. The rain plastered his hair to his head and trickled down the back of his neck.

"Malcolm? Malcolm, don't be silly! You can't go out in this!"

He ignored Caroline, reversed sharply out of the driveway and screeched off down the road. He didn't have any idea where he was going. He just knew he had to get out or he'd kill her.

* * *

"This is nice, isn't it?" Jack nudged Gina.

"Ish very nishe," she agreed solemnly and spilled

her drink in the process. "Oops." She giggled. "Silly me."

"I'll get you another." Jack rose on unsteady legs.

"I'm not sure I should." Gina noticed everything in the room seemed to be moving.

"Course you should!" Jack said firmly.

"Well, maybe a short, then."

"A Muddy Blary?" he asked.

"Nah. I'll have a Bloody Mary instead."

They both laughed uproariously and Jack weaved his way to the bar.

* * *

The pain was getting worse and it was happening every fifteen minutes. "Time to call Marie," Susie muttered when the contraction subsided. She picked up the phone but there was no dial tone. "Ah, shit. Not tonight!" It had happened a few times before. Doug said there was a loose connection between the flat and the main house. "Bloody weather," Susie moaned pulling her coat on and grabbing a brolly. She gasped when she stepped off the last stair and landed in at least three inches of water. "Oh, marvellous! That's all I need." She fought her way around the side of the house battling to keep the umbrella up and trying to ignore the contraction that had just started. She opened the back-door, praying that the alarm wasn't on yet, but all was quiet. She stumbled into the room and sank on to the nearest chair, gasping with the pain. She took slow, deep breaths like they'd told her at the hospital and waited for the pain to pass. "God, if it's like this now, what am I going to be like in a few hours?" she thought, fear gripping her. "Calm down, Susie," she muttered "Didn't Ma do it five times without any problem?" She poured herself a drink of water and made her way into the sitting-room to call home.

"Hello?" It was her da.

"Is Marie there, please?" she said, disguising her voice.

"No, she bloody isn't! And what kind of time do ye call this to be disturbing people?"

"Sorry." Susie hung up. God, what was she going to do now? No Marie and no Doug – she'd noticed on her way around that the car wasn't in the driveway. And there was no way she was going to call Pamela! She picked up the address book by the phone and looked for Gina's mobile. Gina would help her. All she needed was a lift to the hospital and she'd be grand.

* * *

"Sssh! What's that?"

"Your mobile," Jack said helpfully.

"Oh. Right." Gina rooted in her bag and found the phone. "Hello? Hello? What? Oh, Susie! How the hell are you? What? You're not!"

"What?" Jack asked, noticing how Gina's nose kept dividing into two.

"It's Shusie. She's having the baby."

"That's nice."

"Yeah. Thas nishe, Shusie. Best of luck. What? Me?!"

'She tucked the phone under her chin. "She wants me to come and help her."

Jack giggled. "You!"

Gina put the phone back to her ear. "I'd like to help, Shusie, but I think a doctor might be better. What? Oh." She turned to Jack again. "She just wants a lift to the hospital."

"I don't think so." Jack pointed at the TV screen, where a reporter stood knee-deep in water.

"Oh, crikey!" Gina stared at him. "What will I tell her?"

"Tell her the cavalry are coming!"

Gina gazed at him admiringly. "Shusie? We'll be right there."

As they stood up and stumbled towards the door, a soaking wet, white-faced Malcolm Patterson walked in.

"Mal, old son!" Jack hugged him as if they hadn't seen each other in years.

"You're jush in time, Mal. We're going on a mishon of mershy," Gina informed him seriously.

"What?" Mal looked at them, slightly dazed.

"Shusie's having the baby and we're going to help. You can come too." She linked her arm though his and dragged him towards the door. "We can use your car."

"Afraid not, Gina. Doug's neighbourhood is under at least a foot of water."

"Then we'll walk," she said firmly." We can't let Shusie down. Come on, Jack."

"OK. But could I just nip to the loo first?"

* * *

"Susie! What are you doing here?"

Susie jumped as Doug appeared in the doorway. "Jesus, Doug! Ye scared the life out of me! I thought ye were out."

"No. I was in the study."

"But yer car . . ."

"It's in the garage. It was such a filthy night I thought it was safer in there. Just as well I did. The driveway's flooded already. But the house should be OK. Christ, what's wrong!" He jumped to her side as she doubled over with a low moan.

"It's started," she gasped and clenched his hand tightly.

Doug winced. "OK. Well, don't worry. I'm sure you'll be fine. But shouldn't we get you to a hospital?"

Susie sat back on the sofa and closed her eyes. The contractions were taking more and more out of her. They were lasting longer too. "Can't," she said breathlessly. "I rang Holles Street to see if they'd send an ambulance but the roads are flooded. They said either I'd have to get there under me own steam or get the local doctor to deliver it at home."

"Well, there's no way I can drive you in this. Did you call a doctor?"

Susie shook her head her eyes frightened. "I didn't know who to call. I tried Marie but she was out and I don't know any doctors around here but Gina and Jack are on their way."

"Gina and Jack? What use are they?" Doug paced the floor distractedly.

"Well, I don't know, do I? But it was better than sitting here on me own!"

Doug pulled her into his arms and stroked her hair gently. "Sorry, love. Look, don't you worry about a thing. Everything's going to be fine. I'll call my doctor. Joe will look after you. He's a great guy. You'll like him."

"Do ye think he's ever delivered a baby before?"

"Hundreds," Doug said more confidently than he felt. "I'll give him a ring now."

"Oh, Doug, I'm so scared."

Doug cuddled her to him. "I'm with you, Susie. I'll look after you."

"Well, isn't this a touching little scene?"

They looked up to see Pamela standing in the doorway.

"It's not what you think, Pamela," Doug said wearily.

"No?"

They were interrupted by the doorbell. "That'll be Gina and Jack," Susie said in a small voice.

Pamela's eyes widened. "Gina and Jack! What is this? A holiday camp! Are you planning on moving *all* of our staff in here, Doug? And while I can understand Gina's invitation, I was unaware your tastes ran to men too!"

Doug glared at her. "You don't know what you're talking about, Pamela. Go back to bed." He brushed past her and went out to open the door.

Pamela turned her wrath on Susie. "So what is it this time, Susie? Was there a spider on your wall? Did the noise of the storm scare you?"

Susie doubled over and clutched a cushion. "I'm in labour," she replied between grunts and gasps.

Pamela stared at her, uncomprehending. "You're what?"

"Hiya, Pamela!" Gina weaved in and put a friendly arm around her boss. "Isn't this exciting?"

Susie looked at the two of them and wished she'd stayed in her flat on her own.

* * *

"Dick? It's Caroline. I've done it! I've told Malcolm."

Dick O'Toole rubbed his eyes. "What time is it, Caroline?" He tucked the phone under his chin.

"Eleven. Sorry, did I wake you? It's just I had to talk to you."

Dick sighed. Women. They always wanted to talk. A greatly overrated form of communication as far as he was concerned. "That's OK."

"So I told him."

"Told him what, exactly?" Dick asked sitting up in his bed.

"I told him that we'd been seeing each other. That we were in love. That I was leaving him."

"What?!" Dick almost shouted. "Jesus, Caroline! Don't you think you should have talked to me first?"

Caroline was momentarily thrown by his reaction. "Well, yes, I know I should have, Dick. But I couldn't stand it any longer. And, well, . . . I knew you wouldn't want your child brought up by another man."

"What did you say?"

She smiled. "Yes, that's right, Dick. I'm going to have a baby. Your baby."

"Christ!"

"Isn't it wonderful?"

Dick broke out in a sweat and felt bile rising in the back of his throat. "Yes. Yes, of course it is, Caroline. And you told Malcolm all this? About the baby too?"

"Yes. It wasn't easy. But I couldn't live a lie any longer."

"Right. How did he take it?"

Caroline sighed. "Not well. He went rushing out of the house. God knows where to on a night like tonight."

Dick looked nervously at the door and wondered if Malcolm knew where he lived.

"So when can I move in?" Caroline was saying. " I think it should be soon. Rachel could sleep on that little sofa in your studio until we get a bigger place. And we should be able to fit a crib into your bedroom."

Dick felt panic engulf him. "We have to talk, Caroline."

"Yes. Of course. There's so much to organise."

"Right. Let's meet as planned tomorrow. We'll talk then."

"OK, darling. I love you."

Dick listened to the words and felt he was suffocating. "Yeah. Me too. See you tomorrow."

Chapter Thirty-seven

Doug paced up and down the small study. "Pamela, I'm only going to say this once more. Nothing was going on. Susie has gone into labour. We can't get her to hospital because the roads are flooded. When she couldn't find me . . . or you, she called Gina. That's why she and Jack and Mal" – he wasn't sure he understood that bit either – "are here."

"Really?" Pamela looked at him from under heavy lids. She wasn't sure she cared any more. She just wanted to sleep. She swung back and forward in his leather armchair.

Doug noticed the glazed look. "How many tablets have you taken?"

She shrugged. "One, maybe two. I can't remember."

"For God's sake, Pamela! Joe told you that you shouldn't be taking those damn things with alcohol. I'll make you some coffee."

"I don't drink coffee," she reminded him.

"You do tonight," he said grimly and stalked out to the kitchen.

* * *

"How are you doing?" Mal came in and sat down beside Susie.

She shook her head and continued to grip the arm of the chair tightly.

"In the middle of a contraction, eh? Here. Hold my hand."

Susie grabbed onto him with her free hand. When the pain passed once more he handed her the glass of water.

"Thanks." She drank thirstily and then set the glass down shakily. "I don't know how much more I can take, Mal. It hurts so much."

"It won't be much longer, Susie. It will all be over this time tomorrow and you'll have a beautiful little baby . . ." he trailed off.

She gave a bitter little laugh. "Yeah, but for how long?"

"As long as you want, Susie. It's your choice," he said quietly.

"How come yer here anyway?" Susie changed the subject. If she was to get through the next few hours she needed to be strong and if one thing made her fall apart it was the thought of how this was going to end.

"It's a long story." Mal took off his glasses and massaged the bridge of his nose.

"I'm not going anywhere. At least not yet," she joked.

His face twisted into a bitter smile. "Well, the bad news is that Caroline is leaving me."

"What?"

"The worse news is that the baby isn't mine." His voice cracked and tears filled his eyes.

"Oh, Mal, I'm sorry!" She took him in her arms and held him while he sobbed uncontrollably.

"She doesn't even care how much she's hurt me, Susie," he gasped. "It was bad enough finding out that she was having an affair. But then she tells me the baby isn't mine. I just can't believe it." He wiped his eyes and then started cleaning his glasses with the sodden handkerchief. "I was so happy when she told me she was pregnant. Now I don't know what to feel. And then there's Rachel. Oh, God, I don't want to become one of those weekend fathers. Dragging her around the zoo on a wet Saturday afternoon and then on to a burger joint."

Susie doubled over again and it was his turn to hold her. "Sorry, love. You don't need to listen to my problems at a time like this."

She shook her head and when she was able to speak again gasped, "That's all right, Mal. It's a distraction. Oh, sorry, I didn't mean . . ."

"It's OK. I know exactly what you mean." He smiled kindly at her.

"It's not fair, Mal. Yer a great dad and yer losing yer kids – and yeah I know I said kids. I'm not convinced this baby isn't yours. How can she be sure? Unless ye weren't . . ."

"No, we were," Mal said in surprise. It hadn't occurred to him before but their sex life had improved dramatically in the last couple of months. It must have been guilt. Or maybe she got some kind of kick from having two men on the go. "I hadn't thought of that."

"Well, I think she's lucky to have ye and she'd be a fool to leave ye."

"She seems to have made up her mind."

"Yeah, but has he? There aren't many men willing to take on another man's family."

"He doesn't look the settling-down type," Mal admitted. He'd met the bastard a few times when he'd collected Caroline from her class. Dick O'Toole seemed like an ageing hippy who thought he was still twenty. "He's even older than me!" he said in disgust.

Susie smiled. "It probably won't last. Are ye willing to fight for her?"

He thought about it for a moment. "I don't know," he said finally, surprising himself. "I suppose I want to fight for the status quo."

Susie frowned. "The what?"

He smiled. "I'd like to keep things the same," he explained. "I'm reasonably happy with my lot, Susie. The thought of being a single dad at my age depresses me. Coming home to an empty house with no one to ask me how my day was. So yeah, I suppose if she changed her mind I'd take her back. Pathetic, eh?"

Susie shook her head. She knew what it was like. The Clarke household was noisy and her da was unpredictable but it had been better than coming home to a cold silent flat.

Mal looked at her sad face and felt a wave of guilt. The poor girl was going through a rough time and she was in labour to boot and here he was crying on *her* shoulder. He saw her face tense up with pain and he took her hand. "OK, Susie. Breathe deeply and slowly. Don't think about anything or anyone. Just concentrate on your breathing. That's it. That's the girl."

* * *

Gina watched Doug carry the tray back to the study and closed the kitchen door. "I suppose *we* should be having some of that."

"Should we?" Jack shovelled some more curry into his mouth.

"You've an awful nerve," Gina said watching him eat. "Raiding the freezer like that!"

"Doug told us to make ourselves at home," Jack pointed out.

"I'm not sure that's quite what he meant."

Jack shrugged. "It could be a long night. I'm going to need my strength."

Gina giggled. "Why? Are you going to deliver the baby?"

"I might have to," Jack said nodding towards the rain lashing against the window.

"It's awful, isn't it?" Gina stood up and filled the kettle.

Another scream came from the sitting-room and they looked at each other in alarm. Gina sobered as the gravity of the situation hit her. "I hope the doctor gets here soon."

"He will." Jack stood up and put an arm around her.

Gina rested her head against his chest, enjoying the feel of Jack's breath on her cheek.

"Poor Susie," she said.

"Yeah, poor Susie," Jack murmured, turning her around and lowering his head to kiss her.

"Any chance of a cup of tea for the patient?" Mal asked from the doorway. "Oops, sorry! When you're ready."

Gina jumped away from Jack. "The kettle's boiling, Mal. I'll bring it in."

"Grand." He left with a final wink at Jack.

Jack looked awkwardly at Gina. "Gina, I really like you . . ."

"Jack, let's concentrate on Susie for the moment," she said, not unkindly. "We've got plenty of time to, well, figure out what's going on here."

He grinned happily. "Fair enough. What do you want me to do?"

Gina wrinkled her nose. "Well, they always seem to get hot water and towels in the films. I'm not sure why."

"I'll find the towels," Jack said, eager to help.

"OK. And I'll make some tea and coffee and then boil another kettle."

They beamed at each other. Wasn't Susie lucky? What would she have done without them?

* * *

"Feeling better?" Doug asked. The glazed look was gone but she was very pale.

"I feel sick," Pamela said sourly. "You know I hate coffee."

"You should have thought about that before you took tablets on top of alcohol," Doug said dispassionately.

"Shouldn't you be minding your girlfriend?" she asked sarcastically. She started to swing the chair around but stopped abruptly when she felt her stomach lurch.

"If you mean Susie, Malcolm is looking after her. Thank God there's one person in this house who has some idea what to do."

"Why can't she go to hospital?"

Doug sighed. "As I've already told you, we're stranded. There's no way an ambulance or even a car can get down our road."

Pamela's eyes widened. "So how are we going to get out of here? What about when we run out of food?" Right at this moment she'd kill for a dish of chocolate chip ice cream.

"There's nothing to worry about. The weather forecast predicts a dry day tomorrow. The water should have gone down within a few hours."

"And is Malcolm going to deliver this baby?"

"Of course not. Joe is on his way."

"But I thought you said . . ."

"He drives a jeep," Doug interrupted.

"So can't he take Susie to the hospital?" she persisted.

"No. It would be too risky." Doug replied patiently. He'd asked Joe all these questions himself. The thought of the poor girl giving birth in The Sycamores scared the hell out of him.

"No can do, Doug. I have an emergency case to see to first," Joe told him. "But don't worry. I'll be there as quick as I can. It's a first baby. They're never in a rush to come out. From what you tell me about the length and frequency of Susie's contractions, she has a few hours to go yet."

"But she's scared, Joe," Doug protested. "She needs someone to reassure her."

"I'm sure you're doing fine. You can call me on the mobile if you're worried. I'll be there in a couple of hours."

"I wish she'd never come here," Pamela was saying bitterly. "Nothing has gone right since she arrived."

"That's ridiculous, Pamela," Doug said irritably.

"It's true! You'd never have talked to me like that before!" Her eyes filled with tears and she ducked her head so he wouldn't see. She wouldn't give him the satisfaction.

Doug leaned forward in his chair and took her hand. "I'm sorry, Pamela. I'm sorry if you feel I've been treating you badly. It's probably true. I've been a bit . . . confused lately. But you mustn't blame Susie. It has nothing to do with her."

"Hasn't it?" She looked him straight in the eye and her suspicions were confirmed when he couldn't hold her gaze.

"Not directly," he murmured.

"Maybe not," she conceded. "But she's made you question your life. Our life."

He looked up at her in surprise. "How did you . . ."

"Oh for God's sake, Douglas we've been married a long time. I know you a lot better than you think!"

"Then why didn't you say anything?" he asked quietly.

She looked away. "I was hoping it was just a phase.

That maybe with time you would settle down again. That once Susie and her child were out of our lives we could get back to normal."

"I'm not sure that's possible any more," Doug replied honestly.

Pamela's eyes were sad. "That's what I was afraid of."

"But we can make a new life, Pamela. Change things. We can have . . ."

"No, Doug. I'm not at all sure we can. I don't think I can share this –" she waved her hands about, "this new life you're talking about."

Doug took her hands back in his and looked into her eyes. "What are you saying?"

"I don't know what I'm saying," Pamela said, frustrated. "I suppose . . ."

"Doug! Doug! Come quick!" Mal stuck his head around the door and then ran back towards the sitting-room, Doug hot on his heels.

Pamela sighed. "Oh, Susie. Why is your timing always so lousy?" She went out to the kitchen in search of food.

* * *

"Joe? It's Doug. I think you better come now." Doug listened for a moment, trying not to hear the groans coming from Susie. "OK, hang on." He turned to Malcolm. "He wants to know about the contractions."

"Tell him they're only about two or three minute apart and they're lasting over a minute."

Doug relayed the information and put the phone down. "He's on his way, Susie. Don't worry."

"I think ye better get some sheets or something," Susie said faintly. "I don't want to mess up yer couch."

Doug looked at the expensive sofa and the hand-woven rug. "I'll go and find something. Don't you worry about a thing, Susie. You've got Mal here to look after you. And he's an expert." Doug hurried out of the room in search of something old to shove under Susie. Though he wasn't at all sure such a thing existed in this house.

Susie turned desperate eyes on Mal.

"Caroline was in a worse state than you, Susie, honest! Her contractions were *lasting* nearly two minutes!"

"And did she have the baby soon after? And did it hurt a lot?"

"It was another hour or so before she had Rachel but," he hurried on when he saw the look on her face, "the final stage was over in a jiffy and once she was holding the baby she forgot all about the pain." Mal resolutely put the image of Caroline weeping uncontrollably and screaming for painkillers to the back of his mind. "Honest, Susie. Everything's going exactly as it should. You're doing great. Look it's two-thirty now. I bet that you're holding that baby by four."

"Do ye really think so, Mal?" She looked at him trustingly.

"Scout's honour," he said solemnly.

She smiled. "I bet ye were a scout too."

"I was actually. I must show you my medals sometime."

Doug reappeared with some sheets and Mal helped Susie up while Doug draped them over the sofa and across the rug. "Sorry about this," he said, slightly embarrassed.

"Don't be silly. Sure it would be terrible to ruin yer beautiful room," Susie told him.

Doug smiled. "Right, then. I'll go and make more tea." He ducked out of the room again and thanked God that Mal was here. It would be a total disaster without him. Doug wanted to help Susie but he was positively terrified. And when she gave those ear-piercing screams he was sure she was going to give birth on the spot. How in God's name could she put up with all that pain? He'd asked Joe could he give her something but he'd said no.

"She's got this far, Doug. I'd prefer it if she could wait until I got there."

"Hurry up, Joe," Doug muttered as he heard another scream from the living-room. "Please hurry up."

* * *

"Where's Jack?" Doug asked.

"Dunno," Gina mumbled. The coffee was beginning to take effect and her hangover was kicking in. "How's it going in there?"

Doug gave her a cool look. "Why don't you go and find out? I'm sure Susie would like to see you."

Gina reddened. "I'm scared, Doug. And I feel so helpless. What can I possibly do for her?"

"Hold her hand. Tell her everything's going to be fine." He sat down beside her "Please, Gina. It would be nice for her to have a woman to talk to. And I think she probably needs to go to the loo but she's too embarrassed to ask us for help."

Gina jumped up. "Oh, I never thought. Sorry."

He smiled at her. "That's OK. Why don't you send Mal out here for a break and it will give you a chance to have a quiet word?"

"Right. Will do." Gina marched into the sitting-room and pasted a confident smile on her face.

"How are you doing, Susie?"

"Gina! I thought ye'd gone."

Gina looked sheepish. "Sorry. But I thought I'd better sober up a bit before I came near you."

Susie grinned. "Ye were a bit plastered all right. I thought Pamela was going to punch ye when ye started hugging her."

Gina sighed. "I'll probably be out of a job, so."

Mal patted her hand reassuringly. "I wouldn't worry. It looks as if she's had one too many herself."

"Really? She came into the kitchen a while ago and she looked fine. Mind you I didn't get much of a look at her. I legged it out of there as quick as I could."

Susie looked at her curiously. "So where did ye go? And where's Jack?"

Gina blushed. "I locked myself in the loo for half an hour. Jack's probably off having a smoke. Anyway, Mal. Why don't you go and have a cup of tea and let me and Susie have a chat?"

Mal looked at Susie and she nodded. "Go on. I'll be fine. Ye could do with a break."

"Right so. I'll bring you back a cup."

Susie rolled her eyes when he left. "If him and Doug pour any more tea the baby will bleedin swim out!"

Gina laughed and crouched down beside the sofa "Wouldn't you be better off in bed?"

Susie shook her head. "I feel better leaning over the arm of the chair when the pain comes. It seems to help a bit. Oh, shit, here we go again."

Gina watched, white-faced, while Susie went through the contraction, her face contorted in pain. "Are you OK?" she asked when Susie finally sank back against the cushions.

Susie nodded.

"Would you like me to help you out to the loo or anything?" Gina asked helplessly.

"Would ye?" Susie asked.

"Sure. Come on. Lean on me."

Gina brought her out to the loo and after helping her with her panties turned discreetly away.

"I was afraid to go on me own," Susie confided on the way back. "I thought the baby might come out! And there was no way I was going to ask Mal or Doug. Thanks, Gina."

"No probs," Gina said, feeling guilty that she hadn't offered earlier. As she eased Susie back down on to the sofa, the doorbell rang. "That will be the doctor!"

Susie closed her eyes. "Oh, thank God! I was so afraid he wouldn't get here on time."

Moments later Joe McCarthy beamed at her from the doorway. "I'm here! Now, Susie. Let's have a look at you."

Chapter Thirty-eight

"I'll try not to hurt you, Susie. Just relax."

Susie took a deep breath and waited while he examined her cervix. Relax! That was a laugh. This whole thing was a nightmare. She'd never been in such pain – but at least the doctor was here now.

"Excellent. You're doing fine!"

"So when do ye . . . *aagh!*"

Joe took her hand. "OK. Breathe through it. That's right. I'll give you an injection to help with the pain."

"When will it be born, doctor? 'Cos I can't take this much longer."

Joe took a needle from his bag. "I'd say your baby will be born within the hour. You're almost fully dilated. Very soon you should feel the urge to push."

Susie closed her eyes as he stuck the needle in her arm.

"There. That will make the pain a bit more bearable."

Susie gave him a disbelieving look. "Yeah, sure."

He smiled. "It will be over soon. Now which one of that gang," he nodded towards the door, "would you like to help in the delivery?"

Susie stared at him. "Well, it has to be Gina. I mean I couldn't have one of the fellas."

"Maybe Pamela could help too."

"No!" Susie reddened at his questioning look. "We don't really get on," she explained feebly.

"Right. Well, I'll just go and get ready."

When he went outside, Doug, Mal and Gina were standing in the hall.

"How is she, doctor?" Mal asked anxiously. He'd watched Caroline go through a rough time and that was with the help of drugs. Poor Susie was doing it all on her own.

"She's fine. Doug, can I go and wash up somewhere?" He turned to smile at Gina. "You must be Gina? I'm Joe. Susie wants you to help in the delivery."

"Me? Oh no! I couldn't!" she blustered.

"She needs you, Gina. It's less embarrassing for her if a woman helps."

"But I might faint."

"You'll be fine. Trust me," he said cheerfully over his shoulder as he followed Doug to the bathroom.

Mal saw the shocked look on Gina's face. "It's OK, Gina, honest. All you have to do is be there for her."

She looked at him nervously. "I won't have to *do* anything though, will I?"

"Well, you might have to hold one of her legs . . ."

"Oh, blimey!"

Mal smiled. "You'll be fine. Just think of what she's going through and you'll forget all about yourself."

Gina took a deep breath and nodded. "You're right. I'll be fine. Maybe I'll just go and have another coffee first. And I suppose I should wash my hands too."

"You do that. I'll go and sit with her."

Pamela was finishing off a tub of ice cream when Gina walked in.

"Hi," Gina said awkwardly.

"Hi." Pamela raised her head for only a moment before going back to wiping the last scraps off the inside of the tub.

Gina watched her, fascinated. It was hard to believe this dishevelled woman was her sophisticated boss. And she'd never seen her eat like that before. In fact she'd never seen *anyone* eat like that before. "Pamela? Are you OK?"

Pamela laughed hysterically. "OK? Of course I'm OK. Why wouldn't I be? My house is overrun with people. There's a girl giving birth on a sofa that I gave £2,000 for and there's a man asleep in my bed. I'm fine, Gina. Absolutely bloody fine!"

Gina looked puzzled. A man asleep . . . "Jack! Oh, I'm sorry, Pamela! I'll go and get him . . ."

"Don't bother," Pamela said, dumping the empty carton in the bin and searching for the brandy bottle that Irene kept for cooking. "I won't be using it for a while."

Gina watched her shuffle out of the kitchen with the bottle clasped to her chest. She should really go after her, but what about Susie? Gina abandoned her coffee and went in search of Doug. It was his bloody wife. Let him sort her out!

Doug was standing waiting when Joe came out of the bathroom. He stared at the transformation. The man that had arrived in a beautiful, charcoal three-piece suit stood before him in torn jeans and an ancient t-shirt.

Joe grinned. "It's a messy business, Doug. No point in ruining good clobber."

"Oh. Right." Doug paled. It was just as well he'd brought down so many sheets!

Gina met them outside the living-room door. "Doug? I think you should go and check on Pamela."

"Why? What's wrong now?" Doug said irritably.

Gina glanced at the doctor.

"I'll go on in," Joe said diplomatically.

She gave him a grateful smile. "I'll be right with you."

"What's the problem, Gina?" Doug repeated.

"Well, it's just . . . she's not too happy. And . . . and she just finished all the ice cream and . . . and now she's gone off somewhere with a bottle of brandy."

"What?" Douglas took the stairs two at a time.

"She won't be in her room," Gina called after him. "Jack's in there."

"What?!"

"Don't worry. I'll get him," Gina said hurriedly. "You find Pamela."

Doug nodded distractedly and went off to check the other bedrooms.

"Which *is* Pamela's room?" Gina asked his receding back.

"Jack? What the hell are you doing?" Gina shook him roughly.

Jack rolled over and opened one eye. "Gina!" He tried to pull her down beside him.

"No, Jack! You've got to get up. You're in Pamela's bed."

Jack sprung up. "What? *Ugh!* Why didn't you say so?"

"What were you doing up here anyway?"

Jack yawned. "Looking for towels like you said."

"You were hardly going to find them in here." Gina looked around the room curiously.

"It's a very . . . feminine bedroom, isn't it?"

"Well, what would you expect?" Jack stood up and stretched.

Gina rolled her eyes. "A razor? The odd tie maybe?"

Jack looked around him. "Oh. I see what you mean."

Gina shook her head. "It's a weird set-up. Imagine having separate rooms at their age."

"Gina, I believe Joe is waiting for you," Doug said grimly from the doorway.

Gina blushed. "Yeah, right, sorry."

"We were looking for towels," Jack explained.

"Try the airing cupboard," Doug said dryly.

Gina groaned as he walked away. "Oh, bloody hell! Do you think he heard me?"

"No doubt about it," Jack said cheerfully.

"Shit! Look, I better get back to Susie. You get the towels and for God's sake keep well clear of the other bedrooms!"

Jack grabbed her hand as she headed for the door. "Gina? About us . . ."

"Oh, not now, Jack," Gina said wearily. "I've got a baby to deliver!"

Doug knocked on the bathroom door. "Pamela? Pamela are you in there?" He tried the handle but the door was locked. "Pamela? Answer me, for God's sake!" He heard the panic in his own voice. What if she'd done something stupid . . .

"What's wrong, Douglas? Doesn't little Susie need you any more? Has Joe taken over as hero of the hour?"

"Don't be stupid, Pamela. Please let me in."

"Why?"

"I'm, I'm . . . worried about you."

"Has Gina been telling tales out of school?" she said with a bitter laugh.

"Let me help you, Pamela. Please."

"Oh, go away, Doug. Go and find someone else to play with. I'm quite happy on my own."

* * *

"We'll need something to wrap the baby in," Joe told Gina.

"Jack's getting towels."

"Good. That's good. OK, Susie. Are you ready?"

"No! I'm scared!" Susie said tearfully.

"It's OK, Susie." Gina held her hand tightly. "Everything's going to be fine. Isn't it, doc?"

"Absolutely," Joe said as he examined her once more. "Susie, are you feeling any urge to push yet?"

"I don't know, maybe, oh I don't know . . ." she wailed.

"That's OK. The baby knows what to do. You just follow his lead."

Susie smiled tremulously. "Ye said he."

Joe looked at her. "And is it? A boy?"

"They couldn't tell on the scan but I'm sure it is."

Joe smiled. "I'm sure you're right. OK, little boy, we're ready when you are."

"How much longer are they going to be?" Jack asked rocking back and forwards on a kitchen chair.

"Hard to say," Mal told him. "Could be ten minutes, an hour. Every labour is different."

"Were you with Caroline, you know, when she . . ."

"Yeah."

Jack shuddered. "How could you? I'd pass out for sure!"

"It was scary," Mal admitted. "But when I saw Rachel for the first time it was unbelievable." He turned away and blew his nose noisily.

"And you'll be doing it all over again in a few months," Doug reminded him as he opened a bottle of wine. He didn't see why Pamela should be the only one doing the drinking.

"Probably not," Mal mumbled.

Doug looked at him sharply. "What's wrong, Mal?"

"Caroline's leaving me. She's fallen for her art teacher. Laughable, isn't it?"

"So it was true!" Jack blurted out and got a murderous glare from Doug.

"What?" Mal looked at him.

"Nothing," Jack mumbled. "I'd better go and see if they want anything." He hurried out of the kitchen.

"What's he talking about, Doug?" Mal's voice was dangerously quiet.

Doug sighed. This was all he needed. "It's no big deal, Mal. Gina saw Caroline with a man in a restaurant a few weeks ago."

"What? Why the hell didn't she tell me?"

"Because I told her not to. Look, Mal, it could have been perfectly innocent. I told her to mind her own business."

"So instead of telling me she told you, Jack and God knows who else. I suppose you've all been having a good laugh."

"Don't be silly, Mal. We're your friends."

Mal looked at him in disgust. "Some friends," he said and walked out of the room.

Jack came back into the kitchen to find Doug smoking one of his cigarettes. "Sorry," he said, lighting up.

"It was bound to come out at some stage."

"Where's he gone? He's not gone out in this, has he?" Jack said, alarmed. The rain had got steadily worse and the cloths that Doug had wedged against the bottom of the back door were soaking.

Doug shook his head. "I think he's in my study. Well, I heard the door banging and it can't be Pamela. She's upstairs."

Jack looked at Doug's brooding face and slumped shoulders. "Had a bit of a tiff, have you?"

Doug laughed. "More like World War III with a different battle every day. Well, no. That's not strictly true. It's the same battle but from different angles."

Jack smoked furiously. This was more information than he was looking for. "Right. I'm sure things will work out. I wonder how Susie's doing?"

"Oh, God, it's coming, doctor! I'm telling ye, it's coming!"

"OK, Susie. Calm down. It will all be over soon. Now when you feel the start of the next contraction I want you to take a deep breath and push hard into your bottom."

"I can't," Susie wailed. "Not like this." She was half lying on the sofa with her legs in the air.

"That's OK," he said soothingly. "We can try a different position where you feel more comfortable."

Comfortable! Only a man could use a word like that at a time like this! Susie thought irritably.

"Do you think you'd feel better kneeling?"

"Maybe."

"OK. Gina, help Susie down on to the floor." He quickly spread more sheets over the carpet. "Now, Susie, why don't you lean on the sofa for support?"

Susie did as she was told.

"How does that feel?"

"OK," she mumbled, laying her face against the cool of a silk cushion. "Oh, God, here we go!"

Joe positioned himself behind her. "OK, Susie. Deep breath and push as hard as you can."

"What will I do?" Gina asked.

"Eh, you could mop her forehead with a damp cloth."

"Right," Gina grabbed the cloth and shoved it in Susie's face.

"Will ye feck off, Gina!" Susie shoved her roughly away.

"After the contraction is over, Gina," Joe said patiently.

"Oh. Sorry." Gina retreated helplessly while Susie made animal-like noises and Joe supported her from behind.

Minutes later, Susie flopped forward on to her cushion again.

"That was good, Susie," Joe said reassuringly. "Take a rest and when you feel the next contraction start we'll do the same again."

"I can't," Susie sobbed.

Gina mopped her face.

"Get that thing away from me, Gina!"

"What about a drink?" Gina offered a glass of water.

"Only if it's bacardi . . . oh, shit, doctor!"

"OK, Susie. I'm right here."

Gina backed off as Susie pushed and screamed like a madwoman and Joe worked frantically between her legs.

"OK, Susie, don't push again until I tell you. Just pant."

Gina watched, mesmerised.

"OK, Susie. One last time."

"I can't, I can't!"

"You can, Susie," he said firmly. "And I promise after this one it will be all over."

Susie closed her eyes, took a deep breath and dug her nails deep into Pamela's expensive sofa. *"Aaaargh!"*

There was a funny sloshing sound and then Joe called to Gina. "A towel, Gina. A towel. Quickly!"

Gina handed him Pamela's softest white towel.

"That's it, Susie! You've done it! It's all over."

Gina stared down at the tiny figure wriggling between Joe's hands. "Oh, my God! Oh, Susie! Oh, blimey!"

Chapter Thirty-nine

"She's beautiful, Susie." Gina wiped the baby gently the way the doctor had shown her.

"She?" Susie said tiredly.

"Yes. You have a beautiful little daughter."

"I was so sure it was a boy. A little fighter."

Gina grinned. "Well, it may be a girl but I bet she's going to be a little fighter. Just like her mother. What are you going to call her?"

"I don't know," she said as Joe helped her up on the sofa. "I was going to call him Jesse if it was a boy. I didn't pick any girls' names."

Gina wrapped the baby tightly in a new towel and handed it reverently to Susie. "I think Jesse would be a cool name for a girl."

Susie looked down at the tiny, wrinkled face. "Jesse Clarke."

The baby opened her eyes and looked up into her face.

"I think she likes it!" Susie laughed delightedly. "Hello, Jesse Clarke. Nice to meet ye."

Joe stood up. "Right. I've done as much as I can here. Now we need to get these two ladies to hospital."

"But the roads . . ." Gina reminded him.

"I have a jeep. It's not a problem. I'll just go and clean up. Why don't you make Susie a nice cup of tea, Gina? I think she's earned it."

"I'd still prefer a bacardi," Susie said with a grin. "Seriously though, Doc. Thanks a million. Ye were great."

"You did all the work, Susie."

"Tell me about it! Nah, but I felt a lot safer having ye here."

Joe gave a little bow. "Glad to be of service."

He opened the door and smiled at Mal, Jack and Doug. "My God! You're like three expectant fathers! Go on, then. You can go in now."

Doug led the way and knelt down at Susie's side. "Ah, Susie! He's gorgeous!" Doug touched the baby's hand and gasped in surprise when his finger was caught in a strong grip.

"It's a girl, Doug. Meet Jesse Clarke."

Jack leaned in over Doug's head to get a better look. "She's very dark. Not at all like you," he remarked."

"Very like me," Susie assured him. "Before I decided that blondes had more fun."

"Oh. And will she still be called Jesse when she's . . ." Jack's voice trailed away.

An awkward silence filled the room. "I dunno," Susie said quietly. "But she'll always be Jesse to me."

Gina poked Jack hard in the ribs. "Let's go and make some tea."

"What? Oh, right." He followed her obediently from the room.

"Congratulations, Susie," Mal bent to kiss her cheek.

She smiled up at him, her face radiant. "Ah, thanks, Mal. And thanks for everything. Ye were great."

"Sure what did I do?" he said modestly.

"Ye kept me from throwing a wobbly, that's what. It was great to have someone here who'd been through it all before – no offence, Doug."

"None taken," Doug assured her. "I felt a lot happier when Malcolm arrived myself. I'm not used to this kind of responsibility." He stroked the baby's cheek gently. "She really is gorgeous. What colour are her eyes?"

"They're kind of a dark blue."

"They might go brown. All babies are born with blue eyes," Mal explained. "It takes a few weeks for the final colour to develop."

"I never knew that," Doug marvelled.

"Whatever colour they end up she's going to break hearts," Mal assured her.

Susie cuddled the baby closer. "Yeah. And she's going to be a lot smarter than her mother, aren't ye, Jesse? No landing yerself in the family way when yer a teenager. It's university for you!"

Doug laughed. "My God, you're acting like a parent already! Do as I say, not as I do."

"Yeah. Great, isn't it," Susie said smugly.

"Here we are," Jack arrived with a tray and plonked it down on the coffee table. "Lots of Doug's best choccy bikkies for you, Susie!" Gina had torn strips off him for his insensitivity and he was going to make up for it now. "Here. Let me hold junior while you have your tea."

Susie grinned. "Sure," she said, handing the baby over.

Jack took the little girl in his arms and rocked her gently. She looked even tinier against his lanky frame.

Gina watched, amazed at how comfortable he was with the baby. A lot more relaxed than she'd been! He crooned down into the baby's face as he smooched her around the room. The baby gurgled back.

"Where did you learn that?" Gina demanded.

He grinned at her. "I'm a natural."

"Here. It's my turn." Mal held out his arms and Jack reluctantly handed over the baby.

"No, not like that, Mal. She likes being rocked the other way," Jack instructed.

Mal looked at him, eyebrows raised. "I think I can just about remember how it's done, Jack."

"Oh. Right. Of course." Jack smiled apologetically. The last thing he wanted was to upset Mal again. It was great to see him smiling at all.

"Can I have a go?" Doug asked tentatively.

"Sure." Mal went to hand him the baby.

"No. I think I'll sit down first," Doug said hurriedly. Once he was safely ensconced in an armchair, he held up his arms. "OK."

Mal placed Jesse carefully in his arms and Doug looked down at her in awe. "She's so pretty," he breathed, not taking his eyes off her. He examined her soft, downy dark curls, long dark lashes fanning her cheeks, perfect little fingers with nails that looked as if they'd just been manicured. "She's perfect, Susie. Just perfect."

Susie sipped her tea and sighed happily. She had a gorgeous baby. She was surrounded by friends and she didn't even feel that bad. "Perfect," she agreed.

"Perfect," Pamela said from the doorway as she watched her husband cuddle the baby.

He smiled delightedly at her. "Pamela! Come and have a look."

Pamela walked over to his side.

"Meet Jesse Clarke," he announced.

Pamela looked down at the child and then at the tender look on Doug's face. "She's beautiful, Susie," she said finally with a ghost of a smile.

Susie smiled shyly. "Thanks, Pamela. And sorry for taking over yer house and the mess and everything . . ."

Pamela shook her head dismissively. "Don't worry about it. It wasn't your fault."

"Do you want to hold her, darling?" Doug asked.

Pamela backed away. "Better not. I'm quite tired. I think I'll go and lie down. Congratulations, Susie."

They all murmured their goodbyes as she left the room.

Doug smiled around awkwardly. "Those tablets of hers make her a bit groggy."

"They have terrible side-effects," Gina agreed.

"Caroline's have that effect too," Mal assured him.

Jack nodded sympathetically. "Bloody tablets."

Joe came back into the room. "I hate to break this up, folks, but I really would like to get these two to the hospital."

"Could you drop me back to my car on your way?" Gina asked. She was feeling exhausted now and looking forward to a couple of hours in bed.

"I'll come too," Jack chipped in. There was no way he he was letting Gina out of his sight until they'd had a chance to talk.

"I should be going myself," Mal said reluctantly.

"I can't take all of you," Joe protested.

"Of course not," Mal said apologetically. "Why don't you take Gina? Jack and I can walk."

Jack stared at him. "What?"

"Well, you do only live up the road, Jack," Gina pointed out.

"So I do," he said glumly. "OK, Mal. Let's go."

"Best of luck, Susie." Mal dropped a kiss on her forehead. "I'll come and visit you when you're settled."

"Thanks for everything, Mal. And you too, Jack."

"Sure what did I do?" Jack said despondently.

Susie laughed. "Ye got the towels."

Jack grinned. "That's true. Sure, you'd never have managed without me! Eh, Gina? Will I call you later?" he added casually.

Mal and Susie exchanged looks.

Gina looked at her watch. "A lot later, Jack. I'm completely exhausted."

"Me heart bleeds for ye," Susie said dryly.

Gina grinned. "Sorry, Suz. Come on. Let's get you wrapped up nice and warm before we go."

"It's not as bad as it was," Doug reported. "The rain has stopped. But if you hang on a minute, lads, I should have some wellies somewhere. Otherwise your feet will be soaked before you get to the end of the driveway."

By the time the two men were ready to go, Joe was settling Susie into the back of the jeep and Gina was following with the baby.

Doug took her arm, steering her between the puddles. "Careful now, Gina. Mind you don't slip."

Gina sighed. "I'm not going to drop her, Doug. Will ye stop fussing?"

"Sorry," He stood watching until they were all safely on board and waved as Joe drove them away. "See you later, Susie. Take care."

He went back inside and surveyed the sitting-room. It looked as if a bomb had hit it, though Gina had done her best to get rid of all the evidence. It all seemed unbearably quiet now. Doug felt somehow that he'd lost something. He shook his head. "Don't be so damn maudlin, Hamilton." He decided to go and talk to Pamela. But first he had something else to do. He'd promised Susie. He took out his diary and flicked through the pages. When he found what he was looking for, he dialled the number. "Mrs Clarke? Hello. My name is Douglas Hamilton. I employ your daughter Susie."

"Oh, dear God. Is there something wrong?" Florrie's voice was anxious.

"No, no, Mrs Clarke. Only I thought you should know. Susie gave birth to a beautiful, healthy little girl this morning."

"Thanks be to God!"

"I'm sure she'd love to see you. She's in Holles Street Hospital."

"Oh, I don't know . . ."

Doug gripped the receiver and tried to contain his temper. "She needs her mother, Mrs Clarke."

"Don't ye worry about our Susie, Mr Hamilton. She's tough. She'll be grand." Florrie looked anxiously over her shoulder at the sleeping form in the chair.

"Well, will you tell Marie? Ask her to visit?"

"I will, I will," Florrie said hurriedly as Christy stirred. "Goodbye, Mr Hamilton. And thanks for letting me know."

"Don't mention it," Doug said to the dial tone. He put the phone down, shaking his head angrily. Some people didn't deserve to be parents. He headed for the stairs, eager now to talk to Pamela. He'd been so thrilled when she'd come in and congratulated Susie. Maybe she'd finally got things sorted in her head. Maybe now that the baby was born she'd be OK again. He crossed the hall and ran upstairs. "Pamela? Pamela, are you awake?"

* * *

Mal and Jack sloshed their way along the driveway of The Sycamores and out onto the road. "This is more like a river," Jack remarked, glad he'd accepted Doug's wellingtons. "I know I was pissed, but it wasn't this bad when we got here, was it?"

Mal laughed. "No, it wasn't. We're in a hollow here, you see, and what with the Dodder overflowing it would have flooded very fast. It will be better once we get onto the main road."

"I hope Gina will be OK. She's got such a long way to go."

"She'll be fine. Things are a lot better on the north-side," Mal assured him. "So have you two got it together yet?"

"I wish I knew," Jack said glumly.

"You looked very cosy in the pub last night."

Jack grinned. "We were. But then Susie rang and that was the end of that."

"So ask her out tonight."

"You think?" They turned onto the main road. As Mal had predicted, conditions were a lot better up here.

"Well, if you're really interested in her . . ."

"Oh, I am! I mean she's gorgeous and funny and clever. How could I not be?"

"Then go for it."

They walked in silence for a while and then Jack shot Mal a sidelong glance. "Sorry about Caroline."

"Thanks."

"We weren't trying to hide things from you, Mal. It just seemed best to stay out of it."

Mal waved away his apologies. "I know, Jack. I'd probably have done the same thing."

"She's definitely leaving then?" Jack asked.

"She thinks she is."

"What do you mean?"

"Oh, It's just something that Susie said. That not many men would take on a pregnant woman and a small child. Maybe I'm just clutching at straws."

"I don't know. Susie's got a point. I'd have to be really crazy about someone before I'd take on that kind of reponsibility. So what are you going to do?"

"Nothing. For the moment. I'd like a bit of time to get my head straight. Could I stay at your place for a few hours?"

"Sure, of course!" Jack said, glad to be able to do something constructive. "Stay a few days if you like."

"No. Thanks all the same, Jack."

Jack shrugged. "Well, the offer stands if ever you need it."

"Thanks, mate."

"So where should I take her?"

Mal looked confused.

"Gina. Where will I take her for dinner?"

"Somewhere very special."

"How about The Hard Rock Café?"

Mal chuckled. "You've got a lot to learn about women, Jack. A lot to learn."

* * *

"Susie?"

Susie opened her eyes and smiled when she saw her sister standing beside the bed. "Howaya."

"Oh, Susie! Are ye OK? I'm sorry I wasn't with ye? Was it terrible?"

Susie pushed herself up in the bed. "It wasn't so bad and since we got to the hospital they've given me some painkillers."

"What do ye mean? Are ye saying ye had the baby in the flat?" Marie's eyes were like saucers.

"In the house," Susie corrected. "I couldn't get to the hospital. The roads were too bad."

"Oh, God! So ye went through it all without any gas or an epi or anything?"

Susie nodded.

"Mother of God! That's terrible!" Marie gasped.

"I've know better ways to spend a Saturday night. So are ye going to say hello to yer niece at all?" Susie nodded towards the crib on the far side of the bed.

"Oh! I never even saw it! And it's a girl!" Marie hurried around to the other side of the bed and peered in at the baby. "Ah, Susie. She's a little angel! And look at all that lovely hair."

"Her name's Jesse," Susie said proudly.

Marie frowned. "Do ye think that's a good idea? Putting a name on her?"

"Why not?" Susie said mutinously. "Doesn't she have to have a name?"

Marie sighed and sat down on the edge of the bed. "Yeah. But don't ye think her new mother will want to give her a name?"

Susie shrugged. "So? She can call her what she likes but she'll always be Jesse to me."

"OK, love." There wasn't any point in arguing about it. Susie was obviously tired. She'd see things more clearly once she'd had a good sleep.

"Does Mam know? Is she coming in to see me?" Susie asked hopefully.

Marie busied herself putting away the nightdresses she'd brought in. "She says she'll try but little Trisha's got a bit of a cold."

The light went out of Susie's eyes. "Right."

"She sends her love." Marie smiled reassuringly.

"Great. Look, I'm a bit tired now, Marie. Do ye mind if I have a little sleep?"

"No, love. You go ahead. I'll sit here and keep an eye on the baby."

Jesse started to cry as if on cue. "I don't think I'll get much sleep with this one," Susie said, a tender smile on her face. "She's always hungry."

And Marie looked on horrified as Susie lifted the baby and put her to her breast.

* * *

"But she was breastfeeding!" Marie protested.

The social worker smiled kindly. "We encourage that, Miss Clarke. It's good for the baby and it gives the mother some idea of what's involved in looking after a child. It's important that your sister makes the right decision for her and her baby. This time together will help her do the right thing. And if she decides to go ahead with the adoption it will have been after careful consideration. The days of babies being snatched from their mother's arms as soon as they were born are thankfully long gone."

"But it's going to be so hard for her," Marie persisted.

"Yes, it is. And that's where her family and friends

come in. Giving a child up for adoption is similar to a bereavement. It takes time to recover from it and it's very important that Susie isn't told to forget about it and get on with her life. She should be encouraged to talk. To grieve. It's perfectly natural."

Marie sighed heavily. "I didn't think this was going to be so hard. I never thought I'd even see the baby. And she's so gorgeous."

"Has your sister said anything about the adoption since the baby was born?"

Marie shook her head. "Will you talk to her?"

"Of course. I'll be doing my rounds this afternoon. I'll pop in then."

* * *

"It's me," Mal said when Caroline finally answered the phone.

"Malcolm? Where have you been? Rachel's been asking for you. I didn't know what to say."

Mal wondered what Caroline was going to tell their daughter when she moved her in with a replacement dad. "It's a long story. I'm in Jack's at the moment. I'll be back later."

"Well, I won't be here."

"Surprise, surprise," he muttered. "Is Rachel still going to that party?"

"Of course."

"Fine. I'll see you later." He hung up without waiting for a reply. It hurt too much to even talk to her. He thought of her sitting at her dressing-table getting ready to meet *him* and a hot, savage jealousy took hold of him. "Bastard!" He flung the phone down angrily.

Jack, approaching with two beers, retreated back into the kitchen. Poor Mal. Jack knew all about unrequited love. But losing your partner and child – no, children – to another man. That didn't bear thinking about.

He drank his beer and thought about Gina's reaction to his invitation.

"Dinner?" she'd sounded surprised but not unpleasantly.

"That's right," he'd said, trying to sound cool and confident.

"Where did you have in mind?"

"That's a surprise." Mal had suggested that one. "Meet me at eight in the bar of The Westbury."

"The Westbury!" Gina sounded impressed.

"Yes, we'll have a drink and go on to dinner from there." Jack was pleased with that line. He sounded as if he went out to posh restaurants every day of the week.

"OK, then. I'll see you at eight."

Jack checked his watch. That was six hours away. Plenty of time for a decent sleep only he didn't like to leave Mal alone. He brought him in his beer. "All right, Mal?"

"Yeah. Sure. Listen, Jack. Why don't you go and catch some shut-eye? No offence but I'd really prefer to be on my own at the moment."

"Are you sure?" Jack asked, trying to hide his relief.

"Sure. We can't have you falling asleep in your soup, now can we?" Mal managed a cheerful wink.

Jack smiled gratefully. "No. I want to have my wits about me for this one."

"Off you go then."

"Right. Well, you make yourself at home. There's a couple of videos there and there's more beer in the fridge if you fancy it . . ."

"Jack. I'm fine."

"Right, so. Seeya later."

Jack went into his bedroom and Mal flopped into a dilapidated armchair and stared out of the window.

Chapter Forty

"Pamela? Can I come in?" Doug pushed the door open gently. "Oh good. You're awake." He sat down on the bed beside her. "Do you feel any better?"

"I'm fine," Pamela said gravely.

"You're quite pale. Still, it's been an eventful night. Can you believe that a woman just gave birth in our living-room?" He shook his head in wonder.

"Amazing," Pamela agreed.

Doug looked up sharply but there wasn't a trace of sarcasm in her face. He smiled, relieved. "You know you've been terribly silly lately, darling. I can't believe you were jealous of Susie."

"No?" she said, studying the large, strong hands enfolding hers.

"No. I mean as if I'd be interested in someone like her. I just felt sorry for her."

"It was more than that."

Doug looked alarmed. "I swear, Pamela. I never laid a hand on her!"

"I know that!" she said abruptly.

"Then what in God's name is this all about?" Doug jumped up and started to pace the floor.

"You know what it's about, Douglas," she said, her voice sad and tired. "I'm not enough for you any more."

"That's not true," he protested but his voice was unconvincing.

"Isn't it? Come on, Douglas. You're the one who said you wanted to talk. So let's talk. Let's get it all out in the open." She got out of bed, put on a dressing-gown and tossed her long dark hair over her shoulder.

Doug looked at her. So beautiful, so regal, if he could just make her understand . . .

"Well?" She summoned up all her courage and looked into his eyes, half afraid of what she would see there.

He took her hand and led her over to the love seat by the window. "My priorities have changed," he said at last. "The business isn't enough any more."

"I've said we should expand," Pamela reminded him but she knew she was just delaying the inevitable.

"That's not enough," he said his face full of frustration. "I want . . . I want . . ."

"You want a child," Pamela finished the sentence for him. She closed her eyes and prayed that he would deny it.

"Oh, yes, Pamela! I do! I should have known that you'd figured it out. You know me so well."

"Yes."

His mind raced and his face lit up. "And you're still

young. A baby would be a huge disruption to our lifestyle," he laughed, "but we could cope. We could get a nanny to help . . ."

"Stop it, Douglas."

"But it would be fine, Pamela. I'm sure it would. You'd make such a beautiful mother."

"Stop it!" she almost shouted. "It's not going to happen." Her voice was strained, her face pale.

"I know it's a lot to take on board," he said, his voice soothing. "I realise that you might need time to get used to the idea."

"You're not listening, Douglas. It's not possible!"

Doug's expression darkened. "How can you be so dismissive? Don't my feelings count? Don't I have a say in this?"

"No," she said, her voice barely a whisper. "I'm afraid you don't."

"But Pamela . . ."

"Douglas, I can't have children."

Doug stared at her. "What do you mean you can't? How do you know?"

"Because I was sterilised ten years ago."

Doug visibly paled. "What? Why?"

Pamela closed her eyes, shutting out the distraught look on his face. "You made it clear that you didn't want a family," she said simply. "I waited for a while to see if you would change your mind and when you didn't . . ." She shrugged.

"But why something so . . . final?"

"I'd been having terrible problems with my periods and

my gynaecologist said that if I was sure we didn't want a family, sterilisation was the best solution."

Doug tried to absorb what she was saying. "You said I didn't want a family. Are you telling me you did?"

She shrugged. "I don't know. I suppose I thought it would happen eventually. I thought you'd change your mind once the business was up and running. But you made it very clear that children were never going to be part of the plan."

"Oh, Christ, I don't believe this! Why didn't you talk to me first, Pamela? Don't you think we should have discussed such a drastic step?"

She looked down at her perfectly manicured hands, clasping them tightly to stop the shaking. "I was afraid that you'd think I was trying to pressurise you."

"So you did it . . . for me?" he almost choked on the words.

"For us," Pamela corrected, her eyes bright with tears. "And we've done OK, haven't we, Douglas? We're happy?" Her voice sounded desperate even to her.

Doug looked at her blankly. "I've got to go." He stood up abruptly.

"No, Douglas!" She stood up and tried to put her arms around him but he pushed her away gently.

"I need to think. Just give me some time, Pamela. Please?"

She nodded and the tears spilled down her cheeks as she watched him walk away.

* * *

"You look great," Jack said shyly when Gina joined him at the bar. He'd watched her proudly as she'd stood in the doorway looking around for him. The tight suede trousers and clingy, soft wool sweater emphasised her curvy figure. The leather jacket slung casually around her shoulders made her look coolly chic. And her glossy dark hair curled in around her lovely heart-shaped face.

"Hi," Gina said, equally shyly.

"What would you like to drink?"

Gina made a face. "Just a Coke for the moment. I'm still feeling a bit delicate."

"I feel grand," Jack said, taking a gulp of his pint. "The few hours' sleep sorted me out."

"I hardly slept at all," Gina said dreamily. "I couldn't stop thinking about the baby. And the birth. I've never seen anything so amazing in my life."

Jack held up his hand. "Spare me the details, please. At least until after we've eaten."

Gina laughed. "OK. So where *are* we going?"

Jack tapped the side of his nose. "I told you. It's a surprise."

"Are you *sure* you can afford this?" Gina whispered as they were led through the large room to a table in the corner.

"Of course I can," Jack assured her and thanked the gods in heaven that for once he'd paid his *Visa* bill.

"It's very fancy," she said after the waiter had left them to study the menus and gone off to fetch their two Bloody Marys.

"Isn't it just?" Jack looked around him. He hoped that she didn't think he'd gone over the top. It was Mal's idea that they come to The Commons. He'd warned Jack that it would be expensive but Jack didn't care. He looked at the expression on Gina's face and knew it was going to be worth every penny.

The waiter delivered their drinks and they toasted each other and Susie and Jesse too.

"Last night seems a lifetime ago," Gina said, taking a sip of the spicy drink.

"It was," Jack pointed out. "Jesse's lifetime."

Gina smiled. "Jesse. It's a lovely name. It's a pity Susie's giving her up."

"Maybe she won't. Though it won't be an easy life if she decides to keep her."

"But we'd all help out," Gina pointed out. "I'd be quite happy to do a spot of baby-sitting."

Jack laughed. "Have you ever even changed a nappy?"

Gina wrinkled her nose. "Well, no, but it can't be that difficult."

"No. Just smelly and messy," Jack replied.

"Ugh. I think we should change the conversation — unless of course you're deliberately trying to put me off my food."

Jack sighed dramatically. "Darn it, I've been sussed!"

Gina laughed. "So what's all of this in aid of anyway? What are we celebrating?"

Jack smiled. "Well, we could celebrate the new arrival. Or we could celebrate the fact that our hangovers aren't as bad as they could have been or . . ."

"Or," Gina prompted hopefully.

He smiled into her eyes and took her hand. "Or we could celebrate the beginning of a wonderful relationship."

Gina raised an eyebrow. "That's a bit presumptuous."

"Is it?" Jack's expression was suddenly serious. "Don't you think it's time we stopped playing games, Gina? You know how I feel about you. And I think that maybe, you're beginning to feel the same way too. Am I wrong?" Jack felt himself break out into a sweat as he waited for her answer.

"No. You're not wrong, Jack." she murmured.

"Oh, Gina! Thank God for that. I was afraid you might be still pining after Greg."

She shook her head vigorously. "Hell, no! I don't know what I saw in the guy in the first place."

Jack beamed at her.

"Hannah says I always go for guys that will treat me badly. She thinks it's because I don't really want a serious relationship."

"And what do you think?" he asked, his dark eyes searching her face.

Gina grinned. "I think she's talking a load of rubbish and I just hadn't met the right guy."

Jack's face fell. "Oh."

"Or . . . that I hadn't *realised* I'd met the right guy."

Jack looked up into her face, his eyes grave. "No messing, Gina. I can't handle it. I really need to know if there's any chance . . ."

Gina reached over and put her finger to his lips.

"Sshh. I'm not messing, Jack. No more games. I really like you. And I'd like to go out with you."

Jack's mouth fell open. "Really?"

She smiled. "Really."

Jack jumped to his feet and signalled to the young waiter who had been watching from a discreet distance.

"What on earth are you doing?" Gina looked at him, alarmed.

"Celebrating," he said with a broad smile as the waiter returned with a bottle of champagne in a bucket of ice.

"But Jack! This is going to cost a fortune!" she hissed.

"You're worth every penny," he said sincerely. When the waiter had poured the wine and left, he lifted his glass. "To the most beautiful woman in the world."

"Oh, Jack!" Gina flushed as she took a sip of her wine.

"It's true," he said quietly. "And I'm going to make you the happiest woman in the world too. Do you know that?"

She looked into his warm brown eyes and knew, with complete certainty, that he meant every word. She smiled. "You know, Jack. I think you just might."

He leaned over and gave her a long, lingering kiss.

"Jack!" Gina looked at him, wide-eyed, when he finally pulled away. It was as if she was really seeing him for the first time. The cropped, golden hair, those gorgeous dark eyes, the tall, athletic body. How come she'd never noticed how good-looking he was before? She shivered as she saw the look of longing in his eyes. "Maybe we could go back to your place for coffee?" she said, her eyes full of invitation and promise. She had never been so brazen before but this was Jack. And she knew he would never hurt her, or betray her. In fact she'd never felt so sure of anything in her life.

"I wish you hadn't said that," he said with a sigh.

Gina drew back in alarm. "Sorry . . . but I thought . . ."

He grinned broadly at her. "How the hell am I supposed to sit through an entire meal now?"

Gina flapped her napkin at him. "Oh, Jack! You sod! I thought you were having second thoughts!"

He took her hand and kissed it. "Oh, no, love. I know exactly what I want. I have done for a very long time."

Gina sighed as she saw the love in his eyes and wondered why she'd never noticed it before.

She lifted her glass. "To us, Jack. And to our future."

Jack took a quick drink before pulling her into his arms and kissing her soundly much to the amusement of the people around them.

Chapter Forty-one

Pamela stood gazing into the fridge, but nothing appealed to her. Somehow food didn't seem to be the answer today. Her whole life was coming to an end. Stuffing herself wasn't going to help matters.

She whirled around as Douglas let himself in the back door. "Hi."

"Hi." He walked over and sat down at the kitchen table. "Sit down, will you, Pamela?"

Pamela's heart sank. She came over and sat down opposite him, searching his face for clues. "I'm really sorry," she began.

Doug held up his hand. "Don't. Please don't, Pamela. I feel bad enough as it is. You had that sterilisation for me. You wanted children back then but you were afraid to say so. It's true, isn't it, Pamela?"

Pamela stared at him. "I thought you'd leave me. And I couldn't have handled that." Her voice cracked.

Doug put his head in his hands. "My God, can you ever forgive me?"

She shrugged. "It's ancient history. I'm happy now."

"Are you? Are you really, Pamela?"

"Of course."

"Then why the bingeing?"

Pamela's eyes widened in surprise. "I don't know what you're talking about."

"Yes, you do," Doug said wearily. "I should have done something about it a long time ago. Christ, I'm sorry, Pamela! I've done nothing but let you down. And these last few months. Watching Susie get bigger and bigger. It must have been very difficult for you."

Pamela's eyes filled with tears. "I would have traded places with her in a flash," she admitted.

"Oh, my love!" He was round the table in an instant, holding her in his arms, rocking her gently, his tears mingling with hers. "Don't cry, Pam. Don't cry. I love you."

She wiped away her tears and looked into his eyes. "Do you, Doug? Are you sure?"

He smiled. "I'm very sure. You called me Doug. I like that."

She smiled shyly. "It's been a long time since you called me Pam. I like that too." She took his face in her hands and looked deep into his eyes. "I love you, Doug Hamilton."

Doug pulled her very close and kissed her. And for the first time, in a very long time, Pamela returned his kiss, her passion matching his own.

* * *

The social worker stood up to leave.

Susie smiled at her. "I'm glad we talked, Margaret. Everything is a lot clearer now."

The older woman sighed. "There's no rush, Susie. You have to be sure you're doing the right thing. For you and little Jesse."

Susie smiled. "I know."

"I'll come back and see you tomorrow," Margaret promised. "Take care, love."

* * *

Mal walked into the house and threw his car keys on the hall table. It was deadly quiet. *Get used to it,* he told himself. *This is the future.* He went into the living-room and switched on the light. "Jesus! Caroline! you startled me!"

Caroline raised her head to look at him, her face swollen from crying. "Oh, Malcolm. I'm so glad to see you!" She stood up and threw her arms around him.

Mal disengaged himself and moved away. "Really?"

"Yes. Really. It's only when you went missing last night that I realised how much I loved you. That I couldn't possibly leave you."

"Funny that. You didn't sound very worried on the phone. In fact, if I remember correctly, you were still going off to meet lover-boy."

She hesitated. "You . . . you woke me. I was confused. I didn't know what I was saying."

Mal sat down in an armchair and smiled coldly.

"What is this, Caroline? Doesn't Dick fancy playing happy families after all?"

She looked away. "I told you. I realised I was making a mistake."

"Don't give me that crap, Caroline!" he roared, making her jump. "I'm not totally stupid. He's dumped you, hasn't he?"

Caroline nodded, her face pinched and frightened. *Oh, God please don't let him throw me out. I can't go back to typing in some crappy little office.*

"Well, thank you. Some honesty at last." His voice dripped with sarcasm.

"Forgive me, Malcolm. It was just a silly little fling. It meant nothing . . ."

He held up a hand. "Spare me the lies, Caroline."

"No, honestly. . ."

"Shut up!"

She shrank back from the anger in his voice.

"You can stay. But only because of the children. Just tell me one thing."

She stared at him nervously. She'd never seen him so determined, so cold.

"Is the baby his? I want the truth."

"I honestly don't know, Mal."

Mal saw the sincerity in her eyes. He turned away. "I'll go and pick up Rachel."

She ran after him, clinging to his arm. "Mal? I'm sorry. I'll make it up to you." She went to kiss his cheek but he pulled away.

"Give me time, Caroline," he said grimly. "Give me a lot of time."

* * *

Jack arrived back carrying two bacon butties and a can of beer.

Gina giggled as he climbed into bed beside her and handed her a sandwich.

"What?" he asked, smiling down at her.

"I've never had food in bed with a man before."

"That's 'cos no man has ever made you as hungry as I have," he said smugly, taking a large bite out of his sandwich.

"Big-head." She nudged him in the ribs and he started to tickle her. "Oh, no, stop, I'm too tired for this."

He looked at her, disappointed. "Tired? Already? But I'm not finished with you yet." He gave her a lecherous look and ducked his head under the sheet.

* * *

Doug kissed Pamela's hair, enjoying the feel of her naked body against his. "I love you."

She reached a hand up to stroke his cheek. "I love you too."

"I have a favour to ask," he said seriously.

"Oh?"

"Don't look so worried. It's just that I'd like you to see someone about this eating problem."

Pamela stiffened. "It's not a problem. You're exaggerating."

He propped himself up on one arm and looked down into her face. "Maybe I am. I hope so. But humour me, please?"

She nodded silently.

"And there's something else. I'd like us both to see a marriage guidance counsellor."

Pamela stared at him. Douglas had always been such a private person and now he wanted to parade their marital problems in front of a total stranger. "But their objective is to get couples talking and we're already doing that," she pointed out reasonably.

"No, we're not. Not really," he said gently. "Look, Pamela. You've been holding in a lot of feelings for a great many years. A quick chat and a kiss and a cuddle doesn't even begin to sort that out. We need to get everything out in the open. The hurt, the anger, the sadness, everything."

"Don't you think it might be a dangerous can of worms to open?"

He took her hand and kissed it. "Maybe. But I think we're strong enough to do it. And if we're to make a fresh start then I think we have to do it. And I want us to make a fresh start, Pamela."

She gave him a tremulous smile. "I wish I could believe that that was possible."

Doug frowned. "Why wouldn't it be?"

Pamela moved away pulling the sheet up around her. "What about the other women?"

Doug sighed and pushed the curtain of silky hair back off her face. "Why in God's name have you put up with me for so long?"

"For your money, of course," she joked feebly.

He pulled her close to him. "I'm so sorry, Pam. I've been a selfish bastard and I can't give you any reason why you should forgive me. All I can tell you is that I've changed."

Pamela smiled. "I believe you. Once I saw the way you were with Susie Clarke I knew something had changed. I was just afraid that it might mean the end of us."

He hugged her tightly. "Well, it doesn't. Not as far as I'm concerned. It means my priorities have changed. And that means from now on, you come first."

She relaxed against his chest and smiled happily.

"How would you feel about adoption?" he murmured into her hair.

Pamela put a finger up to his lips. "Let's not run before we can walk."

Doug nodded. "You're right. Sorry. We have a lot to sort out before we could dream of bringing a child into this house. Pamela?"

"Mmnn?"

"I want Susie to stay. Both in CML and in the flat."

"That's OK," she murmured.

"Are you sure? What if she decides to keep Jesse? Will you be able to handle it?"

Pamela sighed. "I'll get used to it. Just don't expect me to offer to baby-sit just yet!"

Doug chuckled. "Fair enough."

"Poor Susie. I've given her a terrible time, haven't I?"

"Don't worry about. I'm going in to see her tomorrow. Why don't you come with me?"

Pamela shook her head. "I'm the last person she'd want to see. You go. But tell her – tell her I'm thinking of her."

Doug kissed her. "I love you, Mrs Lloyd-Hamilton."

She hugged him tightly to her. "And I love you, Doug. So very, very much."

* * *

"Susie? Sorry, did I wake you?" Susie's eyes fluttered open as Mal crept into the cubicle.

She smiled. "No, yer OK."

"How are you feeling?" He sat down in the chair and tried to ignore the fact that hers was the only bed with no crib beside it.

"I'm fine," she said but her voice was tired and her eyes were red.

He put a bottle of Lucozade on her bedside table. "I didn't know what else to bring," he apologised.

"That's grand. Thanks. I could do with something to pep me up. How are things with Caroline?"

Mal laughed, but his eyes were sad. "Oh, the great love affair is over, it seems."

"You're kidding! That's great . . . isn't it?"

"It would be if it had been her decision," he said bitterly.

"Oh. So, what are you going to do?"

"Take her back, of course. What else can I do? There's Rachel to think of."

"What about the baby?"

"I asked her if it was mine. But she doesn't know. At least she was honest about that."

"Not before time," Susie said harshly.

"Hi everyone!" Gina's face appeared around the curtain. "Hiya Susie? How are you doing? I brought you some chocs. Medicinal of course. They'll give you your strength back."

"Thanks, Gina."

"Where's . . ." Gina stopped when she caught the look on Mal's face. "Where's Jack got to?" she continued brightly.

"I'm here," Jack appeared behind her. "Hiya Susie, How are you feeling?"

"Grand, Jack. I'm grand."

"I brought you some Lucozade, oh . . ."

"I beat you to it." Mal grinned. We're an imaginative pair aren't we?"

"I'll drink both of them, I promise." Susie smiled at them.

Jack looked around for the baby but said nothing. Mainly because the heel of Gina's boot was planted firmly on his foot. "So, how are you feeling?" he asked again.

"Grand," she said again. "A bit sore and tired, but then that's what you'd expect."

They all nodded in agreement. She looked at Jack's happy face and noticed a positive glow coming from

Gina. "Is there any chance ye have a bit of news for me?" She glanced from one to the other.

Gina blushed and looked at Jack.

Jack grinned back. "Well, I suppose, you're bound to find out sooner or later. Me and Gina are, eh, seeing each other."

"About bloody time!" Mal clapped him on the back.

Susie smiled at them. "I'm delighted for ye. Ye were made for each other."

Jack put his arm around Gina and smiled adoringly down into her face.

Susie watched wistfully. It must be nice to have a man that cared about ye like that.

"Can I come in?" Doug asked.

She smiled affectionately at her boss who'd become such a great friend. "Of course ye can, Doug. Thanks for coming."

"Pamela sends her apologies. She couldn't come but she sends her love." Doug felt a physical pain as he saw them exchange looks. They were all so used to him making excuses for Pam. If only they knew that it was his fault she was the way she was. If only they knew how miserable he'd made her. How would they feel about him then?

Susie looked around shyly. "I want to thank all of ye for looking after me so well. Ye were all really great."

"Sure what are friends for?" Jack said cheerfully.

Susie flushed. "I've never really had friends before. Not like ye."

Doug wondered whether the tears in her eyes were of

gratitude or sorrow. There was no sign of a crib and no one had even mentioned the baby. He decided to say something. They couldn't keep ignoring the issue. It was ridiculous. He was just opening his mouth to speak when the curtain behind him was pulled back.

"Is there room for two more?" Marie asked cheerfully as she pushed her way in dragging the crib behind her.

"Jesse!" Gina's eyes lit up as she leaned over the baby.

"Susie?" Mal looked at her questioningly.

Susie smiled. "I've decided to keep her." She grasped her sister's hand tightly. "Marie says she'll help me."

Gina's eyes filled up and she reached down to give Susie a big hug. "Oh, Susie. We all will. I'm so happy for you."

"Hear, hear!" Jack bent to kiss her cheek.

"Congratulations, Susie. You'll make a wonderful mother. " Doug smiled at her, his eyes unusually bright. He coughed. "So, can I open this now?" He pulled a bottle of champagne from behind his back and a pack of paper cups.

Susie laughed delightedly and Doug popped the cork while Mal distributed the cups.

Marie lifted Jesse out of the crib and placed her in her mother's arms.

"A toast," Doug said when he'd poured the champagne. "To Susie and Jesse!"

Marie tapped her cup against Susie's. "To you and the baby, sis!"

"To the Clarke family!" Jack smiled happily at the two of them.

Mal raised his cup and smiled into Susie's eyes. "To both of you. Enjoy every minute of it, Susie. Before you know it, she'll be out dancing!"

They all laughed and Gina bent over to place a drop of champagne on the baby's lips. "Have a wonderful life, little Jesse. I think we can safely say it won't be dull. Not with a mother like yours!"

THE END

Published by Poolbeg.com

RED LETTER DAY

At the tender age of twenty-seven, beautiful widow Celine Moore has captured the sympathy of the people of Kilmont. When her husband, Dermot, died in tragic circumstances they gathered around her like a protective shield.

However, when they discover that she has been finding comfort in the arms of local hotshot Kevin Gilligan they turn against her and switch their sympathies to Kevin's wife Eileen. Within days Celine finds herself friendless and out of a job.

Unable to bear her father's disappointment and her sister-in-law's rejection, Celine decides it's time to move on.

The offer of a job running a second-hand boutique in Hopefield, on the far side of Dublin, seems exactly what she needs and she accepts it gratefully. Nobody knows her in Hopefield and she is determined to keep it that way.

But soon Celine finds herself caught up in the lives of her new friends and neighbours. And when it comes to the secrets of her past Celine quickly discovers that Dublin is a very small town.

Colette Caddle

ISBN 1-84223-120-0

Published by Poolbeg.com

FOREVER FM

Maeve Elliot, tall, leggy blonde DJ at Forever FM,
Dublin's hottest radio station, has big plans. She goes to
the right parties with the right men, plays the game and
knows the rules. But can she put the past behind her?

Linda Jewell, successful recruitment consultant.
Dumped by her boring husband for a younger model
she invents a lover of her own. But it's only a matter of
time before she's found out and then she'll look even
more pathetic than she feels.

Carrie Lambe, a disappointment to her parents and
a doormat for her boyfriend. Can a new job at
Forever FM help her to take control of her life?

Jonathan Blake, sexy owner of Forever FM.
Changes girlfriends as often as his socks. But his first
love is his radio station and he plans to make it
Number One, whatever the cost.

The station's new talk show is going to affect all of their
lives, but will it be for the better and could it be forever?

Colette Caddle

ISBN 1-84223-023-9

Published by Poolbeg.com

A CUT
ABOVE

'Why on earth did you marry him, Toni?' Chloe asked
suddenly. Toni smiled at the typical teenage bluntness.
'Chloe! What a question!'

From the outside it looks like Toni Jordan has it all.
A successful career as director of a cosmetic surgery
clinic, a husband who is an eminent surgeon, and a
ready-made family in her adorable stepdaughter, Chloe.

But her world is falling apart. Theo has become distant
and cruel since he decided that Toni was not the wife
he wanted. And she is alarmed by decisions being made
at the clinic that may not be entirely ethical.

Just as Toni decides to take action, Theo disappears!

Colette Caddle

ISBN 1-84223-080-8

Published by Poolbeg.com

TOO LITTLE TOO LATE

Stephanie West is fed up.

She has a job in a successful restaurant that she loves but a boss she hates. The only answer seems to be to leave.

Amazingly, an opportunity arises to buy him out and she jumps at it.

So when her boyfriend Sean lands a contract with a software company in Phoenix, Arizona, and wants her to go with him, Stephanie is clear about where her loyalties lie . . .

But ghosts from the past have influenced her decision. Can she come to terms with them? And if she does, will it be too little, too late?

Colette Caddle

ISBN 1-85371-693-6

Direct to your home!

If you enjoyed this book why not visit our website:

www.poolbeg.com

and get another book delivered straight to your home or to a friend's home!

www.poolbeg.com

All orders are despatched within 24 hours.